A Fine September Morning

Date: 8/8/16

BB
B. Bennett Press
San Carlos California

Published by B. Bennett Press
San Carlos, California

Book design by Burche-Bensson
Cover photos used under license from Shutterstock:
Front Cover - © Chyrko Olena (bench), grynold (man & wom-
an), Sattva78 (boy)
Back Cover - © mcseem (churches), Jennifer Gottschalk (Star of
David), Emin Kuliyev (Chrysler Building)

ISBN-10: 1482021617
ISBN-13: 978-1482021615

PRINTED IN THE UNITED STATES OF AMERICA

First Edition

www.alanfleishman.com

To my dear wife Ann,
to whom everything in my life
is dedicated.

and

To my parents,
Ben and Ruth Fleishman,
who saw every flaw in me but
loved me as though I had none.

LIST OF CHARACTERS

MAIN CHARACTERS

Avi Schneider –   A Jewish tailor from Uman in the Ukraine. Comes to America as a young man.   b. 1882

Sara Kravetz Schneider – Avi Schneider's wife.

Lieb Schneider –   Avi Schneider's older brother who stays behind in Uman.

Viktor Askinov –   Avi's childhood tormentor in Uman, and later his brother Lieb's tormentor.

SUPPORTING CHARACTERS

Bettino Rossi –   Avi's friend from his early days in America at the Becker Dress Factory.

Brindyl Schneider – Lieb Schneider's middle daughter.

Chiam Chernoff – Avi's childhood friend from Uman whom he meets again in America.

Daniel Akiva –   Avi Schneider's rabbi and best friend in America.

Duv Eisenberg –   Avi's childhood friend, and benefactor when Avi first arrives in America.

Elias Schneider –   Lieb Schneider's grandson. Son of Lieb's son Joshua.

Ester Schneider Frankel – Avi Schneider's younger sister who marries one of Avi's friends.

Gersh Leibowitz – Lieb's friend and protector in Uman. A local Communist leader.

Golde Schneider – Lieb Schneider's wife.

Hannah Akiva –   Rabbi Daniel Akiva's wife.

Havol Kravetz –   Sara Schneider's younger sister. She stays in Uman, the Ukraine.

Henry Schoor –   Stepson of Sara Schneider's brother Josef. Son of Josef's wife Miryem.

Isaac Schneider – Avi Schneider's son.

Jake Gross –   Avi Schneider's son-in-law.

Josef Kravetz –   Sara Schneider's younger brother. He comes with her to America.

Joshua Schneider – Lieb Schneider's youngest son.

Julia Sorvino –   Avi Schneider's infatuation at the Becker Dress Factory before Sara arrives.

Kay Nolan –   Henry Schoor's nurse.

Manny Weismann – Avi's partner in the tailor shop.

Markus Schneider – Avi Schneider's younger brother, also a tailor.

Max Schneider –   Avi's grandson. Isaac's son.

Mendel Silber –   Avi Schneider's protector on the voyage to America. A revolutionary.

Miryem Schoor Kravetz – Married to Sara Schneider's brother Josef. Henry's mother.

Moishe Stepaner - Avi's childhood friend from Uman who he meets again in America.

Rose Schneider –   Avi's granddaughter. Isaac's daughter.

Sam Lipsky –   Avi Schneider's boss at the Becker Dress Factory, his first job in America.

Sergey Shumenko – Avi Schneider's Christian friend growing up. Then becomes Lieb's friend.

Shaina Schneider – Lieb Schneider's oldest daughter.

Sidney Berman –   Avi Schneider's young, politically connected friend.

Simon Frankel –   Avi's childhood friend. Marries Avi's sister Ester.

Thomas Kelly –   Avi's friend, bar owner, and restaurateur.

Tillie Schneider –   Avi Schneider's daughter-in-law, married to Isaac.

Uncle Yakov –   Young Avi's idol and mentor. A former career soldier. Poppa's brother.

Valerya Shumenko – Wife of Sergey Shumenko, Avi's and Lieb's childhood friend.

Yakira Schneider Gross – Avi Schneider's daughter.

Zelda Schneider –   Avi's youngest sister. Marries an older man and settles in Philadelphia.

A Fine September Morning

PROLOGUE

So why am I in such a hurry to tell this story, you ask? Let me tell you. First of all, I'm an old man and if I don't tell it now, when am I going to tell it? Second of all, I'm a Jew and it's a Jew's duty to remember, especially with everything that's happened. It's the least I can do.

Avi Schneider
October 1947

PART ONE

Avi Alone

CHAPTER ONE

Late November 1905
Uman, the Ukraine

I shot a man the night of the *pogrom*, an evil man. I meant to kill him, but only succeeded in wounding him. I was glad of that, but not of the consequences. If I had killed Viktor Askinov they would have already tried, convicted, and hung me. Instead, they gave me thirty days to settle my affairs and leave Russia forever - expelled. I wanted to leave Uman and go to America, but not like this, not all by myself. Not without my wife, my darling Sara.

The fires from the ferocious mob attacks, the *pogroms*, burned themselves out and the dead were buried. By then the whole town knew there was no longer a place for us Jews in the Tsar's Russia. Sara would join me in America as soon as I was situated and earned enough money to bring her and the children over. The rest of the family would follow. Everyone agreed - Sara, Momma, Poppa, my younger sisters Ester and Zelda, and my younger brother Markus. Everyone but my brother Lieb.

I can admit it now. Convincing Lieb to change his mind and come to America turned out to be my obsession. He was more to me than a brother, more than my best friend. What else can I tell you?

Growing up, we slept in the same bed, went to school together, prayed together, played together, and suffered the torment of Viktor Askinov together. Lieb was a year older but most of the time you wouldn't know it. By the time I was eight years old, I was bigger, could run faster, and read Hebrew better. When we were a little older, I was the one who attracted interest from the girls. But my brother never resented it. In fact, he took as much pride in everything I did as Momma and Poppa. One time when I was about fifteen I threw a rock and knocked Viktor Askinov down, drawing blood. Lieb cheered the loudest and spread tall tales of my great deed.

The day before I left Uman for the last time, Lieb helped me pack my cardboard suitcase, away from everyone else for a few minutes. The smell of Momma's garlic chicken roasting in the wood-burning oven guaranteed a farewell dinner fit for the Sabbath. For a change, there was no sound of crying babies, or of anything else.

Lieb and I talked quietly in my bedroom as he folded my three shirts and my extra pair of pants. I was afraid to look him in the eye for fear I would break down in tears. I handed him my battered copy of War and Peace, a sprig of Sara's golden hair pressed carefully inside the pages.

"I remember the first time you read this," he said. "How old were you, twelve?" He placed it carefully in the bottom of the suitcase.

"Promise me you will come to America," I said.

"America. I wish I could believe in America like you do," he answered. "It would make everything so much easier."

"I need you with me."

"You're the strong one, not me." He looked up from the suitcase. "You're Moses leading your tribe to the Promised Land. So go in good health."

I worried something bad was going to happen if he stayed, but how could I convince my brother of that? "The Tsar's not done with his Jews, you know. He won't be till he's killed, converted, or expelled every last one of us."

"Don't be angry with me, Avi. This is where I belong. I'll be here waiting when the Messiah comes, God willing."

"You sound just like Poppa."

He spoke softly. "I am like Poppa. Is that so bad? And you're like Uncle Yakov. Brave, determined, and discontent with what you have."

"Don't you want a better life for Golde and the kids?" I asked it more as an accusation than a question.

"God will take care of us," he answered. "He has for five thousand years." Lieb smoothed my little bundle of clothes with his hand, then closed the lid of the suitcase and snapped the latch. "Now let's not argue. This may be the last time we see each other for awhile."

Maybe forever, I worried. "But will you think about it?"

"Yes, of course I will think about it." I wasn't convinced he meant it, but I would keep trying to change his mind. If reason didn't work, maybe persistence would.

I hugged him to me when we said goodbye the next morning. He kissed my bearded cheek. Neither of us said anything. We didn't have to. When we pulled back from each other, he raised his left hand and brushed his floppy hair from his eyes, just like he always did.

Even before the *pogrom*s, Uman offered a Jew nothing but a lifetime of despair. America offered hope. But in the dark of the night, as the train I rode rumbled through the driving November ice rain, my certainty wavered. What if Lieb was right and there were *pogroms* in America too, life no better for a Jew there than in Russia? Then I imagined Viktor Askinov leading the mob toward our thinly-defended barricade the night of the *pogrom*, that same wicked sneer on his face I had known since I was a little boy. Life had to be better than that in America, I argued.

Before boarding this train, I had never been more than two or three miles from where I was born. I hadn't even been gone a day and already homesickness for that pitiful place squeezed my heart. I missed my infant daughter, Yakira, and my tiny son, Itzhak as we called him then. I missed the whole family. But most of all I missed my Sara. We made love that last night, mindless of the noise we were making for the rest of the family to hear through the thin walls. Then we held each other and talked quietly until dawn. Such memories were going to have to hold me for at least a year until I could bring her to America.

The hard slat-back seat of the dilapidated third class passenger car tortured my back. Lights were still on in the occasional villages that passed outside my window, interrupting the ink-black darkness. Kerosene lamps at either end of the compartment cast gray lonely shadows. I began a letter to Lieb, the first of many I would write him. I didn't finish and post it until I got to Antwerp.

> *My dear brother Lieb,*
>
> *As I write this, I am surrounded by poor, unwashed Jews, mostly men, escaping the Tsar's grasp, all headed for America. The men look a lot like those from our village with their ragged clothes and scruffy beards. The few women wear faded head-scarves full of holes, little better than the rags Momma uses to wash the dishes. Several men dress in the black of Hassidics, their dreadlocks dangling beneath their black hats.*
>
> *I feel a certain freedom I never felt in Uman. Please do not tell Momma and Poppa, but already I have eaten some unkosher food. When the train stopped in Warsaw for an hour, I bought sausage, bread, cheese and beer from a vendor strolling through the crowd on the platform. I was famished, tempted by the aroma of the sausage. It was delicious, I must say.*
>
> *I met a most interesting fellow not much older than me named Mendel Silber. He is sitting right beside me as I write you this letter. He got on a few stops after Kiev. He swaggered down the aisle, hoisted his huge suitcase into the rack above, and sat down next to me. He is nice enough, and he is sailing on the same ship I am, the Finland, from Antwerp. He told me he left a wife and two children behind, like me.*
>
> *We have had lots of time to talk. He is from Gorotsky, not far from the Polish border, and was a factory worker. He has the big, broad shoulders and calloused hands to prove it. I think he*

is a Bolshevik. He rants on and on about capitalists and bour-
geois. He says they are all vampires sucking the blood out of the
workers, whether they are Jews or gentiles. He says it is the same
in America, but I do not believe him.

The cocksure manner with which he carries himself reminds
me of our friend Duv Eisenberg. He seems to know how to han-
dle any situation. I worry about crooks, police, and bureaucrats
waiting ahead to harry me. I thought I might need a world-wise
ally like Mendel Silber, so I nod and agree with everything he
says.

The only time I saw Mendel waver was when our train stopped at
the Polish border for entry inspections. Two of the Tsar's secret police
in their black leather coats boarded our car, along with two armed soldiers in blue winter longcoats and fur hats. All of the passengers tried
to shrink themselves into their seats, to make themselves invisible. It
was so quiet you could hear a pin drop. The sole sounds were the
chugging of the idling locomotive and the click of the policemen's
boots on the plank floor of our railcar. They stopped five rows in front
of me, jerked a terrified bespectacled young man to his feet, and
dragged him off the train.

Mendel released a long gush of air when they left, and unclenched
his fists. "Pig scum," he snarled. He pulled a tobacco pouch from his
vest pocket, rolled a cigarette, lit it and exhaled the vapor toward the
ceiling. He stared off, his hand shaking.

I went back to writing my letter to Lieb. I told my brother about the
secret police boarding our train.

My tension didn't dissolve until our locomotive issued a blast
of its horn and chugged out of the station. After that, I do not
need any more explanations about why we must leave Russia.
America offers the hope of a better life for our children.

There is too much time to think on this train. One minute I
marvel at the beauty of the rolling Polish countryside, so differ-

ent from the flat Ukrainian plains around Uman. Then the next minute I see Viktor Askinov and the fury in his eyes. When we were children, his brother and his henchmen often looked like they were beating up on us because they were gentiles and that is what they were supposed to do to Jewish kids. But with him, only beating on Jews satisfied his rage.

You and Uncle Yakov and everyone else keep saying how courageous I was for what I did the night of the pogrom. It was not courage. It was something else, but I am not sure what. I see Viktor Askinov's crimson blood pooling on the ground and feel satisfaction. It is a horrible thing to realize I can shoot another man without remorse, but at least for the moment, I suffer none. May God forgive me.

I fear for you, my dear brother, if you alone stay behind in Uman after the rest of the family leaves for America. Uncle Yakov will not be there to protect you for much longer. Come join me, I beg you.

In Antwerp, Mendel found us a barn to sleep in for a few nights until our ship arrived. He quickly discovered a nearby whorehouse that serviced transient passengers and sailors. "Are you a virgin?" he mocked when I refused to join him. "I told you before. I'm married," I answered, as though that might make a difference to someone like Mendel Silber. When I got back to the barn, I wrote Sara a letter to tell her I arrived in Antwerp. Mostly I told her how deeply I loved her and how much I longed for her.

I thought then, and I think now, about the day Sara and I met in the village square on an April market day. The sun turned her hair golden and her eyes a glimmering deep blue. She was the most beautiful young woman I had ever seen, and she seemed to be the only one who didn't realize it. She saw me staring and smiled. I knew in that instant I had to have her, and she let me know she had to have me too.

We waited two days for our ship to arrive, and another for it to prepare to go to sea. Emigrants crowded the dockside, along with stevedores and journeymen workers loading and unloading ships. Many of the travelers looked like me in thread-bare coats and patched shoes, but a few men dressed in short skirts with leggings, funny hats, or billowing dresses in brilliant multi-colors. They spoke languages I never heard before, ate strange foods, and smelled odd. Mendel said they were village Greeks and Turks. Though their oddity made me uneasy, they also intrigued me. I couldn't take my eyes off of them.

During our wait, Mendel protected me from the crooks and con men that would take all of your money in a rigged card game, or sell you fake insurance. They could spot a kindred soul in Mendel as readily as he spotted them.

The day before we departed Antwerp, the steamship company put us through a physical examination, and for good reason. Anyone who failed the medical inspection once we got to America was sent back to Europe at the company's expense. So doctors and nurses poked and explored every inch of our bodies.

When I finished with the examination, I walked to the telegraph office and sent a cable to my friend Duv in New York City to tell him which ship I was on and when to meet me. I was excited about seeing him again. His innocent mischief and naughty wit made growing up in Uman bearable. He had been in America now for nearly three years and, from what he wrote me, he knew his way around. He promised to smooth my path.

The *Finland* rose graceful and powerful in the water with its smokestacks casting gigantic shadows on the dock. On the day of our departure we waited while the five hundred or so first and second class passengers boarded ahead of us. Many of these finely dressed women wore high collared jackets and long satin skirts, and their men sported stylish dark suits with starched high collared shirts of the best broadcloth.

Mendel was late, turning up just before we started boarding. He looked white as a corpse, secreting stale odors of whiskey, cigars and body fluids.

"I didn't think you were going to make it," I said. "You look awful."

He leaned against me for support, one hand on my shoulder. "It was worth it," he moaned. He surely didn't look as though it was worth it.

At last six hundred of us ragamuffins traveling in steerage tramped up the gangplank. The cardboard suitcase I clutched by the handle contained the total of all my belongings, along with the forty American dollars I converted from rubles. At the top of the gangplank, the deck crew pushed us toward the metal steps into the hold, cursing and shouting, menacing clubs in hand, just like Cossacks. We barely started moving when an older man threw up in the middle of the floor.

The dark, smelly steerage compartments divided into separate dormitories for men and women, the narrow bunks we slept on stacked three high. Mendel's bunk was so close to mine we touched shoulder to shoulder. There was no privacy.

How fast the Jewish virgins lost their chastity to the freedoms of America. They immediately forgot everything they had been taught. Men will be men, but how could these women do such things, I wondered? Mendel took full advantage of the situation, as such men will do. He also took advantage of the rigged card games.

Everyone mingled in the dining room one level up. Mendel used his meal times to investigate the women. He eyed every one we passed; many smiled and eyed him back. Maybe it was his air of danger that made him irresistible. It didn't take him long to find what he wanted.

Two or three days after we sailed, I heard some grunting from underneath a stairway as I passed. I could guess by now what was happening and kept my eyes straight ahead, trying hard not to look. I thought I heard a female voice say "Avi." I turned my head and saw a skinny, dark haired woman, her skirt hoisted above her waist, and Mendel behind her with his pants around his ankles, hands on her hips. She fixed her eyes on me, sneering through her grunts. She wasn't embarrassed, and didn't pause for even a moment.

"Get outa' here! Get out," Mendel barked, continuing his thrusts. She moaned louder for my benefit. I hurried away, telling myself this was depraved. I didn't say anything when I saw Mendel a few hours later for dinner. "You can have her next," he said to me like he was offering to share a piece of bread.

"No thanks." I tried to sound disgusted and self-righteous; the truth is when I saw Mendel and that woman fornicating, an embarrassing erection arose. This should have been a warning to me that my needs were no less than any other man's, no matter my determination to stay faithful to Sara. But I didn't hear the warning. I was too certain of my love and my virtue.

Midway across the sea, steerage resembled an insane asylum. Toilets overflowed, the stench mixing with the cloud from unwashed bodies, unchanged diapers, and over-boiled cabbage. Babies cried. Tempers flashed over the smallest provocation.

The worse conditions got, the more Mendel ranted about the capitalists who owned the ship, and the more he ranted the more our shipmates listened to him. On our sixth day at sea, he led a short-lived protest sparked by our daily ration of foul watery soup, moldy bread, rot-pocked potatoes, and the rare glob of fat cloaked as meat. The protest ended immediately when the captain of the ship issued a warning that trouble makers would be sent back home as soon as we landed in America. We were all drained when the final day of our voyage arrived.

The sun sparkled off the water on the crisp December morning the *Finland* entered the mouth of the Hudson River. A bright blue sky shined above. All these years later and still I can't explain to you how I felt when I leaned over the deck railing and sighted the tall buildings of New York City. Then the majestic copper of the Statue of Liberty glided by right in front of me. The other immigrants stood silent and motionless, as spellbound as I was. A few of the older men mumbled quiet prayers, their eyes closed and their heads down, swaying forward and back. There was America. I swore to God I would bring my family to this Promised Land, every one of them, even Lieb. Nothing was going to stop me. But sometimes we take such oaths not understanding God and fate have a say in the matter.

Though still early, the harbor buzzed with ferries and tugboats, while longshoremen on the docks unloaded cargo from the ships that arrived the night before. Going down the crowded gangplank, I bumped into Mendel Silber. "Good luck," I said as pleasantly as I could.

"Yeah, you too." His eyes were cold and distant, his lips tight. I thought I was rid of him, and glad of it.

Our six hundred confused steerage passengers pushed onto small open-air ferries that carried us to the menacing red-brick fortress of Ellis Island. I was so scared I might be rejected my wobbly knees knocked like drumsticks on a Sabbath chicken. For the next hours, doctors, nurses, and immigration officials explored our physical and mental worthiness.

By the time I reached the Great Hall, all I could think about was that I had to go to the toilet so badly I didn't care whether they let me in or sent me back so long as they let me pee. A huge American flag hung from the rafters at the far end of a gigantic room even bigger than the inside of the Warsaw train station. The multitude of incomprehensible languages jumbled together into an out-of-tune chorus of angry street cats.

A row of inspectors in starched collars and heavy blue serge jackets sat at tall desks with the ships' manifests opened in front of them. My trembling hand clutched my medical inspection card in a death grip. The inspector pried it from my fingers, and verified everything on the manifest in about two minutes. He stamped my documents and gave me a landing card for entry into the United States. Just like that and I was in America, too dumbstruck to yet rejoice.

A ferry took the crowd of us over to New York City in a matter of minutes. When we walked onto the dock a red haired, bearded fellow dropped to his knees and kissed the ground.

Do you know how sometimes you yearn for something and pray for it – something really big? Then it happens and it seems impossible it is happening to you. That's how it was for me that cold, sunny afternoon. I bubbled with hope, no longer afraid. Not yet twenty-four years old, I had already lived one lifetime and was about to begin another. Nothing mattered now except working hard so I could save enough to bring Sara over right away. I had no idea how difficult that dream was to fulfill - or the cost of failure.

CHAPTER TWO

Late December 1905

So much had happened since Duv and I said goodbye in Uman three years before, but from the instant we grasped each other in a bear hug, it felt as if we had never been apart. He looked me over from head to toe. "You're a mess," he laughed. "We're going to have to clean you up and get rid of that beard." His own face was smooth as an egg shell. He picked up my suitcase and joined the herd of immigrants swarming from the dock toward the subway.

We jabbered above the noise like a couple of geese, bouncing from the serious to the frivolous. I told him about Sara, Poppa's tailor shop, the *pogrom*, and shooting Viktor Askinov. He told me about the easy virtue of American girls, and how anyone could make lots of money in America if he had an angle. Whatever we talked about, sharing with my friend again felt good. Duv, without a care in the world, always chased mine away too.

"You'll stay with Rebecca and me until we get you set up in your own place," Duv said as we emerged from the subway station into daylight. "This neighborhood's called East Harlem. Most Jews live in the Lower East Side, but East Harlem's better. More American. You'll like it." A few men we passed wore fancy suits and fine bowler hats, and a few women wore well-tailored coats down to the ground. But most of them wore patched coats and worn shoes, little better than the Jews back home.

Duv stopped in front of one of the brown brick tenements. "This is it," he said with a grand sweep of his hand. We walked up the stone steps to the landing; he unlocked the door and led me down a dark hall with a ceiling of ornamented tin. Then we climbed the narrow staircase up four flights, Duv still carrying my small suitcase.

Duv's wife Rebecca was small, dark haired and plain. She spoke softly, her eyes tilted toward the floor, and smiled only in brief flickers. Duv was not unkind but paid little attention to her or their dark haired little boy. She seemed more servant than wife.

He met and deflowered Rebecca on the ship coming over. She was only sixteen then, a virgin. He didn't expect to ever see her again once they landed, but when she found herself pregnant, her father and Duv's father made him marry her. He was not happy about it.

"Sit," Duv commanded. I collapsed into a big, soft armed chair. "We have a toilet down the hall," he bragged. "But we still have to haul water and coal from downstairs." His little boy crawled into my lap and began playing with my nose when I put my arm around him.

My friend must be very rich already, I thought. They had these three rooms all to themselves. A polished wooden table sat by the sofa; a tick-tock clock hung on rose-patterned wallpaper. I hoped someday I could give something like this to Sara.

When he wrote me in Uman, Duv promised he would get me a job where he worked. "I need to start making some money right away," I said the next morning. But it was Sunday and the first thing on Duv's mind was to show me New York City. So we grabbed our coats and headed out the door. He gave Rebecca a perfunctory "goodbye." She mumbled something, not looking up from feeding the boy.

My breath showed in the cold morning air. The streets were already packed. My open-mouthed gawks at the horseless carriages, the clanging streetcars, and the tall buildings amused Duv no end. Everyone spoke a different language. I could understand the Jews and the

Germans, but not the Italians or the Irish. We passed a newsboy hawking Yiddish newspapers on the street corner. Across the street a Negro man played ragtime on an accordion while his little boy tap danced. His big white teeth shined from a face blacker than coal.

"We got everything you want right here in the neighborhood," Duv boasted as if he were the mayor. "Food markets, theaters, free schools, banks, a hospital. You name it." He pointed out the big new library, and then gestured toward the East River. "There's a rubber factory, an iron factory, and sewing factories down that way."

We dodged around one of the stalls selling dented pots and chipped plates. Others peddled beeswax candles and sweets from their pushcarts. The storefronts sold more merchandise than I had ever seen in the Uman market square, even on market day: vegetables, books, feathered hats, meats, fish, breads. I couldn't imagine how so many poor people could afford to buy so much.

"How about a synagogue?" I asked.

"Lots of them. Take your pick." Apparently Duv wasn't spending much time in a synagogue.

He kept on walking and talking, pushing his way past three older women gossiping on a tenement doorstep. "Where are we going?" I asked. Duv gave me one of his devilish grins that growing up usually meant fun, trouble, or both.

We climbed the steps of a once-grand white clapboard house mixed among the stores and tenements. The paint was peeling, exposing bare rotting wood. I tried peering in the windows, but they were covered. "I've picked out a present for you," he said.

Duv opened the door with the familiarity of someone who had been there often. A large-breasted woman wearing too much lipstick and too few clothes met us. "Duv. I thought you wasn't coming." She put her arms out and pulled him to her bosom. "The girls are waiting." Her throaty voice grated like gravel.

The woman led us into a big, over-adorned living room with red flocked wallpaper, two plush red sofas, and a couple of gold stuffed chairs. The lamps on the tables were turned low, the heavy red drapes changing day into dusk. The reek of perfume choked my nose. A woman's shrill laugh carried from the floor above.

"What is this place?" I shifted back and forth, cap in hand, not liking what I was thinking. Uncle Yakov warned me about houses of prostitution. This is what I imagined they looked like.

"Wait till you see this chocolate bundle I picked out for you." Duv took off his coat and hung it on a brass coat tree inside the front door.

"She's our best," the big woman said, amused by my discomfort. "But if you'd rather have a Wop or a blond...."

A middle aged man in a checkered suit and vest came down the steps, one hand on the dark wooden banister. He avoided looking at us. A painted woman in a dressing gown at the top of the staircase waved to him and yelled "come back." He grabbed his coat from the coat tree and hurried out the door.

Duv started up the steps. I didn't move.

"I'm leaving," I said.

Duv stopped, his hand resting on the banister. "What's the matter? Can't you just relax and have some fun for once in your life?" The big woman stood with her hands on her hips as though I had insulted her.

"What's happened to you?" I said.

"Suit yourself." He resumed his climb up the staircase.

I went the other direction, out the door, slamming it behind me. I walked around in circles, disgusted Duv would take me to such a place. Maybe America changed him more than I thought possible. I felt dirty and guilty just for being inside that house. But I have to admit, it had been a little bit tempting. Sara must never know about this, I thought. She was such an innocent; she never could imagine the carnal side of men.

Three days later, the Kiev Gibernya Benevolent Society found me a place to live a few blocks from Duv's apartment. I had heard on the ship about these associations made up of men from the same area back home; they helped their fellow *landsmen* get settled. It was nice to know they were there if I needed them.

Seven of us lived together in a three-room apartment smaller than Duv's. All of us were lonely men in a hurry to earn enough money to bring our wives over. Two slept head to toe in the single bed in the kitchen, three slept across the bed in the bedroom, and two slept with their shoulders on the sofa and the rest of their bodies across a low table. I woke up every morning with a sore back. We rotated positions every week. The apartment itself was dark, moldy, peeling paint and wallpaper, with little furniture. But it was cheap. We split the eleven dollar monthly rent among us.

I immediately wrote a long letter home to Sara telling her about Duv's apartment, the tall buildings, black people, Chinamen, streetcars, and the library. My letter would take three or four weeks to reach Uman.

In the meantime, Sara's first letter to me arrived, delivered through Duv. Actually, she dictated her letter to Ester because Sara couldn't read or write. There were two surprises. First, Lieb decided after I left to join Poppa and Markus in the tailor shop. Poppa said he was a natural tailor and learning fast. It made me wonder why Lieb waited for me to leave before doing that. But I think I knew the answer: He wouldn't compete with me.

Poppa had a tailor shop on the market square, just like his father before him. That would have been my life too if I had stayed. Growing up, Lieb never seemed to like the shop, and when he was old enough, he apprenticed as a baker. I, on the other hand, loved tailoring. By the time I was sixteen, everyone said I was the best tailor in the family. I missed the feeling of the cloth beneath my fingers.

The bigger news was about Ester teaching Sara to read and write. There in Sara's own child-like script she wrote *Sara loves Avi.* I sniffed the paper and I swear I could smell her on it. I ached to hold her and hear her voice. Since I couldn't, I just closed my eyes and imagined her.

I thought about the sunny day I kissed her for the first time in the clearing in the woods at Sukhi Yar, and she kissed me back, trembling. Next I thought about the day she clutched me to her after her heartless father said we could marry – but only after his earlier refusal brought her near deathly despair. Then I pictured the way she cradled Itzhak in her arms while he suckled at her breast, and the way she played with Yakira and made her laugh, as natural a mother as Eve. I thought about how she helped Momma in the kitchen and Poppa in the garden, her precious smile melting their hearts. They loved her as much as I did, and she them. I thought about how shy my fearless Uncle Yakov was around her and how she made him smile when no one else could. I thought about her anxious lovemaking the first time on our wedding night, and then her eager abandon every time after. And I thought about her innocent beauty that made men gasp and women envious; it would have embarrassed her if she ever noticed. My heart ached every time I thought about her, but I could no more stop the ache than I could stop loving her.

One of my roommates, Gideon Katz, reminded me of Lieb, quiet and gentle. He even looked a little like him, with a big nose and hair flopping down over his eyes. The Friday after Sara's letter arrived, he took me to Sabbath services at a synagogue on 113th Street, a short walk from our apartment.

It was the strangest synagogue I ever saw, nothing more than a vacant storefront with a few chairs and benches scattered about the linoleum-covered floor. A clothes wardrobe in the front simulated an altar to hold a Torah – if they had had a Torah. It didn't feel like a synagogue at all until Rabbi Daniel Akiva began chanting the same familiar prayers we said back in Uman. I closed my eyes and let comfort wash over me, the first comfort I felt since arriving in this strange land.

The prayers may have been ancient, but the rabbi was as American as George Washington. After the service, he went to each of the eleven men, the three women and the six children, engaging each in a bit of conversation. He shook every man's hand, patted the women on the shoulder, and bent down to talk to each child.

Daniel was not much older than me. He looked like every other Jew except more handsome and cleaner. When he embraced you, as he often did once we became good friends, it was like the enveloping hug of a bear. He carried himself with a confidence rare among Russian Jews. In the many years since, he sometimes wore a beard, sometimes only a moustache, and more often neither. The day I met him he had neither.

A couple of days later, we ran into each other at the library where I went to escape the cramped apartment while I waited for Duv to get me the promised job where he worked. Daniel invited me to join him for a piece of pie at a pastry shop around the corner. Over an apple strudel and coffee, we told each other our stories. He came to America with his family when he was only six years old, so he missed the *pogroms*. He had gone to American schools and spoke perfect English. His mother and father owned a laundry on Lexington Avenue near 116th Street. They made a good living. We talked all afternoon about our wives, our kids, our favorite books, and our dreams. It seems we talked about everything but the Torah and the Talmud.

Daniel was as eager for my friendship as I was for his. During the next several days, I went to Sabbath services again, met him at the library, and shared a beer with him. "You must come have dinner at our apartment and meet Hannah," he said. I accepted. His wife, Hannah, was plain but pleasant, and as warm as Daniel. She looked like a pixie, with short red hair, a flat chest and a splash of freckles on her face. They fit together like the fingers of interlaced hands.

Many years later and still we're best friends. Who knew then how much I was going to need Daniel? I couldn't have survived this life without him.

In the meantime, I pestered Duv about the job every time I saw him. He worked long hours but always had enough energy for a visit to the Kinsale Tavern on his way home. The first night he brought me there, he stopped about halfway up the glistening mahogany bar. The bouquet of stale beer cut through the haze of cigarette smoke. "This is my spot," he said, rubbing the bar top gently with his hand as though it were the round rump of an attractive woman. He propped his foot up on the brass rail and looked at himself in the big mirror behind the bar, admiring what he saw.

The bar man, a young Irishman named Thomas Kelly, served us. "Thomas will talk your ear off if you let him," Duv said, nodding toward him.

"Aye, and some of what I have to say is the truth." Thomas's dark eyes twinkled from a handsome, dark haired Irish face.

Duv had promised again and again to talk to his boss about me, but hadn't done it as far as I could tell. When I finally lost my temper that night, he promised still again to talk to Sam Lipsky. Tomorrow.

The next night, we met at the tavern. Laughter exploded from the table of Jews seated under the big window. At the other end of the tavern, four Italians sat around a table drinking shots of whiskey, engaged in serious debate.

"Good news," Duv said as he sat down on a stool beside me at the bar. His sour expression didn't match the words coming out of his mouth. "Sam Lipsky will see you in the morning, and if he likes what he sees you start right away. I told him you were good at repairing sewing machines. I guess you'll do that. Maybe some packing and carrying bundles."

Duv's reflection and mine stared back at us in the mirror behind the bar. "You don't look very happy about it," I said.

"It's a different kind of place."

"Thanks for doing this."

A Negro boy pecked out some Scott Joplin ragtime at a piano in the back of the tavern. The Maple Street Rag did nothing to lighten our uncomfortable silence.

"I'm not going to be at the Becker Dress Factory forever," he said. He took a big gulp of beer, draining it. "Another." He motioned to Thomas Kelly who was rubbing the polished bar top with a towel. Duv hadn't smiled a genuine smile since he walked in the door. Whatever was going on made me uneasy, but I would put up with anything if it meant earning enough money to get Sara over here fast.

The next day Duv took me to meet Sam Lipsky. The factory was on the sixth floor of a brick building only a few blocks from Duv's apartment. "We have an elevator, but it's not working right now," Duv said when we went in the door on the ground floor. He looked as sour as he had the night before.

We clomped up the dark narrow staircase. "Sam's a tough man," Duv warned. "No talking back to him."

I could hear the clattering of sewing machines well before we got to the sixth floor. This is what hell must be like, I thought when we went inside. Women hunched over their machines, six rows of ten each, pumping the pedals and moving the fabric under the needles. A few looked old enough to be my mother and a few looked like children. The rest were young women.

A couple of men off to the side pressed the dresses. One of them looked up at us and nodded. A man raced back and forth with bundles of partially sewn garments, carrying them from one operator to another. The building was so cold I could see my breath. The cloud of lint could make a mule gag.

"You get used to it," Duv yelled over the noise, motioning for me to follow him. We passed by the one row of windows. Operators nearest the windows could see what they were doing. Those in the back had only a few gas lamps on the wall to work by. On this gloomy day, the light from the windows didn't carry very far.

The moment I met his boss I knew why Duv wasn't eager for me to get a job at the Becker Dress Factory. Shmuel Lipsky called himself Sam in America, but he was still Shmuel from the *shtetl*. The scorn on his fat, protruding lips gave him a tough, mean look. Horn-rimmed glasses enlarged his hollow brown eyes.

"So this is your hero from Uman." He growled through brown stained teeth clenched on an unlit cigar stub. I held out my hand for a handshake, but he kept his on his hips, examining me. My outstretched hand felt foolish. I dropped it to my side.

"Let's see what you can do, Schneider. That machine's broken." He pointed toward a place at the end of the third row of sewing machines. "Fix it." He reached down behind a table and pulled out a canvass bag of tools. He threw it on the floor in front of me.

"What's wrong with it?" I asked, picking up the tool bag.

"If I knew that I wouldn't need you," he snapped.

He watched me make my way to the machine. Duv hadn't said a word, but now he and Lipsky started talking. Mostly it was Lipsky who did the talking. Duv just nodded his head a few times. The din covered whatever they were saying.

I could fix our old sewing machine at the tailor shop, but I had never seen sewing machines like these. And Lipsky didn't look like a patient man. I felt like my whole future was riding on fixing that one machine.

The aisles between the rows were so close there was hardly enough room for me to push the chair back and squeeze in. The scrawny black haired young woman seated to my right didn't even look up when I sat down. She kept grinding away at the piece she was working on, her purple skirt pulled up to her knees. Her legs pumped hard on the peddle. She paused for just an instant and spoke above the roar.

"That one's a bastard," she said without as much as a glance over at Lipsky. "Be careful." She resumed peddling. I didn't know what to make of it. I said nothing.

I'd never seen a Singer sewing machine before, but it looked enough like the one we had in the tailor shop. I checked the shuttle cover, the feed, the bobbin winder and the needle bar. They all seemed to be working.

"Come on, Schneider. We don't have all day," Lipsky yelled. I took a deep breath and kept working. In a few minutes, I found the problem. It was one of the levers. I tightened a screw, made a few twists and had it running.

Sitting at a sewing machine again felt good. I grabbed a remnant piece of material and ran it through to be sure everything was working. Lipsky had been watching me the whole time. I walked back to him. Duv was gone.

"You can start right now. You get seven bucks a week. You'll repair any machines that break, carry bundles, load the truck, sweep up.

Anything else I tell ya'. Understand?"

"Yes, and thank you." I smiled. He didn't.

"And one more thing, Schneider. Have Duv tell you how things work around here."

I had just met this man, but already I didn't like him. Still, I was relieved to have a job. And it paid seven dollars a week, more than twenty-eight dollars a month. That was a lot of money then. My share of the apartment rent was only two dollars a month. I needed a little for food, a beer now and then, and perhaps a trip to the Lower East Side occasionally. Oh, and a little for some American clothes. I could still save a lot. In a year I should have plenty of money to bring Sara over and set up an apartment. I was going to work as hard as I could; if I did maybe Lipsky would pay me a little more.

Poppa always said you have to judge each man one at a time, and that not all gentiles are bad or all Jews good. I feared Sam Lipsky was going to prove Poppa right about bad Jews.

CHAPTER THREE

February 1906

No one wanted to be late or Lipsky fined you. The elevator never worked, so every morning began at ten minutes before seven o'clock with a six-flight climb up the dark stairs. I felt uncomfortable sandwiched among the pack of women. One day a hand rubbed up and down my leg, the firm stroke not accidental. I thought it must be the Italian named Ladonna, a chesty young woman. She said words I had never heard before but could tell they were foul from her mocking tone. Another time I was pinched on my behind. That time I was sure it was Ladonna. I tried to stay clear of her, but she took too much pleasure in my discomfort to stop.

The starting horn blared at seven and the machines roared like a locomotive. When the horn sounded for lunch, the thunder stopped momentarily. A peddler came through the shop selling rolls, breads and hard boiled eggs. I brought my own stale rye bread, usually with a piece of fruit or a hunk of salami. It was cheaper that way.

Duv was usually by Lipsky's side, so most days I had my lunch with the presser, Bettino Rossi. He was a dark skinned Italian from Naples, a little older than me. He had been in America since he was sixteen, and spoke good English. Bettino never smiled.

Right from the beginning he suggested something wasn't right at the Becker Dress Factory. He had worked there for about a year, and from his station off to the side, he saw everything that went on. One day shortly after I started, we sat on the floor in a corner munching our lunch. "Do you have to give Lipsky a dollar each month for insurance?" I asked. Insurance was one of those things Duv had explained to me about how things worked at the Becker Dress Factory. I didn't understand.

Bettino snickered. "There is no insurance. It's a payoff to Lipsky so you get to keep your job."

"That's like stealing."

"Just pay it. Don't ask questions." He finished his hunk of hard cheese and wiped his mouth on his shirt sleeve. "We've got it easy. The women...."

The blare of the horn interrupted. Lunch time was over. Lipsky moved up and down the aisles. "Back to work. Back to work. Moretti, get going or it'll be a dollar fine," he yelled, pointing a finger at one of the Italian girls in the back row. "Hurry. Hurry." The young woman he had pointed at, Natali Moretti, looked like a frightened rabbit. A dollar would have fed her for a week. She sat down at her machine and began peddling furiously.

My job was hard, but not nearly as hard as the women's. This was before electricity so the machines ran on foot-power, the women peddling as fast as they could, hunched over their work tables all day long. Color was gone from their skin and the light from their eyes. Dark lines crossed their young faces. The unventilated factory smelled from lint and the filthy toilet facilities in back. Sometimes I had to stick my head out an open window just to catch some fresh air.

The piles kept coming all day long. Duv or I stacked unfinished garments on the operator's left. When she finished a garment, she laid it on the right. I picked up the finished garments, moving the bundles along to the next station for the next operation. Some days I helped Bettino with the pressing and swept the floor at the end of the day.

The women came from all over Europe. There was Freida, a big boned, grim German girl who overflowed her chair. Of all the powerful smells in the factory, Freida's stood out. There was Anka, a striking chestnut haired Polish girl with iridescent blue eyes that reminded me of Sara's. She was pleasant looking until she opened her mouth and showed her decayed teeth. Her harsh voice grated like steel on steel. But she was a nice, religious Catholic girl.

Then there were the Jews, Selma and Rose. Selma was timid and shy, with a beaked nose and freckles like Ester. She was thin as a match stick and looked sickly. She didn't say much. Rose, on the other hand, was brash, crude and had the face of a mule. She tried to protect Selma.

The Italians – Natali Moretti and Camella – sat in the third row next to each other. Both of them were from Naples, like Bettino. Natali was quiet, ordinary looking, with a pleasant smile. Camella, on the other hand, might have been pretty if it weren't for her heavy moustache.

Ladonna and Mira were Lipsky's favorites. Ladonna was a seductive blond Italian with big melons for breasts. She was sarcastic and unpleasant. Mira, a Jewess from Hungary, was loud and flirtatious. She and Ladonna took pleasure in embarrassing me. I tried to stay away from them.

They all ended the day with tired eyes and hopeless faces. In dimming light, everyone trudged back down that dark stairway, or out the fire escape. For me, each day was one day closer to seeing Sara again. I fell asleep so tired I could have lay on rocks and not minded. My last thought was always of Sara.

One time when I was gulping air out the window I saw Ruppert Becker, the owner, arrive in his polished horseless carriage with his liveried driver. Both of them sported goggles, tan hats, and tan driving coats. Underneath his coat, Mr. Becker wore a stylish black suit with a black vest, starched white shirt and a black bow tie. His clothes blended well with his full head of gray hair and bushy moustache. A heavy gold watch chain hung from a button on his vest into his watch pocket. He took out the watch and flipped up the cover as soon as he walked into the factory. He stared at it for a second, snapped it shut and moved on to his office.

Mr. Becker only came in occasionally and when he did he stayed mostly in his office at the back of the factory. Sometimes he stood with Lipsky observing the factory floor for a few minutes. Then he secluded himself in his office with Lipsky again. At least while Mr. Becker was there we didn't have Lipsky prowling the factory floor.

I tried to ignore much of what I saw but by the time the spring thaw came, even a naive boy from Uman could tell something wasn't right. Either Duv or Lipsky patrolled the floor. Some of the women were favored and some were harassed. Lipsky threatened the meekest ones with fines or firing over the most trivial infractions, often contrived. Duv wasn't anything like Lipsky, but he played favorites too, and made advances wherever he could.

When Lipsky came near, most of the women shriveled. He singled out Selma and Camella for particular abuse. If one of them had to use the disgusting toilet, Lipsky or Duv yelled at her through the door should she take longer than a minute or two.

Lipsky inspected Selma's and Camella's finished pieces more often than the other girls and rejected many. He made them rip out the stitches and do them over again. Sewing machine operators worked on a piece rate; these re-works cut into their stingy wages. Duv, for his part, would bring over big bundles and say with a threatening urgency, "Lipsky wants these done fast."

A few, like Ladonna and Mira, flirted openly with Lipsky. Duv got his attention from a couple of the other girls. Lipsky never yelled at the favored ones and gave them the easiest operations to do.

One day when everyone was done and I was alone sweeping the floors, I took a look at a few of Camella's rejected pieces. There was nothing wrong with them. Ladonna's and Mira's finished pieces were terrible, with many missed stitches.

Lipsky docked wages if a garment was torn or damaged for any reason. He charged the girls for needles and thread. But Ladonna and Mira were never docked or charged as far as I could tell. What is going on here, I asked myself?

I made up my mind to ask Duv about it, but he had taken to avoiding me. We rarely talked at the factory and hadn't had a drink together for weeks. I waited several days before I asked him to join me for a beer at the Kinsale Tavern. He nodded without looking up from the box he was packing.

We made small talk on the way to the tavern about people back home, and dodged around puddles from the earlier April shower. Thomas Kelly waved to us from behind the bar as we came in and immediately poured two beers. We grabbed them and moved to a table in back.

Duv sensed where this conversation was going and was as reluctant to start as I was. I wondered why he had even come. We drank our beers, chewed on pretzels, and listened to the player piano pump out the Entertainer Rag.

"Becker Dress Factory is a strange place to work," I finally said.

"This whole country's strange."

"Duv, what's going on?" I tried to look him in the eye but he absorbed himself in studying the foam in his glass of beer.

"You get paid, don't you?" His hand squeezed the glass. I leaned toward him; he leaned away.

"Why is everyone so scared of Lipsky?"

"He's a tough boss."

The player piano moved on to Harlem Rag. The upbeat was not in tune with the mood at our table.

"It's more than that."

He finally looked right at me. "Do you want to keep your job?" Duv without a smile on his face didn't even look like Duv.

"You make that sound like a threat."

"Leave it alone." He slammed his empty beer glass on the table.

Thomas Kelly came over to the table to see if we wanted another round.

"We're all done," Duv said, pushing his chair back. He walked out the door without as much as a goodbye. I slumped in my chair, watching him leave.

A few days later I tried again to talk it out with Duv, but this time he refused to even have a beer with me. I didn't want to think the worst of my friend, but he wasn't giving me a choice. I had the terrible feeling that tells you when you've lost someone important to you. His shrouded warning about keeping my job left me feeling unsettled.

So what had happened to Duv, I asked myself over and over again? When we were kids, he might have been irreverent toward our Jewish traditions, but in a playful way. Now he was self-indulgent of his own pleasures, and indifferent to the cruelty of Sam Lipsky. There was a bitter edge beneath his shallow smile. Maybe it was because he had a loveless marriage thrust on him before he was ready. Maybe it was something about America. Or maybe it was because he lost his mother when he was still a little boy, replaced by a harsh stepmother who wasn't reluctant to strike him with whatever was handy.

I tried to make every imaginable excuse for Duv, but whatever the cause, my old friend was gone. And I was all the more lonely for Sara and home.

CHAPTER FOUR

JUNE 1906

Lieb's first letter arrived on a bright spring day. I put it in my pocket unopened and hurried to the library where I could read it in peace. Nobody wanted to be inside on such a magnificent Saturday afternoon so the library was almost empty. I sat down at my table in the corner, pulled out the letter, and carefully opened it. Every page felt like Lieb was there with me, even the dirt smudge in the corner. I was always the only one who could read his left-handed Yiddish scrawl. It looked like it had been scratched out by a wounded chicken.

The first thing he did was assure me Sara and the children were safe, still protected by Uncle Yakov and his army comrades. He went on:

> *Now about Viktor Askinov. He was released from the hospital a month after you left. I see him every now and then. He walks with a crazy limp, a souvenir of his encounter with you. He looks like he's dragging a big tree trunk behind him. We all call him the Kalike – the Cripple. They say he will have this limp for the rest of his life.*
>
> *Some say he's still stirring up trouble. I don't doubt it, but*

don't worry. Uncle Yakov keeps an eye on him and will take measures if it is ever necessary.

Then he told me about our friends. My old teacher, Jeremiah, was gone to Palestine like he promised. Gersh Leibowitz was a Bolshevik and tried to get Lieb to join, but Lieb wasn't political. He told me everyone in the family was doing well, though he did say Poppa had a hard time since I left. Uncle Yakov told him he needs to go to America and be with his son. He went on:

Uncle Yakov tells the story of your glory the night of the pogrom to anyone who will listen, even to his old gentile army comrades. To hear Uncle Yakov tell it, they should build a monument in front of the synagogue to honor you that is bigger than the Tsar's monument on the other side of the river.

When I was finished, I held the pages in my hand and stared out the window. I was the pride of the family, the one expected to achieve great things and take care of all the others. Ester was the dependable one, Zelda the rebellious beauty, and Markus the sweet baby everyone doted on. Momma and Poppa dearly loved us all. But all of us loved Lieb more than we loved ourselves. Maybe that's because we saw in him something so gentle, kindhearted and decent. He was not capable of hate. Oh, he feared Viktor Askinov as much as any of us. But he didn't hate him, at least not like I did.

I wanted to throw my arms around him and beg him to come to America. So I wrote him a letter back while I was still there in the library. I told him how wonderful America was and what a wonderful job I had at the Becker Dress Factory. "Come and we'll open a shop together," I wrote. "But it doesn't have to be just that. Here Jews are free to do whatever they want, just like everyone else." I told him about the nice apartment Duv had, and about the place they called Central Park only a short walk away. "It is like our Sukhi Yar, only better. They have a little pond for the children to play in and horses for them to ride. Can you believe it? Golde will love it here." I figured if I said it enough times I could convince him.

I didn't tell Lieb how my stomach churned every morning I climbed the steps to the Becker Dress Factory, or how much harder it was to save money for Sara's passage than I expected. Everything cost too much. More immigrants were flooding in from Russia and Italy so the landlords raised our rent. The holes in my socks looked like Swiss cheese and my pair of shoes was so worn they were beyond any further patching. I needed new ones. Even day-old bread became a luxury.

When I complained to Daniel, he said, "You have to stop being so generous. Charity is good, but you give a coin to every beggar you see. The beggars have more than you do. They should be giving you a coin." Still, you couldn't turn your back, particularly if the beggar had a child with him, or if it was a woman. I would cut down on trips to the tavern. But if something didn't change I might never get Sara over here. Then what?

Daniel's father understood my frustration better than Daniel, though I never even brought it up with him. Mr. Akiva had Poppa's same sensitivity and gentle humanity. He was a bit older than Poppa, big like Daniel, with a well-tended bushy gray beard and hair. His wife reminded me of Momma, in constant motion, eye glasses perched on the end of her nose. Together they ran their laundry on 115th Street, which did very well. Daniel's wife, Hannah, helped out when she could. I took my laundry there as much for the conversation as I did for the laundry service. It felt like home.

"Come. Come. I have something to show you," Mr. Akiva said one June day when I stopped by to pick up my things. He was excited. He took my arm and led me to a dark corner in the back room. "Look what I found." He pulled a big cloth off a dust-covered ancient sewing machine. "I never knew it was here. The old owners of the shop must have left it when they moved out. Come, let's move it outside so you can see it."

I picked it up and carried it to the counter in front. Mr. Akiva,

Mrs. Akiva and Hannah gathered around the sewing machine as if it were the golden lantern. I dusted it off. It was older than any machine I'd ever seen. "Can you get it going?" Mrs. Akiva asked.

I tried to turn the wheel but it wouldn't move. "It's going to take a little work," I said. "I'll bring some tools tomorrow."

The next day I borrowed what I needed from the factory and brought along some oil. Daniel joined Mr. Akiva, Mrs. Akiva and Hannah hovering around the machine like expectant grandparents. I took it apart, cleaned it, straightened out some bent parts, oiled it, put it back together and put on a new belt. Now it looked like a sewing machine again. Hannah handed me a couple of rags. I placed the machine on a small table and sat down in a chair. After threading it, I ran a rag through. It worked. The waiting audience applauded the rebirth.

"Now I'll need to teach you how to work it," I said. They grinned at each other, intimates in a secret.

"No, it's for you," Mr. Akiva said.

"What?"

"You can start a little tailor shop right here in the corner," he said. "Right by the big window. After work, Saturdays and Sundays, you can work here."

"I don't have any money to pay for it."

"So who said anything about paying?" he answered. "My customers want someone to repair things. Let out a hem, shorten a pair of pants. You'll do me a favor."

I didn't know what to say, so I kissed him on the cheek. Then I kissed Mrs. Akiva, Hannah and Daniel. How do you thank such people? I ran all the way home, laughing and singing. One woman stopped sweeping in front of her used-utensils shop and stared at me as though I was a crazy man.

The next weekend I started. Mr. Akiva put a sign in the window: "Tailor on site." A little business came in. Mostly it was hems, cuffs and repairs. But I made a little money. Some days I was so tired after working at the factory I had to drag myself to the laundry to work another couple of hours. Weekends were gone. But I began dreaming of having my own tailor shop, with Sara by my side. Lots of Jews were starting their own businesses and making good money. A couple of brothers had even bought R. H. Macys, the big dry goods store.

This is where I wanted my children to grow up, far from the Tsar's reach. Here Jews could become citizens, vote, work in government, be a doctor, own a factory or a department store, and do almost anything a gentile could do. No secret police. No anti-Jewish mobs.

I thought with the sewing machine my money problems were solved.

My source of news was usually Mr. Akiva's day-old copy of the New York Times or the Jewish Journal, a Yiddish newspaper. One day a piece on a back page of The Times jumped out. *Priests and Officials in Uman Inciting Peasants Against Jews*, it read. Reports were coming in of continued hostile threats of *pogroms* championed by local authorities. One report specific to Uman said local priests were arming and inciting mobs in our town and surrounding villages, with support from the mayor. Leaflets provoked the crowds to action. Jews were pleading to the central government in St. Petersburg and to the outside world for help.

Bile rose in my throat, along with rage and futility. There was nowhere to turn. By now the *pogrom* might be over. Sara, Yakira and Isaac could be dead by now for all I knew, and the same with others in the family.

I closed my eyes and prayed Uncle Yakov had kept his fighting force strong. My uncle was a much decorated soldier in the Tsar's army until his arm was wounded beyond repair in a fight with Chinese bandits in Siberia some years before. It was Uncle Yakov who organized our band of young men to defend our *shtetl* when the *pogroms* broke out. He armed us, trained us, and developed the plan that saved us. He had appointed me to lead one of the three squads defending the approaches to our village. My barricade was hit the hardest the night of the *pogrom*. It's where we stopped the attacking mob, and when I shot their leader, Viktor Askinov.

But I didn't even know if Uncle Yakov's brigade still existed. So many young men had left Uman for America. Maybe it was time to board a ship and head back to Uman, I thought, if Mr. Akiva would lend me the money.

"Of course, of course," he said when I showed him the article. "But first why don't you send a telegram and find out? Let me help you with that." He pulled out a couple of dollars and handed them to me. "The telegraph office is close by, over on Park Avenue. Or is it Fifth Avenue? Anyway, it's close." I ran out of the shop without taking the money.

My feet couldn't carry me fast enough. The telegraph operator looked over my scrawl to be sure he could read it. "This could take awhile," he said. "Telegraph to Russia is very unreliable." A few minutes later off the telegram went to Uncle Yakov. He would have the best grasp of the situation.

In less than a day, I received Uncle Yakov's reply: *NO PROBLEMS. ALL IS QUIET. BARANSKI IN CHARGE. LETTER FOLLOWS.* Colonel Baranski was the commander of the army troop in Uman who had finally stopped the earlier *pogrom* in Uman.

Three weeks later Uncle Yakov's letter arrived. He assured me again there was no danger. Sara and the children were fine. The alarm had been real, but Colonel Baranski stepped in with force and threatened the mayor and the priests with arrest if they persisted with their incitement.

Uncle Yakov's letter soothed my rash for a couple of weeks, but it returned soon enough. Nothing could satisfy me except having my Sara, Yakira, and Itzhak here with me; that was still a long way off. Maybe I shouldn't have come to America, I sulked through sleepless nights, at least not without Sara. But daybreak brought back my passion for America, rain or shine, even if Lipsky made existence a nightmare.

I won't tell you again how much I missed my wife. Hannah was the only person in America eager to hear me talk about Sara. "I'm sorry I rattle on so," I apologized one night when she and Daniel invited me over for dinner.

"Don't be silly," Hannah answered. "You sound like a man who's in love with his wife. I can't wait to meet your Sara."

But talking about Sara made it worse, not better. I ached for days after. In my mind Sara became someone she wasn't. I tried to remember some of her faults to dull the torture, but I could not think of any. I could remember every detail of the dark freckle near her bountiful nipple, of our love making, of her delighted giggles when I exploded, and the way she clung to me after. I could not satisfy my yearning for her by myself.

CHAPTER FIVE

September 1906

Bettino Rossi and I sat on the steps of the rusty fire escape chewing on our lunch. The pleasant September days weren't going to be around much longer. "Ladonna, Mira and a couple others play Lipsky's game," Bettino said.

"When do they have the time?"

"Watch how long a break they take to go to the toilet. Lipsky closes the shutters in his office and one of them slips in. It doesn't take him long." He smirked. From his vantage point off to the side, Bettino saw everything that went on at the Becker Dress Factor. "You're probably the only one in the factory who hasn't noticed."

"I've noticed," I said.

"Mira, Ladonna, different ones here and there." Bettino sounded like nothing more than an observer. That's how he dealt with ugly things. "Your friend shares 'em."

"Don't lump me in with Duv."

"Well, Lipsky's the disease here. Duv just enjoys the ride." He pushed a hunk of salami into his mouth. The garlic was so strong I didn't need to put it in my own mouth to taste it. "Lipsky goes after the young ones. Fuck him or else. Give him a kickback or he'll work you to death." The disgust in his voice spoiled his attempt at indifference.

"I didn't know Duv was in on the kickbacks." I suspected he was having them, but didn't know about the kickbacks.

"That's why the fire escape exit is locked on pay day and the elevator's turned off. So they all have to go down the steps. Duv is there collecting the money."

"Why don't they quit."

"The same reason you don't. The same reason I don't." Bettino wadded up the newspaper his lunch had been wrapped in. "Where are we going to go?"

The horn sounded. The clatter of the machines roared again.

I trusted Bettino but this didn't sound like the same Duv Eisenberg I knew. Pleasure himself, sure. Even with married women. But not stealing from helpless girls. Maybe Lipsky threatened him or blackmailed him. Duv already told me once to stay out of it, but I had to try one more time before I gave up.

"How about a beer tonight?" I asked him as we were getting close to the end of the day.

"So you can preach to me again? Who needs it?" He turned his back and walked away.

The next morning, Selma was not at her machine. Rose, at the machine beside Selma's, was bent over with her hands covering her eyes, sobbing. "What's the matter?" I asked.

"Selma's in the hospital," she gulped. "She has something like tuberculosis. She could... die." She wailed again.

The horn sounded. The machines roared. "Back to work," Lipsky barked. "Now!" Rose picked up a garment from the pile next to her and began sewing, her body quivering.

The next day Selma's chair was empty again, and the day after that. A week later we heard Selma died in the hospital. Mr. Becker paid for her funeral.

Selma's chair remained empty for a couple of more days. Then one morning Julia Sorvino was sitting there, looking lost and scared. Her pretty brown eyes, wide with wonder, scanned everything around her. Her delicate lips opened and closed without a word coming out. She had a fresh look, not pasty like the women who had worked there awhile. Her long brown hair pulled tight behind her ears amplified her high rosy cheeks.

Right before the horn sounded to begin the day, Lipsky grabbed my arm and pulled me toward Julia. "Teach her how to sew," he ordered, and walked away. I introduced myself. Julia's nervous smile reminded me of Sara. She relaxed a little, relieved someone was there to help.

I explained to her over the roar of the machines how the process worked. I gave her a piece to sew. Her movements were cautious but adequate. She certainly had not been hired because she was a whiz of a sewer. She was delicate and innocent, vulnerable prey for Lipsky.

Julia's machine was the one on the end of the aisle I had repaired on my first day. I couldn't show Julia how to work the machine without being much closer to her than I wanted to be. Every time our shoulders or hands touched accidentally, a shock went through me. And every time we touched she looked up at me with those large doe eyes and smiled her shy smile. "You are very kind," she said in halting English when we were done. I went back to work, glad to be away from her.

Lipsky began circling almost immediately. At first he tried to charm her. He stood behind her for a few minutes, his hands resting on the back of her chair. Then he bent over as though showing her how to do something on the machine. What he was really doing was creating an opportunity to touch her. And every time he did, her body tensed and her face screwed up in revulsion.

I felt protective, as if she were my younger sister. Whenever I saw Lipsky approaching her again, I found a reason to go over to her row of machines and drop off a bundle or sweep up some nearby debris – anything to disrupt Lipsky. She noticed. Lipsky noticed.

I was loading completed garments into a big box when Duv passed by. "Looks like someone found a new girlfriend," he said sarcastically. His insinuation caught me off guard.

"She's barely a woman," I said.

"Look at those pumpkins." He snickered and cupped his two hands as though he were grabbing a tit in each hand. "She's a woman all right."

"Leave her alone."

"Lipsky will get her." He smacked his hand against the side of the box and paraded away in triumph.

I was afraid he was right. With Lipsky, it would be rape. Over the next few weeks, Rose and Camella taught her some new tricks to foil him. She learned quickly but it only frustrated him. She never went to the toilet except during lunch break when one of the other girls went with her, so Lipsky couldn't trap her in the rear of the factory. I don't know how she held it for so many hours. Julia and I didn't speak to each other much, but when we did, I tried to show her not all men were predators like Lipsky and Duv.

The cold of November forced Bettino and me to abandon the fire escape for our lunches. Now most days we used a long work table at the back of the factory. Julia was shy, but one lunch hour she stopped on her way back from the lavatory. Bettino was on an errand for Mr. Becker so I was all alone.

"You are kind to me," she said. "Thank you." Her soft smile lit a gray day.

"Lipsky's an animal." I must have sounded angry. Actually, my reaction to her dark skinned loveliness made me edgy.

Her long black hair fell in her eyes. She brushed it back. Then she put her hand on top of mine and held it there. "You protect me," she said. I looked down. She saw me and pulled her hand back as though it burned. She walked away, still smiling.

Bettino returned as she left. "Now there's a beauty," he said. "Would you look at that perfect ass?" He sounded more like an authority admiring a fine painting than a lecher.

"You can't have her," I joked.

"But you can," he answered, half seriously.

I didn't even consider the possibility. "She's a good Catholic girl," I answered emphatically.

The horn sounded.

Though we had said little to each other before then, after our encounter that day, we were friends. Yet whenever I talked to her I made sure Rose, Camella or Bettino was there. I didn't want Julia or anyone else to get the wrong idea. Sometimes all five of us had lunch together. Julia brought fresh air into hell. She had a kind sense of humor, sometimes bawdy in an innocent way, which she managed to express through her broken English. I learned she was from Naples. She came to America four years ago at age fourteen with her parents and three younger brothers. Her father was sick and she now carried the burden of supporting her family. I told her I was a Jew from Uman, an old married man with two children.

Lipsky behaved like a spurned lover. When he couldn't seduce her, he turned on her. He screamed at her all the time. "Faster! Faster, you lazy bitch!" His face turned red and twisted into a corkscrew. Julia's sewing machine skills improved but not enough to satisfy Lipsky. She made mistakes. I tried to help her out, working at her machine some lunch breaks or after work. Lipsky sometimes sent me on an errand to stop me. He didn't like what I was doing, yet he needed the production. I was as fast on a sewing machine as anyone he had. Duv wouldn't come anywhere near me when Lipsky was in one of his rages.

Julia glanced up. She must have sensed Lipsky approaching. He began yelling at her before he even reached her. "Hurry up, Sorvino. You're costing me money." She tried going faster and when she did she ran the sewing needle right through her finger. She cried out. Blood spurted all over.

"Keep that damn blood off the garment," Lipsky yelled. "You fool," he screamed when a speck of red splattered the piece Julia was working on.

I was one row over, repairing a stalled machine. I jumped over the table behind her and pushed Lipsky away, harder than necessary. At that moment, I didn't care what he did. Tears flooded down Julia's cheeks. She sobbed silently, her body heaving. One by one, the other machines stopped as word spread from one operator to another. Some of them were just curious about what was going to happen between Lipsky and me.

He stood off to the side, baring his yellowed teeth. I grabbed a rag and blotted the blood from Julia's finger, holding her hand as delicately as I could. "Get some water," I yelled to no one in particular. "And some cotton." Someone shoved a glass of water at me. Someone else handed me a bottle of alcohol. I gave the water to Julia. She took a few small sips and handed it back to me. I poured some of the water on the rag and cleaned her finger. She grimaced when I dabbed her wound with alcohol, but I gripped her hand tightly. I gently padded it with cotton and wrapped it.

"Back to work," Lipsky yelled. One by one, the machines started up.

Still holding Julia's injured hand in mine, I reached up with the other one to wipe her tears away and brush her hair back. She smiled with eyes as gentle as a young fawn. She looked down at her hand in my hand and let it rest there for a moment before slowly taking it away.

"You are kind," she said. She looked so fragile.

"Let me run your machine for awhile."

"I can do it." She picked up the garment she had been working on and began sewing cautiously.

Needles through fingers happened, but this one had been worse than usual, and it didn't need to happen. I stared at Lipsky and he stared at me. I clenched my fists. He turned and walked away. "Back to work," he mumbled.

My heart hammered, my breathing heavy. I might have attacked Lipsky if he had said one more word. Who knew how long Julia could continue to resist him, no matter how much she wanted to. She needed this job as much as I did. But I wasn't going to let him have her.

That night when we finished work, Julia waited for me at the top of the stairs. Nearly everyone was gone. She looked very tired.

"How are you," I asked.

"Better." She held up her bandaged finger. "Now I have a medal."

"Clean it again and put more alcohol on it when you get home. Come, I'll see you out," I said. There was more I wanted to say to her, but I didn't dare.

We walked down the steps together, alone in the darkened hallway. Our hands touched. She took my hand in hers, squeezed it, and then let go. When we got to the landing at the bottom of the steps, she kissed me lightly on the cheek and smiled. She wet her upper lip with her tongue. She was so sweet and unguarded; she reached inside me and caressed my heart. I was unprepared for what I was feeling and felt uncomfortable all over.

She slowly pushed open the door into the chilly November night. Rose and Camella were waiting.

CHAPTER SIX

December 1906

Our Christmas present from Rupert Becker was a piece of apple pie and a half day off of work, unpaid.

This was my second Hanukkah away from Sara, and I needed her more desperately every day. One morning I bolted up in bed from a nightmare, only it wasn't a nightmare. I had forgotten the sound of Sara's voice. I could see every detail of her face, feel her gentle touch, and smell the perfume of her white shoulders. But I couldn't hear her voice, hard as I tried. I was losing her a piece at a time.

Daniel and Hannah had me to dinner to celebrate the first night of Hanukkah. It was sweet and sour watching the excitement of their little boys, Nathan and Leo. I stared at the flickering candle in the menorah and thought of Yakira and Itzhak. My children were growing up without me.

I haven't spoken about them much; I don't know why. Maybe because my heart broke every time I thought about Yakira and Itzhak, even more than when I thought about Sara, if that's possible. At least with Yakira I could remember holding her, playing with her, and making her laugh. "Give the child a chance to sleep," Momma would say when she thought my attention to Yakira went beyond common sense.

It had only been a year from the time she was born until the time I had to leave. Itzhak was different. The poor little boy was born in the middle of a riot – a *pogrom* – and now was growing up without a father. I hadn't even gotten to know my son. What kind of man leaves his children behind? I felt so guilty.

Hannah noticed my vacant look. "Thinking of home?" she asked.

I nodded. "I was thinking about Hanukkah growing up. We didn't celebrate it much." She shoveled more potato latkes on my plate.

Sara, through Ester, wrote me about the family and what was going on in Uman. I missed them all but I no longer felt a part of it. Lonely as I was, I had new friends here, a life, such as it was. I had the library, the Kinsale Tavern, and my sewing machine.

Duv should have been my connection to Uman. He should have been the one I could depend on, the person I could talk to about anything. I felt a loss, and lonelier because of it. What happened to the good natured friend I grew up with?

The best part of every day now was when I sewed on my machine in the corner of Mr. Akiva's laundry. I still didn't have nearly enough money to bring Sara, Itzhak, and Yakira over. But my little side business was growing and with it, my savings. I worked ten or twelve hours in the factory, then another two or three at the laundry, even on the Sabbath. Maybe I had an occasional beer at the tavern on Saturday night. Sunday I worked all day. Mrs. Akiva often brought me some of her matzo ball soup or borscht. I might have starved to death without her.

In early January, Mrs. Schulman became my patron. She mothered me like Mrs. Akiva did, and she had money – lots of it. She came into the laundry one Saturday afternoon right after the first heavy snow. She was bundled in a warm black fur, her gray hair tucked under a matching fur hat. She was still a handsome woman for someone fifty years old, built on a tiny frame.

She asked me to make a dress for her from some green taffeta material she had purchased. She brought her own pattern. "It's French," she said watching me cuddle the material between my fingers. "I hope you handle women as well as you handle that," she laughed, almost flirting.

I worked on the dress every available chance. Three weeks later I handed it to her. "It's fabulous," she said, and gave me a hug. Apparently her friends liked it too. A few months later three of them asked me to make dresses for them. The material was always the finest, but now I only caressed it in private.

The more I worked on my own things, the more I hated going into the Becker Dress Factory. When it was freezing outside, it was freezing inside. You could see your breath. Some of the women wore gloves with the fingers cut out. None of them took off their coats. Lipsky's office and Mr. Becker's office in the rear were the only warm places. The willing women were more than happy to meet Duv and Lipsky there for a little respite from the cold. We rarely saw Mr. Becker at this time of year. Bettino said he went to some hot springs in Georgia to get away from the cold.

The morning ascent up those dark steps on a frigid day like this one was a descent into a nightmare. Sometimes I wondered if life in America was much better than life in Uman. On one of those mornings, Julia Sorvino and I trudged up alongside each other. I said hello to her. She tried to say "good morning" back, but she looked terrible. She was pale, sickly. When the five of us gathered for lunch near the presses, she ate little and said little.

She shuffled back toward her machine, every step an effort. I watched her nearly collapse into her chair. The horn sounded. She picked up a garment and held it as though suspended in mid-air. She wobbled for a minute, closed her eyes and keeled over into the aisle. I saw it happen from across the floor and bolted toward her. The machines around her stopped. When I got to her side her eyes were closed and her skirt was pulled up above her thighs. The first thing I did was pull it down to cover her modesty.

I got down beside her and cradled her head with my arm. "Julia. Julia." She didn't move, her eyes closed and mouth slightly open. "Get some water and some rags. Get some ammonia," I yelled as I carried her to the cot off to the side and laid her on the stained, sagging mattress. I put a wet cloth on her head and took her hand. Rose and Camella watched anxiously. Others huddled around.

When I raised my ammonia-wetted finger to her nose, she gulped air and coughed. Then she slowly opened her eyes. She saw me and her lips turned up in a weak little smile.

"What happened?" she asked. She tried to raise her head but fell back down.

"You fainted," I said. She squeezed my hand.

"Back to work. Back to work," Lipsky hollered, flipping his wrist at everyone as though shooing away flies.

"Do you need a doctor?" I asked.

"No. Just let me lie here for a minute."

Lipsky stood over us, impatient. I turned toward him, struggling to control my anger at the whole nightmare of this awful place. "I will sit here with her until she can get up," I said. He looked like he was going to say something. I clenched my fist, my lips pressed together so hard they hurt. He turned and walked away, back toward his office. He would make me pay. Duv, while all of this was going on, went about carrying bundles, avoiding what was going on.

I held her hand and stroked her hair. Some color returned to her face. "You watch over me."

"Like a big brother."

"More." She tried to rise. "I need to go to work."

"You lie here a little longer. I'll run your bundle for awhile."

Lipsky came by again, looked at Julia and stared at me. He didn't like me running her machine, but he needed the production. "She gets back to work tomorrow or she's gone," he said to me.

She stood up, teetered a little, and walked to where I was sitting. I stopped sewing for a minute. "You go home for the rest of the day," I said. "I'll finish here. But Lipsky says you have to be in tomorrow."

She nodded. Then she grabbed my hand and squeezed it. "You are kind."

When I was leaving that night, Duv nearly bumped into me as we started down the stairs. "So, are you having your way with her?" It sounded like a filthy accusation.

"That's disgusting," I said. He snorted.

I walked home in the cold night air, hunched, hands tucked in my pockets, pushing Julia out of my mind. But as soon as I did, she popped back in. I didn't want to think what I was thinking. I tried to force her from my thoughts by imagining what Yakira and Itzhak must look like now. Itzhak was walking. Yakira had a mouthful of teeth, not quite the baby she was when I left. And Sara was waiting to pull me close to her. I shivered, but not from the cold.

Lipsky took his revenge for my belligerence. He probably would have liked to see me gone but he needed me for now. So he found a reason for me to work late every day, late enough so I had no time to work on my own things at the laundry. Maybe Duv told him about my side venture.

He gave me a key to the factory and ordered me to lock up when I left. It was an odd combination of trust and retribution. Every morning the first thing he did was check whatever work he had assigned me the night before. He let me know he also checked to make sure I hadn't stolen anything. My tasks were menial, the more insignificant the better for his purpose.

His favorite torment was to have me clean his office and Mr. Becker's. Mr. Becker was hardly ever there so, even though his office was still neat and clean, Lipsky made me clean it again and again. It wasn't so bad. Lipsky's office was shabby, with only a wobbly gray wooden desk, chair and an old table stacked high with papers and scraps of material.

Mr. Becker's office, on the other hand, was plush and spacious, with two windows looking out on the street below. Stale cigar smoke and Mr. Becker's sweet signature cologne soaked the drapes, the rich blue and gold carpet, and the heavy upholstered couch. Etchings of naked Greek gods and goddesses hung on the walls. I carefully cleaned the personal paraphernalia on Mr. Becker's oak desk and bookcase: family pictures, a heavy crystal ashtray, a fine pen and ink stand.

A few of the women stayed late from time to time to catch up if they hadn't finished their assigned quota for the day. Lipsky was unmerciful and threatened any who didn't. I paid little attention to them unless their machines needed some work, or they needed a fresh bundle of garments to work on.

This one night in early February Julia, Camella and Rosa worked overtime. When one of them had to stay, all three of them stayed so they wouldn't have to walk home alone. They chattered back and forth, often some piece of gossip about one of the other women. I was entertained by their racy remarks when they didn't think I was listening. Occasionally they shouted something to me and I shouted back. I finished my repairs on the one machine and went in back to wash my hands. Then I began cleaning Mr. Becker's office still once again.

The noise from the machines stopped. "Good night Avi," the three girls called out when they left. I yelled back at them. The door to the factory slammed and I was alone again. The Tiffany lamp on Mr. Becker's desk spread a mellow glow on the silence.

I took a close look at the fine tailoring of the midnight-blue brocade drapes, thinking I could make ones like this. Rich women probably would pay a lot of money to decorate their windows. Maybe it paid more than making suits and dresses.

"Avi." I turned. Julia was standing by the door, dark hair falling in her eyes and over her shoulders. One hand clasped the other in front of her, feet close together. She looked like a shy school girl in the presence of her teacher.

"I thought you were gone," I said.

She didn't say a word. She moved to me, and without stopping put her arms around my neck. She wet her lips, looked into my eyes, and kissed me hard. I hesitated for a moment, putting my hands on her hips to push her away. I should have. I didn't. I kissed her back just as hard, wrapping my arms around her. Her eyes closed. Then mine closed too.

She moaned and pressed her body against me. Her tongue flicked out. I felt myself growing. I couldn't stop, I couldn't think, I couldn't help myself. I didn't even try.

She pulled us and I pushed us until we collapsed onto Mr. Becker's couch. She tugged at my pants buttons. I lifted her skirt above her waist. The pale white of her thighs showed above the tops of her stockings. I'm cursed to remember every detail: musky smells, wetness, moans, and the heat from her full body. Our tongues entwined. She wound herself around me and clutched so hard I couldn't breathe. I yanked at her gray under drawers.

"Julia. Julia, are you still here," Rose called from the front of the factory. "We're waiting for you."

We froze, the act incomplete. The whites of Julia's eyes opened wide, her mouth in a silent scream. I withered as fast as noodles in boiling water. Julia released her hold. That very instant I knew I had just made the biggest mistake of my life. I dismounted her and let out a wail like a wounded goat, muted by my hand over my mouth.

"I'll be right there," Julia called out to Rose, her voice strained and husky. She rushed to reassemble herself.

"Hurry up, we're waiting," Rose yelled.

I couldn't look at her. I turned my back and buttoned up my pants, then covered my face with my hands and cried. My body heaved. "Forgive me Sara, forgive me," I whispered.

"I love you," Julia said from the doorway. I didn't even turn around. I heard the clack of her shoes as she ran across the wooden floor. The door to the factory slammed. Guilt pummeled me like angry ocean waves.

Excuse-making began immediately: She had seduced me. I would never have done what I did if she hadn't sought me out in that back office. It wasn't my fault. A man has needs, particularly one who hasn't seen his wife for so long.

The truth waited, not yet ready to show itself: namely, my feelings for Julia Sorvino ran deeper than lust. Yet I loved and longed for my wife more than ever, so this feeling for Julia had to be something other than love, I rationalized in my confused condition. Opposites collided, my mind and heart unable to sort it out.

I staggered out of the factory, and wandered the near-empty streets oblivious to the cold, unconscious of people passing by. A man called out when I mindlessly crossed in the middle of the street and was almost run over by a horseless carriage. A policeman in his blue uniform and helmet walked toward me. I pulled my hat down further, jammed my cold hands back in my pockets, and sloshed through the black patches of week-old snow.

I had betrayed Sara and everything Momma and Poppa taught me. God, please punish me, I begged. But while I flogged myself, never once that night did I think of the injury I had done to Julia Sorvino. Whenever a thought of her began, I pushed it away. By the time I found myself at my apartment, no one else was on the streets. I stumbled into the darkened front room and fell asleep on the floor.

"Avi, wake up." Gideon shook me. "You're going to be late for work." My other roommates had already left. "You look awful," Gideon said, concerned. "You must have had a hell of a night." He poured a cup of strong black coffee and handed it to me. I clasped my hands around it and let the heat burn my hands.

When Gideon closed the door behind him, I pushed some dirty clothes onto the floor and sat down on the sofa. Facing Julia or the Becker Dress Factory today was impossible. I didn't make a decision not to go to work, I just didn't go. It was Saturday. A half day's pay vanished and I didn't even think about it.

The rain came down, beating against the windows. I heaved the cup across the room, crashing it into the wall, shattering and splattering coffee everywhere. I didn't care.

For the next few hours my mind bounded between rage at Julia Sorvino for her seduction and rage at myself. I prayed there was no God to punish me, for if there was, I surely deserved to go to the depths of hell. I couldn't hide what I had done from Sara, and it would kill her if she knew.

The rain had almost stopped when I put on my coat and walked toward the Kinsale Tavern. Thomas Kelly was polishing the brass on the mirror behind the bar. "You're in early, laddie," he said. "Dawn is barely beyond the horizon."

I dumped myself onto a barstool in front of him. "Beer."

Instead of a beer, he pulled a bottle of whisky from underneath the bar. "You look like ya' seen the devil's own brother." He grabbed two glasses and poured one for me and one for himself. He pushed mine toward me and raised his glass. "May your evening bring peace." He drained his glass in one gulp. I did the same. He filled my glass again. By noon I was drunk. I don't remember much more about that day except vomiting violently on the steps outside our apartment building.

By Monday I had entered a permanent stupor. I dragged myself to the factory, and waited across the street until all the women entered.

I hung my coat in its usual place on the hook behind Bettino's. From the corner of my eye, I saw Julia looking at me with the saddest face I've ever seen. I couldn't look back. But later in the day when I glanced over at her hunched over her machine, I couldn't hold on to my anger toward her, only at myself. I should have left the factory that day and not come back, but I didn't. So each morning I got up and went to work, unable to do anything else.

Little memory remains of what happened during those next weeks. I wouldn't eat, and stopped going to synagogue or to Mr. Akiva's laundry. Daniel was the last person I wanted to see, with his sanctimony and compassion. Bettino later told me I worked like a man possessed, but I don't remember it. Lipsky ignored me. Duv ignored me. No one spoke to me and I didn't speak to anyone except Bettino. My roommate Gideon tried to get me to talk about it, but I refused. I couldn't write Sara, and gave no consideration to the worry it would cause her when she didn't receive a letter from me. I threw her letters in my drawer, unopened.

Every day after work I dropped by the Kinsale Tavern and took a solitary spot at the far end of the bar, sometimes drinking beer until I couldn't feel any more. Thomas Kelly gave up trying to reach me, except to bring an egg, a thick slice of black bread, or a lump of sharp cheese. I ate it without as much as a thank you.

Maybe I was thinking if I punished myself enough God wouldn't need to. Then God and everyone else would pity me for my self-inflicted martyrdom. I had no idea how to fix what I had broken, and no will to try.

CHAPTER SEVEN

March 1907

My moral certainty, black and white, could not yet reconcile with the human frailties in even the holiest among us. So I continued to whip myself.

The snow ended. It rained often, and when it didn't rain the days were windy and dark. One Saturday afternoon three weeks later, I took my usual spot at the Kinsale Tavern. Alcoholic indulgence had not yet deadened my tormented mind. Someone sat down next to me. I looked into the mirror at Daniel's handsome reflection, his hands clasped together resting on the bar. His fine black Sabbath suit and tie looked out of place. I hadn't seen him since all of this with Julia happened.

He sat for a minute or two without saying anything. Then he rose from his stool. "Come, Avi. It's time." He put one hand on my arm. He held my cap and coat in the other. I rose and took them. Still holding on to my arm, he guided me out the door.

Neither of us said a word. We walked. He gripped my arm all the way. Someone else had taken charge of me and I was glad. He prattled on about nothing in particular, filling the empty air.

"I have to tell you what I did," I finally said.

"Later." He held his finger to his lips.

"Rabbi, I did something awful."

"I know."

Sabbath afternoon crowds jammed the streets. As we walked, my head started to clear for the first time in weeks. I had to convince Daniel I was worth saving. If I couldn't convince him, I couldn't convince Sara. Losing God was one thing, but my heart broke when I thought of losing Sara.

We walked up the steps to the front door of a neat white clapboard synagogue on Second Avenue surrounded on three sides by tenement buildings. "I know the rabbi," Daniel said in response to my quizzical look. This was a real synagogue, not like Daniel's storefront nearby on 113th Street.

He unlocked the door and we entered into the darkened rear of the sanctuary, empty except for the two of us. A heavy maroon curtain covered the ark for the Torah. Sunlight through two stained glass windows painted a mural on the polished oak pews. We paused for a moment. "It used to be a church," Daniel said. "Come. We'll talk in the rabbi's office."

The office was simple with a desk, bookcase, comfortable flowered couch, and an oak rocking chair accented with a new mustard colored seat cushion. Nothing in the room indicated it belonged to a rabbi except a tallis and black robe hanging on a coat rack on the wall near the door. Unpacked boxes were stacked in a corner. "Sit," Daniel said, motioning with his hand toward the couch. He was as matter-of-fact as if we were there to chat about a good book, rather than how to save my soul.

Daniel took a place in the rocking chair, his hands clasped together, pressed to his lips. "Why don't you tell me what happened," he started.

"I didn't fuck her," I argued in defense, my stare challenging him. Daniel didn't respond. I looked away, knowing full well I would have completed the act if we hadn't been interrupted.

My lips were dry. I was thinking how to tell the whole story in a way that I wouldn't look so bad. Once I started talking, it all gushed out of my mouth as quickly as it flowed into my head. As I did, a great load lifted. I told Daniel everything: our lunches together, how I helped her when she ran the sewing needle through her finger, how I lifted her onto the cot when she fainted, how I protected her from Lipsky. And how she came to me that night in Mr. Becker's office. Maybe I slanted things so the blame was more Julia's than mine, trying to deceive myself as much as Daniel.

Daniel concentrated on every word but said little other than offering encouragement to continue. When I finished, I was exhausted.

"I'm sorry, Sara." I sniveled, my head buried in my hands. "I'm so sorry. God, I'm sorry." Daniel handed me his handkerchief. I wiped my eyes and blew my nose.

Daniel let the silence linger. When he spoke, it was Rabbi Akiva speaking for the prophets. "You could have sought out Julia again and finished what you started. She was willing. You didn't do that. You had a choice to make, and you made the right one." He rocked backed and forth in his chair, his face and voice impassive. "In Ecclesiastes, it says there is not a righteous man on earth who does only good and doesn't sin at all. But you have much work to do if you want to earn His mercy and Sara's forgiveness."

His last words slapped me like a biblical threat. "I confessed everything. I'm sorry." I felt as vulnerable as ice on a hot summer day. My belligerence melted. "What do I have to do?"

He locked his eyes on mine and leaned toward me. "Recognizing we've done wrong to someone or to God is the hardest part. But it's not enough. Sara has no obligation to forgive you even if you do everything you're supposed to do to earn her forgiveness. She's free to do whatever she needs to do to live with her injury. The burden is all on you."

"And God's forgiveness?" I drooped my head.

"Of course you must ask God's forgiveness. But that will come if you do everything you can to repair the injury you caused."

I clasped both hands together, lacing my fingers as though in prayer. I could think of nothing to say. That damn clock on the wall beat louder than my thumping heart.

"Are you in love with Julia Sorvino?" he asked.

His question smacked me in the face. "No, absolutely not!"

"It is possible to love two women."

"She's the one who caused all this trouble."

Daniel let my denial go for now and let me ramble awhile until I stumbled into the place he wanted me to reach. "It's Sara I'm scared about." I said. "I feel I've lost her. That would be hell. But I'll go to hell if it means not hurting her any more."

He got up from his chair and wrapped his massive arms around me in a bear hug. I didn't know what I said to provoke such a suggestion of approval. "Enough for today," he patted me on the back. "We'll talk some more again tomorrow right after work."

On our way out, I sat down in one of the pews for a moment. Daniel sat down beside me. I closed my eyes. "You're a good man," he said. "You will get there."

He locked the door to the synagogue behind us when we left. The sun peeked out, and then disappeared again behind a dark cloud. "How do you know the rabbi here?" I asked.

He laughed. "Because I'm the new rabbi. We've closed the 113th Street synagogue and merged it here, into Ohev Shalom. You're now a member." He was proud of himself, a young rabbi in charge of a real synagogue with seventy-five families, and a few strays like me.

After work the next day I went straight to the synagogue. Daniel was waiting for me. We settled into our places, he in his rocking chair and me on the couch. Hannah had prepared a supper for us of herring, eggs, cheese and cold potatoes in vinegar. The smell of the fish-and-vinegar soaked newspaper churned my nervous stomach. I forced myself to eat a little of it.

Daniel ignored my edginess. "I have to take you to a baseball game," he said as we chewed and swallowed. "The Highlanders have a fabulous ballpark on 168th Street. It's like going on a picnic." I had no idea what a baseball game was but I accepted. He was telling me we were still best friends.

I finished and waited while Daniel stuffed the last piece of bread in his mouth. He crumbled the newspaper the food had been wrapped in, and then turned his eyes on me, waiting.

"I got a letter from Uncle Yakov," I said. It was the first one from home I had read in over a month. The ones from Sara and Momma still lay in my drawer, unopened. I pulled the letter out of my pocket. "Somehow he knows."

"What did he say?" Daniel wiped cookie crumbs from the corner of his mouth.

"He told me how much Sara loves me. How Sara can take any hardship for me. Forgive anything. He said he knew from his own experience what it was like to be so lonely you take another to you. And what it's like when you lose a love because of it. It sounded like a warning."

I turned to the next page of the letter. "Then he told me I'd probably been ill. I should write Sara and tell her so, but that now I was all better."

"He's a very wise man," Daniel said. "You have been ill. You can write and tell her that."

"Uncle Yakov knows God isn't always fair."

"We can't blame it all on God," Daniel said. "He gave us the freedom to make our own choices, good or bad."

"How much do I tell her?"

Daniel had been anticipating my question. He stopped rocking his chair. "It all depends on why you want to tell her. If it's to make restitution to her, then yes, you tell her everything she wants to know. Everything. You answer every question until she has no more. Whatever it takes to win back her trust. If she needs to hear every detail, then your obligation is to tell her every detail." I nodded, but I didn't know how I was going to do that without hurting her more.

"And tomorrow you need to write Sara," he said.

At Daniel's urging, a couple of days later I met him at the laundry after work. Mr. and Mrs. Akiva greeted me like a long gone son. "You look so thin," Mrs. Akiva said. "You must eat." The next day she made cookies for me.

"There's many repairs to do," Mr. Akiva said, pointing to my sewing machine and the clothes piled up on a table next to it. "I've been putting people off. And Mrs. Schulman wants another new dress."

"Monday," I said. "I will start back on Monday."

It was easier to go to work than it had been, but I still couldn't wait for my term in Rupert Becker's prison to end. I was able to grunt a few words to Duv when I saw him, and he to me. I didn't strain so hard to avoid looking at Julia. A couple of times our eyes met, but one of us quickly looked away. Lipsky started up again on her, and he bared his teeth at me. But he no longer ordered me to stay after work.

The day after I visited the laundry, as soon as the horn at the factory sounded I had my coat on and dashed to the library. The streetlamps reflected off the puddles from the day's earlier rain. Crowds of men and women plodded home from work, often in groups. They all looked alike, duplicates of those from the Becker Dress Factory. The men yelled suggestions to the women, and some of the women answered in kind.

I sat down in my usual seat in the library back by the window and pulled Sara's unopened letters out of my coat pocket. Ester was still writing them for her. I read the first one. She said Ester was pregnant again, due to deliver in June, so Simon would not be coming to America right away.

The last letter, the one she wrote only three weeks ago, was heavier and stiffer than the others. I opened it and pulled out a small photograph taken in a studio. Sara looked at me with her sweet smile. Even in sepia I could see her soft blue eyes and feel her there with me. She held Yakira with one hand and Itzhak with the other. They looked adorable, both in checkered outfits matching Sara's. Poppa probably made them.

The wind outside the library window whipped a still-bare tree. I don't even know my own children, I thought. I moved the picture close to my face so I could see them better.

Then I unfolded Sara's note:

> *I know we both feel an emptiness that won't be filled until we are together. Of course I worry when I don't receive one of your beautiful letters for awhile. I had a long talk with Uncle Yakov yesterday. He is so wise. He tells me what it is like to be a lonely man in a far off land, and says I shouldn't fret. He tells me how much you love me, and that is reassuring. All I want from life is you.*

It sounded to me as though she knew what I had done and forgave me. I clutched the letter to me and closed my eyes, praying I was right.

I got up from the table and walked around the library, thinking about what I would say to Sara in my letter. Lost in my own thoughts, I nearly bumped into a woman holding her son by the hand. After a mumbled apology, I went outside to clear my head. The night air was so cold I quickly ducked back inside and took my spot again. An old man with a long gray beard and glasses had seated himself on the other side of my table. He looked at me and pushed his glasses back up his nose.

I took my pen in hand and dipped it in the ink well. *"My Darling Sara,"* I began. *I am so sorry I have not written you in so long. Please forgive me. I have been ill but I am all better now. You must have been very worried. Do not worry any more. I love you with all my heart.*

The following Sabbath the synagogue was nearly full. This was the first time I saw Daniel in front of his new congregation. He looked like a real rabbi in his black robe, with a big wool *tallis* around his neck and shoulders. While Daniel conducted his service, I had my own conversation with God. I begged Him to tell me what was best for Sara. Maybe He answered.

Daniel caught me on my way out. "Let's talk." He walked toward his office, not waiting for my response. I followed, unsure of what was coming. We assumed our usual positions, me on the now-familiar couch and he in his rocker.

"There something else you need to do," Daniel said evenly. "Julia Sorvino."

"What about her?"

"Do you remember the afternoon I came to find you in the Kinsale Tavern?'

I nodded.

"I told you I knew what you had done. You never asked how I knew." I waited to hear the other shoe hit the floor.

"Julia came to see me," he said. "She thought a rabbi was like her priest and that she could confess to me. That I could give her absolution. She took all of the blame on herself. Never once was she critical of you or angry with you." He paused to let his words swell. "All she wanted was for you to be forgiven by our God and by Sara. On her way out, she asked to light a candle. I told her we didn't do that. So she asked if she could pray, right here in our synagogue. She dropped to her knees in the aisle facing the Torah, crossed herself and closed her eyes."

"Stop!" I slapped my hands against my cheeks, hard. Some feeling, maybe love, struck me. I shivered and wanted to cry.

Daniel leaned toward me and placed one of his big hands on top of one of mine.

"She seduced me," I said, but my conviction melted to a whisper.

"She fell in love with you. She didn't mean to. You didn't want her to. Sometimes these things happen."

She didn't seduce me any more than I seduced her. This was the truth I did not want to face. If she didn't seduce me, then I was responsible for what I did.

"What do I do?" I begged to be told, too confused to think any more.

Daniel got up from his seat. "Now we're done here." He put his hand on my shoulder, his expression one of compassion.

"But what are you saying about Julia?" I pulled away from his hand and stood up.

"You'll figure it out. And you will do the right thing."

On the way out, I looked down the row of pews to the sanctuary.

The eternal light flickered over the ark in the half-dark synagogue. What more did Daniel want from me? He was more demanding than God.

CHAPTER EIGHT

April 1907

The next day, Sunday, Gideon Katz asked me to see a show with him at the Grand, a Yiddish theater on the Lower East Side. I'd been there before with Gideon, but today I wasn't fit company. Even I was getting tired of my eternal whining. After he left, I took Sara's picture from my drawer and looked into her eyes, hardly noticing Itzhak and Yakira. I talked to her. Then I put it back in its place, bundled up in my overcoat, and left the messy apartment. I largely ignored my roommates now, other than Gideon.

It was still chilly outside, the barren trees awaiting signs of spring before budding. I walked aimlessly for miles, through the Jewish section to the Irish section and the Italian section. Women in their best clothes, and a few men, paraded on their way to church. The crosses on their churches still provoked a reflexive spasm of fear, as though I was still a child back in Uman.

I allowed myself to think about Julia for the first time since that awful night. Maybe I did tempt her as much as she tempted me. And maybe I wasn't so much the victim as I wanted to believe. An urge to have her stirred at times, and I didn't always suppress it like I should have. I quivered whenever we accidentally touched. And sometimes it hadn't been so accidental. I became attached to Julia. Even now I don't want to call it love, but it was something more than lust. She was alluring but, like Sara, she didn't seem to know it. She was funny and warm. Maybe it was her vulnerability and my need to protect her that drew me to her. And maybe it was nothing more than every man's desire to have a pretty young woman like Julia.

Circling back to the Jewish section, I found a small, ordinary coffee house open and sat down in a wicker chair at a round little table. I was the only person in there. The owner, an old Greek with big lips, cleaned off the tables and counter. The coffee he put in front of me was hot, thick and harsh, much like my reflections about Julia.

Comprehension of what really happened emerged gradually. Put simply, Julia was a heavenly woman, and I had treated her like a common whore. Finally I got Daniel's point. The only way I could make restitution was to restore Julia's honor and her faith in herself. Yes, she sinned too. But by going to Daniel and confessing, prostrating herself to save me, she had already made her restitution. At least she had tried. I hadn't. By the time I finished my second cup of coffee, my responsibility was clear.

Daniel had told me I must make amends to both Sara and Julia. Then I must forgive myself. That was harder than you think. "There are those who forgive themselves too fast when it is not their place to forgive themselves at all," Daniel said later. "It's a cheap forgiveness. Such people feel their victim owes them forgiveness. You're the opposite. You can't forgive yourself even when you should. That's destructive. It's not what's going to make Sara happy." That was a relief. But until now I hadn't figured what I was supposed to do.

I had one more thing to work out: how to leave the Becker Dress Factory but still bring Sara to America as fast as I could. On Monday after work I went to see Mr. Akiva to discuss the possibility of opening a tailor shop full time in the corner of his laundry where I had been working.

He clapped his little hands together and smiled. "You're in luck. I own the little place next door. It's tiny, no bigger than a closet. I just use it for storage, but it's yours. Use it as long as you like."

"I won't have any money for rent until after I bring Sara over," I said.

"So who's asking for rent?" Fortunately for me, Mr. Akiva did very well. "Come, come." He took me by the arm, eager to show it to me as though he was afraid I would change my mind.

The tiny shop had a door and window onto the street, and a connecting door into the laundry. It really wasn't much more than a cluttered closet, but it was better than having a corner in the laundry. There was enough space for a work table, a place to store a little material, and my machine by the front window. I could clean it all up in a couple of days.

But I still couldn't quite find the will to leave. Bad as it was, the Becker Dress Company provided a steady income. Who knew what would happen if I went out on my own? So I kept showing up for work, struggling up the staircase every morning.

For the next few days, I also tried to work up the courage to talk to Julia. A couple of times, during our lunch break, I came close to approaching her, but both times I stopped. I was afraid to ask her forgiveness, afraid she might refuse me. She had reason to.

I looked over at her and saw again the vulnerable, precious young woman. She looked back at me and our eyes met. This time I smiled and she smiled back. I melted. Maybe she's already forgiven me, I hoped.

Lipsky caught our glances. It must have made him crazy. Julia was so busy smiling at me she didn't see him approaching her from behind. He screamed at her so loudly he could be heard above the din of the machines. She startled and knocked her bundle of garments on the floor. That only made Lipsky yell louder. His face moved close to hers. I stopped packing a box and inched in Julia's direction.

Lipsky's contorted face turned hot red, his hair ablaze. Julia cringed, a knot in every muscle. He grabbed her arm and yanked so hard she fell off her chair. I ran right at him and gave him a hard shove with both hands. He stumbled and would have fallen if he hadn't grabbed hold of a work table. His glasses tumbled to the floor. Now it was his turn to cringe. He raised his arm to protect his frightened face.

Spittle dribbled from Lipsky's mouth. I stood over him, both fists clenched, my breathing shallow, ready to attack. Neither one of us moved. Bettino stepped between us and put a hand on my arm. Every sewing machine stopped. All I could hear was my own blood beating in my ears, and my heaving chest.

He picked up his glasses from the floor and backed up a couple of steps, keeping Bettino between us. The women froze in place, watching. "You're fired," he snarled. "Get out of here."

I pushed Bettino's hand aside and moved closer to Lipsky. I poked him in the chest with my finger. "If you ever do anything like that to her again, I will kill you." Duv had told Lipsky the story about my shooting Viktor Askinov; he would take my threat seriously. I stuck my head so close to his I could see every bloodshot vein in his eyes.

"Leave her alone," I repeated. "Do you understand?" His nod was barely perceptible.

Bettino pulled me away. "Pick up my pay, will you?" I said to him. He nodded. The only sound was my clumping feet marching toward the door.

Duv watched the whole thing from the far row of machines. He stood in the aisle blocking my exit, hands on his hips, smug satisfaction on his face. "So was she worth it?" he said.

"Get out of my way." I pushed past him.

"You think you're such a saint, but you're no better than the rest of us."

I turned back toward him. "I pray to God I'm better than you."

I didn't see Duv for a long time after that. It still pains me that our friendship ended the way it did. There were so many times growing up in Uman when Duv alone made existence bearable. Where did my childhood friend go? I still miss him.

My feet walked themselves to the Kinsale Tavern where I told it all to Thomas Kelly. "Eh, lad. You have some fight in you, just like an Irishman," he said, pulling the bottle of whiskey out from under the bar. I only told Thomas the part about Lipsky abusing one of the young women, but Thomas had long ago figured out the rest.

Now I was without a job. I had no choice but to go forward with my own tailoring shop and pray it worked. And I still had an unfinished debt to pay to Julia Sorvino.

Saturday afternoon I waited across the street from the Becker Dress Factory around quitting time. The morning rain had stopped. I paced back and forth, trying to put into words what I was going to say to Julia.

Bettino came out first and walked across the street to me, stoic as usual. He handed me a wad of dollar bills. "Your last pay," he said. "You going to the tavern?" I told him I had to see Julia first. He nodded and moved on.

She came out of the door with Camella and Rose. They were all laughing. One of them saw me and nudged Julia. Her laughter stopped. I waited, hoping she would come across the street to me. Rose whispered something in her ear and led Camella up the street. Julia, arms dangling at her side, stood there for an eternity. At last she came across the street, moving with the beauty and grace of a Kirov ballerina, never taking her eyes from mine.

She stopped a couple of feet from me. "Hello Avi." Her voice trembled.

I stepped closer, swallowed by her dark innocent eyes. I wanted her. A couple of the other women leaving the factory saw us and whispered to each other, looking back over their shoulders as they walked down the street. I raised my hand and touched her soft cheek. She smiled a sad smile.

"Rabbi Akiva told me you came to him." I took my hand away. I had no right to touch her.

"He's a nice man."

"Julia, I am so sorry for everything I did to you." The hurt was written on her face. I wanted to take her in my arms and scrub away the hurt I caused. "I would do anything if I could give back what I took from you."

"Do you love me even a little?" She asked. She looked afraid to move a muscle. A wisp of her hair fell down over one eye. I wanted to brush it back, but I didn't.

"Oh my god, Julia. Much more than a little." I touched my open hand against my breast. "I will always carry you here."

"Lipsky is leaving me alone, thanks to you."

"It was my sin, not yours," I said. "Will you forgive me?" She nodded and wiped away a forming tear. "And will you forgive yourself?" I asked, thinking of what Daniel had said.

"Someday." Neither of us said anything more. We gazed into each other's eyes. I couldn't bear the sorrow on her face. She turned and looked up the street where Rose and Camella were waiting. "I had better go."

I put a hand on each of her shoulders and kissed her forehead. She raised her hand and stroked my beard with the back of it. Then she dropped her hand and scurried away. I watched her go, soaked with the misery of great loss.

From this time on, I was more sensitive to the hurt in others, more tolerant of those who transgressed, and less tolerant of those who refused to make amends to those they wronged.

It was not over when Julia walked away. It will never be over so long as I live. But now my purpose had to be to make restitution to Sara, and that meant the risk of losing her.

CHAPTER NINE

May 1907

Saturday afternoon I sat by the shop window enjoying the sun, blooming trees, and the sweet scent of blossomed flowers. Laundry flew again from the tenement fire escapes. Women donned their most colorful shirtwaist dresses so short you could see their stockings above their ankles. Bettino doffed his straw hat to one of them, and then crossed the street toward the shop, dodging the horse droppings.

A rare smile crossed the corners of his lips when he entered. "Ah, the American Tailor," he said, noticing the sign in the window. "Everyone wants to look American."

It didn't take long to show Bettino around my cramped shop. The sewing machine sat near the window so I could look out at people passing by, just like Poppa's shop. There was a table for cutting out a pattern, a rack for hanging up items I was working on, a little storage bin for some piece goods, and a board on which to press a finished garment. He admired the work in progress, much of it from Mrs. Schulman and the women she brought in with her.

Losing my job at the dress factory set me back, delaying bringing Sara over. But soon I would have enough money. Business had picked up. Mr. Akiva told everyone who came into the laundry about me. I invested in handbills to put up in any willing business nearby. That got me work for a few men's suits.

I wanted to ask Bettino about Julia but was afraid to. He must have heard my thoughts because, right before he left, he told me she was doing well and Lipsky was leaving her alone. He had turned his attention to a couple of the more willing new girls.

A week after Bettino's visit, a fire engine raced down the street in front of the shop. Then another, and two more after that. Some men and a few women ran past the window. I stuck my head out as the fire engines disappeared around the next corner. In the distance, a cloud of black smoke stained the blue sky. Fires in the East Harlem firetraps happened every day. I could smell the smoke, and thought this must be a big one. I went back to work.

Maybe an hour later, a couple of men coming from the direction of the fire stopped in front of my window to talk with a couple of men heading towards the fire. I heard someone say "dress factory." When I heard that, I bolted out the door and ran toward the factory.

The blaring headlines on the front page of the next day's newspaper told the story: 23 DIE IN DRESS FACTORY FIRE. It was nearly quitting time on Saturday, pay day. Other businesses in the building finished earlier in the day, their employees gone – except for the dress factory. The fire galloped so fast because the bundles of garments caught fire and spread like kerosene. The finished dresses hanging on lines combusted, along with the litter of trimmings and cuttings on the floor.

The elevator wasn't working, as usual. The fire escape exit was locked on pay days because Lipsky and Duv wanted to collect their ransoms from each girl as she left the building. The only way down was the narrow staircase.

When the fire broke out, some climbed over sewing tables to get to the fire escape. They tried to break through the locked door but couldn't. By the time they turned toward the inside staircase, their way was blocked by flames. One young girl broke a window and jumped to her death rather than be burned alive. Others climbed onto the window sills. Onlookers on the sidewalk below yelled up at them, pleading not to jump. They did anyway. A couple nearly landed on passersby. Those who jumped were crushed into a thousand pieces. Those who didn't were burned beyond recognition, a mass of ashes and congealed blood.

The fire engines didn't have enough men, equipment or water pressure to do much good. Within minutes, the building evaporated. By the time I got there, the fire was out, nothing left but a smoldering shell. Soot fluttered down on my shoulders. The putrid smell of charred wood mixed with cooked human flesh. I couldn't get the odor out of my clothes for weeks and eventually threw away my shirt as soon as I could afford a dollar for a new one.

Blue-clad policemen pushed back the curious with their nightsticks. I stood in the very spot where I last saw Julia only a week before. Bodies lay in the street, covered with tarps. Two men in white garb loaded them into ambulances. A couple more were brought out of the building and placed on the ground. Not a murmur came from the crowd.

My god, not Julia. Please, not Julia, I begged. She mustn't be dead. I started shaking and groaning. A couple of the men around me looked over. I wanted to scream her name. I looked frantically for someone who could tell me what was going on. I pushed my way toward the front of the crowd and found a policeman. He offered no help. He either didn't know or didn't want to say who died.

Mr. Rupert Becker chatted with a fire chief. His tidy black suit showed he had not been in the building when the fire struck, or he had been the first one out. I started in his direction when I saw Bettino sitting on the stoop of the building next door, a blanket wrapped around his shoulders. A policeman finished his questioning about the time I got to Bettino. His face was splotched with soot, his blood-red eyes as empty as death.

I put my arm around him and squeezed. "How are you? Anything I can do?" He turned toward me. His shirt and pants had rips in them. His hands were black, welts covering his arms.

"Get me home," he said.

I helped him to his feet. He let the blanket fall to the ground, unsteady on his feet. I held his arm as we walked away. The smoke from the fire clung to him no matter how far we got from it.

Bettino looked straight ahead, eyes fixed on the distance. "Julia's alive," he said, answering in a monotone the question I had been reluctant to ask. "She wasn't hurt."

Thank God. I closed my eyes and said a little prayer. We kept walking. I adopted Bettino's monotone. "And Natali, Camella, Rose?"

He shook his head.

"Frieda, Anka, Mira?"

He shook his head again. "Only Ladonna. And the Polish girl, Aniela. But her little friend died."

"How about Lipsky and Duv?" I didn't want anything to happen to Duv, but I would have welcomed the end of Lipsky.

"They were the first ones out the door."

When we reached the front steps of his tenement building, I asked him if he wanted me to come up with him. He shook his head, turned to leave, and then turned back.

"Duv," he said. "He got out right behind Lipsky. Then he ran back into the building. He found three of the girls and led them out. He carried one of them. Burns all over him." He went up the steps into his building. I sat down on the steps, quivering. My friend Duv behaved with courage and decency when it mattered most. I couldn't believe it. Yet Duv was in part responsible for those deaths. There was no way to avoid that.

To calm an enraged electorate, the mayor appointed a commission to investigate what happened and determine responsibility. Duv, Lipsky, and Mr. Becker testified, but nothing came of it. They all got away with murder.

That's how it ended. The Becker Dress Factory was no more. It was a few years before I saw Bettino again. I ran into him at a Benny Leonard prize fight. Still the stoic, he told me Julia married some guy less than a year later and had three daughters. He heard she moved to a place in the Village not far from the little restaurant he now owned. He invited me to stop in for a dinner on the house.

Memories of Julia linger: her smile, her hearty laugh, her gentle touch, those dark inviting eyes – and of course the heat from her that night in Mr. Becker's office. I don't know if it was love or something else. When things are gray, as happens in life sometimes, I find myself thinking of her. When I do, she is again the vulnerable, pretty young woman I once knew. For that moment, I yearn for her. Then I lock the memory away.

The day after the fire, Daniel stopped by my shop. "How is she?" he asked. I told him everything Bettino had told me. He boosted himself up onto my cutting table. He was fidgety, drumming his fingers, something on his mind. I sat in my seat by the window.

"It's time you send for Sara," he said. "Poppa wants to help."

"I can't accept that. It'll only be a few more months if the business keeps coming in."

"You'll pay him back by making suits and dresses for the family when we need them."

Pride made it difficult to accept charity. But a spark jolted me when I realized Sara could really be on her way to me right away. All I had to do was say yes.

I said "okay." But before I left the laundry that day, I insisted Mr. Akiva and I sign a letter agreeing to the loan and its conditions. I think the whole Akiva family was as excited as I was.

The next morning I sent Sara a telegram telling her I was mailing a bank draft to purchase the tickets. I mailed the draft immediately, along with a letter. She sent back a telegram saying she would leave as soon as my letter arrived with the money.

I couldn't afford so fine an apartment as Hannah and Daniel had, but Hannah found something nice across the street and three buildings down from them on 113th Street near Lexington. It was on the fourth floor so we would have a climb, but it had a community toilet on every floor, running water, and a sink in the kitchen large enough to take a bath. We had three rooms all to ourselves. I worried I couldn't afford it on the income of a tailor, but I stretched to make everything perfect for Sara.

Some of the money Mr. Akiva loaned me went to furnishing the apartment. I didn't know anything about making a home. Hannah and Mrs. Akiva did all of that. They gave me pots, pans, and dishes they said were extras they didn't need any more, but I suspect they bought them second hand. When Hannah was done, our new home was much better than what Sara was leaving in Uman.

By the end of June, I had nothing more to do but wait. I worked hard and long at the tailor shop. When I wasn't sewing, I went out to find new business. And when I wasn't doing that, I made two new American dresses for Sara. They were as simple as Sara's modesty, but I could easily add some decoration if she would let me.

Six weeks after I sent off my letter, one came from Sara:

> *My darling Avi,*
>
> *How lucky I am to have you. Nothing could ever make me stop loving you. I am grateful to God our separation will soon be over. You are my life and my happiness.*

It was poetry, created by Sara and penned by Ester. Sara went on to say she was on her way with her brother Josef, so she would have protection and help with Yakira and Itzhak. That was a relief. Uncle Yakov arranged everything. They were sailing from Bremen, Germany on the ship Kaiser Wilhelm der Grosse and would be here almost as soon as her letter.

The New York Times carried schedules of which ships were due to arrive in the next week. So every morning I bought a paper from the newsboy on the corner by the tailor shop, and turned immediately to that page. Not four days after I received Sara's letter, there it was. The Kaiser Wilhelm was due to dock next Monday.

The July day before Sara arrived was warm and sticky. Sun and blue skies mixed with sudden downpours. I couldn't sit still, as anxious as I was on the day before my wedding. I got a fresh haircut and even had my beard and mustache cropped close. I took a proper bath in the kitchen tub, not a quick squirt like usual.

I wandered Central Park and found a bench under the shade of a big maple tree. Children played in the pond under their mother's watch. A band tuned up in the band box across the meadow, the sound of a clarinet counterpointing the tuba.

The past twenty months were an ordeal, a trial I had survived, older, wiser, and badly scarred. Sara and I had been very different people from the very beginning. Sara would have been content to stay in Uman all of her life just like her parents. I wanted adventure, and got more than I bargained for. After this time apart, our differences would be even larger.

In late afternoon I went back to the apartment. At first being alone there felt strange. Not one night of my life had ever passed without a multitude asleep around me. Now I took pleasure in the solitude. On warm, clear days like this one, my perch on the fire escape provided theater on the street below. I watched two young boys chasing a little girl, then two older boys pursuing an older girl. A couple of horseless carriages honked their horns, scattering the crowd in the street.

I tried to imagine what it would be like being a real father to two children I didn't know and who didn't know me. Yakira was only a year old when I left, and Itzhak had just been born. Now she was nearly three, a little person, and he was nearly two years old, walking and talking. I had to admit I really didn't feel much like a father. Yakira and Itzhak were like characters in a novel I only read about.

I must have pulled out the picture of the three of them at least a dozen times. I read Sara's last letter still again and thought about how we met on the April day in the market square. I could see her and feel her the day we first kissed at Sukhi Yar. Most of all, I thought about how close I came to losing her forever because of her father's prejudices.

Reb Kravetz was a bitter man who beat down his wife and children because it was the only power he had. He was a day laborer who brought home barely enough to feed his family and keep a decaying, leaky roof over their heads. Sara and I fell in love and I asked her to marry me. Her father refused to give his permission, as was a father's right back then. He was a dictatorial Hassidic – worse than the Tsar – who deemed me and all open-minded Jews heretics. It didn't matter that Sara withered like a dying rose because of his uncaring stubbornness.

Somehow I mustered the will to persuade him to change his mind. I offered every religious concession I could imagine, with a small financial incentive, layered with an earnest promise to love his daughter and give her a good life. He was full of vodka that afternoon. Maybe it was his usual inebriated state, or a well-concealed love for his daughter, but he agreed. He called out for Sara to join us, and then he immediately left the house with little sign of affection for her. Sara collapsed in my arms, thin and frail after little more than a week of grief when she thought she would be forced to marry a rabbi's son. "You came for me. You came for me," she sobbed. "And now I am going to be your wife." I promised to love her forever and never let her go.

I thrashed around in bed all night. Tomorrow Sara would sleep beside me and I would never be lonely again. At that very moment her ship neared New York, possibly already sitting just outside the harbor, so close I could almost touch her. She might be thinking of me as I was thinking of her, excited and scared.

I had a lot to make up to her.

CHAPTER TEN

July 1907

The rooster hadn't crowed yet when I got up, turned on the gaslight and dressed. I tried to eat but my stomach refused. I drank some black coffee, paced, stood by the window and looked out into the inky night. When the first beam of sunshine unveiled a gorgeous July day, I set out to meet Sara's ship dressed in my best suit.

The main harbor terminal already pulsed with men on their way over to Ellis Island to meet their arriving families. A few piers further down, the four gigantic smokestacks of the Kaiser Wilhelm, Sara's ship, rose above the warehouse roofs. My insides soared and scrambled at the same time.

The ferry ride to Ellis Island took little more than a few minutes, but it was long enough to sniff the deep blue water and follow the gulls gliding across a sunny blue sky punctuated with passing wisps of white clouds.

When the ferry docked on the island, the cluster of husbands pressed through the fortress's giant doors. I took up a position near the pillar at the base of the double flight of wooden steps down from the Registry room. That big room was the last obstacle before immigrants were cleared to enter America.

Other men gathered there to wait, some my age, some much older. They all looked American, no longer the greenhorns dressed in native garb like they were the day they arrived. Now you couldn't tell the Italians from the Greeks or the Russians from the Germans, at least not until they spoke. Everyone smelled like clean Ivory Soap from last night's bath. Most of us talked quietly or not at all, anticipating what was to come.

The first passengers of the day came down the big staircase. Some of the women met their husbands with passionate embraces, and some with the formality of strangers. None were yet from the Kaiser Wilhelm.

I paced and fiddled. The giant clock at the far end of the hall showed it was past noon. I had been waiting for nearly three hours. The thought crossed my mind more than once that possibly she didn't make it through inspection. That sent my insides into a gallop.

"Avi, Avi." I looked up and there she was, bounding down the staircase as fast as she could, her eyes locked on mine. A beam of sunshine followed her, lighting her golden hair.

She dropped her canvas bag and threw herself at me. We hugged tightly, our lips meeting in a long, deep kiss. My heart exploded.

She buried her head in the crook of my shoulder, sobbing. I stroked her hair.

"My darling, my darling," I said over and over.

"Don't ever leave me again." Her body heaved.

"Never. Never."

We pulled away and looked at each other. I was as lost in Sara's soft blue eyes as I was the first time I saw her that April day in the market square. The mixture of tears running down her cheeks and her shining smile made her sparkle, more beautiful than an angel. We kissed again, pulled away laughing, then kissed again, more gently. I touched her hair and her face while I held her close. She stroked my beard, her laugh wrinkling her nose. I had forgotten the gentle touch of her hand.

I hugged her again, this time looking over her shoulder. Her brother Josef stood there holding the hands of these two adorable little urchins. Yakira's face wore a shy smile. Itzhak's eyes darted from side to side, up and down, examining everything going on around him. In that instant I fell in love with my children. "Come," Sara said. She took my hand and led me over to them.

"Give Pop a hug," she said. I squatted down and Yakira stepped into my outstretched arms. I kissed her hair and hugged her gently. Then I held out my arms for Itzhak. He studied me as though deciding whether this was a good idea. Then he moved cautiously into my embrace. Sara bent down and wrapped her arms around all of us.

"Thank you Lord. Thank you," she whispered. I thanked Him too.

There had not been a day for me like this one since the day we were married. No day quite like this one ever came again.

Our modest apartment took Sara's breath away. "Do we live here?" She asked when I ushered her in. Yakira clung to her. Itzhak was absorbed, taking in everything he saw. Josef, again our chaperone, would stay with us until he got work and could afford a place in an apartment.

Sara and I touched every other minute. I couldn't get enough of her. The closer it got to our bedtime, the more my craving for her grew. But I didn't want to force myself on her at such a moment. It had been a long day for everyone. As soon as the light began to fade, Sara put Yakira and Itzhak to sleep, head to toe in a small bed in the kitchen. "Give Pop a kiss goodnight," she said. I hugged them gently, their little arms and hands curling around my neck. I started to feel like a real father.

"I must sleep." Josef covered a big yawn with his hand. He stretched out on the couch in the living room. His snores quickly mingled with Yakira and Itzhak's heavy breathing. Sara took a last look at Yakira and Itzhak before walking into our bedroom. I followed her, turning the gas lamp way down. I felt as awkward as I had on our wedding night, not knowing what to do next.

"You must be very tired," I said.

"I smell awful from the trip."

"You smell good to me." It was almost true.

She smiled shyly. "Go change in the kitchen," she said. I did as I was told, quickly stripping off my clothes and pulling on my nightshirt. I was disappointed I couldn't look at her naked body. I told myself I had to be content just to have Sara sleeping next to me again. Sara took forever to get ready. I peeked in again on Josef, sound asleep. Then I checked on Itzhak and Yakira, also sound asleep.

"Come in, Avi," she whispered.

She stood by the bed wearing a delicate white dressing gown with blue embroidered dots, like on our wedding night. She giggled like a little girl, her eyes opening wide when she looked down at my rising bulge.

"Do you like it?" She twirled around slowly.

"You are so beautiful."

I took her in my arms and kissed her. She grabbed my hair, her kiss fierce. Her body pressed against mine. I traced my fingers over every curve, lingering on her luscious breasts, grown larger with children. She pulled my nightshirt up and grabbed me. I pushed her toward the bed and pulled her nightgown off over her head.

We were done much too quickly, but oh how magnificent it was. Then we kissed gently. Sara snuggled in my arms. I inhaled the perfume of her white shoulders and the aftertaste of her arousal. I traced her hips, her heinie, and her thighs with my finger, kissed her soft hair, and the freckles on her breast.

"Are you alright?" I asked, afraid I might have been too vigorous.

"Wonderful," she sighed. We didn't say any more. I thought she had fallen asleep in my arms. "Don't leave me," she said.

"Never again.... I love you."

This time she did fall asleep. I watched her for the longest time, thinking what a blessed man I was. I shuddered to think she knew what I had done with Julia Sorvino, and how badly it must hurt her if she did know.

The next morning I woke up and moved my hand over to touch her. Sara wasn't there. I heard her talking in the kitchen and stuck my head out. She was sitting at the kitchen table talking to Yakira and Itzhak as they ate their breakfast. Josef still snored on the couch in the living room. When she saw me she threw her arms around me and kissed me. Yakira and Itzhak watched intently. They would have to get used to it.

Sara was more independent and confident than when I left Uman. Maybe it was the long trip across the ocean to a strange new land. She knew everything about being a mother: When to feed them, when to hug them, when to scold them, when to protect them and when to let them run free. It was easy to see the three of them were tied together with a stout rope. I wondered if there would be room for me.

I couldn't wait to show Sara our neighborhood. I wanted her to love America as much as I did. By the time Josef rose and we ventured out, the morning was half over. Sara, Yakira, Izthak and Josef spent most of the time gawking, open-mouthed at all of the strange things: horseless carriages, streetcars, crowded shops, pushcarts, paved streets and sidewalks. Sara was confounded to see churches and syn-agogues mixed together in the same neighborhood. I told her about my Catholic friends, Thomas Kelly and Bettino Rossi. She gave me a skeptical look.

Central Park exploded with summer flowers the colors of the rain-bow and the taste of cotton candy. Sara and I sat on a bench shaded by a big maple tree; Josef chased Yakira and Itzhak on the grass. A pair of bluebirds pecked in front of us, looking for worms.

"It's beautiful," Sara said, squeezing my hand. "Like Sukhi Yar."

I put my arm around her and held her hand. I couldn't get enough of touching her. "Tell me about the family," I said. "I miss them."

She frowned. "Poppa isn't well. The doctor doesn't know why but he's tired all the time. He lost weight. But he and Momma want to come to America as soon as Ester has her baby."

"And Momma?"

Sara brightened. "She's fine. Strong. The same old Momma, in charge of everything."

When she talked about Momma and Poppa, her love showed. But when she talked of her own father, mother, and sister her tone flattened. Reb and Mother Kravetz were miserable as ever, she said. Sara's sister, Havol, was going to marry the rabbi's son, the same one Reb Kravetz had picked out for Sara. I feigned interest in her family, but in truth I had none.

She quickly returned to my family: My youngest brother, Markus, was courting a young woman named Sadie. Momma and Poppa would be very satisfied if he married her. My sister, Ester, and her husband Simon were making plans to come to America. My dear brother Lieb's wife Golde was pregnant again. There was talk Zelda, my wayward sister, had found a man in Kiev and might marry him. I told myself I had a lot to make up to Zelda if I ever got the chance. My own moral failings had earned her my understanding and an apology.

All this talk about the family fanned my determination to get every one of them to America, even Lieb. Sara said persuading him would be hard, but maybe not impossible if everyone else came over.

When Sara asked about Duv, I gave her too great a detail of his sins and failings – and my condemnation. I suppose I wanted to distance myself from him and his immorality, and let her know my sense of right and wrong was still as unyielding as the day I left Uman. I didn't see then that my own failings were teaching me human beings are more shaded than simple black and white. But I still had a lot to learn.

Two little boys came over to Yakira and Itzhak, their mother close by. They examined each other then moved on. Josef took Yakira and Itzhak over to the fish pond where they threw sticks in the water and wet their hands.

"And Viktor Askinov?" I asked.

Apprehension crossed her face for a moment. "He stayed away from me. I saw him every once in awhile dragging his stiff leg around." She clenched a fist to her lips, then spat. "God should visit on him the worst of the Ten Plagues." I'd never heard Sara curse anyone before.

Itzhak came over, cranky. Sara picked him up and fed him some dry bread from her pocket.

"You haven't mentioned Uncle Yakov," I said. "Is he alright?" Sara didn't respond right away, putting another piece of bread in Itzhak's mouth. I held my breath.

"He's fine." She said it as if she didn't want to talk about him. I thought about her earlier letter to me and wondered if Uncle Yakov had warned her about men's carnal weaknesses. I almost hoped he had. Whatever he said, he only would have said it to protect Sara, and me. I had gotten past the first hurdle when she said she loved me and we made love last night. But had she forgiven me, or was I going to have to earn it like Daniel said? I feared what could come next.

Sara looked at me. I hadn't said anything for a couple of minutes, lost in my fears. She got up from the bench. "We'd better go. The children need a nap."

We didn't talk much walking back, letting Josef fill in the silence. I looked over at Sara every so often. When she looked back at me, she smiled, but she looked sad. I held her hand; she let it lie there in mine, limp. I hoped my face didn't show the guilt I was feeling.

A policeman in a blue uniform and gray shell helmet walked toward us. I wouldn't have noticed except Sara pulled Yakira close to her, and Josef moved to the edge of the sidewalk to give him a wide berth. "It's alright," I said. The policeman nodded and smiled when he passed, his eyes mostly on Sara. She didn't return his generous smile.

Two men coming toward us eyed Sara. The one decked out in a blue blazer tipped his straw hat to her as we passed, staring at her breasts. She gave him a polite smile, still unaware of the affect she had on men.

In late afternoon, Hannah and Daniel came over with their sons, Nathan and Leo. They brought a peddler's bundle of food. Hannah embraced Sara. "You are even more beautiful than Avi said you were." Right from the start, Hannah and Sara were the best of friends. America overwhelmed Sara in those first weeks. Hannah taught her what she needed to learn, such as how to shop for food in a grocery store, and about kosher foods that came in packages. Mr. and Mrs. Akiva adopted her like they adopted me.

Sara loved our little tailor shop from the moment she set foot in it. She sat right down at my sewing machine as if she owned it. Then she turned around to find some scrap material, placed it in the sewing machine and ran it off with surprising skill. "Poppa's been teaching me," she said, proudly holding up her work.

Friday we went shopping for food for our first Sabbath together in America. "How can we afford all of this," Sara asked as I loaded up our baskets. "A whole chicken just for us?" I don't remember a Friday after that when we didn't have a whole chicken. After we got home, Sara pulled out candlesticks from her suitcase, Momma's candlesticks. At sundown she covered her head, and chanted the prayer.

Sara went with me to synagogue on Friday evening because it was her first one in America, and because she liked Daniel and Hannah. But she was uncomfortable in a Conservative synagogue like Daniel's. In her Hassidic synagogue back home, she sat with the other women behind a screen in the back. Here she sat across the aisle from me in a pew just like mine. She looked lost, tense that she was upsetting God's natural order. Hannah sat beside her, and every so often I saw her whisper to Sara, probably explaining some ritual. Sara was absorbed in Daniel's service and soon relaxed. Occasionally she glanced over at me and smiled. A week or two later, I offered to find her a Hassidic synagogue, but she was content with Ohev Shalom.

We changed Itzhak's name to Isaac and Yakira's to Kira so they would sound more American. Isaac had no problem, but Yakira wouldn't answer to her new name. She finally got used to it but to Sara and me she was always Yakira.

Josef got a job in a couple of weeks rolling cigars at a cigar factory close by. He was eager to move out on his own and leave Sara and me to ourselves. He also wanted some freedom to chase girls, many who worked in the cigar factory. I wouldn't think of having him live in such an awful apartment as the one I had lived in, so I supplemented his income. He was able to move into a better place with only four other men, a few blocks from us and a few blocks from the cigar factory. He had his own bed.

With Josef gone, Sara and I had time alone. Every evening, Sara tucked Yakira and Isaac into their bed in the kitchen, and softly sang the lullaby *Raisins and Almonds* to them until they fell asleep. Then the two of us sat in our living room for awhile before bedtime, me reading and she knitting, darning or folding laundry. We had never been alone so much since we first met. Sara wasn't interested in much of what interested me, so sometimes it felt awkward when we ran out of things to say. When that happened, I went over to her, put my arms around her, stroked her hair and kissed her. She responded. Sara enjoyed seeing what her naked body did to me. Most nights ended with bed-time play. Fortunately, Yakira and Isaac were sound sleepers.

Maybe it was my imagination, but every time I brought up some-thing that occurred when I was alone in America, she changed the subject. I was trying to make it easy for her to ask me questions, just like Daniel said I should. It was time we talked about it, but the truth is I was afraid.

I started sending money home to Uman to speed the time when the family could come to America. One night Sara asked if we could send a little to Reb and Mother Kravetz just to make their lives a little easier. So I did. After Havol married the rabbi's son, Sara asked me to send a little to her. And I sent some to Lieb, urging him in each letter to join me in my little tailor shop.

We were happy and madly in love. I convinced myself Sara knew what she wanted to know about my sin, and didn't want to know any more. Who was I to spoil everything by bringing up Julia Sorvino? But sometimes I caught her staring out the window, sadness about her. I was scared to ask why.

Daniel wouldn't let me forget. He reminded me that if Sara had questions I owed her an answer to every one until she was satisfied. Only then would my atonement be complete. I told him about every-thing I was doing to bring her joy. He told me it wasn't enough. "You must do what's best for Sara, not what's best for you," he reminded me.

I took to avoiding him but it was hard with Hannah and Sara develop-ing such a close friendship. Besides, I knew he was right. Sara and I could never be one with this lie, this sin, infecting me. I was being selfish, a coward. I can admit it now. But Sara didn't deserve any more hurt than I already caused her. That's the truth too. Believe me.

One nice Sunday a few weeks after they arrived, I took everyone to the Lower East Side to see a little more of New York. The subway ride terrified Sara and excited the children. When we got home, Yakira and Isaac fell asleep immediately. The early September evening was warm, the windows open to catch any breeze. Sara sat on the couch polishing Momma's brass candle sticks. I sat on the chair across the room pre-tending to read. I wanted some distance between us. My stomach knotted.

"You never told me much about Uncle Yakov," I said as casually as I could. "How is he?"

"He's fine." She continued polishing the candlestick.

"Are you upset with Uncle Yakov?

"No."

I didn't say anything for a moment, trying to find the right words to go on. "You wrote in one of your letters how the two of you talked when I was ill."

She didn't look up, rubbing harder on the candlestick in her hand. She wasn't making this easy.

"Do you want me to tell you anything about my illness?" My heart hung in the air, unable to beat.

Sara looked at me with a mask on her face as frightening as her hard father, Reb Kravetz. "Don't tell me you were sick. It's a lie. I know what you did." Her soft blue eyes turned to gray stone.

Her force knocked me backwards. I grasped on to Daniel's words. "Tell me what I need to do to get you to forgive me. Anything. I'll do it. I'll answer every question you have until you don't have any more." I was afraid to stop talking; panic gripped my lungs. "I love you. You're the only woman I've ever loved."

She glared at me, as freezing as damnation. "I will not be like my mother. That night you came for me, I promised no man would ever again own my love as a right." Her voice tempered only a bit, "I love you, Avi, with all of my heart, but...." She shook her head.

"I'll do anything," I begged.

"I'm going to bed." She slammed the candlestick on the end table and left without looking at me. A few minutes later the light went out in the bedroom.

Sara had never gotten angry at me. It made me ready to throw up. I didn't know what to do. I wanted to talk it out, but she was having none of it. When I went to bed, she had her back turned. She was still awake, but when I touched her she didn't respond. I kissed the back of her neck. She didn't respond.

"Can you ever forgive me?" I pleaded.

"I already have," she answered. But she didn't sound like it.

I must have lain awake until the first light of dawn came through the window, and then drifted off.

When I awoke, Sara was bathing Yakira and Isaac in the big sink. I stumbled into the kitchen in my nightshirt unsure of what I was going to face. She brightened when she saw me and met me with an enthusiastic kiss as though nothing had happened. She talked over breakfast about Uncle Yakov, how content he seemed to be, and how proud he was of his nephew in America. "He tells the story of your night on the barricades over and over again. He says when Yakira and Isaac are older I must tell them what a hero their father was."

But she didn't tell me what they had talked about when I was ill. I tried to bring it up again, but again the blood drained from her face. "I don't want to talk about it no more," she snapped. Then she changed the subject.

Our life went on from there. Love never abandoned us, and she forgave me like she said, of that I'm sure. But it took awhile for friendship, sacrifice, sharing, and compromise to soften my guilt and her hurt. Quite a few days passed before our hungry, urgent lovemaking returned. It never left again.

I worked hard to make it up to her. I asked her often whether she was happy. She always assured me she was. I went out of my way to ignore attractive women when Sara was near, and never said anything complimentary about any woman other than family and close friends. She never asked for such a thing. I gave it out of respect and love. Over time I told Sara everything that happened in my life before and after we met, even the most embarrassing. I told her my deepest fears, my greatest joys, and my biggest dreams. I told her about everything but Julia Sorvino.

If life has taught me anything, it's that we can never know another person fully. I never learned how, deep inside, Sara really dealt with it. I never found out how much she knew or suspected. Did she simply have the capacity to blind herself to what she didn't want to see? Or did she have an unfathomable strength to forgive? I suspect it was the latter.

Some months after, I told Daniel I was sure I wouldn't get into heaven unless Sara begged God to let me in. "You've done enough," Daniel told me. "Stop being a martyr. Forgive yourself. Get on with your life." And so we did.

PART TWO

PROMISE MOMMA

CHAPTER ELEVEN

May 1911

Momma's heart fractured the morning Poppa died. Now, three years later, she looked twenty years older. Her hair thinned so it barely covered her pinkish scalp, and deep ruts cut into her weathered face. Her once-robust body shrank, but the formidable woman inside did not. Her children were now spread over two continents, separated by an ocean, and she would not let that stand.

They buried Poppa in the cemetery behind the synagogue alongside his mother and father. The very next day Momma announced she was going to America and all of her children were going with her. She wrote me and ordered me to beg, borrow or steal every cent I could to bring them all over, fast. I did borrow money from Mr. Akiva; and I did beg my customers for more work. But I didn't steal. When I sent money for tickets back to Uman, they all praised me for my generosity, but the truth is I wanted my family here with me.

My sister Ester, her husband Simon, and Momma arrived in America a year later. Not six months after they got here, Ester gave birth to a strong little boy they named Morton, the first Schneider to be born an American citizen. I myself earned my citizenship in time to vote for Woodrow Wilson in 1912.

I helped Markus and Zelda when their turns came. Markus became my partner in the tailor shop, a blessing to have him next to me. He married Sadie Brody shortly before they came over. She was barely a woman, seventeen years old. Markus was twenty-four. Sadie was a sparkly, skinny thing with dimples, freckles and curly red hair. Momma grinned, quite delighted with her new daughter-in-law the first time she saw Sadie cutting Markus's meat for him. Sometimes she even tied his shoelaces as if he were a child.

Momma lived with Ester and Simon in a larger apartment on the ground floor in our tenement. Markus and Sadie moved into an apartment only a block away. But my youngest sister Zelda settled in Philadelphia rather than New York. She had married the man she met in Kiev, a widower named Hyman Horowitz, ten years older with two small sons. She never had children of her own. Every one of us forgave her for her wild cavorting when she was younger. I no longer found it so hard to understand her sins after what I did with Julia Sorvino. Still, Zelda kept her distance, rarely visiting from Philadelphia after the first two Passover *Seders*. Hymie and his sons came to the first one, but we hardly saw them after that.

At first, released from a lifetime of hard work in Russia, nothing could contain Momma. She fussed over the grandchildren and hopped at every chance to take them to Central Park with Sara and Ester. Every few days she made me one of my favorite dishes: potato latkes, pea soup, mandelbrot, noodle kugel, pierogi, you name it. She braved the jammed streets around our tenement, captivated by the plentiful luxuries cramming the peddlers' wagons and shops, like unworn shoes, undented pots, and fresh pretzels. Simon was one of those peddlers. Soon enough he and his father opened a successful dry goods store.

But in the last few months, Momma lost interest. She left the apartment less and less; she stopped cooking. On most days, I stopped by after work to sit with her for a few minutes and give Ester a break. Sometimes Momma was too tired to talk, content to sit together or listen to my stories about Yakira, Isaac, and our busy tailor shop. Other times she wanted to talk about old memories, mostly of Poppa, and when she was a little girl growing up. More and more she wanted to talk about Lieb, who still stubbornly refused to budge from Uman.

The day Momma extracted her promise from me, a fierce May storm thundered in at dawn. By late afternoon when I got to Ester's front door it had turned into a brightening drizzle. What I remember most about Ester's apartment was the way it always smelled of something good to eat. Today it smelled of borscht, just like the dark beet soup Momma used to make. The hunger-inducing aroma of a potato kugel poured out of the oven. Ester's son Willy played nine-pin on the floor in the front room. The little one, Morty, watched the pins go down from his seat on the thick brown rug that doubled as his bed.

"How's Momma today," I asked as soon as I walked in.

"How's Momma? The same as always. She's laying down right now." Ester nodded in the direction of the small bedroom in back. Then she ladled a cup of borscht from the pot and put it in front of me at the kitchen table. "All she ever talks about any more is getting Lieb to come over. I try to tell her he's not coming, but she won't listen."

"They named their new baby Joshua," I said.

"And it's breaking Momma's heart not to be able to see him." She pursed her lips and shook her head slowly back and forth. "You know, I don't understand our brother some times."

Willy took a frayed teddy bear away from his little brother and Morty let out a holler like he was being attacked by Cossacks. "Eh, they've been cooped up all day with this rain," Ester grunted as she went over to settle the argument. "It's stopped for now. I'm going to take them out on the front stoop to play for a few minutes. Have some more borscht. There's plenty."

I filled my cup again and sat back down at the table. I knew Momma was going to start on me again about Lieb as soon as she woke up. In every letter I wrote him, which was often, I begged him to come to America. And in every letter he wrote me, he said he was staying put. *There should always be a Schneider in the tailor shop on the market square in Uman*, he wrote. After he and Golde moved into Momma and

Poppa's old house, my brother pronounced the matter closed. That didn't stop Momma from nagging me to write him again. Her pleading became more desperate. I didn't know how much more of it I could take.

About then, Momma shuffled into the kitchen, her old dress hanging on her like an oversized grain sack. She didn't say anything. I watched her carefully make her way into the front room, afraid she would trip on the uneven plank floorboards. A cleansed after-rain breeze blew gently through the open window, rustling the lace curtains and Ester's bloomers hanging on an indoor clothes line. Momma looked gray, her lips dry and trembling. "Come, sit by me," she said, patting the cushion on the couch with a hand as thin as a chicken's claw. I did as she asked.

"How are you today?" That's the way I usually began our conversations.

"How am I? How is an old lady supposed to be?" Momma had something on her mind and dismissed my usual attempts to leaven her spirits with humor. "I'm worried about Lieb," she said. "Things are going to get worse in Russia."

"Things are better than they were."

"For a Jew? Don't let him kid you." She pushed herself forward on the sofa, her breathing heavy. "And I don't trust that Askinov boy. He's a snake. I pray to God he breaks every bone in his body."

"Uncle Yakov keeps an eye on him. He's a cripple now." I smiled, satisfied to be the cause of Viktor Askinov's affliction.

"You should have killed him. Uncle Yakov won't be around forever." She took my hand in her bony fingers. "You must promise me something."

"Anything." I answered too quickly, thinking only that I wanted to divert her attention.

"Promise me you will bring Lieb and his family to America."

"Momma, he doesn't want to come."

"He's your brother." She raised her tired voice as loud as she could. Her tiny body quivered. She squeezed my hand. "Promise me."

"Let's talk about it tomorrow."

"We will talk about it now."

She stared at me through desperate, determined eyes. She was getting too agitated and I needed to settle her mind. What difference did it make, I thought? Lieb wasn't going anywhere. "Alright," I said, patting the back of her hand.

"Promise!"

"Yes, I promise." I regretted it the moment I said it.

Momma released my hand and sank back into the couch, relieved. She closed her eyes and fell asleep again. I sat with her, thinking about what I had just promised. What she asked me to do was impossible; Lieb could not be persuaded. We would have to have another discussion about this on a better day, and I would need to find a better way to explain the futility of her obsession.

But that night Momma went to sleep and didn't wake again.

We sat *Shiva* at Ester's. I told Sara, Ester, Zelda and Markus about my last conversation with Momma. "She shouldn't have demanded such a thing," Ester said. They all insisted I mustn't take my promise to heart. But they weren't the ones who had made the promise.

I wrote to Lieb and Uncle Yakov to tell them Momma was gone. I also told Lieb about Momma's last wishes. He wrote back at once, his letter full of heartache. He told me how much he missed Momma, Poppa, and the rest of us. Uncle Yakov was taking it hard, he said. He concluded by releasing me from my promise to Momma: *Do not concern yourself with where I choose to live. My life is my life. Uman is my home. I choose to live my life here.*

The first year after Momma died, I could feel her touching me, trying to soothe my sorrow and confusion. Sara grieved more for Momma and Poppa than she did for her own father, who had died at almost the same time as Poppa. She kept saying Momma was now with Poppa. She believed it and it comforted her. I wanted to believe it but couldn't. Then the worst of it eased, replaced with sweet melancholy. But Momma and Poppa left an empty place no one can ever fill.

When they were alive, they spoke as though they could see no flaw in me. Now that they are gone I realize they saw every flaw in me, but loved me as though I had none.

After Lieb's letter of dismissal, I should have felt freed from my promise to Momma, but I couldn't let go. A promise is a promise, my mother's last dying wish. I did not see then that a promise can be a curse.

CHAPTER TWELVE

July 1912

I always blamed Momma for my obsession with Lieb, but I was the one who was so certain he would be better off in America. I wanted my brother here with me. Why not? I loved him. Is that so terrible?

This time I tried enlisting Uncle Yakov's help. My letter to my uncle urged him to persuade Lieb. His answer was quick in coming. First he told me how much Lieb grieved for Momma; his own grief oozed from every word. Then he addressed my request for his help.

> *You, Avi, see your own will as shaping events, much like I used to see things. To you, nothing is impossible if you think it through carefully and act boldly. Lieb isn't like that. He sees events as being beyond his control, something he must simply adapt to. He blames it on fate or God's will. Whatever. He is much like your poppa in that. And he is becoming as skilled in adapting as your poppa was.*

A letter from Lieb arrived before I could write Uncle Yakov again. Sara was out with the children when I got home. The letter sat on the kitchen table where she knew I would see it when I walked in. Lieb had just written me, so another letter so soon after warned me it was something important. I tore it open as I made my way onto the fire escape, hoping to catch a little relief from the humid July afternoon. Down below children ran back and forth playing and yelling, ignoring the heat and sweat.

In the first sentence, Lieb told me Uncle Yakov was dead. *He died peacefully in his sleep, and was buried the next day alongside Poppa in the cemetery behind the synagogue.*

I screamed. Old Lady Lafkowitz stuck her head out the window next door to see if I was alright. I nodded and waved her away, and then collapsed against the brick side. Tears blurred the words on the pages of Lieb's letter too much to finish it. I closed my eyes, the shade of the neighboring tenement shielding me from the worst of the late afternoon sun. For the first time in seven years I let my mind drift back to the night of the Uman *pogrom* when Uncle Yakov, the warrior, saved us.

My uncle marched into my life when I was fourteen years old, a boy struggling to find hope in a place where Jews learned early they were nothing but dirt under the toenails of the Tsar and the gentiles.

I was sweeping Poppa's tailor shop one September morning when a soldier in an earth colored army uniform strutted ramrod-straight across the market square toward us, a big duffle bag slung over his shoulder. He looked as squat and ferocious as a bulldog, with the bushiest black eyebrows I'd ever seen.

Uncle Yakov ended up in the military the way most Jews did. They snatched him. The Russian government forced many Jewish boys into the Tsar's army, often as young as eight years old, and then kept them for twenty-five years. They thought they could convert them to Orthodox Christianity. But the conversion didn't work on Uncle Yakov and didn't work on most of the other Jewish boys.

Nonetheless, Uncle Yakov turned into a fierce fighter, leader, and a decorated soldier without equal. A cavalryman, he waged war in many battles with Turks, Mongolians, and bandits.

By the time I met Uncle Yakov, he was an agnostic, yet still defiantly proclaimed himself a Jew. When he was with his family and army comrades, Uncle Yakov was the most warmhearted, wise, lovable man God created. But when he led our brigade of ragtag Jews into the fight, he was furious as a wild boar, his courage and combat skills infectious.

After his first visit to us, nearly four years passed before I saw him again. In the meantime, he had fought in Mongolia defending the construction of the Trans-Siberian railroad. In a brutal battle, Uncle Yakov was badly wounded in the leg, stomach, and left arm. Everything healed but his withered, useless left arm. The army forced him to retire. After wandering Siberia for a year, he came home to Uman. That was in May of 1900.

Who knows what would have happened to us without Uncle Yakov? He alone sensed the coming disaster after the 1903 anti-Jewish mob riots – *pogroms* – in Kishinev and Gomel. So he did the prohibited. He recruited, armed, trained and led a band of sixty young men to defend our end of Uman. He handpicked every one of us, and then turned us into warrior Jews, just like him. Yakov's Brigade, we called ourselves. I was only twenty-three years old, but he chose me to lead the squad defending the vital southern approach to the village.

In September 1905 the Russian army lost its war with Japan, and the whole country took to the streets protesting against Tsar Nicholas – peasants, workers, intelligentsia, gentiles and Jews. All demanded political reform. To change the subject, the Tsar and his government provoked masses of ignorant Ukrainian peasants and thugs into a rage against the poor and powerless Jews. In late October, only eight days after my son Itzhak was born, *pogroms* scorched the entire Ukraine.

Our makeshift brigade mobilized as soon as it started. Reports from Kiev and Odessa told of horrible atrocities. Hundreds of Jews had already been killed, their bodies left putrefying in the streets. Thousands more were wounded. The mobs of angry gentiles attacked the women and children as brutally as the men, slitting their throats and cutting open their insides. So many synagogues, houses and businesses were on fire the smoke blocked the sun. One of Uncle Yakov's old army comrades warned him Uman would be attacked the next night.

All we wanted was to protect our families. But Uncle Yakov understood if we killed gentiles, the army would join the mob and fighting wouldn't stop until every Jew was dead. So he devised a clever plan to scare the *pogrom*ists into fright and flight.

He had us build stout barricades blocking each of the three main streets into our end of town. That October afternoon he took me on a walk around the market square. "They'll hit us here first and hardest," he told me, pointing at my barricade. "This is where the synagogue is. They'll want to burn it down."

My barricade blocked the near end of Nevsky Street, bordered by two-story buildings on either side. The mob would be forced into the closed end of a narrow horse shoe. We positioned our fighters on the roofs of the houses on each side of the street and behind the barricade. When they attacked, we would fire our pistols and our three rifles over their heads and at their feet. Uncle Yakov promised us this untrained rabble, hemmed in a crossfire, would panic and run. He was sure he could then convince Colonel Baranski, the local army commander, to halt any further *pogrom* attacks – if no gentiles died first.

Uncle Yakov wanted to avoid a fight. I felt otherwise. Viktor Askinov would be leading the mob when they came. That we knew. This son-of-a-whore had tormented me, my brothers Markus and Lieb, and my friends Simon and Duv since we were little boys. He and his henchmen made our young lives a misery with escalating words and violence. Lately he enlarged his quarry to others in my family, particularly Sara. Enough was enough. If I had a clear shot, I vowed to kill him. And if he had a chance, he would surely kill me.

My comrades' fresh young faces appear now right in front of my eyes, as real as yesterday. Mica Rosenbaum was the best shot we had, and Yehuda Barsky the bravest. He climbed up on the far end of the roof knowing he would be trapped if we were overrun. Then there were Moishe Stepaner, Chiam Chernoff, Meier Braun, Shlomo Zilberman and the rest. Of course Simon, Markus and Sara's brother Josef manned the barricade, right by my side. They were all brave young men, as immune to the possibility of their own death as young men tend to be.

My gentle brother Lieb stayed back at the house with the women and children – Sara, Yakira, and newborn Itzhak among them. Lieb and Poppa were the last defense if Uncle Yakov's plan failed.

We waited well into that cold, clear night, crouched behind our makeshift rampart of overturned horse carts, scarred work tables, and oak barrels filled with dirt. Fires from burning buildings lit the sky at the other end of town, the drifting smoke churning my stomach.

When the yelling, screaming mob came around the bend, Uncle Yakov was off inspecting the squads on the other two barricades, blocks away. Simon and Markus say I looked as resolute as a general in full command, but inside I begged Uncle Yakov to hurry back. The attackers' long shadows and determined strides made them look ten feet tall. There must have been a hundred and fifty or two hundred against our band of twenty-five.

I can see Viktor Askinov clearly in the center of the front row, leading, a club swinging from his muscular arm. A thick black belt cinched his long gray shirt, black pants tucked into high boots. To his right a priest in a black robe carried a wooden cross and to his left his father, Constable Askinov, gripped a long metal bar. Behind the first row, a line of big, angry men strode step for step with their leader, clubs and crowbars in hand. Others waved pistols and large wooden crosses. A few carried rifles. A few carried torches.

I tracked Viktor Askinov in my rifle sight, waiting for him to come so close I couldn't miss. He stared right at me, those steely gray eyes excreting hate. I savored the bitterness of my own hate.

Their pace slowed when they saw the magnitude of our barricade. They didn't know how many of us fighters were behind it. They walked slowly forward, hesitant, one step at a time. Their shouts and curses stopped.

When they crossed the designated line, about fifty feet away, I screamed "fire" at the top of my lungs. All twenty-five of us fired simultaneously at their feet and over their heads, from above, left, right, and straight on. Claps and bangs flashed in the night like thunder and lightning.

Each of us fired two rounds, and then stopped. Puffs of smoke from the guns floated like clouds. The smell of gunpowder still clings to my nostrils even now as I tell you about it.

They were snared in a cross fire from above and all around them. They stopped. Most of them crouched down, including Viktor Askinov, the Constable, and the priest by his side. A few fired shots aimlessly into the night, but the Constable yelled at them to halt. Some in the rear of the crowd drifted back down Nevsky Street, ready to run.

When our volley ended, there was silence. All I heard was Simon breathing hard next to me. Viktor Askinov knelt down on one knee. I kept my rifle sight fixed on his head. His eyes darted randomly from one direction to the other, up to the roofs, and back again. He looked confused, scared and as dangerous as a cornered boar.

Viktor Askinov rose cautiously from his crouch, staring right at me again. What I see now is him slowly raising his right arm over his head to signal his men to attack. He opened his mouth to shout something. I sighted down the barrel at his head, took a deep breath, and slowly squeezed the trigger. The rifle's roar exploded the night's stillness.

He screeched like nothing I have ever heard, except maybe a goat being slaughtered. He toppled to the ground grabbing his right leg, blood gushing under him. He screamed and screamed. He cursed. He called for his mother. He bled. I felt the satisfaction of the hunter.

His father and the priest hunched over him. The priest made the sign of the cross, his lips moving as though in prayer. Some in back of their pack snuck away, down Nevsky Street, then a few more and a few more. Others called out to each other, confused and panicky. Then they started running as fast as they could. A couple of them ran into a priest, knocking him to the ground.

I would have shot him again but Uncle Yakov arrived just then and ripped the rifle from my hands before I could squeeze the trigger. "Enough, enough! He's down," he hollered.

Viktor Askinov's cries cut through the madness. Blood puddled.

Two big thugs put their arms under his arms and carried him down Nevsky Street. He shrieked every time his leg dragged the ground. The remnant of the mob retreated, and didn't come back.

Even then we could see the plan was preposterous. We were just a bunch of poor Jews, led by a worn-out war horse. It shouldn't have worked. Wounding Viktor Askinov surely stopped their attack, but I had wanted to kill him, nothing less.

Just before dawn, Uncle Yakov went to see Colonel Baranski. He convinced the colonel to send in the army immediately to preserve order. "It's over. There will be no more attacks," my uncle said to me when he returned.

His voice softened and his shoulders sagged. "Viktor Askinov will live, but they know you were the one who shot him. Now it's you who must pay." He squeezed my hand. "They have given you thirty days to leave Uman. If you don't, they will put you on trial for attempted murder and inciting a riot. You will lose. You have no choice. Leave for America or you will go to prison for twenty years." He looked like he had just condemned me to the gallows, certain he had failed me. The bile of fear rose in my throat for the first time since before the attack. In fact he liberated me, but who would know it then? "I promise you I will protect Sara and the children until they can join you," he said.

Is that the way it really happened? Who can say for sure? It was so long ago. But that's how I remember it, so it will have to do. I nearly killed a man, and the only thing I feel guilty about is that I don't feel guilty about it. Does that make any sense?

By the end of 1905 when the *pogroms* exhausted themselves, they say 10,000 Jews were dead. Many of them were women and children. More than 15,000 were wounded. Over 1,500 sons and daughters were orphaned. Many synagogues were burned. And if they weren't burned, they were defiled and plundered. The number of homes and businesses destroyed was beyond count. Thousands upon thousands of Jews left for America after that. I was one of them.

One thing I know for certain. We would never have survived without Uncle Yakov. Many *shtetls* didn't survive, burned to the ground entirely.

I wiped my eyes with the back of my hand and finished Lieb's letter. *Uncle Yakov loved us all,* he wrote. *But you were the one he was proud-est of. He said you had more courage than any man he had met on a battlefield.*

When Sara returned home, she found me still sitting on the fire escape, my back against the wall, sobbing into my arms. I held up the letter, forgetting she couldn't read. She knew what was in the letter without reading it. She put her arms around me and pulled me to her soft breast. I wept some more.

I guess I always felt Momma and Poppa's love was a given. But I earned Uncle Yakov's. He made me work for his respect, and then gave it to me fully. This was his lasting gift to me. After I shot Viktor Askinov, everyone made me into some kind of hero – David against Goliath. That wasn't fair. Uncle Yakov was the real hero, and I told them so. That didn't stop them from enlarging my role into a fairy tale, a myth which followed me to America.

In his next letter after Uncle Yakov died, Lieb made clear his intension to finish his days in Uman and be buried with Golde right next to Poppa and Uncle Yakov. The way he said it convinced me it was no use trying to get him to do what I wanted. If he was ever going to change his mind, he would have to do it himself.

Frequent letters between Lieb and me traveled across the ocean on into the years. We often wrote another one even without waiting for the previous one to be answered. We poured out our most secret thoughts and feelings, things we would never reveal to anyone else. In many ways we came to know each other better than ever before.

I was certain I would see him again, in America, even if he didn't know it yet. For the moment, I trusted God would make it happen in His own way. But don't get me wrong. I hadn't given up.

CHAPTER THIRTEEN

May 1913

In his letters, my brother tried to hide his anxiety beneath clever ridi-
cule of Viktor Askinov. He labeled him "the Cripple."

> As long as Uncle Yakov was alive, the Cripple stayed away
> from us. Uncle Yakov terrified him. But the day we buried our
> dear uncle, I saw him lurking at the edge of the cemetery with his
> younger brother Olek and his puppet, Igor Czajkowsko. I swear
> he brought the dark clouds and rain that day. He never married,
> you know. Who would have him? They say even the whores des-
> pise him. He brutalizes them, beats them up, particularly the
> Jewish ones. It's hard to figure why he even wants a Jewish
> whore the way he hates Jews. Lately he's taken to obstructing
> customers as they try to enter my tailor shop, sitting in front
> whacking a truncheon in the palm of his hand like his father the
> Constable used to do. You know he is a clerk in the tax collector's
> office. He threatens people, exaggerating his power to increase
> their taxes.

In most other ways, Lieb spoke like a man content with his life, proud of his children. *Shaina is kind like Golde,* he wrote. *Brindyl has Zelda's beauty, and little Joshua has your smart mind.*

My dreams for Yakira and Isaac were more ambitious than his were for his little ones. Still hoping to entice him to America, I told him here Jews could go to college, work in any profession, buy property, get a government job, or serve as officers in the military. None of this was possible in Russia. Here Jews were entering politics and leading unions made up of both Jews and gentiles. We worshiped however we wanted without paying any special Jew taxes.

Our tailor shop thrived. Markus and I had more work than we could handle, and the money was more than enough. Whenever I wrote about these things, Lieb responded with genuine pleasure at my good fortune, but I don't think he entirely believed all of this could be true. Sometimes it was hard for me to believe it.

I didn't tell him many Americans still didn't like Jews being in their country. Whenever they could, gentiles restricted which companies we could work for, what colleges our kids could go to, and where we lived. Those things didn't affect me, and I was sure they would get better by the time Yakira and Isaac grew up.

Lieb liked to talk about old friends of ours who remained in Uman, like my first love, Bayleh Zuckman, and Gersh Leibowitz, the tough guy who led one of the three squads the night of our Uman *pogrom.* My good friend Sergey Shumenko married a wonderful girl named Valerya. She now came to the tailor shop for Lieb to make her dresses and coats, much as Madam Shumenko had done with Poppa. *She is as pleasant to look at as Madam Shumenko was,* he wrote. *And just as courteous to Jews. I look forward to her every visit. Sergey comes with her often. I think it brings back childhood memories for him. He always asks about you and sends his best wishes.*

Letters to Sara from her sister Havol were rare. She herself couldn't read or write, so she had to have a professional letter writer do it for her. Lieb told us about Havol in almost every letter he wrote.

When I see her she is most gracious and always says a kind word about your generosity. She is proud to tell everyone she has a big sister Sara and little brother Josef in America. She is as devout a Hassidic as the day you left. Unfortunately, her severe dress and countenance hide what could be an appealing woman. She always looks as sad as Mother Kravetz used to look. They say that rabbi she married is severe, like her father was. I believe it. I've met him a few times.

Lieb was the one who first wrote to tell Sara her mother had died. Havol's letter arrived soon after. I had been sending Mother Kravetz a little money every so often to make things easier for her. Havol's biggest concern was that I not stop those stipends. When I wrote back to her on Sara's behalf, I assured her I would keep sending them.

Sara did not weep when her mother died, nor did Josef. Neither of them wanted to sit *Shiva*, but we did say *Kaddish*. Sara was quiet for several weeks, lost in thoughts she could not share. She welcomed my more frequent hugs, but in bed her passions were banked to the point where I began to doubt my urges would ever be satisfied again. Then one blustery evening after Yakira and Isaac were in bed she sat down next to me on the couch. She wore a death mask, so pale and sickly looking she frightened me.

"I went to see Rabbi Daniel today," she began. She closed her eyes for a long moment as though she were praying. I waited. She took a deep breath and gulped.

"My mother did the best she could," Sara continued. She spoke so softly I strained to hear her above the windy rain rattling the windows. "She didn't have a husband like you. But she loved me. I know she did." I put my arms around her, and she collapsed into my chest, heaving great sighs as grief burst through her. I kissed the top of her hair and held her closer.

"She loved Josef too," she said between sobs. "And Havol." I pitied Mother Kravetz her sorry life, but she could have done better for her daughter. Unfortunately she didn't have her daughter's strength.

A cloud lifted after that. A few nights later, Sara leaped on me as soon as we climbed in bed, hiked up her night gown and straddled me. She grasped hold and guided me in. Sara was so loud old lady Lafkowitz must have heard us, because when I passed her in the hallway the next morning she gave me a bawdy smirk and the wink of an eye. I gave her a guilty look like a schoolboy who had been caught behind the barn.

In the fall of 1913, we were surprised to find Sara pregnant. The word joy doesn't begin to describe what we felt. Sara had gone through a wicked time when Isaac was born. Her midwife, Fradel Grunwasser, told us then it was not likely Sara could have any more children. Now Sara glowed like a new bride, except for moments of the morning sickness. The doctor prescribed some Lydia Pinkham which took care of that problem. I couldn't wait to write Lieb.

But it didn't last. In the third month she miscarried. To make it worse, the doctor warned us in no uncertain terms Sara must never have another baby or it might kill her. We cried on each other for weeks. My heart ached for the unborn baby I already loved, and twice for Sara. She felt damaged as well as aggrieved.

I had to stay away from her most of the time after that. We picked our moments carefully, me more cautious than Sara. I would not endanger her to gratify my own needs, and I didn't trust God any more. So the spontaneous passion ended, but my love for her deepened, if that was possible. Many nights we fell asleep in the comfort of each other's arms.

Sara was not one to linger long over life's disappointments and tragedies like I do. Her spirits rebounded but the miscarriage left us with a melancholy that still lingers. I try not to, but sometimes I wonder what our child would have been like. We almost never talk about it, but the same haunt remains with Sara as it does with me. I find it hard to talk about so don't expect any more from me on it, but it's always there, believe me.

Such *tsores*. So much death. How do you go on living, you ask? How can you ever be happy again? Because we loved each other more than we loved life itself. Because Yakira and Isaac gave us such joy, and America gave us such hope.

The first gray hairs appeared in Sara, though she was only thirty years old. The tragedy showed in her smile and in the deepening lines across her brow. But maybe because of it, Sara grew more beautiful inside and out.

About that time Lieb sent me a nice photograph of him and Golde dressed up in their best Sabbath clothes, she sitting in a chair with baby Josh in her lap, and he standing behind her. Their daughters, Shaina and Brindyl, stood next to their father. Lieb looked the same to me, the shaggy lock of hair waiting to drop down over his eyes, and he ready to brush it away with his left hand. Golde looked prettier than I remembered her, if a bit heavier.

That night I tossed and turned, my mind arguing back and forth between Lieb and Momma. In my nightmarish slumber, I yelled at Lieb to recognize the never-ending misery of Uman. Then I begged Momma to understand my helplessness. Daylight relieved my distress, and in a few days frustration's scabs dropped off.

Weeks later Sara, Yakira, Isaac and I sat for a photographer's portrait which I sent to Lieb. The one he sent me still sits on top of my dresser, a bundle of his letters stuffed in the drawer below.

CHAPTER FOURTEEN

August 1914

"WAR! WAR!" The newsboy at the subway entrance barked this hot August morning. "Kaiser declares war on Russia." A dozen men swarmed around him, arms outstretched to grab a newspaper. I gave him a nickel and grabbed mine.

I read as I walked toward the tailor shop, scanning for any news about Kiev or Uman. There was none. A big picture of Kaiser Wilhelm of Germany in full ceremonial regalia dominated the front page. We would become very familiar with that gigantic handlebar mustache in the years that followed.

Germany was mobilizing, Russia was mobilizing, France was mobilizing, and Austrian river gunboats had already shelled Belgrade according to reports from Serbia. President Wilson declared American neutrality. Our president's sentiments were with the democracies, but he detested their allied Russian autocracy almost as much as he did the German and Austrian versions.

Markus heard the news and was beside himself when I walked in the door of the tailor shop. "Lieb's in trouble," he said. "You've got to do something." All morning long he hatched one scheme after another to get our brother out of Russia, each more preposterous than the other, and each requiring me to be the one to do it.

The telephone rang in mid-morning, Zelda calling from Philadelphia. "Hyman and I will help financially," she said. "But you've got to get Lieb out of there."

Ester charged into the shop in the late morning with little Max in tow. "So what are you going to do?" she demanded, hands on hips.

"What should I do? Send a warning to the Kaiser?" Sweat from the hot August wetness rolled down my back, puddling in my underwear.

"Would it hurt to try?"

I had had enough. "You all expect me to do the impossible." I smacked my open hand on the presser's table, hard enough to sting.

Little Max started to cry. He wrapped his little arms around his mother's legs and buried his head in her dress. Ester knelt down and picked him up, comforting him with soft, soothing purrs, her eyes shooting spears at me.

"You'll figure something out," Markus said, playing his usual peacemaker.

But I had no idea how I was supposed to do that. On my way home I thought about Russia's last war with Japan. When Russia was defeated, *pogroms* followed. Another Russian defeat and who knew what could happen? Probably more *pogroms,* and this time Lieb wouldn't have Uncle Yakov or me to look after him.

That night, unable to sleep, the sheets drenched, I got out of bed about four in the morning. I crawled out the window onto the fire escape to catch a little breeze. Here I was, safe in America, the new war far away. Sara was safe, my children were safe. I told myself Lieb was in a stew of his own making. I had begged him to come to America; he wouldn't listen. Now I was expected to somehow rescue him. But like it or not, I was my brother's keeper.

Day after day I tried to send a telegram to Lieb, but each time the officious looking telegraph operator gave me the same response: "There will be no telegrams to Europe today. Too much official traffic. Try back tomorrow."

Germany declared war on France and invaded Belgium. Great

Britain declared war on Germany, and the ancient Austrian Emperor Franz-Josef declared war on Russia. President Wilson reaffirmed American neutrality, to my consternation. Turkey also declared its neutrality.

Six weeks after the beginning of the war, Lieb's letter arrived, his left-handed chicken scratch an impossible relief to see. It was dated August 5, 1914, just a few days after the start of the mayhem.

> *My dear brother,*
>
> *By now you must certainly know we are at war. Do not worry about me. We are safe. Russia is strong. We will beat those Huns.*
>
> *What a glorious day it was today.   The first of the troops from here marched off, led by General Baranski. He looked so fine in his blue and red jacket, his saber strapped to his side. You may remember him from the pogroms. But today there are no Jews, no gentiles, no Bolsheviks, no Monarchists. Today we are all Russians.*
>
> *There must have been thousands of people along the route to the Uman Station where the soldiers boarded the train, everyone waving their Russian flags, cheering. All of the young men are hurrying to enlist, afraid the war will be over before they can get there.*
>
> *I bumped into Sara's sister Havol in the crowd. She was so excited she threw her arms around me and kissed me right on the lips, then hugged me close, laughing and laughing. Her headscarf had come off and her hair flew in every direction. The day was hot and she was covered with sweat. But don't get me wrong. Her embrace wasn't at all unpleasant. I was startled, that's all. Golde wasn't so amused.*
>
> *I saw the Cripple standing at the base of the rostrum where the mayor spoke before the troops departed, trying to look important. He was wearing some silly looking green uniform, not of a soldier but of a town clerk. You can be sure Viktor Askinov*

will find some way to profit from this war.

Rest easy, dear brother. We are well, and hopeful something good will come for the Jews from the Russian victory I pray comes quickly.

Patriotism intoxicated my gentle brother. Had he forgotten what happened last time when Russia lost a war? *Pogroms*, that's what! What made him think this would turn out any differently? Tsar Nicholas hadn't suddenly become the friend of the Jews. Any hope this war might stir Lieb to leave Uman vanished beneath the waving red, white and blue stripes of the Russian flag.

I feared for my brother but there was little I could do for Lieb now, even if he decided he wanted to leave. Not as long as the war went on, and not with America keeping a safe distance. Still, this is why Momma extracted her promise from me. I hadn't forgotten it.

Tense letters from Lieb arrived one after another. The only difference between now and before the war was their journeys took longer.

He wrote about the long roll of dead and wounded Uman boys posted outside the post office every morning. Even when the harsh winter winds blew in across the plains, anxious mothers, fathers, and wives crowded around the moment the postmaster pinned up the latest list. But many names weren't on the lists. They marched off to fight. After awhile their letters stopped coming. They just disappeared. *That's what happened to Izolda Redko, Arkady Rothstein, and the Ziskind's sons. All three of them,* Lieb wrote. *How awful not to know.*

The army requisitioned foodstuffs from the countryside. Grain all but vanished, and the younger peasants born to plant and harvest instead became meat for the cannons. By the early summer of 1915, Lieb's severe situation showed.

Thank goodness the garden in back of the house still gives us some vegetables. We have a few chickens left, who work hard to give us eggs, but most of those that haven't been stolen have been eaten or confiscated by the military. Wheat is rare. A piece of bread is now like a piece of cake to us. Sergey Shumenko's wife Valerya brings us some produce nearly every week. She is a kind, gentle woman, and nice to look at. You wouldn't know she and Sergey were so well-off. Besides their town house, Sergey owns a small estate at the edge of town on our side of the river. In truth, it's not much more than a small house and a small piece of land. He grows vegetables and fruit trees, and raises a few milk cows.

Russia threw millions of men into the battle along a long front from the Baltic in the north to the Black Sea in the south, a distance of nearly a thousand miles. In Poland and Lithuania, Russia enjoyed early successes against the Germans at enormous cost in lives. Then the Germans gained the upper hand until things settled into deadlocked carnage.

In the south, the area closest to Uman, Russia attacked the Austro-Hungarian forces, advancing well beyond its borders. Lieb was in no great danger from Austrian cannon, as far as I could tell. The Tsar's mother, the dowager Empress Elizabeth, remained planted in her palace in Kiev, well protected. Lieb wrote of the Tsar's frequent visits to her when he toured the southern front.

Sara said I was living Lieb's ordeal, suffering more than if I were actually there. Lieb himself tried to be encouraging or matter-of-fact in most of his letters. In March of 1916, he wrote about common things to remind me of my old home. *The river is thawing. Big blocks of ice crash into each other as they rush past town. The noise sometimes scares people who think it sounds like cannons firing near us.* He always included a mention about how beautiful his daughters Shaina and Brindyl were becoming. They were nearly women. But his son Joshua was his great blessing.

Several weeks later he wrote of the first flowerings of spring, the budding of the fruit trees, and the fragrant sky. *It is surely the hand of God bringing us hope,* he wrote. This was also the letter in which he told me Gersh Leibowitz disappeared. Gersh was a tough guy, the leader of one of the three squads the night of our fateful 1905 Uman *pogrom.*

> *One day I noticed he was just gone. No one seems to know what happened to him. The Cripple detected his absence immediately. Now he hovers closer. He bumped into Golde in the market the other day. The sack she was carrying split open and its contents spilled all over the ground. Do you think our crippled friend helped her pick up her things? He just snarled and told her to tell you hello. Why does he still think about such matters that happened all those years ago? Not with a war going on. I don't know what job he has in the government, but it must be more important than the one he had before. He wears a better uniform with a nice short-billed hat, a revolver in a holster, and a truncheon like his father the Constable used to wield. It's a blessing you are in America. He might kill you if he had the chance.*

As long as Gersh was around, I didn't worry too much about Viktor Askinov hurting Lieb or his family. I knew if he ever got too far out of hand, Gersh would step in. He never liked Viktor Askinov any better than I did, and would take any excuse to thump him. Now that he was gone, Sergey Shumenko was the only protector Lieb had. Sergey was a good man, a gentile with influence. That would have to be enough.

Meanwhile, Russian troops ran out of food and ammunition. German and Austrian cannon and machine guns slaughtered them by the hundreds of thousands. Tsar Nicholas took to the field, he himself replacing his uncle as Commander-in-Chief of the Imperial Army. By the middle of 1916, the mountains of dead were biblical. With the Tsar away from St. Petersburg commanding the troops, chaos choked the capital and mushroomed everywhere in Russia. Strikes and political protests drained the hungry, angry country of its strength. Some well-intentioned politicians worked to convert the autocracy into a democracy, but anarchists, Bolsheviks, and monarchists worked equally hard to grab power for themselves. To me it read like 1905 all over again, with *pogroms* soon to come.

Troops in the field deserted in masses, many just walking away, killing their officers if they tried to stop them. Troops in the cities refused to fire on striking workers and protesters, instead turning their guns on the police. The Tsar was losing his grip.

Lieb's letters alarmed me. He wrote more and more about gangs of desperate deserters who roamed the countryside ringing Uman, looking for food and anything else they could steal.

The fallen had to be replaced, so by 1916 the Tsar's army started calling up recruits who were younger and younger, and older and older. *I don't have anything to worry about,"* Lieb wrote. *Thank our Lord, Joshua is only five years old, and I am 37. Who would want such an old man to fight?*

I shared Lieb's letters and everything I learned about what was happening in Russia with the rest of the family. Havol's rare letters sent Sara into a dark mood for days. Markus drained me of every bit of information I had while we sat in the shop sewing. Some days I had to go for a walk to get away from him, or go talk to Mr. Akiva in the laundry next door. Ester was more reasonable, but no less voracious. Zelda phoned Ester all the time for the latest news until her husband Hymie protested about the size of their phone bills. Occasionally she called me. All of them begged me to do something.

Josef alone ignored any mention of his sister Havol or Uman. His attention focused elsewhere. He continued to work at the cigar factory, but his anger at the owners' mistreatment of their employees pushed him more and more toward engagement in the labor unions. I feared he might go too far. "Mendel Silber says to tell you hello," he mentioned whenever he ran into my old shipmate from the Finland. I warned him every time that Silber was a Bolshevik who transmitted trouble to everyone he touched.

Mendel Silber showed up in the neighborhood from time to time. Now and then we exchanged nods of recognition from a distance, but nothing more. Usually he was picketing in front of some sweatshop, handing out radical circulars, or exhorting workers to join the Bolsheviks. He was ready to bring his Russian revolution to America. On more than one occasion, policemen with truncheons chased after him and his compatriots. They must have caught him because a few times I saw his name in the newspaper, arrested. I wanted nothing to do with him and his kind, and I didn't want Josef involved either.

Hanukkah that December was more like sitting *Shiva* than it was a celebration. We gathered at Ester's place as usual. Simon's dry goods store prospered, and they had moved to a bigger apartment in the building down the street from us, so we weren't as packed.

When Ester lit the menorah, I pictured Golde lighting the same candles on the other side of the earth. Here we were with Hanukkah gelt, presents for the children, potato pancakes, roast beef and chicken, and sugar covered doughnuts filled with strawberry jam. And in Uman Lieb, Golde, Havol and their children were lucky if they had some bread.

I had no way to get Lieb out of Russia until this war ended, and even if I could, he might not be so welcome here. More and more Americans were saying there were already too many Jews in the country. Then there were those who wanted to send all of us back to the old country, war or no war. They claimed Jews were born with certain undesirable traits and had no business being in America, pure and simple. One powerful newspaper published an editorial advocating Jews be restricted to living in certain areas and at certain jobs. It sounded like the Pale of Settlement all over again. But that couldn't happen in my America.

CHAPTER FIFTEEN

November 1916

With a mighty war destroying Europe's youth, and my brother in mortal danger, it is shameful to admit how happy Sara and I were most of the time.

Sara blossomed like the springtime lilies in Central Park. She wasn't reluctant to tell me how blessed she was to have such a wonderful husband, and happy to be living in such a wonderful place. She yielded to more American style dress, but always modest solids, never prints. She still wore a muted scarf on her head whenever she went out, and mannish laced shoes with the short, solid heels of a laundry maid. Whatever she wore, she couldn't hide her simple beauty.

Fashions changed just before the war and my patron, Mrs. Schulman, and her friends liked what I did with them. The corsets and severe tailoring disappeared, replaced by flared skirts and softer pastel materials. I wanted to see more ankle. Mrs. Schulman obliged. She was a handsome woman for fifty, still slim, graceful, and elegantly sensuous. But her good friend, Mrs. Rockland, was a challenge. She was plump as a pumpkin but wanted me to make her look like Mrs. Schulman, impossible as that was.

I never imagined we could make this much money. We were so busy we had to expand. Markus and I moved to a larger, nicer shop around the corner on 116th Street. We had room now for three sewing machines, work tables, storage bins for the material, and hanger racks for the garments we were working on. Markus took days arranging all of the threads by color, the buttons by size, and the material by fabric. Thereafter, orderliness in the tailor shop became his mania. My pleasure was I could still look out on the street through the big window from my seat at the sewing machine and watch people passing by.

We added another tailor, Emmanuel Weismann. Manny was a pleasant man, older than us. His bald, fringed head sported a short, groomed beard and mustache. In the old country, Manny owned a tailor shop in a village not far from Vilnius. He didn't talk about it, but I gathered he lost his family in a *pogrom* in 1903 and escaped to America with only his sister and her husband.

Sara and I spent nearly every day working together in the tailor shop, except on Sabbath eve when she cooked, cleaned and prepared dinner. The children thrived in school, Isaac the smartest one in his class. Yakira, a year older, reminded me so much of Momma. She even looked like Momma, stocky and plain on the outside, but inside she was as beautiful as Sara. Isaac, on the other hand, was handsome and looked much like Sara with sandy hair, chiseled jaw and soft blue eyes. Sara doted on him.

He made friends easily and often brought home his Irish, German, and Italian pals. Sometimes he brought home his black friend, Amos. He was so much like Poppa in that way. He liked everyone and never seemed to notice their differences. By the time he was twelve, Isaac worked a sewing machine like a skilled tailor.

Yakira was very mature and responsible. She admired and took pride in her younger brother. They both went out of their way to be as American as apple pie: how they dressed, their confusing slang, their comic book heroes, and the games they played – stickball for Isaac and hopscotch for Yakira. Sometimes they got upset with Sara because she still dressed old-world and spoke little more than a few essential words of English.

Sara was content. But in those years, she seemed afraid to venture outside the boundaries of our safe Yiddish neighborhood. At times I started to get frustrated with her. Then I reminded myself of my promise to God to love her just as she was. When I finally coaxed her into a brief venture into the Italian section, she found a greengrocer to beat all others. Sara and the greengrocer's mustached wife smiled, gestured, and talked, each in her own language, not understanding anything more than the common kindness that connected them. In the following weeks, they both picked up a few words of English with which to communicate.

Thank goodness for motion pictures. Sara loved going to the movie show. She clutched my arm when Mary Pickford was in peril and exploded with a squeaky laugh at Charlie Chaplin's Keystone Cops. "What does it say. What does it say," she begged, eyes wide, when the subtitles flashed across the bottom of the screen. She did it until those around us joined a chorus of "Ssshhhhhh." She did the same with the comic strips in the newspapers.

Daniel's wife Hannah of course spoke English. Ester and Markus's wife Sadie learned soon enough. Sara steadfastly refused. "Smart people learn English," she said whenever I brought it up. "Not people like me." She asserted her right to decide in the way she always did – silence or smiles. That might have all been fine, but as the United States crept closer to entering a world war, its citizens grew more disapproving of immigrants who weren't fully American. In 1917, Congress passed a law forbidding entry into the country of anyone who wasn't literate. Sara was aware she would have been denied entry if that law had been in effect when she came to America. It concerned her, but she did nothing about it.

At my urging, one day Isaac invited his friends to a sit-down Sunday dinner. There was Frankie the Italian, Timothy the Irish kid, the colored kid Amos, and Isaac's cousin Willy. Sara prepared a meal fit for the Sabbath. The four of us and the four invited boys all squeezed into our small apartment. Yakira liked Isaac's friends and fit right in with them. She even played stickball with them, the only girl who would ever do such a thing. The other girls were more into ogling the boys and giggling.

That afternoon, all of the boys were on their best behavior. They came dressed in clean shirts, hair combed, and scrubbed behind the ears. They were young gentlemen, about twelve years old, more quiet and polite around the table than I had ever seen them. "Mrs. Schneider, this is delicious," Amos said as he scooped up another mouthful of honeyed brown beans. Sara nodded and smiled, understanding a compliment had been given, even if she couldn't understand what the words meant. Unable to communicate in English, she said almost nothing during the meal, wearing a painted smile on her face, uncomfortable every time a question or comment came her way. Isaac occasionally translated. Yakira scowled, more and more frustrated with her mother.

When dinner was over and the boys were gone, Sara and Yakira tackled the cleanup. Sara washed while Yakira cleared the table and dried the dishes. The clanging and banging warned the world Yakira was about to detonate. She slammed the last pot on the counter top. "You're an embarrassment," she yelled in Yiddish, her face red and scrunched. "You didn't understand a word any of them said and you didn't say a word. You couldn't. When are you going to be an American?" Sara looked stunned, a limp dishrag hanging in her hand. Her mouth dropped open and her eyelids drooped.

"Yakira. Stop that," I barked. "Apologize to your mother. Now!"

She took off her apron, threw it on the kitchen table and thundered out the door. Isaac rushed after her, mortified.

I went over and put my arms around Sara, but she was as frozen as a statue of ice. "I'll take a belt to her when she gets home," I said, an idle threat because I never could spank my children.

Sara shuffled into our bedroom, head down, and quietly closed the door. I went in to check on her a little while later. She was just sitting on the edge of the bed, lost in thought. She looked up at me. "Yakira is right," she said.

Yakira and Isaac came back a short while later. Yakira was contrite and eager to apologize. When she began, Sara put her finger to Yakira's lips to stop her and shook her head. Then she gathered Yakira in her arms. Yakira melted and started to sob. Her mother held her and stroked her hair.

Without a word to anyone, soon after that Sara began taking English classes afternoons and evenings. She didn't try to hide it but didn't want anyone making a fuss either. She struggled, but slowly the words came. Sometimes when we were outside, I caught her moving her lips, sounding out the words on a poster. Every now and then I came into the room and found her reading one of my newspapers. Then one day we met the Italian greengrocer's wife on the street. These two friends said a few sentences to each other in English, both of them all smiles. It turns out the greengrocer's wife was Sara's regular companion at the English classes.

When Sara learned to speak, write and read English, she also surrendered the last of her Hassidic garments. She no longer wore a scarf on her head except when it rained or snowed. Modest shoes of an American woman replaced the ugly workman's shoes. She allowed me to make her a bit more stylish dresses, if kept to quiet tones. Sara still wore no jewelry except her wedding band and a pair of small pierced pearl earrings. With the tailor shop doing so well, I could afford to give her a diamond, but she would have none of it.

Markus and Sadie had first one baby boy, then another and another until that winter they finally had a baby girl. Ester also gave birth, another boy. Sara spoiled them all as though they were hers, and they loved her for it. Then Havol sent a letter to tell us she had a new baby girl to go with her son and daughter. Sara was happy for them all, but each one brought a scent of sadness for the baby we lost. I'm no longer so selfish. Now I thank God for giving me Sara, and I still find God's perfection in Yakira and Isaac, even when I doubt Him. I have been blessed enough.

That year I joined the Anti-Defamation League. I had to do something to fight anti-Semitism when Leo Frank, a young college-educated

Jewish businessman, was lynched in Georgia over the murder of a Christian girl, Mary Fagan. Prominent citizens of Marietta, Georgia were so proud of the lynching they took pictures of each other with the body of Leo Frank dangling from the tree limb where he had been hanged. They made postcards of his corpse and sent them around the country. Leo Frank was an innocent man, and this was America. Such things weren't supposed to happen to Jews here.

"They hate us here too," Simon said over a beer at the Kinsale Tavern. "Did you see where our own police commissioner said half of New York's criminals are Jews?"

I took it personally when family complained about this country. "We don't have *pogroms* in America," I said. "In Russia we worked hard and nearly starved. Here we work hard and we make money. Our kids go to school. We can vote." I downed my beer, satisfied with my rebuttal.

Simon waited a minute before he said anything, then he responded. "Don't forget the Ku Klux Klan. They're ready to bring *pogroms* down on us whenever they get the chance, or hang us one by one."

But no matter what skeptical Jews like Simon had to say, or incidents like Leo Frank's hanging, our landsmen were making it in America. Irving Berlin conquered Tin Pan Alley. Gentiles were paying good money to watch Al Jolson, Eddie Cantor, and Fanny Brice perform. A few Jews were elected to Congress, and in 1916 President Woodrow Wilson appointed Judge Louis Brandeis to the Supreme Court. "If a Jew can be a Supreme Court justice, you can be anything in America," I told Isaac.

Europe tore itself apart, but in America the sun shined. Macy's and Gimbel's, both owned by Jews, opened grand department stores across the street from each other. The first subway could get us to City Hall in the lower end of the city in about twenty minutes. The New York Public Library on Fifth Avenue opened and immediately became my synagogue. I treasured Sunday afternoons there whenever Isaac asked to come along. He was as thirsty for books as I had been at his age.

There were electric streetcars you could jump on for a ride to anywhere you wanted to go. There were so many automobiles you had to watch yourself crossing the street or you could get run over. We had electric lights in our apartment, and our first radio. Sara liked our new gramophone and the telephone best of all. Sometimes she raced home before me just so she could call me in the tailor shop. "Hello, this is Sara Schneider," she said formally, as though we were strangers. "Who am I speaking to?"

In 1916, we moved to a nicer apartment on 118th Street between Fifth and Madison Avenues, not far from the shop. It was much larger, with its own bathroom and separate bedrooms for Yakira and Isaac. The neighborhood was better. There was a small park only a couple of blocks away. Sara said she loved it, and I'm sure she did, but she would have been just as content to stay in the old place. I still tried giving Sara everything I could to make her happy; she kept telling me she didn't need anything more.

One blustery early January day soon after our move I had lunch with Daniel at a small kosher delicatessen store around the corner from his synagogue. There wasn't anything I didn't share with him and him with me. We talked politics, philosophy, literature, women, kids – you name it. That day we sat at a booth by the big window watching East Harlem pass by. The wind blew the women's skirts up to their knees, earning our appreciation.

I turned my attention back to Daniel. "I don't even look at another woman if Sara's around," I said.

"You're a wise man," he chuckled, and then became more serious. "But it's not so much what you think that matters. It's what you do." He sounded like a rabbi warning a man not to do anything stupid. His warning was unnecessary.

"At first my disinterest was forced," I said. "I didn't want her to feel threatened. Now it's second nature. Still, she watches anxiously whenever I speak too long to another woman, even a customer. She occasionally comments that this one is pretty or that one's smart. I always tell her she's the prettiest and the wisest, and I mean it. When we're in a crowd, like at synagogue, she grabs hold of my arm." I took a long sip of my coffee before finishing the thought. "I never forget I gave her reason for her possessiveness."

"My god, have you ever tasted such corned beef?" He had already devoured his sandwich while I was working on my first half.

Daniel was earthier than any rabbi I ever met, but still pure. I teased him about it often. He took my kidding in good humor. But that day he told me about his own imperfections. As a teenager, he stole coins from the blue tin box his parents kept for charity. Twice he was too aggressive with girls, and even cheated on a test in divinity school. He woke up to his shortcomings after he married Hannah.

"I tried to make amends. One of the girls forgave me." He examined the half eaten pickle on his plate, ashamed to look at me. "She said she wasn't even offended, at the time or since. The other one still won't forgive me no matter what I do. I have to live with that. I confessed to my teacher at the divinity school. He was surprised and disappointed. He made me work for my atonement. I'm still working at it." He gave me a melancholy smile. The more flawed Daniel revealed himself to be, the more I liked him.

As we were getting our coats on to leave the deli, Daniel asked me about Lieb just like he always did. "He's fine," I said out of habit.

Daniel gave me a puzzled look. "You heard they killed that mad monk, Rasputin, didn't you?"

"So, are they blaming it on the Jews?"

"Not this time. Apparently some prince named Yusapov killed him. In St. Petersburg."

"Lieb's a long way from St. Petersburg," I answered.

But the boiling pot in St. Petersburg cooked the whole Russian empire, including Uman.

CHAPTER SIXTEEN

March 1917

Lieb's letters no longer pretended optimism. It didn't take much to see in my mind the January snow gusting across the Umanka River, mounding into mountains on the *shtetl* side. Lieb broke apart the chicken coop in back of the house for firewood. There wasn't much left to burn after that.

In spite of President Wilson's declared neutrality, goods from America helped keep the Allied armies supplied. So in January Germany resumed unrestricted U-boat attacks on all merchant ships. At first I had wanted America to get into the war to help Lieb. But this sinking of our ships was something else. America was my country now, and I for one was ready for a fight.

Big events happened so fast that winter they mixed in your mind like scrambled eggs. We gathered in the Kinsale Tavern after work every day to learn what we couldn't learn from the newspapers, and weigh in with ill-informed opinions that made no difference. So many Russian Jews crowded the bar those days that Thomas Kelly even learned how to say "Fuck the Tsar" in Yiddish.

My old roommate, Gideon Katz, had a sister living secretly in St. Petersburg. He read us a letter she wrote about the hunger, bread lines,

agitators imploring soldiers to mutiny, and flimsy coats giving no protection from the arctic snows. Fuel bins for the stoves and coal bins for
the factories were empty. Unemployed workers milled about the
streets aimlessly, waiting for something to happen.

On Monday, March 12, the New York Tribune ran a small article on
page two dismissing a food riot in the Russian capital, St. Petersburg,
as "groundless." It didn't sound groundless to me when frantic mothers broke into bake shops hungering for a loaf of bread, and mounted
troops were called out to cut them down.

The next day's press dispatches from St. Petersburg described a city
staggering toward revolution. The Tsar suspended the Duma, their
congress, ending all hope for conciliation. Our group of regulars gathered around a table in the corner of the Kinsale Tavern, the cigarette
smoke and spilled beer thick enough to chew. "Shut the door," someone yelled whenever a new patron opened the door and let in a March
gust.

"The revolution's coming," Josef said, his eyes burning with certainty of the Tsar's end. "That ass licker's finished, I'm telling you."

"From your mouth to God's ear," Simon responded. "You watch.
The bastard's going to call out the Cossacks, some loyal battalions, and
that's the end of that."

"There are no more loyal battalions," Josef answered.

Everyone argued about what was going to happen next but the
truth was none of us understood the situation in St. Petersburg, and
we certainly didn't know what was going on in Uman. One thing was
definite; there would be a tsar in Russia for as long as there were stars
in the sky. He wasn't going away.

Over the next few days there was hardly a word in the newspapers
about Russia, and our attention turned elsewhere. Headlines talked
about a threatened nationwide railroad workers' strike in the United
States, passage of women's suffrage in New York State, the nineteen
percent rise in food prices, preparation for war, and loyalty oaths. On
Thursday the lead headline was about the German U-boat sinking of
the U.S. freighter Algonquin.

There hadn't been a letter from Lieb in weeks.

The streets were nearly empty that Friday morning when I left the apartment. It wasn't such a cold day for the middle of March. The last of the nearly-melted clumps of snow hung around the trees, black as much as white.

The few men passing by the Tribune newsboy bought a paper before heading down into the subway or hurrying on up the street. "EXTREE! EXTREE! READ ALL ABOUT IT. TSAR ABDICATES." One tall woman with a pheasant feather in her hat shoved me out of the way to grab her copy, and then glared at me as though I had been the pushy one. I waited my turn, handed the newsboy a nickel, and took my paper.

A short man with a potato nose grabbed my arm and looked at me with vacant eyes. "The Tsar's gone," he said quietly. "*Kaput.*" He walked off shaking his head.

How could there not be a tsar anymore? The headlines might as well have said there was no more moon or no more ocean. I had been on my way to the tailor shop. Instead, I turned around and walked home to be with Sara and the children.

The newspaper said the Tsar abdicated for himself and his hemophilic son Alexis. Prince Michael, the Tsar's brother, had been named Regent, but authority rested with the new Provisional Government of the Duma and the Soviet of Soldiers and Workers. The next day we learned Prince Michael also abdicated. The monarchy was gone. A republic was declared. The Provisional Government announced its intension to prosecute the war vigorously, with the full support of the army commanders. In their first proclamations, the new government promised to dissolve the Pale of Settlement and free the Jews. Everything turned upside down. Who was I supposed to hate now? Who was I supposed to fear?

We sat around the kitchen table and talked quietly, just the four of us. Sara and I rarely discussed life in the old country in front of the children. The memories were too ugly. But today was different. They listened, somber and understanding. Occasionally they would ask a question.

"Why did the Tsar hate the Jews so much?" Yakira asked. I tried to put it in plain words they would understand, but didn't succeed. Yakira continued to ask "why" until we had no more answers. "Because we're Jews," Sara said at last, as though that was the final, logical explanation. When Sara started talking about the night of the *pogrom* and me on the barricades, I cut her off. "They don't need to hear that," I said.

"I want them to know how brave their father was," Sara said with a resolve she didn't often show. "I want them to know you fought for them." I nodded. She proceeded to tell them everything she knew beginning with the moment Isaac was born.

"Did you shoot anyone?" My twelve year old son asked, his eyes wide as silver dollars.

"One man."

"Did he die?"

"No, but he still walks around with a limp from where I shot him."

"Why did you shoot him?"

"He was a very bad man, worse than the Tsar." I got up from the kitchen table and looked out the window to see what the commotion was on the street below. A crowd of men, women, and children moved in the direction of Jefferson Park and the river. They shouted and cheered, some waving American flags and others waving the red banner of revolution. We joined them. They say a million Jews jammed our New York City parks that day to celebrate the fall of the Tsar.

Rabbi Daniel's synagogue will never again see such a crowd as it did that Sabbath evening. All of them were Jews from Russia. For the first time in my life I saw women sitting with their men, holding their hands. Even Sara didn't seem to mind. She held tight to my hand.

"You can't do away with hate," Simon said on our way out. "The Russians hated Jews before the revolution. They'll hate us after the revolution." I couldn't disagree with him.

Not three weeks later our high minded president, Woodrow Wilson, went before a joint session of Congress to demand a declaration of war on the German Empire. They complied. With the Tsar gone, Wilson could now tell the American people we were joining the Allies to fight to make the world safe for democracy.

Young men ran down to recruiting offices to enlist. We hung American flags out of our windows and wore American flags painted on thin tin buttons clasped to our shirts. Sara, Ester, Sadie, and Hannah wore red, white and blue scarves on their heads until they got tired of looking at them. Bond rallies, rallies to support our soldiers, newspaper editorials, entertainers, and politicians drummed up patriotism and money.

Word got out that Teddy Roosevelt was raising a volunteer infantry division. When we gathered at the Kinsale Tavern, we old men fantasized about joining his division like we joined Uncle Yakov's Brigade. But it was only a short-lived fantasy. President Wilson quickly dismissed Roosevelt's offer.

We still didn't know what was going on in Uman. That tormented all of us until Lieb's next chicken-scratched letter showed up in the mailbox. It was dated March 10, nearly a week before the Tsar's abdication.

> You will be as amazed by this latest news as if I told you I saw the Messiah walking down Potocki Street. The Tsar has sent me a letter. He asked me to join his army. Well, not so much asked as ordered. Yes, I have been drafted. That tells you something. There is no one else left. The young men are all gone, the older boys are gone, and now the old men have been called. I'm thirty-seven years old. Maybe that's not so old. But can you imagine me carrying a rifle? Even the noise scares me. I have never been outside Uman and never been on a train, so my adventure should be of great interest.
>
> The worst part of this whole catastrophe was when I had to go down to the draft office to accept my orders to report. Who should I find in charge but none other than Igor Czajkowsko, the

Cripple's little toad. Well, maybe he's not so little any more, but he is still a toad. He paid you a compliment. He said he hoped I could fight as well as my brother. But the next words were not so nice. He said Yids were cowards, and if I would not fight I would still make good kosher meat for the German meat grinder. I signed the papers and wished him a good day.

Of course I worry about Golde and how she will care for herself if I do not return. She says she can run the tailor shop but I don't know. I am hoping Valerya Shumenko will look after her. Sergey Shumenko was called up a few weeks ago and he was running a factory before that. If they would take away such an important man as him, of course they would take me. They made him an officer. Valerya says she will write him a letter right away and tell him about my situation. Maybe I can serve under him. That would be nice. I won't ask you not to worry about me. I know you. You worry about everything, particularly your thick-headed older brother. God does not make mistakes, and that brings me comfort. Still, maybe you can say a little prayer. Carry me in your heart always, as I will you, my dear little brother.

I could not imagine Lieb in the army. He was the gentlest man I knew. His letter took me back to the day we were hiking to our favorite hiding place in Sukhi Yar. I must have been about ten or eleven. We came across a small deer with a broken leg. It wasn't much more than a fawn, probably abandoned when its mother was shot by a hunter. Simon, Duv and I hung back. Lieb bent down and petted the deer gently between its big ears. "You'll be okay," he kept saying. The deer looked back at him with its big black frightened eyes as if it understood. Lieb turned to the rest of us. "We have to get Poppa." With that, he sprang up and raced as fast as he could to the tailor shop. Simon, Duv, and I chased after him. Poppa made us wait on the edge of the clearing while he went alone to look after the deer. But it seems the wolves got to it before Poppa could. Lieb mourned for weeks after that.

Finally it comes to this, I thought. How ridiculous. My brother was going to be a soldier, all because of his stubborn refusal to leave Uman when he had the chance. He wouldn't last five minutes in a fight. I was angry with him. I yelled it at Sara, then called Ester, Markus and Zelda so I could yell it at them too. Why hadn't he listened to me?

I stomped around the apartment, upsetting Yakira and Isaac. When I at last threw myself down on the couch, Sara brought me a shot of *schnapps*. I threw the shot down in one gulp. The warm current reached to my knees and my fingertips. She poured me another one. That's when I began grieving for Lieb. I had no doubt he would die on a muddy battlefield for a country that had no place for him or any other Jew.

"You are a good brother. Lieb knows." Sara put her arms around me. "But you are not God, so leave these things to God." I needed her to tell me that. Ester, Markus and Zelda said the same thing. I still needed to convince myself his death would not be on my head.

CHAPTER SEVENTEEN

May 1917

Soon after Lieb's last letter arrived, Alexander Kerensky took over as Chairman of the Russian Provisional Government. He vowed to keep fighting the Germans and launched a last desperate offensive. The Allies cheered it. But troops continued to dessert in gigantic numbers, and the army rotted away. The Bolsheviks bit at the belly of the Provisional Government, promising the exhausted Russian people peace, land, and bread. In the Ukraine, which was all I cared about, nationalists advocated formation of their own independent republic.

I watched the mailbox expecting a letter from Golde any day telling me Lieb was dead, a nameless soldier killed like a lamb on a forsaken field of death. When a letter did come, it was addressed in Lieb's left-handed chicken scratch. I pulled it from the mailbox, tore it open, and read it right there on the stoop of our tenement, numb to the backfires of passing automobiles and the shouts of neighborhood boys in their knickers playing stickball.

> *The Tsar is gone, thanks be to God. Can you believe it? May he die a hundred times from fire and plague. I am still alive as you can tell from this letter. I was supposed to report the week*

after the Tsar fell, but everything was in such confusion I decided to just stay home and wait to see what happened. Nothing happened. After awhile the new government decided it didn't need me. Or else they just forgot about me. Anyway, I'm not going anywhere.

The day the Tsar fell was magnificent. Only the day I married Golde was better. It was a sea of red everywhere, red banners, red flags, red armbands, and red scarves around people's heads. I had some red material and made a flag to hang outside the tailor shop. Bands played and everyone danced in the market square. I found myself dancing with a pretty black haired gentile girl. It was altogether very nice.

We weren't Jews and gentiles that day, just Russians. We are free, Avi. We are free. All the Jews. The Pale of Settlement has been abolished. I can go anywhere I want and do anything I want. But who wants to go anywhere? And what else would I do? I'm a tailor, like you, like Poppa, like Grandpoppa. But it's nice for my children. Things will get better from now on. Maybe you should think about coming home. Would you consider such a possibility?

Sergey Shumenko was back. When the Tsar was deposed, Sergey's troops all deserted. He had no one left to lead, so he came home. He was only in a few battles, but he said he saw enough of death. Gersh Leibowitz survived too, a declared Bolshevik who used his speechifying skills to convince soldiers to desert. The Cripple was a monarchist one day and a republican the next, Lieb wrote. Now he served the new government. Who would expect anything else?

I sat down on the stoop steps, closed my eyes and held Lieb's letter against my chest. A hand touched my shoulder. "Are you alright, Avi?" our neighbor Mrs. Rabinowitz asked.

I opened my eyes and looked up at her, smiled, and nodded. "My brother's alive," I said, standing up. Telling her made it so. I carried her shopping bag full of the day's produce up to her apartment, and then went home to tell Sara the good news.

In the months that followed, the paradise Lieb imagined for Jews in Uman did not come to be. The Pale was gone, but not the Jew-hate behind it. The political situation all over Mother Russia was like a hurricane followed by a tornado followed by an earthquake. Nothing was settled. Was the Ukraine trying to become a republic separate from Russia, or not? I didn't know whose side I should be on, as though it mattered. Lieb was no help. He kept writing that he was fine and he wasn't political. Our debates at the Kinsale Tavern after synagogue Sabbath services raised more smoke than light.

"So what," Simon said when the newspapers reported Russia was losing the war. "The Germans can't be any worse for the Jews than the Russians." We were about to find out.

In early November, the Bolsheviks seized control of the government in the capital of St. Petersburg, overthrowing the Provisional Government. Lenin was now in charge. Not only did the Bolsheviks immediately withdraw from the war, they began a crusade to replace capitalism with communism everywhere in the world. The United States refused to recognize the new regime. Overnight Russia became an outcast, despised among the democracies. The Bolsheviks were bad, but I couldn't fathom my former country and my brother being on opposite sides from me. Anyway, it was impossible to tell where the Ukraine fit into all of this.

Nonetheless, my brother seemed satisfied with the situation, so satisfied any idea of convincing him to come to America was out the window. But I remembered how Uncle Yakov warned us about the Bolsheviks. I wished he were still alive to stuff some sense in my brother's head.

Soon enough, ruthless retribution followed, more violent and vengeful than anything done under the Tsar. "Bourgeois" and "counter-revolutionary" became curse words that could get you killed. The United States and the other democracies feared this germ would spread to their countries.

Civil war scorched Russia as soon as the Bolsheviks took over.

There were too many sides to keep track of, except that everyone was against the Bolsheviks: nobles, ex-government bureaucrats, industrialists, liberals, moderate social democrats, ethnic nationalists, and alienated army officers. The Allies turned on Russia, sending assistance to what became known as the Whites, a loose association of those opposing the Communist government. The United States, France, Great Britain, and Japan even sent troops to scattered areas of Russia. They stayed until the civil war ended a couple of years later.

Lenin was in no position to bargain with Germany when he sued for peace. His Communist government couldn't keep fighting, and he needed every resource he had to resist the counter-revolutionaries. So under great pressure, and to his shame, he sacrificed the Ukraine. Germany grabbed it and took immediate control.

Regardless of the chaos, Lieb's letters kept coming, if a bit slower, perhaps routed through the Far East or Sweden. When the hated Huns marched in, Lieb said they treated the Jews and all Ukrainians better than the Tsar had ever done. Uman was calm. He, Golde, and the children mixed comfortably with the German soldiers. His oldest daughter Shaina, now fifteen years old, had her eye on one particular good looking blond private. That passed quickly when he was ordered to the Western Front. Rudolph was his name, and Lieb liked him even if his interest in Shaina troubled him.

His every letter mentioned his appreciation for the money I continued to send him. Havol was not so grateful and, in her rare letters to Sara, she asked for more. Of course Lieb had to mention the Cripple; Viktor Askinov transferred his loyalties and now served the new German-sponsored government.

American soldiers didn't start arriving in France in any numbers until October of 1917. The first ones died in early November. By the end of the war a year later, over 116,000 Americans were dead and another 200,000 wounded. A lopsided number of them were Jewish kids. The Schwartz boy, who had his bar mitzvah in our synagogue, was one of them. His father, Isadore, never wore anything but black again after he got the horrible news. Neither did his wife. The Shapiro boy fell at the battle of the Marne, along with Tina and Harold Grossman's son Stanley. Maybe we had to give the blood of so many of our young men if we expected to be Americans. But I thanked God Isaac wasn't old enough.

Thomas Kelly posted a huge map in the Kinsale Tavern so we could locate these foreign places in France we had never heard of. Thomas himself was an Irishman through and through, so he found it hard to cheer for the British. But he had embraced his new country like the rest of us, an American bound by choice, and grateful for it. He raised a glass in cheer with every new Allied victory.

By the summer of 1918, nothing should have surprised me any-more. I awoke that mid-July Sunday to see Isaac waiting patiently for me to open my eyes. "The Tsar is dead," he said softly, pointing to a front page article. He handed the newspaper to me. The Bolshevik government in St. Petersburg announced they had shot the Tsar to spoil a plot to rescue him and overthrow the new government. The Bolshevik government also reported that the Tsar's family had been taken to a secure place. It was awhile before we learned that all of the Tsar's family had been executed too in some god forsaken place in the Urals, their bodies dumped down a mine shaft. When I mentioned the Tsar's final fate to Sara, she puckered her lips and spit. "The worms should eat him," she said.

Our telephone rang a couple of hours later. It was Markus telling me Thomas Kelly opened up the Kinsale Tavern and everyone was headed over there to celebrate the death of the Tsar. I declined. In-stead, I crawled out the window onto the fire escape to be by myself. Sara brought me a glass of lemonade. She saw I was in one of my moods so she left me alone. On the street below men cheered and car horns honked, celebrating a murder.

I thought about Lieb and what this turn of events meant for him. Probably nothing. Uman was no longer Russian, but a semi-indepen-dent republic under German occupation. Lieb wrote that all was well for him. Then why did I have this unsettled feeling, I asked myself?

On October 12 of that year, our son Isaac became a man – his *bar mitzvah*. He was still such a little squirt. He could hardly see over the podium on the *bimah*, the raised platform in the front of the synagogue where he and Daniel read the Torah that morning. He wore a fashionable brown tweed suit I made for him, complete with a belted jacket and the latest style of knickerbockers. It was the first time he ever wore a tie.

I was so proud of him. He was a good boy in every way. He studied hard, was well liked by his friends, and treated his mother, father, and sister with respect and warmth. His sense of humor and fun sometimes got under Yakira's skin when he teased her, but she loved him. A little peach fuzz formed on his cheeks and above his upper lip. Sara prodded me to have that conversation with him about girls. He already paid a lot of attention to them, and they to him. I was no more ready for that conversation than Poppa had been with me at his age.

The Armistice came a month later, on the morning of November 18. We had done what we could for the war effort. Markus, Simon, Daniel and I raised more money for more causes than the Rothschilds. Josef, now an ironworker and union steward, actually built army vehicles. Sara, Sadie, Ester, and Hannah volunteered for the Red Cross, rolling bandages and stuffing boxes for the American soldiers in France. Yakira and Isaac helped them after school and weekends. Sara also prayed. Then there were those like my old friend Duv Eisenberg who profiteered in ways legal and illegal.

Lieb's letters arrived less often. He wrote the one I received in February 1919 a few days after the armistice the previous November. He said the defeated German troops started withdrawing, on their way home. Some of the men heading the newly-independent government in Kiev were Jew-haters of the worst kind. He didn't say so, but in his letter I read apprehension over what would happen next.

Our newspapers carried stories about the civil war which began immediately after the Germans left. The Bolsheviki Reds in St. Petersburg invaded the Ukraine in December 1918. Then monarchists determined to re-impose the old order formed an army to the south.

They called themselves Whites. Meanwhile, a French force landed from the Black Sea and took Odessa. I hoped Lieb would realize he and his family would be better off in America. And if he did, I would find a way to bring him here, no matter how impossible the task.

A few months later, victory parades to honor our American soldiers returning home became a weekly event. I joined the crowds hooting and waving their small American flags at every battalion marching by. Bands played Souza marches that tickled your spine. It made me feel good to be an American.

No one in the crowds knew the returning soldiers brought home more with them than just themselves. When Lieb's letters stopped coming, I didn't notice because soon after the parades ended, Yakira came down with the flu.

CHAPTER EIGHTEEN

March 1919

Doctor Goodson put his stethoscope back in his traveling bag. He was a stout little man with a balding gray head and wire rim spectacles. He had been our doctor since the children were small.

We stepped outside Yakira's bedroom door. He pulled down his gauze face mask. "There's this illness going around called the Spanish Flu," he said. "That's what this looks like."

"Will she be alright?" Sara asked. Worry lines etched the corners of her eyes.

"She's young and strong. Give her lots of fluids. Clear soup. Wipe her with a cold cloth."

"And the bleeding from her nose?" I asked.

"It will stop as she recovers," he said. "Be sure to wash your hands every time you're near her or anything she's touched. And wear these." He handed us gauze masks.

Sara did not leave Yakira's side for days, sleeping fitfully in an uncomfortable chair by her side. She mopped Yakira's brow with cold cloths, cleaned up the bloody bed, changed the linens, tried to feed her, and held her hand when there was nothing else to do. I was scared to death about Yakira, but I was also scared for Sara. She looked thinner and paler every day.

In a week, Yakira improved and a week after that she was back in school. Then Isaac got sick. Doctor Goodson became a regular visitor to our house. "It's the same flu. Do the same as you did with Yakira," he said, his words muffled by his gauze mask. "And be sure you get plenty of rest," he admonished Sara. "We can't have you coming down with it."

The Spanish Flu devoured New York City that year of 1919. Many died, several in our congregation. Daniel was busy with funerals all of the time. In our building, a young boy and his mother who lived on the first floor died. So did a man on the second floor and two children on the third floor. The gauze masks everyone wore when out in public made the streets look like a parade of mummies. The city health authorities shuttered the synagogues, churches, and many factories, including the iron works where Josef now worked.

Isaac got better, just as Doctor Goodson promised. I told Sara to take some time and rest up. She had lost weight. I could see it in her face and in her sagging body. But she wanted everything back the way it was, and that included working in the tailor shop.

Mrs. Schulman had just left when the phone on the wall rang. Sara picked it up. I couldn't tell what was going on from the fragments I heard on Sara's end, but her rigid body and pursed lips told me it wasn't good. She hung up the phone.

"I have to go help Hannah." She grabbed her coat.

"What's the matter?"

"Leo and Jonathan are both sick." She slipped on her coat and grabbed her purse.

"Sara, you can't," I said. "You need some rest. Let Mrs. Akiva help."

"She's sick too." She gave me a kiss on the cheek, put on her gauze mask, and left.

The crisis passed in several weeks, but Sara had exhausted herself. I tried to have a stern talk with her one night after the kids went to sleep. When I started, she got up from the couch, came over and sat in my lap. She ran her fingers through my hair. "I love you," she said.

As if to prove a point, she then got up from my lap and took my hand. Without a word, she led me into the bedroom, and then slowly undressed. Her body was aging. She had thinned during this ordeal and it showed, but she was still delicious to the eye.

When we were done, she cuddled in my arms. "Satisfied?" she asked playfully. And that was the problem. I could never stay upset with Sara when she was this way. So we fell asleep in each other's arms.

Fear of the Spanish Flu hung over a beautiful summer, gripping the city like a mouse in the jaws of a cat. In August we celebrated our sixteenth anniversary with only a walk through Central Park. We kissed in the shadow of the maple tree by the pond and held hands all the way home.

In the fall, Ester's son Willy got the flu, and then Ester's other kids. Simon got it, and finally Ester. We took their kids in. Ester ended up in the hospital for a week. Next it was Markus, Sadie, and all four of their kids. And each time, Sara did the nursing. She even helped nurse Mimi Katz, whose temperature rose so high her hair turned gray, and then fell out.

"You have got to stop," I yelled at her. This time she was not going to seduce me.

"You heard Doctor Goodson," she said evenly. "No one knows how to take care of this better than me."

"That doesn't mean you're the only one who can take care of the whole world. You hardly know Mimi Katz."

"I have to do this." Usually Sara did whatever made me happy. Not this time.

"Well, you're not taking care of your own family," I snapped. This stung her like a slap on the face. Good, I thought. Maybe she'll stop. But she didn't.

By late fall of 1919, Josef and I were the only people I knew who the monster hadn't bitten. Black hearses crowded the otherwise empty streets. I held my breath every time one neared. The Spanish Flu wiped out one whole family in our building - mother, father, two daughters, and a son. The same thing happened in Markus's building. Our congregation lost four entire families. No one wanted to rent their empty apartments.

I had only been in a hospital a couple of times. And I had never been in an ambulance until the October night they rushed Sara to the hospital, blood dripping from her nose. I tried to be calm and encouraging to Sara, but I was scared. She shivered so violently her bones rattled, hot to touch, and too weak to respond.

They put her in a room by herself though there was an empty bed beside hers, one recently vacated. Everything was stark and sterile. The nurses wore white uniforms. The doctors wore white coats. The sheets and coarse blanket were white. Even the bed was painted white. The smell of alcohol clung to my nose, bitter to the dry taste on my lips. A small light cast a yellow shadow over half of Sara's face.

After he examined her, Doctor Goodson motioned me to follow him into the hall. He lowered his gauze mask. "She's very weak," he said.

"Is she going to die?" I was so terrified I could barely whisper.

Doctor Goodson cleared his throat. He patted my shoulder. "Let's pray it doesn't come to that. We'll know in a couple of days."

I sat by her side all through the night. Nurses came in every so often, took her pulse, checked her breathing, and felt her forehead. Sara slept. The night was so lonely.

Josef shook me, waking me with a start. The sun shined through the window across the room. "How is she?" he asked, his face scrunched with apprehension.

Sara was sleeping as deeply as she was when I nodded off. "The doctor says we'll know in two days," I said.

A stocky middle-aged nurse in starched white blouse and skirt entered the room, a phantom in a gauze mask. "One of you will have to wait outside," she ordered.

"Get some rest," Josef said. "I'll sit with her."

Josef came every day after that. So did Ester and Hannah. Markus and Manny took over running the tailor shop while I spent most of the time at the hospital. When she wasn't at the hospital, Ester took care of Yakira and Isaac.

"The kids are worried to death," Ester said to me. "Spend some time with them."

I did go home to explain to Yakira and Isaac what was happening. Yakira at fifteen took over running the house, cooking and cleaning. Isaac was like me, silent and fretful.

I touched his shoulder. "She'll be alright in a few days," I said. "Then you can come see her." I took a bath, changed my clothes, and tried to eat something, but nothing would go down. Yakira was disappointed I didn't like her cooking. Isaac stayed by my side, his big blue eyes begging. He watched me shave. "She'll be fine," I said. "I promise." I tried to sound more confident than I was.

Visiting hours were usually strict at the hospital, but I had plied the nurses with cookies and candy. They liked me and they liked Sara, so they let me in whenever I wanted. I don't know how long Sara was at her worst. Maybe it was only the two days Doctor Goodson predicted.

However long it was, I walked into Sara's room and found her sitting up in bed. She smiled at me. "I prayed you wouldn't be mad at me for not listening to you," she said quietly, struggling to speak.

"I can never be mad at you," I said. I bent down and kissed her on the forehead. I stroked her soft face. She looked drawn, her hair a tangled mess, but she no longer looked whiter than her sheets.

Doctor Goodson came in to check on her. He took her pulse and put his stethoscope to her chest. When he was done, I followed him into the hallway. He told me she had turned a corner, and if she kept improving she might be able to go home in three or four days. The big knot in my stomach loosened for the first time since the terrifying ambulance ride.

I went back into the room. Sara had her eyes closed again. I watched over her, thinking how precious she was to me. I would die without her. Her eyes flickered open. She smiled. "You're still here," she said. She sounded and looked so weak in spite of Doctor Goodson's optimism.

"You'll be going home soon." I held her frail hand. She squeezed as hard as she could, which wasn't very hard.

"I...love...you." She had trouble getting her words out.

"And I love you." I bent down and kissed her, ignoring her foul breath, then pulled her blanket up and tucked it around her. She closed her eyes. I waited a few minutes to make sure this time she was actually asleep. Then I tiptoed out.

When I walked into the tailor shop, Markus and Manny greeted me like a long-gone sojourner. I told them everything Doctor Goodson and the nurses had told me. After that I sat down at one of the sewing machines and worked on a half-finished dress. The familiar feel of the soft cloth through my fingers was balm on a pestered sore. Then the jangle of the ringing telephone jarred me out of my reverie. Doctor Goodson was on the other end of the line.

I don't recall his exact words, but I remember he told me Sara was dying. I don't think I answered him. I just slowly hung up the hand piece. I asked Markus to watch after Isaac and Yakira before I bolted out the door. The streetcar I jumped on moved slow as a turtle.

Dr. Goodson waited for me outside the door to Sara's room, his hands in the big pockets of his white coat. His lips tightened. "I'm sorry," he said. "There's nothing more we can do but hope for the best."

"But you told me she was getting...."

"This happens sometimes. We don't know why." He led me toward her room. "She's sleeping. You might want to say anything you have to say to her now."

I did that. I talked to her deep into the night, holding onto her hand, but she couldn't hear me. The hard-backed chair produced a pain of appropriate penance. Every so often Sara interrupted her soundless, shallow breathing with a gasp for air. I picked up the rhythm and could tell when the next gasp was coming. Fear choked me whenever she missed a gasp. I bent down close to her, sure she was gone. Then the gasp; I relaxed again for a few minutes. A somber nurse came in now and then but did no more than check her pulse, as though waiting for the ordeal to be over. She entered and departed without a word.

The night was soundless, with the only light the glow from a single small lamp near her bed. I lowered my head to her side and began my negotiations with God.

First I begged Him to take me rather than she, certain if God took Sara it would be to punish me for my sins. I had tried to kill a man, even if it was a man who deserved killing. I nearly committed adultery. How many of His other commandments had I broken? Then I chastised Him for putting one of his own angels through such trial. I reminded Him she still had two young children who needed her.

I made every promise to God I could think of making, and meant every one. I would honor Sara like never before, and be a better father. No more jokes about Him behind His back. No more sneaking pork fried rice at the Chinese restaurant around the corner from Joe & Harry's Barber Shop. No more missing Friday night services to go to a Yankees baseball game. I knew in the dark of my mind I had made such promises to Him before which I hadn't kept. The Devil mocked me, telling God I would never keep these new promises either.

She couldn't die alone. But as the night wore on, exhaustion defeated me. My struggle to keep my eyes open failed.

A hand ran its fingers through my hair. I lifted my eyelids uncertain of where I was. My head rested on the white sheets of Sara's bed, my bottom still on the hard chair. I looked up at Sara's smile, her blue eyes alive like they hadn't been in weeks.

"You've been here all night," she said, her voice gentle but sturdy.

I nodded. When I embraced her, she hugged me back with some oomph. And when I kissed her she held the back of my head to deliver a full measure in return.

She sat up in bed for the first time, and ate like a starved pony. After that, I knew I wouldn't lose her. Sara was convinced it was my prayers that did it. She insisted she could feel them that night through her unconsciousness. Who was I to doubt? I kept most of my promises, except the one about eating pork at the Chinese restaurant. And the Yankees games on Friday night, but only if Bob Shawkey was pitching. I no longer made jokes about Him behind His back.

It took another couple of weeks before Sara could come home. It rained that November day, but who cared. Her recovery was slow. For the first time in her life, she let other people take care of her. Yakira took over the running of the house. She sounded and acted more and more like Momma. Taking care of Sara gave Isaac maturing purpose. Ester, Sadie, and Hannah cooked and ran errands to relieve me. But I was the only one Sara would let bathe her, dress her, read to her and, when she was ready, take short walks with her. By then winter's first snowfall had arrived and the gauze masks had disappeared from the streets.

Shadows of Sara's illness showed. A few gray hairs mingled with her beautiful blond. Lines creased the corners of her mouth and eyes. For the first time in our married life she didn't want me to see her without her nightgown on, hiding her frail, thin body and sagging breasts. Yet now she had a more handsome, deeper beauty. Other men, and even some women, still stopped and stared. And she still didn't notice the affect she had on them.

It was many more months before Sara, one evening, took off her night shirt and stood naked before me in all her beauty. Her eyes twinkled. She took my hand and rubbed it over her breast. I gently squeezed.

"You don't have to be so careful," she cooed. "I won't break."

She took care of me with enthusiasm I had longed for and thought I would never know again. I finished in no time. She was very satisfied with herself.

CHAPTER NINETEEN

January 1920

While I was consumed with worry about my family and the Spanish Flu, civil war laid waste to the Ukraine. Stories ran in the New York newspapers about it, but news of flu deaths dominated the front page; and I was too consumed to read any further than the front page. Can anyone blame me if I missed the back-page paragraphs about the two *pogroms* in Uman?

The Bolsheviks – the "Reds" as they became known – might control St. Petersburg and Moscow, but not the rest of the country. Everyone who opposed the Reds joined the counter-revolutionary army of Whites. In the Ukraine, where much of the fighting took place, a strong separatist force, neither Red nor White, sought to establish an independent country. Added to this complicated stew, gangs of criminals, anarchists, and former army soldiers roamed the countryside, pillaging Jews and reaping fear.

During the Spanish Flu's summer lull, the extent of the *pogroms* in the Ukraine finally got through to me. I tried to cable Lieb, but lines were not working most of the time. I sent him a couple of letters but got no reply. I visited the Red Cross Center and some Jewish relief organizations active in the Ukraine, but only learned the *pogroms* were worse than those of 1905. The American government protested; there was no one on the other end to listen. Soon enough, I was lost again in the flu's assault on our family. That's when I nearly lost Sara.

Months went by until she fully recovered and some normalcy returned to our lives. By then Lieb hadn't written me a letter in over a year, not since the Germans left Uman.

One dark January day I went to the big public library to scrutinize every back issue of every newspaper and magazine I could lay my hands on that had any information about the fighting in the Ukraine. The librarians got tired of my requests for another batch.

One thing was clear: Jews were being plundered and murdered by every side – the Whites, the Ukraine nationalist Green Army, the Anarchist Black Army, warlords, roaming bands of well-armed ex-soldiers, Cossacks, and the Reds in the beginning. Later the Reds became the only defenders the Jews had against the *pogroms*.

When I voiced my frustration to Daniel, he told me about a special Red Cross committee composed of Jews sent to investigate the *pogroms*. They were over there for months and traveled everywhere. He knew the committee chairman, a man named Ezra Heifetz. He suggested I go see him and promised me an introduction. At that point I had nothing to lose.

The gray building on the east side of Forty-Second Street housing the committee looked like it hadn't had a coat of paint since it was built. A plaque on the side of the main entrance indicated that was in 1881. I went in through a glass paneled door off to the right and climbed the worn, narrow, dark staircase to the second floor. The mildew smell reminded me of climbing the stairs at the Becker Dress Factory.

The landing opened into a large room where three middle-aged women at desks pounded away at typewriters. Bare light bulbs hanging from the ceiling illuminated the cavernous space. Each of the women wore nearly identical white ruffled blouses and black ties. Each sat ram-rod erect in her chair, looking down at material to the side of her typewriter. Only their fingers on the keyboards moved.

The woman nearest to the entrance looked up when I approached. The clatter of her typewriter stopped.

"I'm Avi Schneider," I said. "Here to see Ezra Heifetz." She gave me a skeptical look as though such a request was odd. "Rabbi Daniel Akiva sent me," I added.

"Mr. Heifetz isn't here right now," she answered. She wasn't unfriendly, but neither was she helpful.

"When will he be back?"

"Mr. Heifetz is out of the country and won't return for several weeks. Perhaps you can come back sometime in March."

I fell on her mercy, explaining I had a brother, my wife's sister, and both of their families trapped in the town of Uman in the Ukraine. I heard from Rabbi Akiva about the heroic work the committee was doing, and thought maybe Mr. Heifetz might have some information about them. Whether it was flattery or sympathy, I don't know, but she softened.

"Let me see if someone else can help you." She got up from her chair and walked down a short hall lined with a handful of offices.

She returned a few moments later. "Mr. Lipsky can see you," she said. "Please follow me." She did an about-face and proceeded back down the hall from which she had come, me trailing behind.

She stopped in front of a closed door and knocked firmly. A man's voice answered, "Come in." When she opened the door, a cloud of cigar smoke mucked the corridor. She stepped aside and gestured for me to enter.

There on the other side of the desk was Sam Lipsky, the same bastard Sam Lipsky from the Becker Dress Factory. The same horn rimmed glasses and sweaty balding head. The same brown stained teeth clenching a smoldering cigar stub. I stopped dead in my tracks, my mouth open. But his bared fangs were gone. A warm smile and kind eyes replaced the evil sneer and evil eyes. When he rose, he placed the cigar stub in an ashtray on his desk littered with files. What's a son-of-whore like Lipsky doing working for a noble cause like this, I asked? My consternation surely showed.

"Avi. It's been a long time," he said as though I were a dear old friend. He motioned toward the worn leather chair in front of his desk. "Please, please. Have a seat." The typist closed the door behind me.

In a few moments, Sam explained his spiritual conversion. It happened in the days right after the fire at the dress factory in 1907, he said. He went to his rabbi for relief from the burden of a guilty conscience, confessed, and took responsibility for what happened. He couldn't give those girls their lives back, but he had been working ever since to make amends. He would for the rest of his life. He told his story with such candor and sincerity he earned my pardon.

He was convincing, and I needed him to be a redeemed Sam Lipsky if I was to find out anything about my brother. So I sat down in the chair and told him about Lieb and Havol.

He listened patiently, asked a few questions, nodded and voiced a sympathetic word here and there. He scribbled a note now and then. When I finished, he put his hand to his mouth and thought a moment. "I won't kid you, Avi. The situation's not good. Let me tell you what's going on. Then we'll look through some files to see what we can find about Uman and your brother."

"The Committee went over there to offer money, food, medical aid and all that. Help the orphans. But we also wanted to investigate. Get a firsthand look at what's going on. See what caused all these *pogroms*. Our investigators talked to a lot of people in a lot of places. I think we have a better understanding of the scope and cause of this thing than anyone. It's complicated. You should know that. You lived it." I watched his eyes and measured his words as he talked for any signs of the treacherous old Lipsky. I found none.

He picked up his cigar from the ashtray, stuck it in his teeth and relit it. "We've verified every piece of information in our report. Not verified? Not included. Where there were questions, we sent legally trained people to the scene. It's dangerous work with the civil war still going on, but being a Red Cross organization has helped."

"And in Uman?" I fiddled, eager to get to what I came here for. He was in no hurry. He had to tell his whole story.

"I think the killing's over in Uman. But other places? Who knows." He closed his eyes and shook his head. Then he continued.

"The society's broken down, completely. There's Petliura's Ukraine independence army, the White's under Denekin, and the Bolsheviks. Then there's the bandits, peasant gangs, army deserters, and Cossacks. They roam the countryside plundering Jews for their money and belongings, killing them out of nothing less than hate."

"And what about Uman?" I asked again.

"In a minute. In a minute." He examined the chewed end of his cigar and stuck it back in his mouth. "The center of this whole thing was in the villages and smaller towns, though of course the fighting took in cities like Odessa and Kiev too. But Jews in the villages are nearly all gone, annihilated. Jews were blamed when the Germans occupied the Ukraine and carted the wheat back to Germany. Then when the Soviet government took over, some Jews were put in government positions. This was something totally new, Jews in government positions. The gentiles didn't like that, particularly when the Soviets requisitioned grain and other crops and paid in worthless paper money."

"So how many of these Bolsheviks are Jews?" I asked.

"Not many. A handful. But everyone knew Trotsky was a Jew, and a few of the others at the top, like Litvinov, Zinoviev and Kamenev." The only Bolsheviks I personally knew were Gersh Leibowitz and Mendel Silber. Gersh was a good man, but it wasn't hard to believe the worst about someone like Mendel Silber.

"All it took now to unleash this bloody butchery was counterrevolutionary leaders like Petliura and Denekin. They linked this hate for Jews to the Bolsheviks. That's all it took to get the gentiles to join their armies and make them fight. Of course the Bolsheviks weren't blameless. At least at first. They did their share of plundering and violating women. That stopped when their commanders executed some of them. After that, the Bolsheviks were the only ones who protected the Jews." He shook his head in dismay.

"What can you tell me about Uman," I asked again.

"Yes, yes. Uman." He opened a file on his desk, and leafed through a number of pages with his tobacco stained index finger.

He found what he was looking for. I held my breath. "It doesn't look good," he said, not raising his eyes from the page. "Two big *pogroms*, one in May and one in July. Several smaller ones. The Bolsheviks now have firm control."

"How many dead?"

"I'm sorry Avi," he said, looking up from his paper. "Close to 200 in the first one, and 170 in the second."

A fist punched my gut. "Worse than 1905," I muttered. I lowered my chin to my hands clasped in front of me and closed my eyes. There had to be people among those dead who I knew, maybe Lieb and Havol.

"Much worse than 1905," he said. "Sometimes whole villages. Every Jew killed, all the children. Every woman violated. My whole village was massacred."

"Is there any way I can find out about my brother?"

"Maybe. We have some lists but they're incomplete. There are some mistakes on them. But it's worth a look." He turned to one of the big file boxes on the floor behind him.

The phone on his desk rang just as he removed a thick file. He picked up the earpiece from its hook and answered. He grunted a few words into the mouthpiece and hung up. "I'm afraid I'm needed next door for awhile. You can sit in the vestibule and read over these lists." He handed me a file titled "Uman," and then guided me out of his office to a chair and table in a corner of the large room where the three women pecked at their typewriters. He left me there to sort through the lists, and disappeared down the hallway past his office.

I scanned one page after another, searching for Lieb, Havol or anyone named Schneider. Needles shot through me every time I recognized a name on the handwritten Uman death lists. Some were childhood classmates or their sisters, brothers or parents. In many cases whole families were on the list: the Shapiros, the Goldsteins,

Yossef Berkov and his sister.

I must have gone through fifteen or twenty pages. My eyeballs grew weary. The rhythm of the typewriters in the background irritated my scratchy nerves, as did the turning of every page, none with Lieb's name on it. Then boredom set in. I wasn't prepared when I turned the page and saw the unmistakable name *Schneider,* preceded by a scripted initial that looked like a capital "*L*" followed by a period. But the handwriting was barely legible and the black ink runny. It could as easily have been an "*I*" as an "*L*." I gulped to hold down the nausea surging in my stomach.

"Are you alright, sir?" the typists closest to me asked.

I nodded, then got out of my chair and carried the piece of paper to her. "Can you tell if that is an *L* or an *I*?" I asked.

She studied it. "It looks like an *I* to me," she said. "But I can't be sure." The other two typists took a look. One said it looked like an *I* and one said it looked like an *L*, but neither could be certain.

I chose to believe it wasn't Lieb. There was no one else named Schneider on the list. Havol and her family weren't on the list.

Lipsky came back down the hall, his vest flapping open and his shoes smacking on the wooden floors. He carried another thick file under his arm. When I showed him the Schneider name on the page, he insisted it was *I*. "I know that investigator. That's how he writes," he said.

"Can you ask him whether it's an *L* or an *I*?"

"Sorry. He's in the Ukraine and won't be back for at least another five weeks."

I winced.

"Here," he said handing me the file from under his arm. "These are a few first hand reports written by our agents who took part in the investigation. I'll be back in a few minutes." He walked back down the hall. I turned my attention to reading the first report. It was in fact a draft of the final report of the All-Ukrainian Relief Committee under the sponsorship of the Red Cross. The title on the first page read: *The Slaughter of the Jews in the Ukraine in 1919.* I flipped randomly through the pages, settling on one chapter entitled Pogrom Pictures – A Few Episodes:

> *On the 9th of June a peasant brought to the Jewish hospital the two last Jews of Ladyzhenka (before the pogrom there were 1,600 Jews in that town.) They were two young girls, frightfully mutilated, one with her nose broken off, and the other with broken hands. They are now in Kiev, suffering not only from external injuries but also from venereal diseases contracted from their violators.*
>
> *In Uman five Jews were killed in the fields. One of them, an old man with a white beard, was not killed at once, but met his death in a long agony and great torture. This attracted the attention of Christian children, who gathered around him and threw stones at him, thus hastening his death. Not far from there the bandits murdered a Jew, who fell down dead. He was then lifted up, tied to a tree and made a target at which the fiends kept shooting a long time.*
>
> *In Uman a woman tried to protect her husband and father with her own body, and received a bullet in the breast. The woman was in an advanced stage of pregnancy and on the following day gave birth to a boy, so that there were four dead bodies lying on the floor of the house.*

The big room in which I sat had been an icebox only a few minutes earlier. Now it seemed as hot as Hades. Not even my own experience from Kishinev and our 1905 *pogroms* prepared me for this. I loosened my necktie and took off my jacket, then forced myself to resume reading the testimony.

> *It may be said that in all of the places which were visited by the pogroms the possessions of the Jews were completely destroyed. We have a typical report in this connection from the village of Orlovetz (District of Kiev), which reads as follows: The*

*plunderers rushed at the Jewish houses. Here they were helped
by the whole Russian population. Everything was loaded on
wagons and carried away. After they had completely emptied
the houses and squeezed out in every possible way the last savings of the Jews, they proceeded to destroy the houses and the
shops. Shutters, window panes, doors were taken out, roofs were
torn off, and so on. In the town of Zlatopol, of 285 shops, 275
were plundered and then burned down.*

Revulsion came first, then anger. I knew my brother. He was a gentle man. He would have died without a fight if it was only his life he
was protecting. But if it was Golde and the children, he would have put
up a fight to make even Uncle Yakov proud. Of that I had no doubt.

I read till the end, then closed the file, slumped in my chair, and
shut my eyes. Our home – Momma and Poppa's home – burned in my
mind, and the tailor shop a charred rubble. Sweat drenched my forehead and stained my white shirt. One of the women-typists brought
me a glass of water. She herself had probably read many of these reports while preparing them. She dressed like she was in mourning.
The next report I read was testimony by a student named B. Z.
Rabinovich. I wondered if this Rabinovich was related to a tin maker
in Uman named Amshel Rabinovich.

*The pogrom, which took place May 12-14, 1919, was perpe-
trated by Klimenko's bands, which were joined by a part of the
city bourgeoisie and various criminal elements. They stayed
about ten days, and on May 22, under pressure from Soviet forces, left Uman. They took away mainly money and valuables, and
searched everywhere for weapons. "Give us the Jew-
Communists," they yelled. Then they killed them and looted their
places. Although they were searching for Communists, Christian
Communists were not touched.*

*There were many cases of Jews whom Christians concealed in
their homes. But the average Russian intellectuals were hostile*

in their attitude and refused refuge. Many were content with the pogrom and among some parts of the population there was even exultation.

Lipsky returned. I followed him to his office, too drained to say a word. When we sat down, he patted me on the forearm and looked at me with the compassion of the Messiah.

"How many?" I asked.

"What do you mean – 'how many?'"

"You know what I mean," I said. "How many Jews have they murdered altogether?"

He looked down at the pile of folders on the desk in front of him and shook his head. His angry red-rimmed eyes softened to sadness. "I don't know. At least a hundred thousand. Probably a lot more. It could be two hundred thousand before we're done counting."

We talked for a few minutes more. When I got up to leave, I apologized for taking so much of his time. He would have none of it. "I owe you," he said. "Restitution. This is part of it." He didn't need to say he was talking about his sins of the Becker Dress Factory.

"You're okay with me," I answered. He patted me on the shoulder.

Sam walked me out; he promised to keep a lookout for any more information about Lieb or Havol. Then he asked about Duv. I told him I hadn't seen him in years.

"I hear he's hanging out with some rough characters, gangsters like Arnold Rothstein and Joe Amberg. He's going to land in jail," he said. I didn't say anything as we walked toward the front of the reception area.

We stopped to say goodbye at the top of the flight of stairs leading down to the street. I thanked him for everything.

He looked back to see if the receptionist was watching. She was engrossed in typing something. Then he put his hand on my arm and leaned his head toward me like a conspirator.

"So tell me," he whispered. "Did you *shtup* her?"

"What?"

"Julia Sorvino. Did you *shtup* her?" For a moment, that vulgar smirk appeared just like the Shmuel Lipsky I knew so well in the old days.

I didn't answer him. I just stared until he looked away. "I'll stay in touch," I finally said, my voice as flat as I could force it to be. "Let me know if you hear anything about my brother."

The sympathetic smile of the new Sam Lipsky returned. "I'll do that," he said as I clomped down the staircase. He waved goodbye.

The cold of the late afternoon slapped me in the face. Snowflakes began to fall, lightly dusting the sidewalk. Even if he was still alive, Lieb could never be the same. And if he died, the horror of how he died made me stop by the entrance to the subway and wretch. Passersby stared at me and gave me a wide berth.

During the subway ride, I pondered what I was going to tell Sara, Markus, Ester, Zelda, and Josef. The truth couldn't be hidden from them, but I needed to give them only enough details to prepare them for the worst. I had to give them hope too. Lieb wasn't dead as far as we knew, and neither was Havol. Their names weren't on any of the lists.

One important thing Lipsky told me was that the fighting was over and order restored to Uman. The Bolsheviks were in charge. It was time for another letter to Lieb. And time I wrote to Sergey Shumenko. If Lieb was dead, Sergey would know about it. If he was alive, I had to figure a way to get him out of Russia. Surely now he would be ready to leave.

Viktor Askinov must be drenched in the blood of these *pogroms*, I thought. How could he help himself? This time there was no Uncle Yakov to lead a ragtag self-defense brigade of Jews.

Equal measures of terror, frustration, grief, and hope stewed inside me on the cold, wet trek home from the subway. When I walked in the door of our apartment that afternoon, Sara took one look and held her arms out to me. Then she asked the question.

"Is he alive?"

"Yes. And so is Havol."

Why I said that I don't know. Maybe it was willful blindness. I really had no idea whether they were alive or dead.

CHAPTER TWENTY

July 1920

Months passed with no letter from Lieb or Havol, and no reply from Sergey Shumenko to my urgent letter. Sam Lipsky offered no encouragement. I finally had to admit to everyone that there was no evidence Lieb was alive. But there was also no evidence he was dead.

One hot, humid day, Ester phoned me at the tailor shop and asked me to come over. She said she had something important she wanted to talk about. The first thing I thought of was her health, but she assured me she and everyone in the family was fine. I loved my sister but didn't always like being around her. The more successful Simon was, the more generous they were. Ester took care of everyone in every way, but that gave her permission to butt into everyone's business with condescending suggestions and implied criticism. It might be about what Sara fed the children, how Sadie dressed, or how unfriendly Zelda's husband was. Simon was just as critical, but on a grander scale – America.

As I walked in the door of Ester's apartment, I was greeted by the aroma of fresh lavender, which had replaced the smell of fried potato pancakes and blintzes since she and Simon moved to this fancier place. Ester showed off Simon's business success in the lavish furnishings.

After a hug and a peck on Ester's cheek, I sat down in the over-stuffed sofa, trying not to disturb any of the doilies decorating the tops of the cushions. Ester poured me a glass of lemonade, and then plunked herself on the leather-padded chair next to me. The two of us hadn't been alone like this in a long time.

Ester started. "I've been thinking a lot about Lieb," she said.

"Me too, all the time." I wasn't sure where this was going.

"I'm eating my heart out." She fiddled with her fingers, her eyes downcast. "We have to have a memorial service for Lieb," she said. "Sit *Shiva*."

"Why? He's not dead."

"Avi, we have to come to terms with this."

I leaned forward in the couch and stared at her. "I'm telling you he's not dead."

"How long has it been since you heard from him? Two years? How many letters is it you've written? How many telegrams? How many visits to Congressman LaGuardia's office? You must have visited every Jewish relief organization in New York City. Even the Russian Consul General. You're driving yourself crazy. Sara's worried about you." She sounded like she was lecturing one of her children. It annoyed me.

"The Bolsheviks now have firm control of Uman."

"But I ask you, have you heard even one word about Lieb?"

"If anything happened to Lieb we would have heard from Gersh or Sergey or someone."

"But what if they're dead too, God forbid." It was hard to argue with her logic, so I changed direction. "Look. I've talked to Lipsky three or four times. He keeps checking new lists. There's no Lieb Schneider on them, and there haven't been any new *pogroms* in Uman in months."

"So tell me, why haven't we heard from Lieb?"

"Why are you so eager to put him in his grave?"

Ester's face furrowed, first around her mouth, then her brow. She let out a moan as though her heart was breaking. I went over to her and put my arms around her. "I'm sorry," I said.

She sniffled a few times and blew her nose. "You're strong," she said. "I'm not. If he's gone, the least we can do is say *Kaddish* for him."

"We will say *Kaddish* for him if it comes to that."

The handsome grandmother's clock on the wall opposite me bonged four times. Ester waited for it to stop. "I talked to Rabbi Daniel. He thinks now is the time. So does Markus, and even Zelda, mind you."

I was nowhere near ready to give up. Lieb was alive, even if I was the only one who still believed it. I left soon after with nothing resolved, except my vague promise to consider what Ester said if another month went by and we hadn't heard from him. But she punctured my iron-willed denials. Why hadn't my brother listened to me, I asked myself on my slow walk back to the tailor shop? Because he was Lieb.

That Fourth of July we had a lot to celebrate. Two days before, I pulled a letter from our mailbox and saw Lieb's left-handed chicken scrawl. I charged up the steps, burst through the door, and picked Sara up and swung her around. "He's alive," I yelled, waving the envelope.

Sara threw her arms around my neck and kissed me hard. Tears streaked her cheeks. I tore open the envelope and started reading. "He says he and all of the family are alive. And to tell you Havol and her family survived, and that's all we can ask." I read the rest aloud.

When the Reds 8th Regiment came to Uman, they looted all of the Jewish homes and businesses. That wasn't so bad. All they wanted was plunder. There were even Jewish bandits with the 8th, robbing their own landsmen. But they didn't kill us. The Reds' plundering stopped after the officers shot a few of the culprits.

But in May and July, the Reds lost control of Uman to Petliura's bandits, and then the Whites. We wouldn't have survived if it wasn't for Sergey and Valerya. He knew what was coming and brought us all to his country home on the edge of *town. We hid in the cellar whenever there was any noise outside. That worried us too because we had heard about instances where these pigs broke into a house, found Jews hiding in a cellar, and threw a bomb down, killing everyone.*

One such night we hid in the cellar when a gang on horseback rode up. It was so dark in there I couldn't even see Joshua whose hand I was holding. Sergey had given me a bayonet to defend us with, but that was no protection against a bullet or a bomb. Anyway, I heard someone calling my name. "I know Lieb Schneider is in there," he yelled. "Come out or we'll burn this place down." I could tell it was Olek Askinov, Viktor's younger brother. Someone must have told him where we were hiding.

Shaina started whimpering. I crawled over to her and clutched her head against my chest, afraid her noise would give us away. She stopped. I thought I had smothered my daughter. Sergey went out to confront the bandits. He told them he was "Count" Shumenko. Somehow he convinced them a count would never hide Jews. They left. There were other close calls before and after but God watched over us and delivered us, may He be praised. Sergey and Valerya should be sainted by their church. They fed us, clothed us, and hid us, at risk to themselves and their children.

Other Jews in Uman weren't so lucky as us. Many people you know are dead. They killed all of the Hiecklen family. Moishe Pinsky was bayoneted from behind, the blade going through him and impaling his little daughter who was clinging to him.

Sara gripped my shoulder all the time I was reading, giving off groans and moans with each dark passage. Her brow and crows-feet wrinkled. She couldn't stand it anymore. "What does he say about Havol? Does he say any more?"

I scanned down until I saw Havol's name and resumed reading aloud. I wished I hadn't.

I am reluctant to write more about Havol but Sara and Josef must know. Tell them it is enough that she is alive and we should rejoice in that. She is a courageous woman. You see, Havol was violated repeatedly, first by the Petliura filth, then by the Whites filth. The worst part is she was raped in front of her husband. She beseeched her rapists not to harm her husband or her children. Havol was a prize and so they granted her wish. She saved their lives. But her husband, the rabbi, was shamed. Now he won't touch her, and barely speaks to her. Golde heard about it and went to see her. She said that when she offered Havol her sympathy, Havol broke down and cried in her arms. She is a strong woman and refuses to be shamed or destroyed by what happened. But Golde is afraid her heart has been hardened. I pray for her to find peace and beg you to do the same. Letters from Sara and Josef would be appropriate.

Sara wrapped her arms around herself, frozen. She looked in my direction, but her glazed stare put her somewhere else. She wore the same anguished look her wretched mother always wore.

"I hug Ester and Sadie, but I never hugged Havol," she finally said. "Your family hugs all the time. Mine never did."

Sara's still-frail body shook, and yet she didn't break down. I moved to her and gathered her in my arms. She melted into me, her head nested against my shoulder.

"Havol never had any happiness," she said.

"God will take care of her," I replied with more conviction than I could give reason for.

Ester screamed when I phoned her about Lieb. Markus thanked God. Zelda said that I had willed it with my irrational hope. Their delight turned cold when I told them about Havol and how hard Sara was taking it.

When Josef came over that evening, Sara threw her arms around him, startling him. I had never seen them hug before. He wrapped his arms around her and hugged her back. Tears still wet her eyes, but she smiled a small smile for the first time since hearing of Havol's fate. The two of them sat at our dining table and together wrote a long letter to Havol expressing their regrets, voicing their love, and offering whatever they could do to help her. Sara kept touching Josef's arm, and every so often he stopped writing and grasped her hand.

Havol answered their letter several months later putting into words love for her sister and brother she had never uttered before. She also told us how brave Lieb had been throughout the attacks on the Jews, and how generous he and Golde had been since, though they themselves had little to share.

Before I fell asleep that night, I prayed for Havol and cursed her shameful husband for abandoning her in her time of trial. For the first time, the condolences I felt for Havol were for her and her alone, no longer a byproduct of my concern for my wife. And with it came a responsibility to do what I could for her from the same distance and state of helplessness as with Lieb. My last thought before I drifted off was how strange that Lieb and Havol should have become good friends. They were such different people, but now family.

The next morning I finished reading the rest of Lieb's letter, the part I had skimmed on my way to the part about Havol. He talked some more about Sergey and Valerya's generosity and courage. In his telling, he unintentionally revealed his strength. He was the one who went out to scavenge the town for supplies and to help other Jews in more desperate situations. And it was he who kept everyone in the house calm during the most frightening moments. I could see Lieb doing that.

He wrote about the night they knew they had been delivered. They again heard the hoof beats of a troop of mounted horsemen, and scurried down to the basement. Again he heard someone calling out his name, ordering him to come out. He recognized the voice this time. It was our old friend Gersh Leibowitz commanding the Red soldiers who had come to liberate Uman.

I went out. There he was on his horse, the red star of a Bolshevik officer centered above the brim of his brown cap. For a moment he reminded me of Uncle Yakov. We have been safe and cared for ever since. Gersh is a political commissar of a big region, so he is not always in Uman, but he has given us the name of someone to go to in his absence if we need anything. He is a good man, even if he is a Bolshevik. He has also helped Sergey get a job as the managing director of a new tractor factory in Uman. They converted it from the old iron works where Gersh used to work. This is good news because it means Sergey has been accepted by the new regime, even though he is of old wealth. Sergey's heart is with the Bolsheviks and the Jews. He's a good man, that Sergey Shumenko. And his wife Valerya is a good woman.

The Cripple, Viktor Askinov, led a bunch of peasants and some Black Hundreders when they pillaged, raped and killed. I know it was him. Then at just the right moment, he switched sides when he saw the Reds were winning. The Communists need followers so they accepted him. He now has a nice job in the government, as a tax collector I think. He will enjoy that job and will be vigorous in carrying it out. If I have learned anything, it is that the Communists are as cruel as the Whites or the Greens, just in a cause more favorable to us Jews.

During the gentiles' pillaging of Uman, our house and the tailor shop were stripped bare of everything except the big dining table in the front room. Not a chair or a rag was left. But I had concealed my new sewing machine just before we went into hiding, and the thieves never found it. So as soon as we repaired the window, the tailor shop was ready for customers again. Of course no one has any money, but I am able to barter clothes I make for what we need.

The Shumenkos and many other Christians have provided us with so much. They have given us furniture, utensils, clothing, and food to eat. May God be praised for our good fortune.

The Reds were now firmly in control. The civil war was over. Lenin declared anti-Semitism illegal in the new Soviet Union. Maybe a better day was ahead, the one the Bolsheviks promised. All I could do was pray for it to be so.

As more and more of our congregants received family letters from Russia, Daniel's Sabbath sermons took on a mix of deliverance and sorrow. He struck just the right tone. Gideon Katz said *Kaddish* for his brother and nephew, slain by the sword of a Cossack. Harold Berkowitz mourned for his sister and her whole family – a husband, mother-in-law, and five children.

I talked to Sam Lipsky one more time to tell him I heard from Lieb. He told me the committee's final report estimated over 150,000 Jews had been massacred across the Ukraine and Belarus.

After a couple of months, we were ready to store the Spanish Flu and the *pogroms* in a pouch in our hearts and get back to living. But it seems God wasn't yet done with the Ukraine.

CHAPTER TWENTY-ONE

October 1921

Famine descended on Russia like the plagues on the Pharaoh. And if that wasn't enough, hordes of lice infested with typhus accompanied the starvation. Some blamed it all on the civil war, some blamed it on the drought, others on farmers protesting Soviet collectivization of their farms, and still others on the wrath of God. No one could say whether He was punishing the Communists for their godlessness or Christians for their *pogroms*. One thing was for sure; millions of people were starving to death, Jews along with gentiles. My brother was one of them.

Lieb never asked me for anything before, but this time he did. For the first time he hinted at a willingness to leave Russia.

> *People are eating the thatch off the roofs and bark off the trees. Dogs, cats, and most of the horses are gone. I haven't seen a cow, a goat, a chicken, or a goose in weeks. What are we to do, I don't know. Our small plot in back of the house still produces abundantly but not enough to take us through the winter. Sergey and Valerya give us what they can from their small farm, but they aren't much better off than we are, and they need to take*

care of their own children. Gersh tries to help, but he is often away from Uman on official business. He is a political commissar. I think I told you that before.

I took a walk to Sukhi Yar yesterday. There is peace there, and so many good memories of us growing up. I sat in our secret clearing in the woods and could hear Duv, Simon, and you laughing with me, and see us chasing squirrels. Do you remember when Duv got caught up in a tree and couldn't get down? It is sad to say that for now Sukhi Yar is not what it was then. Every plant that can be eaten has been eaten. Some peasants have even been eating the grass until nothing but dirt remains. The only birds left are the crows, and they have grown fat as flying pigs.

We see many children with bloated bellies, their clothes little more than rags that barely cover their behinds. Winter is coming, and I wonder how many of them will die. There have been so many tales of cannibalism one is inclined to believe them. The authorities of course deny it. Yet they still issue harsh warnings about such practices, pass new laws, and arrest people for it. It is too horrible to imagine. But all you need to do is look in the crazed eyes of some of them to know it is true.

Please, my dear brother, I beg you to help us. I have nowhere else to turn. I am ashamed to ask and would not do so even now if it were not for Golde and the children. I should have listened to you and followed you. I made a mistake. I hope you and my family will forgive me. The pain of looking in their helpless faces is too much for a father to bear.

How could my brother be starving when here we go to sleep with full stomachs and leftovers in the ice box? And how could my brother be embarrassed to ask me, of all people, for help? Growing up, hadn't he been the one always there with a generous hand and understanding heart every time any of us needed it?

The first job was to keep them from starving, and Havol's family too. Then I would turn my attention to getting him out of Uman and to America, if he survived.

That very night I took the first step to rescue my brother. I assembled the family in our front room: Markus and Sadie, Ester and Simon, Sara, and Josef. They trembled when I read them Lieb's letter, particularly the part about cannibalism. Ester cupped her hands to her face. Sadie gagged. Sara closed her eyes and mumbled a prayer. Josef cracked his knuckles. Simon and Markus looked away. They each vowed to help with money, food, and anything else they could do. We didn't know if we could even get food through to them. The Soviets weren't admitting there was a problem.

The first thing we did was telegraph and mail money to Lieb. Sam Lipsky used his Red Cross contacts to help us get a stream of packages of food going to Uman: beans, flour, and rice above all. Lipsky also taught me how to bribe whoever we needed to bribe. Most of what we sent made it through. We considered the shrinkage a worthwhile expense.

Before I knew it, I was leading the synagogue's relief efforts, covering all of East Harlem. We set up something we called The Russian Famine Relief Committee. Approaching others for money was something new for me, and I didn't like it one bit, but I did it. I went after everyone. Most people gave generously. Those who weren't so eager to contribute hid. I hunted them down like thieves, then begged or embarrassed them until they gave more than they wanted to.

Lieb wrote again when the packages started to arrive. He mentioned that Havol was also receiving our money and packages. She was as grateful as he was. Golde had lost much weight, he wrote. *She's now thinner than Sara or Zelda as I remember them. If it weren't for the circumstances, I might even say she looks better than before. The Cripple is, of course, the only one who looks well-fed. He should be embarrassed, but he isn't.*

In a few months, generous aid from America arrived in Uman from both the U.S. government and private citizens. When the worst of the crisis passed, Lieb said American corn had saved them. *America must be as prosperous and generous a country as you have said,* he wrote. *I don't understand that. It's not what we are told.*

With disaster averted, Lieb hinted again about coming to America. In a couple of letters he alluded to my good judgment in choosing where I made my home. Who knew if his mind opening would last? But by then powerful forces had mustered legions to lock the gates of America to the likes of Lieb Schneider and the Jews of eastern Europe.

A bill was making its way through Congress to close Jewish and Italian immigration. Exclusion of Chinese, Japanese and other Asians had already been taken care of earlier. The well-organized eugenics movement gave a scientific rationale to many decent people and to political leaders for what was a racist immigration policy. This so-called science provided evidence of the superiority of one particular race – northern Europeans.

The eugenics nonsense troubled me, but Henry Ford was the hater I feared. He was a respected industrialist with the power, money, and influence to take away everything. Not just my security, but Yakira and Isaac's future place in America. Ford blamed Jews for Communism, pornography, alcoholism, American foreign intervention, the Great War, and just about everything else wrong with the country and the human race.

In 1918 he bought a newspaper, the Dearborn Independent, which he used day after day to spread the alarm about the treachery of Jews and their sinister influence. Circulation rose to some 700,000, but its force reached well beyond.

Ford wrote that *"One of the strongest causes militating against the full Americanization of several millions of Jews in this country is their belief – instilled in them by their religious authorities – that they are 'chosen,' that this land is theirs, that the inhabitants are idolators, that the day is coming when the Jews will be supreme."* It sounded to me a lot like the Tsar's newspapers before the *pogroms.*

His propaganda persuaded many citizens and elected officials of the dire consequences that lay ahead if America did not immediately stop further Jewish immigration.

I was only a little pipsqueak, but I had to do what I could to stop the new anti-Immigrant law from passing Congress. Otherwise Lieb wouldn't have any chance to come to America. I turned over the operation of the Russian Family Relief Committee to Gideon Katz and enlisted Bettino Rossi to join me in launching the East Harlem Immigrant Advocacy Committee. Bettino and I hadn't seen each other in a few years, but some friendships never dull.

Together we enlisted battalions of Jews and Italians to circulate petitions, and raise money for advertisements and handbills. We initiated a campaign of letters to Congress, civic leaders, clergy, and newspapers. I collared the same people for money I had pursued for famine relief only a few months before. The same ones volunteered time and money, and the same ones had to be rooted out from their hiding places.

We fought back against Ford the way you fight back in America: with boycotts of Ford automobiles, articles in newspapers, rallies, and ultimately a court of law. It wasn't only Jews who joined our cause. It was compassionate Christians too, in great numbers.

In a few months, we gathered over 8,000 signatures for presentation to Congress. When it was time to deliver these petitions to our own congressman, the Honorable Isaac Siegel, I decided to take a young man from our synagogue, Sidney Berman, with Bettino and me. Sidney had good looks, good manners, and a good wardrobe. He looked, acted, and spoke more like an American than Warren G. Harding. This ambitious young man was going places; he already had a job in the Bank of the United States. It was only a clerk's job in a Jewish bank, but still, we could introduce him as a banker.

Congressman Siegel was as American as apple pie, a Jew born in the United States. Though he was a Republican, when he ran in 1920 he was nominated by both the Republicans and the Democrats. I voted for him, but I didn't know him, and I didn't know anyone who did. I kept telling myself this wasn't Russia, and that congressmen in America worked for the people. That didn't diminish my awe.

Congressman Siegel's local Congressional headquarters opened onto the street in one of the nicest buildings on one of the nicest streets in East Harlem. A huge American flag flew on a pole by the entry door. Siegel welcomed us into his well appointed oak and leather office. He wore the confident posture and strong voice of the powerful. My tailor's sense told me his solid blue suit and vest were custom made by a skilled tailor using fine material. His strong brown eyes and solid eyebrows focused on me. "Gentlemen, I am at your service. What can I do for you?"

I delivered a short rehearsed speech about the injustice of the anti-immigrant law, and how it would be a betrayal of the American constitution and the rights of all people to the pursuit of life, liberty, and happiness. Bettino and Sidney later praised it as "inspiring." I was too charged by the importance of the moment to judge.

When I finished, Congressman Siegel leaned back in his swivel chair and lit a cigarette with an elegant Parker Beacon lighter. He took a long puff and bellowed first one cloud, then another. He patted our stack of petitions and promised to deliver them to his colleagues.

"Let me tell you what I've said in the halls of Congress," he said with the certainty of those who know the real facts. "This whole bill is un-American and against the spirit of American institutions. And all this talk of Bolsheviki and radicals from Europe is ridiculous and hysterical.

"Now let me put your mind at ease. It will be a hard fight, but I don't believe for a moment Congress will enact this bill. There is not the slightest necessity for anti-immigration legislation. I regard such legislation as ill-advised, to say the least." With that, he rose from his chair, signifying our meeting was over. I could have kissed him.

Bettino, Sidney and I were as pleased as if we had just elected the first Jewish President of the United States. We did a victory march down the street just as the brilliant orange sun sank below the western ridge of tenements.

"Speakeasy," Sidney hollered, pointing his finger emphatically in the direction of the sunset. "I'm buying."

"Then I'm drinking," Bettino shouted loud enough to catch a glance from the policeman walking his beat on the other side of the street.

To reach this fine establishment, we had to sneak down the side alley next to Harvey Hornstein's grocery store, knock on an inconspicuous weathered door, and descend four steps into a dark half-basement. A couple of dirty windows and bare light bulbs overhead gave the place as much charm as a warehouse by the docks. Fancier neighborhood speakeasies were still a few months away. The Kinsale Tavern and other legitimate taverns had been boarded up the night Prohibition began.

The workday hadn't ended yet, so the place was only half-full. On our way to the bar I spotted someone I didn't care to see deeply engrossed in conversation at a back table. I turned my face away hoping he didn't see me.

We each ordered a whiskey and sat at a table near the front. We toasted our victory; Sidney and Bettino saluted my oratorical performance in front of the congressman. Bettino left quickly without finishing his drink; his wife was going to a suffragette meeting, so he had to get home to the children. I wished Sara took such interest, but to her women voting was as unnatural an act as women reading the Torah on the High Holy Days.

Sidney and I finished our drinks, making awkward small talk. Sidney was a kid really, a few years younger than Markus and only a few years older than Yakira. We had little in common, and Sidney couldn't put his formal manners aside. He kept calling me Mr. Schneider and sir even after I told him to call me Avi several times.

I finished my drink and let my silence tell Sidney I was ready to leave. Just then a strong hand grasped my shoulder from behind. "Avi Schneider." I recoiled from the hard voice of Mendel Silber. "What's a swell like you doing in a juice joint like this?" His mockery never failed to annoy me.

"We were just leaving," I said, picking up my hat from the vacant chair.

Silber sat down in the chair, depositing his half-full beer glass on the table. He introduced himself to Sidney, because I wasn't going to.

"To old times," he raised his glass to me in toast. I nodded.

"I hear you did quite a job with those petitions," he said to both Sidney and me.

"Mr. Schneider put it all together," Sidney answered, as if currying favor. "But Congressman Siegel said the anti-immigrant bill isn't going to pass any way."

"It'll pass," Silber said. His certainty irritated me. "And a worse one is on the way. They don't want no more Jews in this country. And they don't want no more guinea wops neither." Silber leaned back in his chair and lit a Lucky Strike, blowing the smoke in my direction. He stuffed the pack back in his vest pocket.

Sidney took it all in as though Silber was more of an authority than Congressman Siegel. "We're all equal in America," I said, unable to come up with any rebuttal other than a cliché.

"Well, at least we have the right color skin. Better than being a Chink, or a Jap or a nigger." I don't know why I allowed myself to be pulled into a debate with a Communist like Mendel Silber. Maybe it was fear he might actually convince a nice young man like Sidney Berman that America wasn't what he thought it was.

"Millions of good Christians in this country joined us last year to protest the *pogroms* back in the old country."

Silber ignored my comment. "That other congressman, Johnson's his name, wants to stop interracial marriage too. And that includes us. No more Jews marrying Christians." There was that sarcastic sneer again. "I guess we can still fuck 'em. We just can't marry 'em."

I wanted to remind Silber that American charity and the American Congress provided over twenty million dollars and tons of American corn to relieve the Russian famine. But it wouldn't have done any good. He denied there even was a famine. So I just stood up and said, "I've had enough of this charming conversation." Sidney stood up with me and put on his fedora.

Silber remained seated, arm draped across the back of the chair. "Why don't you talk to that brother-in-law of yours," he said, referring to Josef. "That union of his fights us more than the capitalists. We should be brothers. Those big shit owners are bleeding our brothers and sisters." He said it without passion, like a memorized speech.

I turned and left, Sidney tagging after. "Tell the kid about Henry Ford," Silber yelled after us.

We walked back toward the tenements. A gust of wind blew paper wrappers and autumn's dried yellow leaves about the sidewalk. When the sun set, a chill inched in. Instead of telling him about Henry Ford, I told him who Mendel Silber was and how I first met him on the ship on my way over. Sidney put my mind at ease; he would have nothing to do with Communists.

"But some of what he said is true," Sidney said when we turned on-to his tenement-lined street. "I want to go to college. I tried getting in Columbia but they told me their Jewish quota was full. But they liked me and said to try next term. And when I went to get a job in Madison Bank they told me they don't hire Jews. Just told me outright. No excuses."

"So go to City College. Then do what you're doing. Keep your job in a Jewish bank. What's wrong with that?"

"And if we try moving out of these tenements, where do we go? They won't have us living in their neighborhoods or joining their clubs or marrying their daughters." A tiny speck of anger showed itself in my well-mannered friend. That's not so bad, I thought.

"So what's wrong with Jewish girls?" I chuckled. "I don't want to sound like your father, Sidney, but he's right. In the old country we couldn't go to college, couldn't work for the government, couldn't vote, couldn't go anywhere except where the Tsar told us we could go. We were prisoners. With all of its problems, America isn't Russia. And it'll get better. You watch."

We stopped in front of his building. A shapely young woman with bobbed black hair and a short flapper dress came out of the front door. She smiled and said hello to Sidney. He ignored her, studying his shoes. "If there's one thing I did right in this life," I said, "it was bring-ing my wife and kids to America."

"Thanks for taking me along today," the young man answered. "I'll remember what you said." He stuck out his hand to shake before climbing the front steps.

I walked home thinking more about Mendel Silber than what we accomplished with Congressman Siegel. Silber never failed to upset me. He saw the dark in people, not the hope. I couldn't live like that. The only thing to do was to stay away from him, and keep everyone I cared about away from him – good kids like Sidney Berman. Josef would take care of himself.

Mendel Silber proved right about the anti-immigrant legislation, a bitter herb to swallow. Not long after our visit to Congressman Siegel, Congress passed the Emergency Quota Act, the House by acclimation and the Senate by seventy-seven votes to one. President Warren Harding signed it and it was the law.

Senator Hiram Johnson of California tried to push through an amendment that would have allowed admission to victims of political and religious persecution; it failed by sixty votes to fifteen. Johnson's amendment could have saved many Jews from the *Shoah* twenty years later. In spite of what I told Sidney Berman, a mean spirit dirtied our land, blinding most to the consequences, as if they would have cared anyway.

After 1921, the torrent of Jews from Russia shrunk to a dribble, as it did for Italians and nearly everyone else. Canada closed its borders too, with its own new anti-immigrant laws. An even harsher immigration bill passed Congress in 1924 and was signed into law by President Coolidge.

We deserved the small satisfaction we felt when Henry Ford lost a libel lawsuit for defaming Jews in his newspaper. On top of paying damages, he had to make a humiliating public apology which must have made his blue blood boil. He ended up closing the Dearborn Independent, but in the thirties he led an even meaner epidemic of anti-Semitism. As a reward, Hitler honored him in 1938 on Ford's seventy-fifth birthday with the highest medal Nazi Germany could award to a foreigner, the Grand Cross of the German Eagle. Is it any wonder no Jew will be caught dead driving a Ford?

My worry, of course, was Lieb, now that America barricaded its doors to Jews like him. But there were still options open, difficult as they would be. Getting him to Palestine remained a possibility. So was Mexico. I knew people whose families had gone there, welcomed. And Mexico wasn't so far from America. I could visit him. It had to be better than Russia. Lipsky said Lieb and his family could try getting out through Turkey or Romania. If that failed, he could try going through Poland. Lipsky knew people who might be able to help smuggle them out.

I didn't need to even think about Havol. She was a lost cause. Her lout of a husband was a Hassidic rabbi who wanted above all to die and be buried in Uman next to the great Rebbe Nachman. He almost got his wish, but that was some years away.

The famine in the Ukraine ended. At a critical moment, Americans had donated generously and our government had supplied the means to relieve the Russian misery. Some might say things in Uman and the Soviet Union improved after that. For the first time in Russian history, Jews stood as equals in employment, education, and citizenship. But five million Ukrainians lay dead from starvation or from typhus, the disease that piggybacked on famine.

Lieb's younger daughter, Brindyl, was one of those typhus victims. Torment saturated every word of his letter telling me about it.

> *Brindyl was only sixteen years old, and the sweetest little girl God has ever put on this earth. I will never again feel her little arms around my neck and her gentle kiss on my cheek. She will never know a husband or hold her child. But maybe she has been spared the tragedy that seems to always descend on the Jews of Russia. May God bless her soul and grant her eternal peace.*

They buried Brindyl next to Poppa and Uncle Yakov in the cemetery behind the synagogue. Gersh, Sergey and Valerya came to the service together. Havol came all alone. She entered our old synagogue in defiance of her husband. Like her father, her husband considered us Haskalah Jews blasphemous, worse than gentiles.

Grief for my brother and Brindyl ripped my insides. When Sara came home, she found me still sitting in the stuffed green chair, Lieb's letter on my lap, staring mindlessly at the grape-leafed wallpaper.

She took the letter from my hand and read it. "I held that little baby in my arms," she sniffled, recalling a time years ago before she left Uman for America. "She babbled to me and smiled every time I picked her up." Sara's lips quivered. "She can't be dead. She can't be." We held each other for awhile. Then I had to call my brother and sisters to tell them. I couldn't imagine losing Yakira and Isaac like that, or what it would do to Sara.

After Brindyl's death, despair extinguished my dear brother's resilience and good humor. He no longer hinted at leaving Russia. It wouldn't have mattered anyway. The Soviets made it impossible to leave, and the door to America was barred. My own mind turned elsewhere.

CHAPTER TWENTY-TWO

May 1922

One morning I awoke and found myself in the middle of the Roaring Twenties. Every day brought something new, whether it was the radio, speakeasies, or Yankee Stadium. Jews were getting ahead, opening stores, factories and other businesses. We had a few more Jewish mayors, judges, and government officials in Washington. On the other hand, gangsters like Arnold Rothstein and the Amberg brothers embarrassed us as much as if they were members of the family.

Women got the right to vote. They raised their dresses up to their knees, bobbed their hair, wore makeup like prostitutes, and started smoking in public. I certainly enjoyed a glimpse of a woman's thigh getting in or out of a car, but looking was all I did. Sara didn't change much except she raised her skirts up to her calves. The flat-chested look couldn't work on her even if she tried. She still stood out in any crowd of women, young or old, flapper or not.

Congress's passage of Prohibition forced all bars to shut in 1920. No more liquor. Josef, Simon, Markus, and I threw down one last whiskey at the Kinsale Tavern just a few hours before that midnight. Thomas Kelly wasn't sorry to see it go. He told us he was opening a simple café called T T Kelly's on 5th Street and Third Avenue, but in the back there was going to be one of those new speakeasies. "Come visit," he said. "Go down the alley on the north side, knock on the door and tell them Tommy T sent ya'." He winked.

One night, Markus, Manny and I snuck down that back alley to the hidden door Thomas told us about. Inside, Thomas had created a plush place with red-bricked walls, checkered table cloths, a stage for a band, polished wooden floors, electrified lanterns hanging from the ceiling, and the long polished bar from the Kinsale Tavern, with the same big mirror behind it. Thomas had a big success on his hands, a real moneymaker. Police raided other joints, but they never raided his. The word was he paid off the police to leave him alone.

In the tailor shop, fashionable women paid us more to make those tiny flapper dresses than they had for the old long ones. We were so busy we had to hire another tailor. Solly Birnstein was young, little more than an apprentice really, but he had the talent to be very good if we taught him right. Mrs. Schulman and her aging friends took to him like schoolgirls in an all-boys school. Every time he flashed his toothy smile, they fluttered their eyelashes.

Solly mid-wifed my brother-in-law Josef's social awakening. When Solly joined us in the tailor shop, he and Josef began hanging around together. He tempted Josef with stories of booze and the loose women who frequented speakeasies; he invited Josef to come along. Apparently a young, good looking guy like Solly had an abundance of opportunities he didn't mind sharing.

By then Josef was a hardened bachelor of thirty-four years, used to a world of hardened men. He was a tough guy himself, still small in stature but with the muscled body of an iron worker. His whole life went into his battles as a shop foreman and union leader. His fiery curse-laced speeches always roused his brethren into a frenzy. But workers and owners knew he fought to keep the Communists from infiltrating his union with the same passion he fought management. On the other hand, attractive single women mortified him.

Sara wanted nothing for her brother as much as she wanted him to find a good wife who would love him and take care of him. Sara,

Hannah, Sadie and Ester did their best to find eligible widows for Josef. The women they found were nice but not what he had in mind. One Hannah arranged was so fat she would have killed Josef if she got on top of him. And one Ester arranged had a darker mustache than mine. Sadie's pick was dumber than a dead horse. Josef concluded being alone might in the end be a more satisfactory condition.

The roar of the Twenties saved him, thanks to Solly. Josef's first gratification was with a gentile girl; he had had to drink a lot to numb his inhibitions. When he finished, he felt guilty for doing it with a *shiksa*. When he did it a second time, it was easier and better.

My guess is it was Josef's first regular experience of this sort. Proud and perplexed, he shared every intimate detail with me. I tried to just listen, but he expected me to offer my wisdom on the subject of women and sex. I tried to tell him I didn't know much more than he did. It didn't occur to him I had little experience myself beyond his sister.

One night he and Solly ventured into an overheated T. T. Kelly's. Sweat dripped off the women's naked arms and legs. The erotic scent of booze, bodies and smoke mixed with the charged beat of the band. Solly spotted a lanky blond sitting at the end of the bar with her friend. The tops of their rolled stockings showed when they crossed their legs. "She and her friend eyed us," Josef recounted to me. "Solly asked the blond to dance."

The darker haired one sat alone on the stool smoking a cigarette and sipping her drink. She watched her flaxen haired friend do a Charleston, occasionally sneaking peeks toward Josef. He still didn't know the signals of a woman in heat. When the music ended, Solly and his new friend led the dark haired girl in Josef's direction. He tried to look nonchalant, but he didn't know how to do that.

"This young lassie is dying to meet you," Solly said with a mock brogue.

"I'm Maggie Flynn." Her lilting Irish accent sounded like an exotic harp to Josef. She held out her hand for him to shake.

"And I'm Brigit," the lanky blond said.

Maggie's gray front tooth and drooping left eyelid marred an otherwise pleasant Irish face; her tempting body and short chestnut hair aroused Josef. She bent way over and took a big gulp from his drink, standing close enough for him to peek down her dress. She looked up into his eyes at close range and smiled. Josef was embarrassed at being caught. She wasn't. Her ruby red lipstick stained his glass. "My thirst is powerful," she said. He had no experience with such provocative intimacy.

They slept together that night and many others over the next couple of months. A quick meal or a short visit to a quiet speakeasy let them both pretend they were together for something besides an eager trip to bed. She taught Josef things he had never imagined, primed by a lust he didn't know a woman could possess.

Maggie was as Catholic as she was Irish, frequently lacing conversation or climax with a "Holy Mary, Mother of God," or reference to some saint. But her piety didn't interfere with her bodily hungers. Josef wondered out loud to me if she confessed their sins to her priest. He never mentioned he was Jewish. "I guess she figured it out from my circumcision," he said to me. "She viewed it close up." That might have been part of her pleasure, he speculated.

Solly couldn't keep himself from teasing Josef about Maggie whenever Josef stopped by the shop. But as time went on, his teasing took on a serious tone of warning. You would have to be blind not to realize Maggie Flynn was no innocent, and Josef was entangled in something he didn't know how to end. As Solly said, "nice girls don't go to T. T. Kelly's unescorted." It fell to me to have the serious talk with Josef.

My affection for my then-young brother-in-law began when I first met Sara. He took my side when her father rejected my marriage proposal. And he was right next to me on the barricades in 1905 when the mobs attacked the Jews of Uman. Then two years later, he was the one who escorted Sara, Yakira, and Isaac to America. He was my brother as much as Lieb and Markus. There is nothing I wouldn't do for Josef, including keeping his secret about Maggie Flynn from Sara when that's what he asked. I didn't want to hurt him, and I knew making him face the truth about Maggie would do just that.

He wasn't at all happy when I confronted him. First he denied she was a fast woman. Then he denied his involvement with her was anything more than a dalliance. But my words sunk in. Much as he enjoyed his time between her legs, she embarrassed him. He hid her from me and everyone else he knew. By the time we were done talking, he could no longer deny what he hadn't wanted to admit. Yet you can't blame him if he was confused and a little anxious about what to do next. He had no experience.

So he didn't call Maggie or see her for several days. When she couldn't get a hold of him any other way, she called him at the tailor shop knowing he stopped by sometimes late in the day. I gave her feeble excuses for him. She called many more times at his apartment, at the union office, and at the tailor shop, each call more desperate. He kept hoping she would give up. She didn't.

Solly finally said to him, "Just tell her it's over." So the next time she called, he did. Josef was unsettled by how he ended it. He knew whatever Maggie was she deserved better treatment from him.

Josef had never known a woman in the way he knew Maggie, but this indulgence was enough. He didn't say it, but what he was looking for was a good woman, one like his sister. He realized if he wanted to find her, he was going to have to find her somewhere else than in a speakeasy. His forays with Solly paused while he was entangled with Maggie. They didn't start again.

The end of Josef's affair with Maggie coincided with the close of Yakira and Isaac's childhood. They were almost adults now, and Sara and I were very satisfied with how they were turning out. Our daughter was a self-assured, independent young woman at just the moment people began accepting that. School held little interest, and she stopped only a year before she would have graduated from high school. She got a job selling shoes at Macy's. Her girlfriends loved her; young men showed little interest. Poor Yakira was short and squat like Momma, with Poppa's big nose, but she was the most lovable young lady you could meet. I prayed a good man would find her.

Girls, on the other hand, flocked to Isaac like butterflies to sugar.

He was good looking and gentle, with Sara's deep blue eyes. He graduated from high school in May 1922, the smartest one in his class. He strutted across the stage to get his diploma, head high, spiffed up in his new double breasted coat, tie, and knee-length knickers. I was not surprised when on the walk home he told me he wanted to go to City College and become an accountant. What a waste of his tailoring talent, I thought, but it was his choice. It was for moments like this I came to America.

Sara never once asked me what was going on with Josef and Maggie. Yet she must have known, because she and her sisterhood stopped pestering him about finding a woman. Still, she worried about his vulnerability - and with good reason.

CHAPTER TWENTY-THREE

December 1922

"At least she's not a *shiksa*," Sara said, an unusually spiteful look on her face. She finished drying one of the pots and clanked it on the washboard next to the big metal sink.

Josef had just left our apartment with his new girlfriend, Miryem Schoor. Both Sara and Miryem had been on their best behavior during dinner, eager to please each other. I was intrigued by Miryem. She was a well-educated, well-read woman, probably seven or eight years younger than Josef.

"She smokes too much." Sara shoved a stack of dishes in the cabinet so hard they should have broken. "Did you notice how she kept handing the matches to Josef to light her cigarette for her? Just so she could touch him."

"They're in love."

"And that so-sophisticated English accent of hers. Talking to Isaac all night, bragging about all the books she's read. As though she's the only woman who's ever read a book."

Miryem's passion for Edna Ferber and Scott Fitzgerald actually impressed me, but I wasn't going to say that to Sara right now. "Yakira and Isaac liked her," I said.

"Let them." Sara ripped off her apron and stomped into the bedroom. I turned off the lights and followed her.

Josef and Miryem made an unlikely couple, I thought, he rough and she polished. "He's going to marry her," I said.

Sara slipped her wool nightgown over her head. "I'll be nice to her, but I don't have to love her." She turned off the light.

Josef and Miryem's first encounter happened in early October when he was on the way out of our apartment building. She was mopping up a spill on the black and white tiled entryway. She paused to let him pass, an embarrassed look on her face. They exchanged a few words.

The next day Josef picked through a bin of apples at the corner grocery store. She was doing the same. They looked over at each other. She smiled. He went back to his search for the best apple in the bin.

"I was bringing Mrs. Brickman some groceries," she said to him. "I dropped a bottle of milk."

Josef stopped picking and looked over. "What?"

"You thought I was the cleaning lady, didn't you?" She snickered.

Now he was the one embarrassed. He apologized. They chatted briefly about the price of milk and the state of the fruit at this time of year.

They laughed when they told us the story of their first meeting. She claimed he tried to give her a tip. He insisted he did no such thing. Mrs. Brickman was a feeble old lady and Miryem worked for a charity, the Women's Support Agency. She was there to look in on Mrs. Brickman.

The next afternoon Josef stopped by the grocery store again, hoping to bump into her. He was loitering among the vegetables when she tapped him on the shoulder. "Hello," she whispered. "Are you following me?" She was smiling. He was embarrassed again.

Her dark eyes and coal-black hair grabbed him and wouldn't let go, even though her rail-thin body made her look like little more than a teenager. Her flat chest hinted at breasts that were the size of small potatoes.

They had a cup of coffee together that afternoon, dinner the next, and many more after that, until it was time to meet Josef's family. Miryem was a widow with a six year old son named Henry. Other than that, she herself had no family in America.

Josef stopped by the tailor shop on his way home from work the day after we met Miryem for the first time. He was eager to hear how Sara and I took to her. I put on my heavy wool coat, scarf, and knit cap before we headed out in the cold to a local speakeasy.

An icy wind swept up the street, forcing passersby to grip their hats and clutch the top button of their overcoats. A frigid couple crossing in the middle of the street dodged passing automobiles, ignoring their honking car horns. Shriveled brown leaves littered the sidewalk.

"She liked both of you very much," he said as we walked past the Padilla's restaurant. The neighborhood was changing: Restaurants named Sanchez and Collazo, a greengrocer named Luis Campos, a barbershop owned by Pedro Mendez. Most of the Jewish pushcart peddlers who once jammed the streets had moved to the Bronx or Brooklyn and opened real stores there. Sara seemed to be the only one who hadn't noticed how many Puerto Ricans were moving in.

"We liked her very much," I lied as we turned the corner. Josef was too much in love to have noticed Sara's lukewarm treatment. I noticed. Sara was polite, but responded to every attempt at conversation by Miryem with an abrupt reply. After dinner, Miryem had grown quiet. She just chewed on her fingernails and held her son Henry in her lap.

When we went down the three steps to the speakeasy, Josef gave the door a loud knock, paused and then gave it two more. A small man with glasses and a bald head let us in. The place was small and spare, but convenient for our needs. We took a small table in the corner under a picture of Jack Dempsey, the new heavyweight champion. While we waited for our drinks, Josef filled me in on more of Miryem's story.

"She grew up in Budapest. Her father was a teacher at the high school. But then her mother died when she was ten and her father died four years later. Her mother's sister and her husband took Miryem in, but them fuckers treated her like god damned garbage."

She had an older sister and a younger sister who were sent to live with relatives in other parts of Hungary. She rarely saw them after her father died. These sisters still lived in Hungary. They wrote infrequently, maybe once every couple of years, and no longer meant anything to Miryem.

"She felt all alone, unwanted," Josef said. "That's why she took up with her husband, Theo. To get away. He was twenty years older than her. She didn't love him, but that son-of-a-bitch seemed to be the only one who wanted her. It was a brief, bad marriage. Henry's the only good thing that's happened in her life, she says, until I came along."

They left for America right after they were married and landed in Hartford. She didn't know it yet, but she was pregnant with Henry, so she was trapped. He was born seven months after they got here. There was a nice older couple who lived in the apartment next door. They could hear Theo whipping Miryem night after night, and Henry crying. They told her about the Jewish Women's Support Agency in New York, which took in women like her.

The neighbor woman knew the director, Harriet Miller, and rang her up on the telephone. They gave her money for a bus ticket, and she snuck away one day when Theo was at work. It's the last she ever saw of him. He knew where she was, but he never tried to follow her. The Women's Support Agency got Miryem a place to live and a job as a governess. Theo died of a heart attack a year later.

Josef looked pensive. He drew a Lucky Strike from its package and lit it, the smoke drifting toward the hammered tin ceiling. "So you and Sara liked her?"

"What about Henry?"

A little sunshine crossed his clouded face. "He needs a father. I love the little guy, and he loves me. Miryem doesn't want any more children, and I think I'm too old to start."

Sara came around quickly once she heard Miryem's story. "That poor girl," she said. "The flames of hell should torture that bastard husband of hers for eternity."

Later that evening, she softened a little more. "Maybe I can love her a little. And if he marries her, I'll be nice to her."

Josef and Miryem went on seeing each other every day. The snows melted. The heavy late April rains that year yielded to bright May days. They took long walks in Central Park with Henry. The park was crowded again, young women showing off their shapelier garments, young men in heat pursuing them in blue blazers and straw hats. Flocks of returning birds crossed the sky. The sweet smell of budding flowers ignited Henry's hay fever.

On one of those walks, Miryem asked Josef to marry her. Rabbi Daniel performed the ceremony two weeks later. It was a simple affair. I stood up for Josef and Miryem's friend Harriet, the hard-edged agency director who rescued her, stood up for Miryem. The only other people there were Sara, Henry, Hannah, Markus, Sadie, Ester, and Simon. There was no canopy and no breaking of the wine glass. Miryem clung to Josef all day like she was afraid he was going to get away from her. They left immediately after by train for a weeklong honeymoon at Asbury Park on the coast of New Jersey.

I had written Lieb about Josef's escapades, beginning with Maggie. He seemed to enjoy the stories as much as he enjoyed reading Chekhov. When I told him Josef had married Miryem, he asked me to convey his congratulations and joy, as well as his hope to one day meet her. He enclosed a plain white handkerchief Golde embroidered with Miryem's new initials, MK, a generous gift from someone who had so little.

When they returned from their honeymoon, Josef came over to the apartment alone to tell us he and Miryem were moving to the northern part of Brooklyn. He took a job in the union office there, mostly organizing the ironworkers in the Brooklyn Navy Shipyard. It was a nice job for Josef, and one he was eager for.

"Brooklyn? It might as well be the end of the earth," Sara said when he told her. "Why does everyone want to go to Brooklyn?" She looked so sad. Josef wasn't the only one leaving East Harlem. Simon and Ester had already told us they were moving to a neighborhood called Manhattan Beach. Simon was opening another dry goods store there.

It would be his fourth.

Around this time, Markus also brought up the idea of moving out of East Harlem. "The Spics are moving in," he said. "And the *shvartzers* are taking over everything north of 125th Street. It's dangerous. You want your daughter living with this? Your wife? I don't." But Sara was in no hurry to leave.

CHAPTER TWENTY-FOUR

June 1923

Markus offered to sell me his half of the tailor shop, and I was not happy about it. He and Sadie decided to move to Brooklyn, not far from Ester and Simon. Markus said he was tired of tailoring and wanted to try something different. Maybe he was also tired of living in his brother's shadow.

I couldn't imagine tailoring without my little brother next to me. The shop was his as much as mine. I tried to persuade him with every imaginable argument, finally invoking our father's name when all else failed. "We're *schneiders*, for goodness sake. Tailors. What would Poppa say?"

"I know what Momma would say," he answered. "The same thing she said to you when you wanted to come to America and Poppa didn't: Go! Do what you have to do.'" In the end, Manny bought a small share of the shop from Markus for a too-generous sum, and I bought the rest.

Everyone we knew was leaving East Harlem. Markus, Sadie, Ester and Simon begged us to join them. I couldn't imagine how I was going to convince Sara. She liked it just fine where she was.

Markus and Sadie moved into a nice big apartment, one with colorful flower boxes and a garden courtyard. Sadie still came back with Ester once a week for their card games, but when they suggested they have a game now and then in Manhattan Beach, Hannah was willing but Sara refused. Ester's house, Markus told me, was bigger than the New York Public Library.

Markus took a job as a teller at the Brooklyn Bank, a few blocks from their apartment, while he figured out what to do next. It was only supposed to be temporary. Years later he was still there. The job was adequate. Mr. Hill, the owner of the bank, was a decent enough boss. Markus earned a few promotions, and the pay was sufficient. But it was never more than a way to make a nice living. Tailoring still beat in his blood, and every so often he had to come to the shop to sit down at a sewing machine and feel the softness of the cloth. Much as I liked Manny, life was not the same without Markus sitting next to me.

Rosh Hashonnah felt lonely that year without my family and friends around me. In synagogue, I kept looking across the aisle at Sara, but her head was usually lost in prayer. She still had Hannah to sit next to her, but even that was about to change. When we were cleaning up after the second day, Daniel told me about a new synagogue they were building in the Sheepshead Bay part of Brooklyn. The synagogue wouldn't be open until next summer, but they were looking for a rabbi now and had promised him the job.

If our neighborhood continued to decline, the tailor shop would decline with it. The Puerto Ricans moving in did not have as much money as the Jews and Italians moving out, and I was not in step with the styles they liked. Something had to be done. So in October I took a trip by subway out to visit Markus and Ester. Sara knew about it, but wouldn't join me, waging a war of resistance to any move.

Markus took me right to the beach. "Look at this," he said, waving his hand toward the glistening water. "Bring Sara here and she'll never want to go back to East Harlem." Gulls glided through the cobalt blue sky toward the green fields on the peninsula across the bay. The taste of salty ocean seasoned the coming and going of the gently lapping waves. I reached down and scooped up a handful of chilled sand, letting it dribble through my fingers. I was sold.

On my second visit, Markus handed me off to a real estate sales agent, Irving Polansky. Irv was a courtly, graying gentleman in a well-tailored gray stripe suit who never stopped talking. He had lived in Manhattan Beach for over two decades, since back when it was a rich man's haven. It still felt like a little village. Here you could smell the sky and taste the ocean, unhindered by light-killing blocks of tall tenements and the farts of too many automobiles.

There were more kosher restaurants and meat markets in Manhattan Beach than grains of rice in a rice bowl, most with signs in Yiddish and English. There was a nice grocery store, a barbershop, a movie theater, and a soda fountain. Irv pointed out the local speakeasy, down a small alley. He said they were building a new synagogue in Sheepshead Bay, only a five minute walk. Daniel and Hannah would be close by.

One thing Manhattan Beach didn't have was a good tailor shop. Irv showed me three or four storefronts just off the main street which would do nicely. Then we got to the hard part, finding a house Sara would fall in love with. In late afternoon Irv showed me one on West End Avenue.

Some would call it modest, but it felt like home the minute I saw it. Gray-blue shutters framed the freshly painted white clapboard. A small evergreen tree guarded the two steps up to the porch. The windows in the upstairs bedrooms looked out on the tree-lined street. The front lawn only had space for a few rows of flowers, but the backyard was bigger. For the first time, Isaac and Yakira could each have their own rooms, even though they wouldn't be at home much longer.

Sara wouldn't even look at the house I picked out no matter what I said, and I said plenty. But one night, just when I had given up, she relented. "You were right to bring us to America," she said. "We'll go to Brooklyn, make a new life." I put my arms around her and kissed her gently. She laid her head on my shoulder. "I'll be happy," she said. It sounded more like an aspiration than an expectation, but once Sara made up her mind there was no going back.

It took until the spring to work out the purchase of the house in Manhattan Beach and the sale of the tailor shop in East Harlem. A nice man named Reynoso Campos bought the tailor shop and asked to keep my original name, *The American Tailor Shop.* I agreed. Manny joined me as a junior partner in our new shop in Manhattan Beach, a short walk from our new house. He was eager for a fresh adventure.

Sara tried not to show it, but she grieved when we left East Harlem. So did I. A week before we were to move, I took a final stroll by the empty lot where the Becker Dress Factory once stood. I was just a young man then, a greenhorn, twenty-three years old and all alone in a strange country. My only friend, Duv Eisenberg, had already proven himself a rogue. I could smell the sweatshop, taste the fear of Lipsky's lash, hear Bettino Rossi's detached commentary, and see the faces of the girls who lost their lives in the factory fire that awful day. And I felt Julia Sorvino. They were awful days except for her. At that moment, I would have given anything to see her again, but it could never happen.

The hardest goodbye was when Sara and I visited Momma's grave. I closed my eyes and said a prayer, begging Momma to forgive me for failing to get Lieb out of Russia. It was the last thing she asked for, and the one thing I couldn't give her. We each placed a pebble on her headstone, and one for Poppa. I would always feel closer to Momma in this cemetery than anywhere else. I still go there to talk to her, and she hears me.

The taxi dropped us off at the new house so early in the June morning little was stirring. Yakira and Isaac carried our old cardboard suitcases up the front steps. Sara's face was impassive, not grim but not smiling either, hiding whatever was going on underneath.

When I unlocked the door, she stepped inside and looked around for the first time at the hallway and barren living room of her new home. Her shoes clanked on the empty polished oak floors as she made a tour, beginning with the upstairs bedrooms. Yakira, Isaac and I trailed up the staircase behind her, the children as eager for Sara's approval as I was. They had both spent time at nearby Coney Island, and to them, fun and beaches went together. They couldn't figure out their mother's absent passion.

"How do you like it?" I asked as Sara inspected the large master bedroom.

"It's nice," was all she would say. She had yet to smile.

We followed her back down the stairs like three lambs, each of us afraid to make a sound to spook her. She stopped at the entrance to the kitchen. The muted morning sun flitted through the window, settling gently on her golden hair and deep blue eyes. She didn't even notice the new ice box, the freshly painted cabinets, or the modern gas stove. Instead, her gaze fixed out the window toward the back yard. An angel must have whispered in her ear because she let out a noise somewhere between a squeal and a screech. She pointed. Her lips unwrapped into a big grin. She ran out the kitchen door, down the steps, and across the still-damp grass toward the back corner by the fence.

She fell to her knees amidst a garden of budding squash, carrots, lettuce, and tomatoes the previous owners had left behind. "Look, Avi, look!" she yelled, embracing the plants in her hands. "A garden. Just like back home." She ran her fingers through the dark earth and raised a handful to her nose as if inhaling the scent of the black soil of the Russian plain.

She threw her arms around me and kissed me hard. "We're going to be very happy here," she said.

When Ester and Sadie arrived later in the morning, she led them first to her garden. All she talked about was the borscht she was going to make from the beets, the horseradish from the radishes, and the bouquets from the roses and daffodils.

After that, the garden became a place where Sara went to work her hands in the soil, meditate and communicate with the divine. She also grew enough vegetables to fill a large root cellar. I wondered then and still wonder why I have been given so much. No dreams of my youth included such a good women and such abundance.

That first week we were exhausted by the end of every day from unpacking and setting up our new home. By the second week we were ready to discover a little bit of Manhattan Beach. Sara fell in love with the ocean, just like Markus said she would. We started taking long walks along the beach carrying our shoes in one hand and holding hands with the other. Sara always had to stick her feet in the water, the gentle lap of the waves splashing her ankles. The only time she didn't do it was in the cold rain or winter's freeze.

That Saturday night we went to the moving pictures to see the new Douglas Fairbanks film. Sara clutched my arm all through the show and all the way home. When we got home, she hung up her coat on the tree in the entry, took off her shoes, and beckoned me with a seductive finger as she climbed the stairs. Her face was covered in mischief, as though she owned a spicy secret she was about to share.

She took off her clothes and presented herself to me like she did the first night we were married. A little child-bearing paunch and etchings around her eyes made her more inviting than a virgin. As my eyes ate her up, I worried the rest of me might be getting too old to respond adequately. But that night Sara did things I never guessed were possible. When we were done, she was very pleased with herself. It didn't happen as often as it used to, but I was very satisfied when it did. We fell asleep in each other's arms, fully sated.

Until now, Sara would never spend money on anything but second hand furniture, second hand shoes, second hand pots and most anything else. She couldn't remove the tattoo of poverty she grew up with, or trust we would have ample food for the next Sabbath. But something good was happening to her, a birth of some sort. She let Ester take her to buy a new household: a spindly legged cherry telephone table for the entryway, a big mahogany buffet in the dining room, an overstuffed blue velour sofa, and pictures of Grecian urns and flowers for the walls. That was enough for now. She wouldn't even consider replacing our tired old bed from the East Harlem apartment. "It has too much experience," she laughed.

Her clothes changed. Now she wore whatever colored dresses were fashionable, but always modest. Stylish pumps replaced her laced oxford shoes. She studied pictures of Mary Pickford, and when she saw something she liked, she asked me if I could make it for her. But she had her limits. With the daring new styles, many women her age showed their bare arms. Sara couldn't.

Finally, she cut her hair short and started wearing close fitting cloche hats that resembled upside down buckets. She looked adorable. The fashion enhancement I enjoyed most was when she modeled her first brassiere for me, one of the new modern-style Nemo-flex. No wonder men still gawked when they saw Sara for the first time. She never noticed their hungry stares.

Sara also stopped speaking Yiddish about then, even when we were alone at home. The only time she relapsed was when an emotional tempest, good or bad, strained the limits of her English.

With all of her new daring, Sara refused to don the immodest bathing suits now in style. At first the Manhattan Beach police chased women wearing these form-fitting outfits from the sands, Yakira and her friends among them. But women who had just won the right to vote weren't about to back down. After some unwanted publicity, law enforcement officials surrendered.

I can't explain the change in Sara. It could have been the village life of Manhattan Beach and the ocean. Russian Jews dominated the town, but they all seemed as liberated from their past as I was. Perhaps it was because for the first time in her life there were no Hassidic men around in their severe black cloaks and dreadlocks ready to judge her and remind her of her disapproving father.

One thing didn't change: Sara kept her unshakeable reverence for God and her obligation to honor Him. Every Friday evening she lit the candles and said the prayers, holding the palms of her hand over the flames. She insisted Yakira and Isaac show up for Friday's chicken. They came without objection. She preferred kosher restaurants, but conceded to a trip to Devito's Seafood Shack in Sheepshead Bay or a dinner at a nice Manhattan restaurant; she ordered only fish with gills to satisfy her conscience. The rest of the year she scrupulously observed the rituals of every holiday from Passover to Purim, Rosh Hashonnah to Tish'a B'Av, and even the little festivals only she and Rabbi Daniel seemed to remember.

The biggest surprise was when Sara began to read an occasional novel, an interest she reserved for comic books before then. We both followed Scott and Zelda Fitzgerald's opulent, untamed lives like everyone else did. Most days she grabbed Walter Winchell's gossip column in the Daily Mirror before I could lay my hands on it. Zelda Fitzgerald's promiscuous ways reminded me of my sister Zelda in her younger days. When I read about one Zelda, I sometimes saw the other. I found myself missing my little sister. So I phoned her more often.

Daniel got his new congregation in Sheepshead Bay, but not until the spring of 1925. Rain or shine, I walked the ten blocks from the house or the shop whenever I needed a private visit with my friend. As time went by, I felt less and less connected to the god I grew up with. Maybe it was our prosperous lives, or the desperation of Lieb's. Or maybe it was a desire to be wholly American, no different from Christian Americans. Nonetheless, I still clung to the comfort of the rituals and the rightness of His commandments.

Daniel brought his old rocking chair with him, refinished as well as it could be. It didn't blend well with the polished mahogany desk, plush Persian rug, and dark wainscoting of his spacious office, but it bore witness to his less affluent past. The first time I visited him in the new place, I found him seated behind his desk studying the draft of his first sermon. His hair was gray now, and his moustache gone. Eyeglasses were a necessity.

"You've come a long way from that first store front synagogue," I said.

"Sometimes I felt God there more among those poor, desperate men than any time since," he answered. I felt the same way.

Hannah completed Sara. Now the old card game could resume as it did back in East Harlem. The four women tried to include Miryem, but after a few tries she stopped coming and they stopped inviting her. Nevertheless Miryem, Josef and Henry were included in everything the family did. She and Sara were too different to be close, though Sara wanted to be. Miryem and Josef loved each other, and that was the important thing. She stopped biting her fingernails, but a cigarette still dangled from her lips most of the time. The whole family adopted Henry. He was a polite, pleasant boy.

Manhattan Beach was so full of Russian Jews it was becoming a Russian village. Still I was astonished to find a couple of people in our synagogue who I knew from years ago in Uman – Moishe Stepaner and Chiam Chernoff. I had gone to school with them. We had fought together and shared fear on the barricades that night in 1905 the *pogrom*ists came to kill us. But we had little else in common back in Uman and we still didn't here in Manhattan Beach.

They spread exaggerated tales of my deeds the night of the *pogrom*, which always climaxed with my shooting Viktor Askinov. That came in handy when I tried raising money for the Anti-Defamation League or support for the Jews in Palestine. Few men in our congregation and that end of Brooklyn had the nerve to turn me down. After all, I was the hero of Uman and a cold killer none dare cross.

Otherwise, the night I shot Viktor Askinov had become a night I would just as soon forget. These days I thought about it less and less, and usually only when I received a letter from Lieb talking about the Cripple. It wasn't who I was any more. In America I didn't need to summon that kind of courage.

The Roaring 20's were a great time to be alive. I had more money in my pocket than I ever imagined. Sara was at last brave enough and interested enough to venture into Manhattan to see the Ziegfeld Follies. She clapped when Eddie Cantor pranced across the stage, snorted out loud at Will Rogers, and sang along with Fannie Brice when she belted out Second Hand Rose. On our next trip to the city, we were among the first to see Al Jolson in the first talking moving picture, the

Jazz Singer. Sara cried.

By the second year we had to hire five new people in the tailor shop, three men and two women. We became known for our fine craftsmanship and for pleasing our customers. I designed elegant collections for sale to a few exclusive boutique stores in the city.

My old and best customer from East Harlem, Mrs. Schulman, had protested when I moved, vowing never to see me again. But she changed her mind. She and a few of her friends made a holiday of their twice-annual trips to Manhattan Beach for some new outfits and to be pampered at the spa of one of the expensive beach hotels.

I kept asking Markus to come back to the tailor shop. We needed him. But he contented himself with his work in the Brooklyn Bank. The bank's owner, Edmund Hill liked having a Jew working with his money. "Jews'll turn a nickel into a dollar. Gentiles'll turn a dollar into a nickel." Mr. Hill's prejudices didn't bother Markus; I didn't like it. Hill was happy to have a Jew deposit his money in his Brooklyn Bank, but if a Jew asked for a loan, he told him to "go to the Jew bank," the United States Bank in Manhattan.

For our anniversary that August, I planned a special night in the city at the elegant old Waldorf Astoria on Fifth Avenue, where the Empire State Building is now. It was the first time we stayed overnight in a hotel alone since our wedding night.

I wore a tuxedo for the first time ever. Sara looked stunning in her black crepe evening dress, a simple gold chain and small rosebud earrings her only adornments. I caught a glimpse of us in a long mirror as we walked down the hallway at the Waldorf. We looked as fabulously elegant as Scott Fitzgerald and Zelda. When we were all dressed up, she was no longer the young Hassidic girl I had married, and I wasn't so much the middle aged man with the graying hair and expanding waist.

At a time when we were usually going to bed, we grabbed a taxi and headed for T. T. Kelly's. Tommy's speakeasy had a big reputation as an elegant place frequented by Broadway stars, gossip columnists, politicians, and gangsters. Sara hoped she would catch a glimpse of someone famous. I wasn't sure this was the place for Sara, but she was eager, and I missed Thomas Kelly. I hadn't seen him in nearly five years.

When we walked in, he was where he always was, wiping the big mahogany bar. He had gotten older in those five years, with bountiful gray hair and deep wrinkles creeping into his handsome face.

"My goodness. And look who the devil's dug up," he said when he saw me. "My heavens, laddie, I thought you were dead and in your grave. And who is this gorgeous lady?"

"You haven't lost any of your Irish blarney," I said, grasping his outstretched hand in both of mine.

"I'm Sara, this lucky man's wife," she laughed, putting out her gloved hand to shake his. Her twinkle captured Thomas. When Sara went to the powder room, I asked him about Duv. I hadn't seen my childhood friend in a very long time. I still mourned my loss a little.

"He comes in here now and then," Thomas said, serious for the moment. "He usually has a lassie or two in hand. He hangs around with a rough crowd, if you get my meaning."

I nodded. Stories about Duv got back to me. Some said he was into the numbers racket. Others said it was moonshine. Either way, it spoke ill of him.

When he saw Sara returning, Thomas leaned toward me. "He keeps this up and he's good as gone," he said. "They'll kill him."

In the spring of 1927, Isaac graduated from City College, the first Schneider to do so. I have to admit, at times like this I took some credit for my obsession to leave Russia. If I hadn't, my life would have turned out like Lieb's, and my family would have suffered for it.

After graduation, Isaac got a good job with one of the Jewish accounting firms in Manhattan. The gentile ones still weren't hiring our kind. Babe Ruth hit sixty home runs that year, and my Yankees won another world series. That same year Lindberg flew across the Atlantic all alone and became the most admired hero in America. We all cheered him. Who knew then what a Jew-hater he was?

The stock market kept going up and up. I was making good money like everyone else. Stock tips came from all over: Simon, Markus, Moishe Stepaner, my butcher, and even the guy who owned the newsstand near the Brighton Beach subway entrance. Everyone had a hot tip, and many of them paid off.

The summer of 1929 was the last of easy times. We didn't know it, of course. Everyone believed these good times would go on forever. Yakira married Jake that June, to my great relief. We had been so worried about her. She was twenty-five years old and still hadn't found a husband. But when she did, she found the right one.

Jake Gross had the big paws of a butcher, and someday would take over his father's kosher shop in the Bronx. He didn't thrill me the first time I met him. Yakira brought him down to Manhattan Beach to spend a weekend with us. He never stopped talking. He knew everything about everything. He had a puffy face to go with the rest of his body, and he walked around the house in bare feet and a sleeveless undershirt, his hairy chest flowing out the top.

But Jake always had a smile, and when I got to know him I learned he was a good, decent, generous man who would do anything to make our daughter happy. During the difficult times that were in store for us, Jake was the one always ready to help any of the family who needed it. I waited eagerly for Yakira and Jake to give us our first grandchild, but it never happened. It wasn't because they didn't try. They talked every now and then about adopting. One time they almost got a pair of twins. That never happened either, and the time passed. Yakira was made to be a mother, like Momma. I wondered what God was thinking when he denied her a child.

Yakira's wedding should have been enough good fortune for one year. But that was also the summer Isaac brought Tillie home for us to meet. Sara and I fell in love with her. They met one weekend on the boardwalk in Brighton Beach, next door to Manhattan Beach. Tillie was from the Bronx and worked in Manhattan not far from Isaac. They started seeing each other regularly.

She had gone to City College for two years and now worked as a stenographer for a lawyer. She loved reading books and talking about them. She read all of Hemmingway and Sinclair Lewis.

Tillie was adorable. Maybe it was the look on her face that said she enjoyed being with us. Or maybe it was the tender looks she gave Isaac. She had that olive Mediterranean skin, walnut hair, and dazzling dark eyes. Her pointed Sephardic nose added a touch of glamour.

When she said goodbye she gave Sara and me a big hug and a warm kiss on the cheek. She promised she would see us again. The moment they left, Sara and I started to gossip.

"She's wonderful. Wonderful!" Sara yelped, clapping her hands together.

"No wonder Isaac went after her."

"He's going to marry her," she bubbled.

"Hey, they just met. Isaac says her father's not crazy about his daughter dating an Ashkenazi."

"And what's so wonderful about the Sephardics?"

There's never a bad time to fall in love, but they could have picked a better one. Tillie's father would be the least of their problems.

CHAPTER TWENTY-FIVE

August 1929

We thought no one could be worse than the Tsar, until Lenin. The new Soviet dictator slaughtered tens of thousands of innocents, Jew and gentile, with no attempt to conceal his indiscriminate murders. The radical changes he envisioned for Russia demanded the people understand resistance was hopeless. My brother was not political, but still I worried for him.

In the wink of an eye, the government seized factories and abolished private property. Churches and synagogues were desecrated, their property confiscated, and clergy brutalized. From the safety of America, the violence in Russia seemed like wanton bloodlust, though some sympathizers in our press tried to justify it. Just when we thought no one could be worse than Lenin, he died and Josef Stalin succeeded him. That was in 1924.

Lieb first started inserting coded messages in his letters in 1927 or 1928. I'm not sure which. Stalin's paranoia about spies and counter-revolutionaries motivated a suffocating censorship on the whole country. I imagine my letters got in and Lieb's got out because of the money I sent. Soviet authorities would have preferred no contact with foreigners, but they needed the foreign currency.

My brother was clever. He constructed his code from a conglomeration of Russian, Hebrew, Yiddish, biblical references, and childhood memories. When combined with his illegible, left-handed scrawl, his messages would have confused even the most patient Soviet censor. It must have taken two years and more than ten letters back and forth for me to figure it all out.

There were times in the early Stalin years when Lieb seemed a little hopeful, though he continued to mourn his daughter Brindyl. Russia was changing, even if he wouldn't take advantage of it. He said as much in one of his letters.

Many Jews have moved out of our town, eager to be a part of the new world the Communists are creating. There are better jobs in the big cities. Chiam Shapiro's son moved to Moscow and Boruch Ramberg's son to Petrograd. I hear Ramberg's son has married a Christian, but that is not so unusual any more. If you join the Communist Party, you're not going to be a Jew, or any religion for that matter. Some Jews have become atheists even if they're not Communists. I don't understand it.

Many of the younger people are giving up Yiddish. They only want to speak Russian. So Golde and I speak Russian to Shaina and Joshua, but we still speak Yiddish to each other. When I think of Momma, Poppa, and Uncle Yakov – may the Almighty bless their souls – I think of them only in Yiddish.

There are fewer and fewer synagogues now. I fear ours will be next to close. But we have Jewish doctors, lawyers, government officials, business people, writers, and even Jewish army officers. That's something.

All of this change is difficult to keep up with some times. I pray it will lead to a better life for Shaina and Joshua. Golde and I ask for only enough to eat and a chance to worship as we see fit. The Soviet constitution guarantees us that right, but it gets harder.

I sit at the sewing machine by the window in the tailor shop and look out across the old market square. At times I can feel Poppa and you there beside me. When the day ends I go home, Golde greets me with a hug and a kiss like Momma used to greet Poppa. We sit down to eat at the old dining table. I see you, Uncle Yakov, Markus, Ester and Zelda around the table, and I am comforted. Those were wonderful days. But I am blessed with a good daughter in Shaina and a good son in Joshua. Shaina is twenty-one years old now, and quite attractive. She will find a man soon, I'm sure. Joshua wants to be called Yuri. He says Joshua is a Jewish name and he wants to be Russian like everyone else.

You may like to know our good friend Gersh Leibowitz is now supreme leader of the Kiev Gibernya Jewish Workers Council. This is an important job for the entire district, including Uman. I don't see him much anymore. Sergey is now a favorite of the Communists and I see him all of the time. He is very helpful.

The New York newspapers carried stories of churches and synagogues being destroyed all across Russia. The piles of splintered Orthodox icons reached higher than the piles of tortured Torahs. Authorities confiscated all prayer books and burned them. They turned our old synagogue into a shoe factory. Lieb wrote me when it closed. His sentimental letter recalled our school days, our teacher Jeremiah, the Shamash, and our Rabbi Rosenberg.

I still put on my tallis and tefillin and pray at home. It is only open worship that is forbidden. Joshua wanted a bar mitzvah. So we did it in the house with barely enough men for a minyan. We only had nine Jews so we borrowed Sergey Shumenko. The Soviets outlawed the study of Hebrew, but Joshua learned enough Hebrew words to read a few prayers and a small passage from the Torah. It is enough. He is a Jew. Now he and I sometimes go to Sukhi Yar on nice days, to the clearing in the woods where we used to play. That beautiful, quiet place is our synagogue. All of the wildflowers have grown back since the famine.

Sometimes I sit by myself under the oak tree in front of the old synagogue and contemplate the Almighty. One time when a policeman stopped and asked what I was doing staring at the sky, I told him I thought I saw an image of Comrade Stalin in one of the clouds. He liked that and praised me for my dedication to our great leader.

Letters from Lieb came less frequently after Stalin took over, and in between letters I could almost forget I still had a brother in Russia. Then another letter arrived, and I was yanked back. Sometimes I resented him for not coming to America when he had the chance. I told myself he made his pot and he could cook in it. The next minute I was creating impossible schemes to get him out. But they were nothing but daydreams and I knew it. The ache for my brother lasted for days after one of his letters, sometimes longer. Then it faded, along with my guilt.

It must have been the summer of 1929 when Lieb sent that picture of himself, Golde, Shaina, and Joshua. The snapshot was well-posed in a flowering field, maybe at Sukhi Yar. I spent hours looking at it, examining every detail with a magnifying glass.

I was confused at first. I couldn't believe the old man in the picture with the big smile on his face was my brother. His hair was completely gray and not much of it. He looked thin and fragile, but then Lieb never was a big man. What confused me was the young man in the picture, Joshua. He looked exactly like Lieb looked at that age, with black moppy hair, parted on the right, falling down over his left eye. After the camera clicked, I imagined him lifting his left hand to push the mop back, out of his eyes, just like Lieb used to do. My brother as I remembered him was in Joshua, not the old man.

Golde smiled from the picture, now thin except for her big bosom. I remembered her as round and plump as a stuffed pillow. Their daughter was pretty, much like Zelda, but severe and unsmiling. She looked

like the good Communist Lieb said she was. They all had their arms
around each other revealing a closeness one could not pose. I sent him
another picture of our family by return mail. I tried not to brag about
how well we had it in America. And I kept from him the truth about
the restrictions, insults, and anti-Semitism we still dealt with.

Lieb was as proud of Shaina and Joshua as I was of Yakira and Isaac.
Shaina wanted to be a teacher. She first joined the Young Pioneers and
then, when she was older, Komsomol. Lieb said she went around singing the latest patriotic songs all of the time. When Stalin rose to
power, she became a disciple. In her eyes, Stalin could do no wrong.

Joshua admired his big sister and followed in her footsteps, though
Lieb implied Joshua never let go of a piece of Judaism born in him. He
became a Komsomol member in 1927 like most of the other young
people, tasked with spreading Communism to worker and peasant
youth. He was soon voted secretary of his Komsomol unit.

Many Jews have left Uman for other parts of Russia, Lieb wrote in
early 1928. *Of those still here, you would hardly know they were Jews
any more. They speak Russian. They dress like Russians, and so many of
them marry Russians, soon you won't be able to tell a Jew from a gentile.*
Joshua and Shaina had both Jewish and Russian friends; Lieb claimed
they didn't face anti-Semitism any more in school or at work. I sensed
my dear brother was trying to prepare me or himself for something.

That very summer he wrote to say his daughter Shaina had married
her Russian boyfriend, a young man named Dmitri Baikov. He was a
manager in a small local glass factory. There was no wedding ceremony. They simply went to the registration office, filled out some forms,
and began living together as husband and wife. They were both good
Communists, so this is the way it had to be. With housing still in short
supply, the newlyweds moved in with Lieb and Golde.

In the following six years, Shaina gave birth to three girls: Perle,
Arina, and Kalina. There was no doubt Lieb and Golde showered their
little granddaughters with love, and tried to give them something of
their Jewish legacy without offending Dmitri and Shaina. Golde lit
candles every Sabbath for a long time. She only stopped later when

she was very afraid, and they didn't have any money for candles.

Joshua, Shaina and the grandchildren joined Lieb and Golde for Sabbath dinners and celebrations of Jewish holidays, even if they didn't believe entirely. All of them devoured Golde's chicken, gefilte fish, and matzo strudel. Dmitri often exited to the local tavern at such times.

Not long after Shaina married Dmitri the government launched the NKVD – the state police and the secret police – to directly execute Stalin's terror. One of their missions was to extinguish religion through force and fear. They liquidated Zionist organizations and exiled thousands to Siberia. New edicts mandated everyone work on the Sabbath, Saturday for Jews and Sunday for Christians. The Communists feared all religions, and the NKVD played no favorites.

I wanted to scream when Lieb repeated Soviet propaganda about America, but just when I thought my brother had been completely taken in by the lies, his true thoughts came through. The sorrowful letter about Brindyl arrived sometime before the second famine. I don't remember exactly when.

> I find Brindyl on my mind more and more. My heart aches. I dare not talk to Golde about our departed daughter. It only brings her more pain. Our little girl has now been gone eight years, but it gets no easier. I only thank the Lord she has been spared so much of the torment. She was such a sweet, gentle girl who delighted in all things Jewish. She loved to help Golde with the preparations for Hanukkah or Pesach – the cooking, the cleaning, washing the floors. It made no difference to her. She could recite the prayers over the Sabbath candles better than Momma used to do. She was only sixteen, not yet fully a woman, when the Lord took her. I miss my little girl so much my heart is breaking.
>
> Forgive me for burdening you, my dear brother, with my troubles. I have nowhere else to turn since they chased off all the rabbis. Couldn't they have left us just one? Uncle Yakov used to

say "You can't run away from the Devil, and you can't bargain with him." Our uncle was a wise man.

    As they say, if you lie down with fleas, you get bitten. I have been bitten over and over again. My whole family has been bitten. Havol's whole family. I suppose every nation has its good and bad people. Why should ours be any different? But the Ukraine is my country. I chose to stay here and now I must live with it.

    All I want is to spend my days on earth with my God, Golde and my children close to me. Is it too much to ask that I be allowed to put on my tallis and tefillin, and say a few prayers once in awhile with ten other Jews?

    And when my days near an end, I will still raise my eyes to the sky and say Sh'ma Yisraeil Adonai Eloheinu Adonai Echad. Hear, O Israel, the Lord is our God, the Lord is one. *Thank the Almighty you and your family are safe in America.*

In less than ten years, the Communists destroyed what had survived for two thousand years of Jewish exile. How could that be?

"He's given up," I said to Daniel after telling him about Lieb's latest letter. "The things he writes are more and more reckless. It's dangerous." We had just finished our Sunday morning poker game in the synagogue annex. I won a nice little bundle again. The other men had gone, leaving Daniel and me to clean up the last of the lox and bagel Hannah brought over.

"We are blessed here in America," Daniel answered.

"Where is God? Why isn't He fighting back?"

"Don't blame it all on God," Daniel answered. "He gave us free will. Lieb had the same choices you had. You know it and he knows it. That's what haunts you both."

But more trials were still to come and Lieb would need his faith to get through them. There was nothing I could do about it but pray for him, at a time when my own faith was brittle.

Sometimes Lieb's letters dragged me down, and sometimes they burned me up. "Why does he always have to write about Viktor Askinov?" I snapped at Sara, slapping Lieb's latest one on the kitchen table. "I'm getting sick of it."

Sara washed the last of the dishes and stacked them on the drain board. Dinner's fried onions basted the air. The taste of the liver they covered lingered on my tongue. "So who should he talk to, the sky?" she asked. "Not Golde. You Schneider men protect your women."

"Listen to this." I read my brother's letter aloud.

> *Viktor Askinov and I are comrades. He always calls me Comrade Schneider when he comes into the shop to collect the taxes. You know he has been appointed the tax collector for our end of Uman. He is a cunning man who owes his allegiance to Satan, not Stalin. Now he gets to wear a blue uniform with red stars on the lapels. All he needs is a truncheon and he would look just like his father, the Constable. May worms eat his eyeballs in his grave.*
>
> *I can always tell it's the Cripple coming down the sidewalk by the sound of him dragging that mangled leg behind him. It gives me satisfaction to know you, dear brother, gave him such a souvenir. He brings his brother Olek or his toad, Igor Czajkowsko, with him whenever he pays a visit. Could it be I frighten him? I can't imagine. I think he just wants an audience to witness his spite. Not everyone gets the honor of a personal visit from the tax collector. Such an honor I would just as soon do without.*
>
> *The government keeps raising taxes on the tailor shop. It's now so high it may soon be impossible to keep it open. Business is not good for a little shop like ours. I may lose it in any event. I had a visit from the local NKVD. I am certain it was Viktor Askinov who put me under suspicion. They accused me of being a bourgeois because I own a tailor shop. Even worse, I have brothers and sisters in America. I called our old friend Gersh Leibowitz. He stopped anything more from happening for now,*

but the Cripple won't give up, and I can't always ask Gersh for help. He is a very important party leader now and hardly has time for me.

Today the Cripple came to tell me of another tax increase. He enjoys my misery, of that I am sure. It is entertainment to him. It also wouldn't surprise me if some of my tax rubles go into his pocket.

You used to say he was the Devil. I used to argue that he was nothing more than a big bully whose father beat meanness into him with his fists and thick leather belt. But now I think you are right. I know of no one more evil.

It's ridiculous to admit it, but even after almost twenty-five years I still hated Viktor Askinov like no other. I couldn't allow him to have his victory. So, the next morning I sent Lieb money to pay the taxes, and promised to send whatever he needed to save the tailor shop.

Then I went back to enjoying my own life. I had never imagined it could be so good. Earlier in the Twenties the banks introduced this thing called consumer credit, and everyone took advantage of it to buy something. It seemed stupid not to. We bought ourselves one of the new electric refrigerators, a washing machine, and an electric iron. Fabulous inventions came along every day to tempt you out of your money. One of them was an underarm deodorant for women; even Sara tried that one. I had liked the way she smelled before just fine, like Ivory Soap.

We lived in a time of permanent prosperity, or so they told us. Our mayor, goodtime Jimmy Walker, insisted everyone go out on the town and have some fun. He made it sound like a civic duty. Most New Yorkers listened to the Mayor.

CHAPTER TWENTY-SIX

September 1929

The summer of 1929 a heat wave gripped New York, but who cared? The stock market kept going up and up in step with the thermometer. Watching the market ticker was a better sport than watching the Yankees chase the Philadelphia Athletics for first place. Whenever I walked into the barbershop, someone yelled out, "How's the market doing?" Everyone was getting rich: school teachers, shoeshine boys, secretaries, garbage collectors, and even tailors.

That summer was also the summer when Sara wore a real bathing suit for the first time. Trips to the beach during the hot days were particularly bothersome for Sara. Seeing all of that skin showing embarrassed her, whether men or women. She feared for the modesty of Yakira and Isaac the first time she saw them in their skimpy one piece bathing suits. For the longest time, she covered up nearly every part of her own body. But the movies brought her along, particularly Mary Pickford. She wanted to look just like her.

So she donned the most modest granny suit she could find; then she hid herself in a big towel until the noonday sun forced her to unwrap. Now approaching fifty years old, Sara was still the most appealing woman on the beach. Her beautiful legs, ample breasts, and gorgeous face drew too many stares and cad whistles for her to ignore. After a quick dip in the bay, she was ready to retreat home. But the next day she ventured out again. And the next bathing suit she bought was less modest. Mary Pickford would have been proud of her, and Douglas Fairbanks interested.

When the summer of 1929 came to an end, we were well set. The house I paid $10,000 for was now worth more than $23,000. Nearly all the rest of my money was in the stock market. Sara, who knew nothing about handling money, pestered me about having all our eggs in one nest. I started feeling edgy too, so I sold about half of it and put the proceeds in our bank account at the Brooklyn Bank.

The stock market started down on a Thursday, October 24, 1929. Then it plunged on Monday and Tuesday. For months and months it went down, then up, then down again. Every time it went down I felt good I had half my money in the bank. And when it bounced up, I felt good I still had half of it in the stock market. I never imagined it could go so low. We thought we were out of the woods when the market rose sharply in April. Then it plunged again. By the time I finally got out entirely, I had lost seventy percent of the half I had left in the market. I was lucky. Those who stayed until the bottom in 1932 lost ninety percent.

It was all my fault, but Sara held no resentment. When I complained, she said "It's done. We can't do anything about it." She was like that, putting the past in the past and moving on.

Mr. Edmund Hill, who owned the Brooklyn Bank where Markus worked, was a cagey and ruthless man. That's why he survived. The gray granite bank was austere, the very image of strength and stability. But inside it was only a small town bank and Mr. Hill a conservative small town banker. He took in money mostly from the savings of the townspeople in Manhattan Beach and Brighton Beach, usually at low interest rates. He lent it out primarily to stable businesses and well-considered home loans. He never got into lending money to people who used stocks as collateral.

The New York Bank of the United States collapsed on December 11,

1930. Everyone panicked, not just in New York but everywhere. They wanted to get their money out of their banks. People were already lined up around the block when Markus got to work that day. But Mr. Hill saw it coming, and stopped the run on his bank. He personally greeted every depositor at the door with a big smile and a handshake. "Come in, come in," he said. "We have all of your money right here, safely kept." This wasn't exactly true but most people didn't under-stand that. These were mostly small depositors, uneducated in the ways of banking. When the depositors entered the bank, they saw a group of tellers and managers sitting at temporary desks in the lobby with piles of money in front of them. Who knows where Mr. Hill got so much cash overnight?

They paid any depositor who wanted his money back in small bills, so when he left he had his pockets and hands stuffed to overflowing. Mr. Hill said goodbye to each depositor, offering to re-deposit their savings whenever they were ready. By late morning many of the men waiting in line changed their minds and decided to leave their money on deposit. Those who withdrew their savings came back a few days later to put it back in their accounts.

Markus had worked for Edmund Hill now for seven years, but Hill still didn't know anything about him except what he saw of him at the bank. He greatly admired Markus's special skill with numbers and the way he dealt with people. By the time the panic arrived, Markus man-aged all of the tellers and five or six others. Even in these treacherous times, he had the most secure job in all of New York City, he thought.

Then one morning, a few days after the panic at the Brooklyn Bank, Markus tapped on the window of the tailor shop. I looked up from the evening dress I was working on, surprised to see him. He should have been at work by now. His face looked like he had just been chased by Frankenstein. He motioned frantically for me to join him outside. I grabbed my overcoat and hurried out.

Markus guided me to the entrance to the alley that ran alongside the tailor shop. His face was as pale as a bleached sheet.

"I lost my job," he said. "Fired."

"What?"

He grabbed his stomach, turned his head away from me and vomited, splattering his black wing tips. He turned to speak but wretched again, this time splattering the front of his coat.

I handed him my handkerchief, then took him by the arm and led him deeper into the alley, away from the puddled vomit. The warm morning sun beat on the peeling yellow paint of the hardware store across the alley from the tailor shop. "What happened?"

Markus composed himself as best he could. "Hill fired every Jew in the bank, the nine of us. All he said was Jews knew better than anyone how to make a dollar, and we'd do just fine. He said Christians had no such advantage."

The way Markus described it, nothing in Hill's manner suggested he felt even a little sympathy for the people he put out on the street. Their paychecks stopped at the close of the day, and there was no unemployment insurance back then. Markus looked at me with panicked eyes, pleading for his brother to fix it. I stepped back, afraid he was going to throw up again.

Markus was the most responsible person imaginable, determined to provide for Sadie and his children. Now this. I didn't know how I was going to do it, but I had to find a place for him in the tailor shop. Our income had plummeted by now. Still, I couldn't leave my brother out on the streets selling apples. I assured him I wasn't going to let that happen.

After a brief conference with Manny, we agreed Markus would rejoin us as a full partner. He would pay us back when he could. At first splitting the income with Markus put a big drain on our own shriveling means. Sara assured me we would make do with what we had. She squeezed every penny out of our weekly budget, except for the Sabbath's Friday night chicken. She also comforted Sadie and tended to Markus's sense of humiliation.

Markus appreciated what Manny and I did for him, and wasn't afraid to say so. He was happy to be back tailoring. "Sadie says I just had to grow up to realize I'm as much a tailor as any Schneider." One of the first things he did was organize the bins of threads by color, the buttons by size, and the bolts of material by weight. We needed it. And Manny again enjoyed teasing him by mixing them all up when he wasn't looking. But where before it frustrated Markus, now he took it in good humor, laughing along with us. Then he put everything back in its proper place.

Markus earned his keep all during those hard times. My little brother was creative and industrious. He figured even in a depression people needed newer clothes sometimes. So he bought up used clothes cheaply, and then with a little imaginative tailoring turned them into nice garments people could buy for not much money. He began selling them on racks in front of the tailor shop, then on consignment through Simon's Brighton Beach dry goods store.

Simon himself had to close five of his seven stores, but hung on to the ones in East Harlem and Brighton Beach until things began to turn around. He was a good man. As long as he was able, he extended credit to everyone who needed it even when he knew they were not likely to pay him back.

Everyone in our congregation held together during the Great Depression, better than most. Those who had any income helped those who didn't. Daniel made sure of it. But that doesn't mean there weren't Jewish families evicted from their houses, just like the gentiles. Many ended up living in tents and huddled around camp fires in the dead of winter. I tried not to look. Eventually they became invisible.

People were desperate for anything that would produce a dollar. At first I was embarrassed when I met an acquaintance near the steps to the subway selling pencils, used kitchen utensils, or second hand clothes. Some sold their own households, a piece at a time. After a few years, no one was embarrassed any more. We had breadlines and soup kitchens right in Manhattan Beach. A shanty town of derelicts cropped up under the elevated subway in Brighton Beach. The police would chase them away, but they'd just find another place in town.

The worst moment came when I found myself eye to eye with

Charlie Klein, one of the men I had let go from the tailor shop. He bared his teeth like a mad dog about to attack me. His wife was holding the hand of a little boy, their son presumably. She grabbed Charlie's forearm with the other and turned him away. I wished he had hit me. The next day I found him and gave him a few dollars. He took the money but refused to say thank you. How could you blame him?

Business at the tailor shop took more downturns. Even Mrs. Schulman wasn't coming in as often. And I still had to send money to Lieb and Havol. Both of Daniel's sons lost their jobs at one point. To keep his store open, Simon had to cut back so far on the merchandise it looked like an unoccupied warehouse.

Money was tight for several years, but we got by better than most, though there was once when we thought we might lose the house. Sara and I still took walks on the beach, sometimes with Isaac or Yakira, sometimes just the two of us. I liked it best in the late fall and early spring when we were the only ones there. Sara and I read books, listened to our radio shows, and saw an occasional movie to entertain ourselves until the worst passed. We rarely went into Manhattan any more. On occasion I found some spare change to take Josef's stepson, Henry, to a baseball games at Ebbets Field. The Brooklyn Robins changed their name to the Brooklyn Dodgers about then. Still they lost.

The Depression destroyed many families. I myself look back now and don't remember that time as being as awful as it was. For us, it might have been the trial of those years that brought Sara and me so close. Sara was strong. She accepted whatever came our way, good or bad. But I always felt I had let her down, not providing for her as well as I should have.

On a warm evening in June of 1930 Isaac told us he wanted to marry Tillie. Her father was a prosperous, arrogant Sephardic Greek. He didn't much like Ashkenazim – those of us from Russia. So he didn't like Isaac. He made them wait to get engaged until Isaac earned enough for a proper engagement ring, a near-impossibility given the

Depression. Isaac wouldn't be deterred. In a year he had enough to buy Tillie a full karat diamond.

In spite of his feelings about Isaac, Tillie's father loved his daughter and wanted her to have a high-class wedding. He passed out invitations as though he was printing money. More than two hundred people filled the temple on the Grand Concourse in the Bronx that cold afternoon in January 1932. It snowed for days before, but on this day the sun melted the sidewalks by late morning.

It was a good thing we were in the front row so people couldn't see me crying. This magnificent synagogue was so different from the pitiful Hassidic synagogue in Uman where Sara and I were married. I could still see her smiling at me that day just the way Tillie smiled at Isaac now. We loved Tillie and Tillie loved us. Sara squeezed my hand and sniffled.

A couple of years later Isaac left his safe accounting job and started a business with cousin Willy, a garment factory making children's clothes. Tailoring was in his Schneider blood, he told me. "Even in a Depression, parents are going to buy their kids clothes," he reasoned. I gave him a little money to get started and so did Simon. Tillie's father provided most of the investment.

Isaac asked me to join them as a partner. He said they needed my help with designing. I couldn't, but I did design a few things for them now and then. The only bad thing about it was they opened up in the little industrial town of Berkinbury, about two hours north of the city by train. Isaac said they had to do it there to get the cheap labor they needed to make a go of it. That didn't sit well with his Uncle Josef, now a leader in the local ironworkers' union.

There were only a handful of Jews in Berkinbury. Sara worried he would forget he was Jewish. But it made me think at last a Schneider had escaped the *shtetl*. He was a full American.

The next year, Tillie had a little girl. They named her Rose, after Momma. She looked so much like Sara: the golden hair, the soft blue eyes, and the way she crinkled her nose when she laughed. She loved her Grandpa Avi and Grandma Sara. Max, who came along three years later, was smart, like his mother and father. They named him after Poppa.

The Depression never seemed to reach its terrible hand into T. T. Kelley's. Whenever I had to run into mid-town on business I tried to stop by for a beer or a shot. As soon as Roosevelt took office in 1933, he repealed Prohibition. Booze was legal again. Thomas remodeled the front and back into one big bar and restaurant with a small jazz band on Tuesday and Friday nights. The long bar from the Kinsale Tavern, now refurbished many times over, still ran along one wall. Thomas was always glad to see me, ready to give me free drinks or dinner. Whatever gloom and doom there was outside, there was none inside. Those who had money, and there were more than a few, came to T. T. Kelly's.

This one particular day was hot and muggy. So many panhandlers begging or selling pencils turned the once-fun city into a dismal place. But Thomas's place was half-full even at two o'clock in the afternoon. A Negro piano player tendered a quiet set of Gershwin. I strolled up to the bar as usual and greeted Thomas. Deeper etches crossed his warm smiling face every time I saw him. He probably said the same thing about me.

He nodded toward a dark corner. "Your old friend's here," he said as he poured me a shot of his good Scotch from the bottle under the bar.

"What old friend?" I turned in the direction of his gesture.

Duv sat in a red velvet booth with one arm around a skinny blond flapper to his right and the other arm around a bosomed brunette who displayed her assets. They looked like children wearing their mothers' bright red lipstick and overgenerous makeup.

More than a decade had passed since I'd last seen Duv. I might not have recognized him with his slicked back hair and pencil mustache if it wasn't for his infectious cackle that still pronounced life a big joke. As soon as he saw me, he unwrapped himself from the women and sauntered over to the bar. I didn't know what to expect. Was this an old friend, a foe, or a stranger?

"My friend," he said, sticking out his manicured pink hand for me to shake. He gripped with authority, a manufactured smile on his still-handsome face. Thomas poured him a drink from the same bottle of Scotch mine came from, and then moved to the other end of the bar to cater to two other swells.

Duv pulled out a gold cigarette case from his inside pocket, re-moved one, and lit it with a classy black enameled lighter. There was a Depression on, but you'd never know it looking at Duv. Elegant black and white wingtips topped off his richly tailored gray gabardine suit. A gold wristwatch hugged his wrist, and a diamond pinky ring encir-cled his manicured little finger.

We made small talk for a few minutes, staying away from reminis-cences, and making insincere inquiries about each other's families. While we talked, his eyes scanned back and forth across the room. Maybe it was my too-active imagination, but rumors of Duv's involve-ment with Meyer Lansky's gang suggested he might be alert to an unexpected assault from a rival organization. He made me nervous.

We didn't have much to talk about. "I'd better go," I said after a po-lite interval. "It looks like your lady friends are missing you." He glanced over at the red velvet booth. His two floozies giggled and waved at us with their white gloved hands.

He nodded in their direction. "Want one of them? Take your pick."

"No thanks."

"Still a Boy Scout. You don't know what you're missing."

"I like what I have."

Just as I turned to go, he put his hand on my forearm. The painted leer washed from his lips for a moment. "Do you hear from Lieb? How's he doing?" This was genuine.

I gave him a brief version of Lieb's old tribulations and new ones.

"Those fuckin' Communists. We should kill the whole bunch of them." He said it with the menace of a gangster to whom the word "killing" was more than just a slang term. Then the compassionate friend reappeared, the one I used to know.

"I'm sorry to hear it," he said. "Lieb's a good man. Too bad he didn't leave when he had a chance." He pointed a finger at me. "You call me if Lieb ever needs help. Got it?" I nodded and thanked him.

When we separated, we promised to keep in touch, but we both understood that wasn't going to happen. I thought about Duv all the way home on the subway. I don't know if I could have survived the misery of growing up in Uman without him. There were still traces of that mischievous young prankster in the mobster I just met, but the young and the old Duv weren't really the same person. I missed my old friend. But some people change for the worse as they get older, some for the better. And there's nothing you can do about it.

I expected to pick up a newspaper one morning and see where Duv had been killed in a gangland shooting. I already mourned him.

CHAPTER TWENTY-SEVEN

March 1933

Manny closed the door behind him, leaving me alone to brood over my brother's latest letter. Steam hissed through the radiator, pushing back against the last winter freeze of the year.

The flimsy paper rested heavily in my hand. *I've lost the tailor shop,* Lieb wrote. *How can I tell you, dear brother, how ashamed I am? It was our Schneider legacy, yours and Markus' as much as mine. Please forgive me.*

The legacy mattered not at all to me; Lieb's anguish did. He had already suffered more than any man should suffer; first civil war, then famine, the death of his daughter, and now this. The Soviet government stole that shop from him, just as they stole the life and spirit from everyone. Cursing the Bolsheviks did nothing to release my toothless temper.

> *It would have been difficult no matter. But it was Viktor Askinov who got to deliver the death sentence. He sneered like a jackal, pleased by the misery he inflicted. You've seen that look yourself. It can't get any worse.*
>
> *I managed to hide away Poppa's old sewing machine, some-*

where no one will find it. I still used it, right up until the end. I
will use it again when things quiet down. We Schneiders need to
feel the cloth beneath our fingers. It is as much a source of our
strength as Samson's hair was to him.

Lieb went on to say he now had a job in a tannery, working alongside our old friend Shlomo Zilberman. It must have been difficult work
for a man our age. *Golde is my strength,* he wrote. *Thank the heavens*
above our children are grown.

"Don't torture yourself," Ester said when I telephoned her with the
news. "He made his bed. Let him lie down in it." Zelda and Markus
were indifferent, if less harsh in their judgments. I cursed all three of
them for their stone hearts, then apologized. Lieb seemed to be slip-
ping away from them, no matter how hard I tried to hug him close to
all of us. Only Sara understood. She gave me what I needed most: a
shot of whiskey and the warmth of her bosom.

It pained me to write, but I told Lieb it didn't matter that the old
shop was gone. This was a different time from Poppa's. He would
understand. All that mattered was he and Golde should be well. I told
him Markus, Ester, and Zelda felt the same way. I couldn't tell him
they no longer cared one way or the other. To them, Uman was not
something they even wanted to think about any more.

After the shop closed, I increased the amount of money I sent Lieb.
What else could I do? He wouldn't leave. He couldn't leave. And if he
did, where would he go? My country didn't want him or his kind. That
door was shut and locked. So Lieb did what he always did. He accepted his lot, adjusted to it, and put his faith in the coming of the Messiah.
But God wasn't yet done tormenting His most devoted servants.
Sometimes I got angry at God, but what good did it do? Other times it
was just easier to stop believing.

I should have known something strange was happening when Lieb
wrote in the spring of 1933 that he had eaten *some delicious horsemeat*
sausage, just like Momma used to make. It was red and moist. I enjoyed
it. Momma would never have thought to make such *traif,* and Lieb

would never have eaten such unkosher meat if she had.

It wasn't like the famine of the twenties. Even though millions were dying, this time Soviet spokesmen denied there was a famine, daring anyone to challenge them. The story got out anyway. Reports about starvation in Uman appeared first in New York's Yiddish newspapers.

Some said the famine was a consequence of state collectivization of farms. Others said Stalin provoked the famine to stamp out the peasants who opposed the collectivization. The state police shot thousands who resisted or tried to hide grain.

Typhus again hitchhiked on the calamity. Cannibalism spread across the countryside, parents eating their weakest children. Lieb's encoded messages said dogs, cats, frogs, mice, and birds disappeared again, and so did the leaves and bark on the trees.

In Europe, Canada, and America, people tried sending in food, but it was stopped by the Soviets at the border. I sent several large packages of canned goods and other foodstuffs before Lieb told me to stop. It was causing trouble. Instead I sent money, and more money, hoping he could bribe someone. We sent Havol more money too.

Sergey and Valerya Shumenko tried to help Lieb with produce and an occasional animal from their meager supply. But even in his prominent position as director of the tractor factory, Sergey had to watch his step lest his generosity be construed as a treasonous act against the state.

My chest beating only brought tears to Sara, and did no good for Lieb. So when I needed to cry for my brother, I walked down to the sea and screamed into the wind and the waves. So much the better when a thunderstorm cracked lighting off the shore and soaked me.

In the fall of 1933 Lieb wrote in his code to tell me the worst was over.

My son-in-law, Dmitri Andropov, was a godsend. He is a good Communist and would never think a bad thought about Comrade Stalin, but he saw what was happening to people and did what he could to help them. He makes sure we always have enough to eat, such as it is. He is a good boy.

You know I was opposed to Shaina marrying him. Momma and Poppa must have spun around in their graves. Thanks be to the heavens they did not live to see their granddaughter marry a shaygetz – a gentile boy. But now I must admit I love him like a son. He and Shaina have given us the most beautiful grand-daughters, Perle, Arina, and Kalina. It is nice to have them living here with us and get to watch them grow up. Maybe they will even have another. Dmitri says he would like to have a boy, may God answer his prayers. So who knows?

Joshua has joined the Communist Party: We are very proud of him. Usually it takes a year to go from candidate to member, but Joshua was admitted in only eight months. He obtained a recommendation from Gersh, and that helped. Sergey also rec-ommended him.

Still, he answers to the Lord, and takes walks with me to the clearing in the woods at Sukhi Yar. There we both exalt silently in His presence. From the rise you can see the wheat fields stretching to the horizon, turning to gold in the morning sun. Soon the peasants will begin the harvest. At such moments I feel His divine presence and thank Him for leading us through this trial. Let us know peace now and for the rest of our days.

Amen, I said, putting the letter back in its envelope for storage along with all of his other letters. I don't know why I saved them except they were the thread to my dear brother, penned by his hand. Sometimes I smelled them or held them to my cheek just to feel my brother close to me. At moments like that I knew I would see him again. I said a little prayer hoping He would hear me.

That November the United States formally recognized the Soviet Union for the first time. You couldn't say they were friends, but at least my old country and my new country were talking again.

In every letter, no matter how dire his own situation, Lieb was sure to ask about my family, as well as Ester, Markus, and Zelda. He sent his blessings, and worried about us like a good older brother would. The picture the Russian people received of America was what Josef Stalin and his government wanted them to have – a mash of truth, distortions, and lies intended to disparage capitalism. But I couldn't always justify to Lieb the human suffering of our Great Depression any more than he could justify his country's famines.

In the summer of 1934 Lieb's son Joshua graduated from university near the top of his class with a degree in engineering. He went to work in Sergey's tractor factory. A year later he married a Jewess named Leya Tombak. Her family was typical of those assimilated Jews who surrendered their Jewish religion to the new Communist state. He wrote soon after the wedding.

> *Leya is a nice girl and we like her very much. She says that if they have a son he can be circumcised according to our traditions. They registered their marriage in a registry office. It was just a day like any other. There was no ceremony, no celebration. But that weekend they let us put on a small party for them with only close relatives, and a few prayers.*
>
> *Joshua and Leya moved in with us as soon as they were married. We already had Shaina, Dmitri and their three children. It is getting crowded. The house hasn't gotten any bigger since you and I slept in the same bed.*
>
> *I think Shaina is a little jealous because Leya fusses over me and helps Golde with household chores. Shaina should be relieved because she is getting so large even tending to her children is a difficulty. Leya helps with that too. Did I tell you Shaina is going to have a baby? The size of her belly tells me this time I will be blessed with a grandson, praise the Lord. Golde cautions me not to be so certain.*

Not a month later, Lieb wrote to tell me he had a new granddaughter who they named Natalia. *What can I say,* he wrote? *The Lord has chosen to honor me with a fourth granddaughter. I am overjoyed. She is a blessing, healthy and beautiful. You should hear her yell when she is demanding to be fed. Such lungs! I am the only one who can calm her down. When she is done with the tit, I hold her again and she grabs my finger until she falls asleep. I pray the Lord will watch over her and give her a good life.*

Ten months after that Joshua's wife Leya gave birth to still another granddaughter, Lieb's fifth. They named her Rebekah, after Momma. His joy came through in every word he wrote, undiminished by any disappointment at not having a grandson. *The Lord in his wisdom grants me so many blessings. He will give me a grandson in His own time and for His own reasons. I will be patient.*

I finished reading the latest of Lieb's letters and stuck it in my pocket. No matter how much good news he stuffed in it, something told me it couldn't last.

I never told Lieb about the times I thought my own adopted country was turning on me. As we entered 1936, Anti-Semitism infected every corner of America. A growing number of gentiles blamed the Jews for the Depression, inflamed by popular radio commentator Father Charles Coughlin, and others.

Coughlin reached millions of Americans through his broadcasts on CBS. A Catholic priest, he had a built-in audience of believers to whom he railed against an imagined conspiracy of Jewish bankers who caused the Depression. His rhetoric resurrected narratives of Christ's fight with the money lenders in the Temple, and wove in Shakespeare's Shylock as evidence of the treachery inborn in Jews.

Then Coughlin turned around and blamed the Communist takeover of Russia on Jews, a twist in logic and illusion reminiscent of Houdini. But sometimes I thought about Mendel Silber and shuddered. He was a Communist and the type of Jew who gave a grain of validity to Father Coughlin's bigoted charges.

Coughlin praised Hitler and the Nazis. "When we get through with the Jews in America," he said, "they'll think the treatment they received in Germany was nothing." He advocated restrictions on Jews and even suggested Jews be deported just for being Jewish. Legions flocked to his calling. Many politicians fell in line as his influence on their electorates multiplied.

I listened to Coughlin's broadcasts now and then just to hear for myself what he was saying. Sara begged me to stop, but I was like a fly drawn to the spider's web.

From Atlanta to Altoona, many Catholic priests fought to keep Coughlin off their local radio stations. Sometimes they succeeded, but too often the local station owner stood to make too much money to concede. Eventually Coughlin was challenged and brought down by more powerful liberal voices in the Catholic Church, like Cardinal Mundelein of Chicago. But that was some years away. In the meantime, he fertilized fear and hatred.

The German-American Bund aimed another spear at the hearts of Jews. This home-grown organization of Storm Troopers, led by their Fuhrer Fritz Kuhn, recruited a menacing mob of Americans. When I saw newsreels of marching men in their brown Storm Trooper uniforms, I saw Viktor Askinov, and the vision of *pogroms* coming here. A big Madison Square Garden rally a couple of years later drew over twenty thousand American Nazis.

But we fought back against the Bund peacefully, in courts and in public opinion. And we won. Others weren't so peaceful. Newspapers reported instances where men armed with clubs and crowbars attacked columns of Storm Troopers. They didn't report on it when a few of the Bund leaders and troopers were gunned down by Jewish mobsters, ordered by the likes of Meyer Lansky. I heard whispers of it from Josef and wondered if Duv, now one of Lansky's lieutenants, was involved. I hoped he was, but didn't want to know.

In spite of all this, I held fast to my conviction that the number of committed anti-Semites in America was small, despite their loud voices. I wouldn't let the people I loved lose faith in our country. "Hate can't kill hope," Daniel kept preaching.

When threats of physical violence increased, so did Jewish anxieties. It got bad enough by early 1936 that Markus, Josef and a few others urged me to assemble a brigade and be ready to fight. Josef said he could find us weapons, just like Uncle Yakov did.

But I was getting too old for that. My fifty-four years showed in my thinning hair and my widening waistline. Even walks along the beach winded me and made my heart thump. Besides, I couldn't believe it would ever come to that. Not here. Not in America.

PART THREE

GET HIM OUT

CHAPTER TWENTY-EIGHT

JUNE 1936

One sunny June morning Sidney Berman phoned and asked me to join him for a ballgame at Ebbets Field. He had some free tickets and something on his mind.

Sidney was the most politically connected friend I had. He left his job as a banker some time ago and was now a Brooklyn district coordinator for President Roosevelt's re-election campaign. Like many of us, Sidney hero-worshiped FDR because of all the Jews he appointed to important posts in his administration.

The crowd at the ballpark was bigger than what usually turned out to see the pitiful Dodgers. Regardless, Ebbets Field was a great place to spend a dandy of a June afternoon. The St. Louis Cardinals were in town with Leo Durocher, Joe Medwick and the rest of the Gashouse Gang. All during the game, Sidney seemed preoccupied. He hardly noticed when we took an early lead against Dizzy Dean, deaf to the roar of the crowd. He just kept cracking peanuts and stuffing them in his mouth, the pile of shells accumulating at his feet. I waited between innings for him to unload whatever was troubling him. He didn't.

The game ended with a rare five to one win for the Dodgers. The crowd exited around us, and still Sidney sat there staring at the empty field. "What's eating you?" I asked, half expecting him to tell me his wife ran off with his barber or his mother-in-law was moving in with them.

He shrugged. His shoulders sagged like a man whose dog just died. "We could lose this thing," he finally said. I guessed he was talking about FDR's re-election. It's all he seemed to have on his mind any more. "And if he loses, we're going to be blamed. The Jews."

"That's ridiculous," I said.

"Haven't you been paying attention?" His voice rose, and his left eyebrow twitched. One of the Negro janitors sweeping four or five rows below us looked up, puzzled why we were still sitting there. "Republicans are calling the New Deal the Jew Deal. Lots of people don't like it that FDR appointed so many Hebes to big jobs, particularly Henry Morgenthau as Secretary of the Treasury. Jews and money. How's that for playing into their catechism?"

I wasn't sure what he meant, but I said "They're not going to vote for Alf Landon, for god's sakes." Roosevelt's Republican opponent was governor of Kansas at the time, a small mind from a small state.

"It's already getting ugly and it's going to get worse. They're spreading rumors Roosevelt's a secret Jew. That his real name is Franklin Rosenfeld." The stadium was nearly empty now. Groundskeepers groomed the infield.

"Nobody's going to believe that *drek*."

"You're not listening," he snapped, his face frozen in a scowl. "Some of our own people, right inside the party, are saying he has to fire a few Jews and do it right now. Maybe Felix Frankfurter. Maybe Abe Fortes or Bernard Baruch. We're in trouble in upstate New York, and if we lose New York we lose the election. Landon'll undo the whole New Deal. We need to win big. Bigger than in '32, or it's the Jews' fault."

The way Sidney was acting, you would think he held me personally accountable for this state of affairs. He was starting to scare me. "So what do you want out of me? You're the politician here."

"Get off your ass and do something, for Christ's sake. You've got influence. Get out there and raise some money. Get Jews working, not sitting on their asses praying the messiah will come to save them. Speak out. Hand out flyers. Get 'em registered and get 'em out to vote. If we lose it'll be because people like you sat around and did nothing." Sidney's face turned deep red, his soft hands tightened into fists.

"That's bullshit!" Shadows settled over the stadium. I stood up. "We'd better go."

Sidney pissed me off for days. To make it worse, that Sunday my brother-in-law Simon and I got into it again after our card game at the synagogue. He was always finding reasons to fan the fear of fascism coming to America. I don't know what life had done to my brave childhood friend to make him so afraid.

I took his cancerous criticisms of America personally. After all, this was the golden land to which I had led my family, the best thing I'd done in my life, and now Simon was saying it didn't count for anything. He looked under every rock for even the smallest piece of anti-Semitism. Then he used those turds to exaggerate fascist infiltration. I refused to let him get away with it.

"Did you see that job ad the Strand Theater ran?" he asked after the last hand was played. "It actually says they're looking for ushers with blond hair and straight noses. It's right there in writing. Know any Jews that look like that? Huh?"

"So start your own movie theater," I answered. "There's no secret police stopping you. I'll even buy the first ticket. This is America, for god's sake." Markus tallied the winnings and losses silently while Daniel and Abe Cohen cleaned up. All three of them wanted to stay out of it.

There was some truth to what Simon said, though I would never admit it to anyone but myself, and maybe Daniel. Many schools restricted the hiring of Jewish teachers. Colleges had Jewish quotas. Corporations wouldn't employ Jews. Small businesses posted ads that said "No Jews need apply." Clubs wouldn't admit Jews. Some gentiles wouldn't sell their houses to Jews, or even rent to them for that matter. Times were still so desperate some Jews looking for work changed their names to ones that didn't sound so Jewish. Others wore a St. Christopher's medal or a crucifix to job interviews. Sara said she could understand why they did it. I couldn't. Pride still counted for something, I answered.

On the other hand, new laws now required civil service hiring and promotion based only on merit. Hordes of Jews landed good paying jobs in government. And bad as the Depression was, I have to tell you life was paradise compared to what it had been under the Tsar. Jews prospered in America like they hadn't prospered since the Romans threw us out of the Holy Land two thousand years ago. So how could you complain?

Simon wouldn't yield an inch. He argued big shots like Henry Ford, Congressmen Hamilton Fish, and Charles Lindberg were doing all they could to convince their fellow gentiles Jews were greedy, dishonest outsiders who could never be true Americans. I must say, they did sound a lot like the Tsar's propaganda ministers just before the *pogroms.* But I reminded Simon we now had two Jews sitting on the Supreme Court, Louis Brandeis and Benjamin Cardoza. The governor of New York, Herbert Lehman, was Jewish. And how about Gimbel's and Macy's, both owned by Jews?

For the next couple of days I chewed on what Simon had said and what Sidney Berman had said. In America, the haters hadn't yet translated their intolerance into actual discriminatory laws like they did under the Tsar and in Nazi Germany. Deep down Americans believed in the promises made in the Constitution, even if they hadn't all been realized yet. Some day they would be. Many gentiles believed it as deeply as I did, and worked just as hard for it as any Jew. The thing is, all that progress we made under Roosevelt would be turned upside down if Landon beat him, or even if it was a close call.

So I decided Sidney was right. I called him and told him so. Then I did what he asked me to do. I demanded donations and campaign help from every Jew I knew, and many I didn't. I did the same with gentile friends like Bettino Rossi and Thomas Kelly. It got so bad even friends and family ran and hid in their closets when they saw me coming.

Sidney kept egging me on with calls of alarm, each one more hysterical than the one before. Some of it was just to crank my engine, but most of it was real. Markus and Manny didn't complain too much, but they let me know they had to work longer hours to cover for my absences from the tailor shop. When they finally annoyed me enough, I reminded them I was doing it for them too. Then I badgered them with guilt until they donated some time and more cash.

A third party candidate, William Lemke, got on the ballot in many states. Lemke, a populist congressman from North Dakota, was sure to pull votes from Roosevelt. Father Coughlin, a vicious Roosevelt antagonist, threw his substantial support and his radio platform behind Lemke. He promised his audience that Lemke would put the Jews in their place.

In September, Maine held its election for governor. The Republican, Lewis O. Barrows, won and Sidney worried it forecast a national trend. Following that, Jesse Owens, the American track star and hero of the 1936 Berlin Olympics, endorsed Alf Landon. "We're going to lose all of Harlem," Sidney fretted. "And that could cost us New York State."

"Don't worry," I joked. "Negroes don't vote." But enough Negroes voted to make a difference, and we both knew it.

Roosevelt did his part. He crisscrossed the country by train non-stop and spoke to the people by radio. Alf Landon, on the other hand, knew he was going to win, so he didn't venture far from his home in Kansas. He didn't need to. The rest of the Republican Party assaulted the New Deal, with particular venom for the new Social Security program scheduled to go into effect in 1937. They called it socialism or worse yet, Communism brought to America by Jews and other Europeans.

October was a disaster. The respected Literary Digest published the results of a massive poll of its readers in that month's issue. They forecast an overwhelming victory for Alf Landon. The poll even had FDR trailing in New York State, but close enough that our little group of campaign workers in a corner of Brooklyn might make a difference.

By then I had a small army of volunteers working out of a makeshift campaign headquarters in an abandoned storefront two blocks from the Brighton Beach El station. It used to be Polansky's Hardware Store before the Depression. Sara, Yakira, and Miryem brightened it with streamers, red, white and blue bunting, posters of FDR, and a huge American flag pinned to the back wall. Each new piece of alarming news drove us to more frantic effort, panicked that our dreams for Jews in America would disappear with a Roosevelt defeat.

Every friend and every one of the family did something, even Simon. So did nearly every member of our congregation, led by Daniel and Hannah. We walked door to door. We stood on busy sidewalks and rode streetcars, passing out handbills and affixing campaign buttons to total strangers. We exhorted new voters to register, and begged for campaign contributions. I must have spoken in front of twenty clubs, sometimes joined by Sidney Berman or a Democratic candidate for local office. I must say, I wasn't too bad at it. And I enjoyed the applause.

Josef spent every hour of every day directing his own Ironworkers Union campaign in Brooklyn, an effort much bigger than ours. But his wife Miryem threw herself into our campaign more than anyone. She was tireless, always at my side to run any errand or carry out any assignment, no matter what it was. And she did it well. She glowed with excitement at what we were accomplishing, radiating an appeal I had rarely noticed before. To this tired fifty-four year old man, the youngish forty year old woman brought bountiful energy.

In earlier times, Sara occasionally criticized my indifference toward Miryem. I appreciated Miryem's cultured mind, but at family gatherings we rarely had much to say to each other besides a few comments about the latest book we read or movie we saw. Now in this election we had something important to share. Politics held no interest for Sara beyond baking batches of cookies for the campaigners.

During breaks between stuffing envelopes and plotting strategy, Miryem and I went to the coffee shop down the street from our campaign headquarters. We were both reading *Gone With The Wind* and gossiped about Scarlet and Rhett as though they were our next door neighbors. "If you ask me, what Scarlet needs is to know what a good man feels like," she whispered. Her mind fascinated me; her suggestive sense of humor tickled me.

One day I was particularly worried. Al Smith, the former Democratic governor of New York and former supporter of FDR, had come out with statements in the press critical of the New Deal.

"Alf Landon, president? Don't worry," Miryem said with a straight face as she poured cream into her coffee. "Presidents don't come from Kansas. Kansas is where brothers and sisters have babies together, isn't it?"

I laughed. She smiled at the corners, stirring her coffee. She pulled a pack of Camels from her purse and handed me the matches to light her cigarette for her. She cupped her fingers around mine, and then blew the first puff of smoke out the side of her ruby lipsticked mouth.

When we got up to leave, I helped her on with her coat. As she pushed her arm into the sleeve, her blouse gaped open revealing her brassiere. She noticed my gaze and paused before thrusting her arm fully into the coat. Her dark eyes glistened. She glanced down at the wooden floor and smiled. I imagined what this small-breasted woman would look like with no clothes on.

That night when I came home Sara was in the kitchen busy ironing. A pile of laundry sat on the chair beside her. She looked tired. Her age was showing as much as mine. I told her about my newfound admiration for our sister-in-law, expecting her to applaud our improved relationship.

"She's your brother-in-law's wife," she said, pressing hard with the iron on the pair of my shorts she was working on.

"He's lucky to have her," I said.

"Humph." The iron sizzled when she raised it and spit on it.

Maybe my praise of Miryem had been too enthusiastic. I didn't mention her again.

"Look at all of them," Miryem said one day when twenty-five or thirty volunteers crowded the campaign headquarters stuffing envelopes. "They're all here because of you. Just like you did the night of the *pogrom*." I looked at her with what must have been a puzzled expression. "Josef told me about it." She squeezed my arm. Her touches no longer made me uncomfortable. "You're my hero," she laughed.

I hadn't thought about the *pogrom* in a long time, and had trouble seeing it as similar to a presidential campaign in America. But I was pleased it inspired Miryem's admiration.

In the closing days, I spent every waking moment working on the campaign. I hardly saw Sara except for a late supper before collapsing into a deep sleep.

On November 3, I voted at the fire station as soon as the polls opened. Then we threw everything we had into one last effort getting people out to vote. Some of us walked the precinct street by street, knocking on doors. Others positioned themselves at key spots, like near the stairs to the El station or on the sidewalk in front of Abe Cohen's grocery store.

Soon after sunset the polls closed. My engine kept running, but there were no more wheels to turn. The only place to wait was at our little campaign headquarters. Only a few people were there, but others straggled in.

Miryem spotted me approaching through the display window in front. As soon as I walked in she handed me a salami sandwich. "You look exhausted," she said. "Sit down and eat this." I did what she said.

Someone set up a radio in the far corner, and a huge chalkboard along one wall to post the results. The big room began to fill up. Markus and Manny closed the shop early. Sara brought me another sandwich, egg salad with some Wise Potato Chips. The early returns gave us hope. But then results came in from Maine. We lost there. "As Maine goes so goes the nation," Simon reminded us. Results from Rochester and Syracuse were not promising. We needed a big victory in the city to pull out a win in New York State. If FDR lost his home state, it was all over.

In the early evening the radio said a huge crowd overflowed Times Square, hooting and hollering each time new results flashed on the Times tower. Police estimated the crowd at over a million people. Sidney Berman called to say the turnout in Brooklyn and the rest of New York City was tremendous, particularly the Jewish neighborhoods. Cheers went up when I stood on a chair and shouted this tidbit to our growing crowd. They were itching for any reason to let off steam.

Early returns from Massachusetts showed it close. The same for New Hampshire. Vermont came in. We lost Vermont. Alabama and the rest of the South were never in doubt so huge wins there did little to unknot the apprehension. I held my breath until Connecticut posted a comfortable win for FDR, followed by Pennsylvania. It was the first time Pennsylvania voted Democrat since James Buchanan in 1856.

Above the noise, Miryem leaned on me and yelled in my ear, "we're going to win this." I could smell the scent of pine in her midnight hair and feel her warm breath in my ear. She squeezed my hand. Her eyes shimmered. Moisture glistened on her forehead and over her ruby lips. Ohio, Illinois, and Indiana went our way.

Roosevelt spent the evening at his Hyde Park estate. The President made a brief appearance on the porch, and then went back inside to get the returns from California. Robert Trout, the CBS radio commentator, reported they had started celebrating along the Hudson. By about nine o'clock it was clear Roosevelt was winning an overwhelming victory. Still Alf Landon wouldn't concede.

Josef was, naturally, spending election night with his campaign workers at the Ironworkers Union Hall, but he sent over a few cases of champagne and whiskey, courtesy of the Teamsters. Someone in our hall popped the first bubbly bottle. What did I feel; disbelief, relief, exhaustion, exaltation? All of them, crashing into one another.

Miryem handed me a water glass half-filled with bourbon, no ice. She clinked glasses and we both threw down a big gulp. She giggled like a schoolgirl when someone jostled her making her spill a little on the front of my shirt. She took out a handkerchief and wiped it off. She giggled some more, and I laughed with her. The heat of the bodies, the excitement of the night, the noise, fatigue, and the glow from the whiskey put me in a fuddle. Smoke veiled the room.

"Hold me up or I'll fall over." Miryem grabbed my sleeve to steady herself. I grabbed her tiny waist and held on. She licked her ruby-red lips. "I need a refill," she said looking into the bottom of her empty glass, and was off.

By now cheering men and women packed our campaign headquarters so tightly you couldn't turn around. I had never met most of these people before the campaign. I couldn't spot Sara in the crowd though I knew she was there somewhere. Flowing booze, consuming fatigue, and steamy excitement lowered inhibitions. Someone set off firecrackers.

Sidney phoned again. "It's over! We won! We won! We won!" he screamed above the noise on his end of the phone and mine. Just about that time the CBS newscaster on the radio made it official.

An accordion, clarinet and drums banged out Happy Days Are Here Again as loud as they could. Streamers soared through the smoky air. People sang, screamed, hugged, and kissed – some much more than just celebratory. I got my share of passing smacks on the cheeks and touches on the lips from doughty grandmothers and enticing granddaughters. A leggy dame with a Lauren Bacall look climbed on top of a table and did the Charleston to hungry hoots and whistles.

Simon thumped me on the back. "We did it!" he yelled. "We beat those fuckin' Jew haters. We beat 'em good." I received more than my due share of applause. You would think I had won it for Roosevelt all by myself.

I retreated to a corner near the exit to the alley to catch my breath. I looked for Sara but couldn't see her. More than a hundred fifty people crushed into that storefront, some pushing to get in the front door and some pushing to get out. I no longer saw anyone I even knew until Miryem shoved her way through to my protected corner.

"Congratulations," she said with a throaty voice hoarse from screaming. Then she looked me in the eye, put her arms around my neck, and pressed her wet lips against mine. She tasted of bourbon, tobacco, and appetite. I began to pull away, but she grabbed the back of my head in her two hands and kept her lips locked on mine. Every part of her hot body pressed against me. I responded. Then she stuck her tongue in my mouth.

This time I jerked my head back in surprise and pushed her away. She laughed and patted me on the chest. "C'mon, Avi. Celebrate. We won!"

Markus appeared from nowhere and grabbed me by the elbow. "Time to go," he said. He drove me through the throng toward the front door. I looked back to see Sadie gripping Miryem by the arm and speaking earnestly into her defiant face.

"Wipe the lipstick off your mouth." I did what Markus said.

Sara was waiting for me by the door, a big smile on her face. She put her arms around me and gave me the familiar kiss of a proud wife. "You did it Avi. You did it." She hugged me and held on.

"Take him home," Markus said. I was in a state of mind to do whatever anyone told me to do.

Sara clutched on to me all the way as though afraid I was going to escape. I wondered if she had seen Miryem's kiss. Crowds roamed the streets cheering, marching, and setting off fire crackers and sparklers. Car horns honked and trolley bells clanged. Bonfires blazed here and there in the downtown, figures dancing around them, worshipping the sparks that rose in the night. Happy days were indeed here again.

When we got home and climbed the stairs, I was too tired to move but too excited to sleep. I sat down on the bed. Sara undressed. Then she undressed me. She left the reading light on and climbed atop of me. She grasped me that night as though asserting primal possession, and I cherished being possessed by her and her alone.

The next day we learned the historic scope of Roosevelt's victory. He carried every state except Maine and Vermont with sixty-one percent of the national vote. In New York City, we won by seventy-five percent. The Democrats swept Congress, winning 331 of the 423 seats in the House and, with a gain of seven, now held seventy-six of the ninety-six Senate seats.

Sidney Berman stopped by the tailor shop a couple of days later to thank me. "We couldn't have carried Brooklyn without you," he said. Markus told me later I beamed like a Cheshire cat even while trying to voice humble denials.

"Tell me," I asked Sidney. "When we talked after the ballgame back in June, did you really believe we might lose this?"

"Yep, I really did." He smiled a sly smile, paused and went on. "But I would have said anything if I knew what an army you would muster."

After Sidney left, I sat at my sewing machine and mended a torn dress, lost in thought about what had happened. This victory was every bit as sweet as seeing Viktor Askinov's blood on the street the night of the *pogrom*. From it all, I learned that even at my age I could rally a brigade behind a just cause. Our victory was the answer to Simon and his declarations of despair about America, and Henry Ford's campaign of hate. Roosevelt continued to appoint Jews to key positions, and nominated Felix Frankfurter to the Supreme Court.

In spite of our great victory, many Jews remained silent in the 30's, afraid that taking action against anti-Semitism would provoke more animosity from American gentiles. Not me. I saw what silence earned us back in Russia – *pogroms*. So once we re-elected Franklin Roosevelt, I went on a new mission. This time it was raising lots and lots of money for the Anti-Defamation League to fight discrimination. I learned from debates with Simon that we had to use public opinion and the legal system if we were ever going to achieve full equality for Jews in America.

Also, we had to venture out of our safe New York City Jewish havens, like my brave son Isaac. When he moved to Berkinbury, he didn't hide that he was Jewish. He proclaimed it. He pushed the small community of Jews in his town to buy an old, abandoned church and turn it into a synagogue. That was progress. Daniel helped them set it up and buy a Torah. He conducted their first Sabbath service one bright spring morning in May of 1937. Sara and I joined him.

As for Miryem, nothing changed. The next time I saw her was the first night of Hanukkah at Ester's house. She was the same Miryem, distant with no connection. Only once did she look my way. She winked, with a slight smile. I smiled back and nodded.

Sara was another matter. Somehow she and Miryem got into a row about whose gefilte fish was better. Sara rarely argued, and usually with the light touch of a butterfly. This time she punched and counterpunched like Joe Lewis, landing blows I hadn't seen her throw since a bully boxed Isaac's ears when he was eight years old. Sara and Miryem might have gone a few more rounds if Sadie hadn't changed the conversation to one about how to make rugelach. Sadie made the best, and no one would think to argue about it.

Sara was still grumbling about Miryem when we got home. "What does a Hungarian like her know about making gefilte fish," she snapped, as though country-of-origin was the ultimate argument clincher.

I suppose my brief encounter with Miryem made me feel good, that I could still appeal to a younger woman and that maybe there was more to Miryem than met the eye. But she also scared me. She was a warning that even at my age I could still make a huge mistake. Sara, for her part, made sure I never forgot how much I was loved.

The 1936 election diverted our attention for awhile from what was happening in Germany. Beginning that day in June when Sidney Berman first warned me about Roosevelt's vulnerability until the day after the election, there wasn't time for anything else. Now that the election was over, we could no longer look away.

Most of us Jews were slow to react when Hitler first grabbed power. "It can't be any worse than the Tsar," Abe Cohen said. "So they'll have a little *pogrom* and it will be finished." But when Germany passed the Nuremburg Laws, we noticed. Hitler stripped Jews of their citizenship and all protections. The whole world knew then about the menace to the Jews, and they can't say now that they didn't.

The Anti-Defamation League tried to rally Jews and other Americans to challenge Hitler. We wrote letters, lobbied our congressmen, and petitioned President Roosevelt. Not much happened other than lame American government protests to the German government.

There were times I wanted to believe what was happening in Germany wasn't my fight. We had enough to deal with in America. And Lieb was safe. I was thankful for that. Germany and Russia were mortal enemies and the Russians were just as powerful as the Germans, I thought.

I never considered the possibility the threat to Lieb and his children might come from inside Russia before it came from outside. Stalin could have been Hitler's brother.

CHAPTER TWENTY-NINE

April 1938

Sara loved going to the movies. If it was a musical, it was hard to keep her from tapping her foot and singing along, annoying everyone around us. But not tonight. We waited weeks to see Fred Astaire and Ginger Rogers in *Shall We Dance.* Now she sat quietly without so much as a small smile. Occasionally she raised a hand to her troubled lips or closed her eyes.

"Didn't you like the movie?" I asked afterward, as we crossed the rain-wetted street in front of the theater.

Sara buried her hands in her coat pockets. "Do you think it's true?" she asked. "All those men shot?"

She was referring to the newsreel before the main feature showing the third Moscow espionage trial. Stalin wanted the whole world to witness these proceedings. That's how we got to see them in our newsreels. They were much the same as the ones Lieb watched when he went to the cinema in Uman. This was indeed a strange experience my far off brother and I shared.

In the first of the show trials back in 1936, sixteen Soviet leaders were found guilty of treason and shot within hours of their conviction. The charges included a plot to kill Stalin, and then turn over Soviet territory to the Germans and Japanese. The Soviets said Trotsky was behind the failed coup, but he fled to Mexico City and barricaded himself behind tall walls, safe for the time being from the reach of Stalin's assassins. In the second trial last year, the same thing happened to seventeen more high ranking officials as happened to the first sixteen.

Now this time twenty-one more defendants were found guilty, eighteen of them executed, including the former chairman of the Communist International, Nikolai Bukharin, former Premier Alexei Rykov, and former head of the NKVD Genrikh Yagoda.

After the first trial, many American correspondents and the American ambassador thought there was proof beyond a reasonable doubt, credence added by the confessions of those charged. But by the third trial, even Western journalists sympathetic to the Communist revolution doubted the integrity of these purges. Clearly the many confessions were coerced through torture.

"Stalin's killing off all of his opponents," I answered Sara, holding my hat on against a sudden gush of April wind. Sara's hair blew back behind her ears.

She shivered and put her arm through mine. "So much death. It's worse than the Tsar. Do you think Lieb and Havol have anything to worry about?"

"No."

Lieb and Havol were not political. But Sara's simple questions made me think Stalin was more infected with suspicion than any of the tsars. No one could be truly safe; I worried a bit more than I let on to Sara.

We didn't know it at the time, but that same year Stalin's secret courts tried and executed scores of high ranking Red Army generals. It wasn't long before even low level Party members and common people across the Soviet Union were under suspicion of treason. Still, Lieb did not question the authenticity of the charges against them. At least not yet.

Thank heavens for comrade Stalin. He knows what he's do-

ing. There are announcements on the radio and in the newspapers almost every day of new arrests, some of them right here in Uman. Editors of our newspapers have been charged with being enemies of the people. They did such a skillful job of hiding their treason that no one ever suspected. We were completely surprised.

At first it was just high officials, party activists, and military men. Now they are finding more and more enemies of the people hiding everywhere. Young children of ten or eleven are uncovering heretics, even turning in their own parents.

Everyone is busy searching for traitors. The Cripple is proving to be very skillful at it. He has rooted out dozens of them and turned them in to the state police, the NKVD. I am told he is an important witness and testifies against many of the spies and saboteurs. It puts him in great favor. But I don't trust him.

Almost all of Joshua's former teachers have been arrested. It's all justified. I am sure of that. It's a shame so many of them are Jews. There are no longer any Jews at the top levels of the Party, the government, or the army.

These are troubling times. It is not always looked favorably to have relatives abroad if you are arrested. But please do not stop writing me under any conditions. I have nothing to worry about. I am a loyal Soviet citizen, and I am not political. I put my faith in God, knowing even Abraham had doubts.

My brother's last comment about Abraham's doubts puzzled me. I wondered if he had even small doubts about the validity of Stalin's purges.

Lieb's next letter a few weeks later calmed my unease. His every word bubbled. Joshua's wife Leya had given birth to a daughter who they named Anya. *She is as pretty as a snowflake,* he wrote. He also said the house was getting more crowded with him, Golde, Shaina, Dmitri, Joshua, Leya and all their children. *My cup runneth over,* he wrote. *Six granddaughters I have been blessed with. I am a rich man, dear brother. Now don't get me wrong. A grandson would be nice too, one to carry on the Schneider name in Russia. That will come in God's own time. I'm sure of it. Praise Him and pray for us.*

The next Sabbath I asked Daniel to say a special prayer for my new great-niece Anya, and another one for Lieb. But my brother needed more than prayers.

Not long after, the Ukraine Prime Minister Panas Liubchenko committed suicide. He had been accused of planning to separate Ukraine from the Soviet Union and turn it over to Hitler and the Germans. A new man named Nikita Khrushchev was personally appointed by the supreme leader, Josef Stalin, to head the Communist Party in the Ukraine. He was directed to stomp out the Trotskyites, a task he approached with enthusiasm. His reach extended to Uman.

The groups purged mounted like cords of bodies: more party leaders, kulaks, priests, military officers, and even those who drew suspicion only because they had traveled abroad. "It's amazing how many poets, authors, artists and actors have proven to be spies and terrorists," Pravda reported. Lieb would have to be blind to keep believing these fairytales of Soviet propaganda.

Innocence such as that of my brother no longer mattered. Gersh Leibowitz and Sergey Shumenko provided him some protection, but if they went down, he could go with them. Viktor Askinov would be sure of that. Fear for him rose like leavened bread, and I again chewed over how I could persuade him to leave. He ignored the hints in my letters.

Meanwhile, everyone but those with family back in Russia paid less and less attention to the Soviet purges as Hitler became a more threatening story. Earlier in 1938 Germany annexed Austria. Then in October, they grabbed Czechoslovakia's western Sudetenland following the capitulation of British Prime Minister Neville Chamberlain at Munich. What next?

In November, a young Jewish refugee murdered a German diplomat named Ernst von Rath in Paris. *Kristalnacht* – the night of the broken glass – followed immediately. We huddled by our radios and ran to buy every newspaper with accounts of the mass attacks on Jews across

Germany. Nazi propaganda presented the attacks as the instinctive response of the German people to von Rath's murder. It only took the well-prepared Storm Troopers a few hours to ravage nearly every synagogue, Jewish home, and Jewish business in Germany. They killed close to a hundred Jews and injured thousands. They sent tens of thousands to concentration camps in Buchenwald, Dachau and Sachsenhausen.

That year we gathered at Ester's for Hanukkah as we did every year. The family had expanded with the arrival of grandchildren. Isaac and Tillie brought their little ones, Rose and Max. The candles glowed, prayers said. The younger children spun their dreidels, and *gelt* was given. The tables sagged under the load of potato latkes, chicken, meatloaf, roast beef, cooked spinach, beets, potato kugel, and kreplach in chicken soup. When that was finished, everyone forced down a couple of jam-filled donuts and fritters. Even with all of that abundance, it was hard to celebrate Hanukkah with a jubilant heart.

The younger ones with children left early. When the dishes were all cleared, I brought up my uneasiness about Lieb and his family.

"Stop! I don't want to hear about it," Ester snapped. "It's Hanukkah. Leave it alone for once."

"Besides," Markus said. "Lieb can't just walk out of there. And how are you going to get him out? There's no way." He put the emphasis on "you," as though it was only my responsibility.

"If they tried to get out," Zelda added, "they'd be shot before they could get ten feet."

"What's the matter with all of you," I yelled. "Don't you give a damn if your brother's killed? Or one of his kids?" I felt ganged up on, and I resented all of them for their indifference. My half-full coffee cup rattled in my hand when I tried to put it back down in its saucer.

"He made his decision," Ester countered. "Now he has to live with it."

Sara said later my face turned red as an apple. Before I could respond again, she grabbed me by the arm and pulled me up from the table. "We have to go," she said. "Avi has to mow the lawn tomorrow morning." Everyone laughed a nervous laugh. There was an inch of snow on the frozen December ground.

Sara took my hand on the walk home. A few snowflakes wet my nose. I boiled like a hot turnip. It would have been nice if Sara had stood up for me for a change. Sometimes she was just a doormat for Ester, and I didn't like it. But that was Sara, eager to please everyone, me most of all. So I kept my mouth shut about it. "They just don't care," I said instead.

"They care," she answered, "just like I care about Havol. But some things are not for us to say. God gave them the same choices he gave you. They decided to stay, Lieb and Havol. I never told you I offered to bring both Josef and Havol to America when I first came. Josef said yes. Havol said no." I pondered her words the rest of the way home.

What I resented most was that Lieb had slipped away from Ester, Markus, and Zelda. They showed it through their indifference. It had been over thirty years since they last saw their big brother, and he wasn't even a real person to them anymore. All they knew of him was from his letters to me. They hadn't written to him themselves in years. I still knew him, and felt him, and loved him more than the day I left Uman. I couldn't relieve myself of my responsibility to Lieb or the promise I made to Momma to bring him to America. The world was breaking into pieces and I wanted my brother by my side, for my sake as much as his.

"When the time comes, they'll help," Sara said when we climbed our front steps. I questioned to myself whether she was right.

I wrote Lieb a letter the next day telling him in no uncertain terms to get the hell out of Russia. Then I thought better of it. Every one of my letters was probably scrutinized by a censor, and my words could land him in front of a firing squad. So after taking a few deep breaths, I tore it up and burned it in the stove.

CHAPTER THIRTY

JUNE 1939

They ripped Lieb's heart out when they arrested his son-in-law Dmitri. It was almost as bad as when he lost his daughter Brindyl.

I loved that boy. It's a pity Shaina had to divorce him, but the Party demanded it. She said if he is a traitor like that, who needs him anyway. Still, she is in great pain and it is hard to see that in your child. She and her daughters are shunned by many in Uman. The Cripple torments her because she was married to an enemy of the people. He uses his influence to make it difficult for her to get work. He will not surrender the hatred he has for the Schneider family even down the generations. My suspicion is that monster turned Dmitri in with false testimony. They have sent Dmitri to Siberia for six years. I will miss him. He was a good father, a good husband, and a good son. I know Shaina is still in love with him. She will miss him too.

My hand shook as I read his letter for the second time. A big burst of wind and rain slammed a tree branch against our living room window making Sara jump. She pulled her sweater closer to her and went back to her knitting, a blue and green scarf for our granddaughter. Tchaikovsky's Symphony Number Six played quietly on our new Philco radio. Business in the tailor shop had picked up lately so we could afford a few luxuries, while in Russia my brother was going through an orgy of terror.

"Can I get you some tea?" Sara asked.

"I don't understand my brother." I held the letter out to her to read. "He criticizes the purges and the trials in every letter now. I warn him not to write such things to me. He knows government censors read everything. But he doesn't listen anymore."

Sara put down her knitting and came over to sit on the arm of my chair. Her soft golden-gray hair against my cheek comforted me like a mother's breast. "You can't judge him," she said softly. "We don't know what they've been through since we left. How many years has it been? Thirty?"

"Momma always said Lieb came out of the womb quietly, and I came out screaming. Now he's the one who's screaming."

"Let me get you some tea," she said. She got up and went in the kitchen.

I turned back to Lieb's letter: *People just disappear. Some of them have relatives abroad. If you do not hear from me anymore, perhaps I too have disappeared. But please, in the name of God, do not stop writing. Do not abandon me.* Lately every letter from him contained that same desperate plea.

Lieb took to writing every few weeks as the purges piled up, but after this latest letter several months went by without another one. I began to worry his remark about disappearing had been a premonition. Our apple tree in the back yard hung heavy with ripe fruit by the time his next letter arrived in mid August.

First they got Gersh Leibowitz. Then they got Sergey Shumenko. They are consuming their own like crazy monsters. Where can this end?

They arrested and tried Gersh in secret. All I know is he was sentenced to five years in jail. Thank the Lord they didn't shoot him. I cannot prove it, but I feel Viktor Askinov had his hand in it, just like with Dmitri. It is not just us he torments. He troubles Meier Braun, Shlomo Zilberman, Mica Rosenbaum and their families every chance he gets. But he torments no one so much as he torments the Schneiders. Why? Why did he choose to curse this family?

Gersh has been a loyal Communist from the beginning. How long is that? Thirty-five years? They convicted him of being a Trotskyite. I remember he knew Trotsky when we were all very young but I don't think he even saw Trotsky again after about 1915 or 1920.

Gersh is not a young man anymore. By now he is in Siberia. I pray he can survive such an ordeal. Selfishly, we have lost our benefactor. Many said he was as brutal as any of the Communist Party chiefs, but to us he was a caring friend. He intervened many times over the years to help us.

Sergey's situation is an entirely different matter. They hold him in our jail in Uman but have not charged or tried him. They say he is voluntarily providing information about traitors and counter-revolutionaries in the tractor factory where he is the director. They have converted that factory to making tanks now, so it is even more important than it was before. Rows and rows of tanks sit in the yards surrounding the main assembly buildings. Joshua is one of the engineers working on them. I trust the Lord to keep Joshua safe and out of harm's way, but I worry about him in this insanity. I'm afraid our friendship with Sergey will be held against him.

The day after Sergey was taken in, his wife Valerya came to see me at our house to beg for my help. She had nowhere else to turn. Golde was at the market at the time. Valerya even at fifty years old is a stunning woman, made more striking by her grief. She cried in my arms, hugging herself to me. What could I do but embrace her in return and stroke her soft hair. She is such a saintly person with a pure soul, kind and brave. She has helped me and my family more than anyone alive, sharing whatever they had with us as though we were her family, even when they had little themselves. That we are Jews does not bother her for a moment. She speaks more than a few words of Yiddish. Yet she remains an observant Christian worthy of the noble Shumenko family name.

So I went with Valerya to the police station to find out what we could find out. They made us wait on a hard bench by the front desk for nearly four hours. When a police officer did finally see us, at first he denied Sergey was being held there. I insisted he was there, though I wasn't sure. I don't think I would have been so foolish as to contradict an NKVD officer if Valerya wasn't with me. She expected me to be brave. So then they said he was there voluntarily, but he could not see us. He was on an important mission for the state.

While we were waiting on that hard bench, the Cripple came out of one of the back rooms. I think they have made him some kind of Party political commissar. He glanced at me with the look of the devil. I swear fire was coming out of his nose and smoke from his ears. He made a vulgar gesture with his hand and arm in our direction. In normal times I would have been embarrassed that Valerya would see such obscenity, but in such a situation that was the least of our worries.

We left the police headquarters that day without an answer to Sergey's circumstance, or when he might be released. That was three months ago. All I ask is for my family to be safe and have enough food to eat. Is that too much to ask?

I wonder when it was that the God of Avriham spoke to Moses and sent him a sign. How else do you know when He is speaking to you?

His last paragraph puzzled me. The codes my brother imbedded in every letter had gotten so complicated I sometimes worked for hours to translate them. This one seemed to suggest he was Moses preparing to lead his tribe out of Russia and wanted a sign from Avriham. Me, Avi. I hoped it was so, at last, but I had no idea how I could help him. Exit from Russia was impossible and the castle gates to America were locked to immigrants.

Ester, Simon, Markus, and Sadie came for Sabbath dinner that week. The men sat around the dining room table after and talked while the women cleaned up. I read them Lieb's letter.

"I think he's stronger than any of us," Markus said. "He just wanted something different. To be left alone and allowed to be safe in his own home. In Uman."

"He'll never be safe in Uman," I said.

Simon smoothed out his napkin on the table, and then picked up a salt shaker, studying it as though it were a valuable icon. "I think he's realized that," he said. "But what can you do about it? Hitler or no Hitler, they aren't letting Jews into this country, if that's what he's thinking about."

"Roosevelt would be tarred and feathered if he tried," Markus answered. "Look what happened to that German ship, the St. Louis. A thousand Jews on board. Turned away from America and forced to go back to Europe. Hitler will get them all."

"You don't know that," Ester said, breezing in from the kitchen with a sponge cake on a platter. "The ship docked in Belgium and most of the passengers got off there." Sadie followed Ester from the kitchen with plates and fresh forks. Sara brought the coffee. Sadie poured Markus a cup, added milk and sugar, and then took a sip to make sure it wasn't too hot.

"What are we going to do about Lieb and his family?" I looked over at Sara. "Havol too."

"Havol will never leave," she said, her voice flat.

"There's nothing we can do," Ester said, as though closing the subject. Everyone around the table agreed with her.

"We have to do something," I persisted.

"Well then you figure something out, Mr. Big Shot," Ester retorted.

"Let it go," Markus said.

I couldn't let it go. Call it premonition, or maybe it was the obvious evidence stacked in front of us: Hitler, Stalin, Kristalnacht, Czechoslovakia, purges. Something big was going to happen, and it was just around the corner. Lieb must have sensed the same thing. Now what?

First thing Monday morning I contacted Sidney Berman. He had said he owed me after I helped him carry Brooklyn during FDR's 1936 campaign. It was time for him to pay that debt. Right after the election he went to work as a key aide to Congressman Ezra Breuer. He worked out of the Congressman's Brooklyn office most of the time. Sidney was the only person I knew with any political influence. When I phoned him and told him it was urgent, he promised to meet for lunch the next day.

We talked over chicken salad sandwiches in a small coffee shop near his office in mid-Brooklyn. The tiny fan above the cash register did nothing to mitigate the August humidity. My wet shirt clung to me. Sidney had taken off his dress jacket and loosened his tie as soon as he came in the door. Otherwise, he didn't sweat.

I told him right off what was on my mind. He was not encouraging. "Avi, this country is locked down tighter than a virgin's chastity belt," he said when I told him about Lieb. "Besides, getting out of the Soviet Union is just about impossible."

I pushed away my half eaten sandwich and nibbled on a fried potato. "Is there going to be a war?"

"It looks like it, doesn't it?"

"And us?"

"We'll stay out of it. At least for now."

"So why can't we get Lieb out?"

"I know you don't want to hear this, but even if you could get him out – which you can't – then where does he go? Our State Department is full of Ivy League anti-Semites who would just as soon see Hitler put every Jew in Europe behind barbed wire before they would help them."

"And Roosevelt?"

"Who knows? Americans aren't too generous in their attitudes toward Jews right now, and FDR wants to run again. You saw the polls. Most of the people think Jews have too much power and should be restricted. Hell, ten percent say we should all be deported."

"So what do I do?"

He took a breath, and then casually looked around the restaurant to be sure no one was listening. "I probably shouldn't tell you this, but I heard about a small group trying to smuggle some Jews out of Russia. You might know one of the guys. Sam Lipsky."

I smiled. "That's the first encouraging thing you've said all day. I knew Sam years ago. He worked on the Red Cross committee investigating *pogroms* in the Ukraine. Haven't seen him since the early twenties. Where can I find him?"

"I can't promise you anything. I'm not even sure he's legit." Sidney wrote something down on a slip of paper, looked around the restaurant again to be sure no one was watching, and slid it over to me. "Just don't tell him I'm the one who sent you."

Doing business again with Sam Lipsky wasn't something I looked forward to. The man I knew at the Becker Dress Factory was a ruthless son-of-a-whore. The one I met at the Red Cross committee was better, but still no saint. I wished Sidney could have given a more enthusiastic endorsement. Still, I didn't have any other option.

The next day I went to see Lipsky. The rickety stairs up to his office above an abandoned car repair shop reminded me of the Becker Dress Factory. The odor of stale cigar smoke told me I was in the right vicinity. His rundown office wasn't an office so much as a space little bigger than a small bedroom. The only furnishings were a beat up desk and swivel chair, a wobbly hard backed chair for a guest, and an empty bookcase. An old two-piece phone sat on his desk, along with a large overflowing glass ashtray. The windows hadn't been cleaned since Taft was president. He was the only one there.

When he saw me, Lipsky jumped up from his seat with a big smile on his face and thumped me on the back like I was his long lost cousin. He seemed smaller than I remembered, but with the same horn rimmed glasses on a sweaty head as bald as a ripe honeydew mellow. His brown-stained teeth clenched a well-chewed cigar stub.

I sat down and in ten minutes explained Lieb's entire situation. He sat back in his chair, hands clasped behind his head. Every so often a cloud of stinky cigar smoke belched from his mouth. A long ash formed, ready to fall off. He leaned forward and flicked it into the ashtray.

He was completely familiar with the terror in the Ukraine, including Uman. He remembered Lieb from my search when Sam was with the Red Cross. He wasn't at all happy that I heard about his clandestine operation rescuing Jews who wanted to escape.

"Will you help?" I begged.

He took the cigar stub out of his mouth and stared at the end. He made a face. "I'm sorry, Avi. I really am. This is tragic, what's going on over there. But you have to understand, so many people are trying to get their people out...."

"You've got to help. I've got nowhere else to turn."

"I'm afraid I have to say no."

My only chance to get Lieb out rested right now with this foul human being sitting across the desk from me. I wasn't leaving until I got what I came for. "We have a long history, you and me," I said. "If my brother dies...." I didn't need to remind him he wore the blood of those young women who died in the Becker Dress Factory fire, but it was on the tip of my tongue.

He spun around in his chair, his back to me, and gazed out the grimy window. Then he turned back. "It's very expensive," he said. "Maybe two thousand bucks to rescue four or five of them."

My eyes must have looked as wide as silver dollars. Whatever I was expecting, I hadn't expected it to be so much. A new Buick would have cost a lot less.

"Look. For you, I'll see what I can do," he said. "Let me talk to my guys. But so many want to get their people out. And there are risks.

Many, many risks."

We shook on the deal. The money was staggering, but for the first time since I made the promise to Momma, I felt Lieb had a chance. I wished his fate was in better hands than those of Sam Lipsky, but what else could I do? Now, armed with this option, all I needed to do was give Lieb the final shove to get him to move. That moment had come at last.

Before I left I promised to give Lipsky a two hundred dollar deposit to hold a space until Lieb agreed to leave. Lipsky cautioned me about mentioning our arrangement to anyone. "The fewer who know the better. Soviet agents operate all over New York City." He glanced around as though there might be one hiding next door. "When we get closer I'll introduce you to the man who will actually carry out the operation."

"How will you get them out?" I asked.

"The less said the better. You'll know when they're safely out." He looked around again to see if anyone was listening. Then he whispered, "Turkey."

I thanked him and promised to have the two hundred dollar deposit in his hands by the next day. I would need to tell Markus, Ester, and Zelda if I expected them to help pay the full two thousand dollars, but I didn't mention that to Lipsky.

We met the following afternoon at the El station in Brighton Beach. Before I turned the two hundred dollars over to him, I insisted he tell me who the big boss was behind his operation. At first he refused, but when he saw how determined I was, he relented. "Menachem Veinberg," he whispered, again looking around to see if anyone was close enough to hear. He had me spooked. I looked around too, wondering if I could still move fast enough to escape a pursuer, whoever that might be. "You must not say a word to anyone. You could jeopardize people's lives." I took his warning seriously.

The next step was to get Lieb to make the decision to leave. Lipsky urged me to take care of that right away. The situation in Europe deteriorated more and more by the day. I had no illusions about the difficulties and dangers in front of Lieb and his family, but at last there was hope. Who would have ever guessed Sam Lipsky would turn out to be Lieb's savior?

That night I wrote Lieb.

CHAPTER THIRTY-ONE

September 1939

Everyone reacted like a cuckold husband when Hitler and Stalin signed a pact that August promising not to attack each other. What did they expect? But it gave me reason to worry a little less about Lieb. It seemed whatever happened in Russia next wasn't going to be because of Hitler. I should have known better. And Lieb should have known better too.

The first Friday in September Germany invaded Poland from the south and the west. Hitler claimed Polish forces attacked a radio station inside of Germany. No one believed such an absurd charge. Two days later Britain and France declared war on Germany, but they did nothing to halt the German blitzkrieg. Tanks slaughtered the Polish horse cavalry; Stuka dive bombers pounded Polish towns and villages into piles of dust.

Two weeks later we celebrated Rosh Hashonnah, the Jewish New Year. Some celebration. Half our congregation still had relatives in Poland. Daniel's sermons were flat and irrelevant when they needed to offer more than platitudes. He did mention Poland, if only to pray for these Jewish people in their time of trial. Simon and a few other men dozed off on the second day. Some of the women carried on their own muted conversations, as bored as their husbands. I was disappointed in Daniel, and I told him so the next day in no uncertain terms.

"So what do you expect me to do? Preach war?" he shot back. "The American people are already screaming that Jews are trying to draw America into this mess. There's enough hate out there toward us. We don't need to invite any more."

I tried to argue with him, but his mind was made up. He accepted the wisdom of many American Jews at the time: pushing for even the smallest American role would just make the situation worse. It sounded to me a lot like the arguments made before our *pogroms* in Uman thirty-five years earlier. During my walk home, I thought what Daniel needed was someone like Uncle Yakov to give him some courage.

By the time we gathered for Yom Kippur eight days later, the Germans had penetrated to the Polish city of Brest-Litovsk. That's when Stalin launched his army into eastern Poland, taking his bite of the Polish rump state. Along the way, he also took Estonia, Latvia, and Lithuania.

From reports in the newspapers, that year most rabbis were even more timid in their Rosh Hashonnah sermons than Daniel. They acknowledged the plight of Polish Jews but stuck to spiritual themes and prayers for God's forgiveness. Anti-Semitism reached a new high that fall and rabbis were reluctant to inflame it further by advocating American involvement. Rabbinical silence did nothing to stop anti-Jewish groups from accusing Jews of warmongering. This propaganda line played to the country's desperate desire to stay out of another European war.

Then Daniel surprised me during his Yom Kippur sermon. He wasn't ready to call Jews to the barricades yet, but he did talk about courage. He even mentioned Joshua, Gideon, Judah Maccabee and King David – all of them Jewish warriors. It was a start.

After services, I complimented him on our way out and shook his hand. He smiled, pleased by my praise. "I thought about you and the night God tested you," he said, referring to my Uman *pogrom*. "What it must have taken for someone like you to shoot another human man."

"Anger and fear," I answered.

After that, Daniel pushed further and further, in spite of reluctance by some in our own congregation and criticism by many of his rabbinical brethren. He recruited more and more rabbis to speak out, arguing American military involvement was morally right. It did little good at the time, but it made a lot of us feel better. And who knows? Maybe it helped us keep our self respect when the worst happened.

By October Poland was gone, partitioned as savagely as Catherine the Great and Prussian Emperor Fredrick Wilhelm had done a century and a half earlier.

Lieb's letter was the only one in our mailbox the week after Thanksgiving. It was dated September 18, the day after the collapse of Poland. *I am happy to tell you, dear brother, that the Lord has at last blessed us with a grandson. His name is Elias. Joshua and Leya thought about naming him Elijah, but that sounded dangerously biblical. Still the sentiment is there. Say a prayer for him.*

That was all he wrote, after waiting years for a grandson. He showed no joy, and he didn't tell me whether they had a *bris* – a ritual circumcision. His reference to Elijah intrigued me. Daniel, ever the rabbi, said his meaning was obvious. "Elijah defended God, which brought him into constant conflict with the Kings of Israel. One time he had to flee for his life. Could it be that's what Lieb's trying to tell you?"

"Or what Joshua and Leya are trying to say."

That afternoon I wrote a letter to Lieb telling him as clearly as I could that I had found a means to rescue him and his family. All I needed was a clear sign he had reached a decision and I could put Lipsky in motion. It was time to act. I had only heard from Lipsky twice since I turned over the first two hundred dollars to him. Both times he assured me they were still rescuing people in spite of the war. In the second call, he pressed me hard for a decision to move ahead.

The day after I wrote Lieb I phoned Lipsky to make sure his people would be ready to go as soon as Lieb said yes. He picked up on the first ring. "Good thing you called," he said, his words garbled by the cigar clenched between his teeth. "Things have changed because of the fighting. More dangerous, more people to bribe. I'm going to need some more dough to hold your place." He sounded edgy, no doubt the result of the escalating hostilities. "Three hundred dollars more."

"It's going to take me a couple of days to round up that much cash," I said, startled by the amount and the urgency in his voice. "Should I bring it to your office?"

"No, no," he said. "Do you know the Famous Odessa? It's a kosher deli near the El station in Brighton Beach. Right next to the candy store."

"Everyone knows the Famous."

"Meet me there Thursday at one o'clock. Be on time. I can't wait around. And bring the money. Small bills." He hung up before I could say another word.

Sara let me handle all our money, but she was not happy I was carrying this financial burden by myself. "He's their brother too," she said, referring to Ester, Markus, and Zelda. "Let them help." She was right, but I wasn't yet ready to bring them into it until Lieb committed and Lipsky needed the rest of the two thousand dollar payment. I wasn't sure how my brother and sisters would respond, and wanted the plan to be too far along for them to try to talk me out of it. Even I had some doubts, not about Lipsky but about his unknown accomplices. I had to accept Lipsky's faith that they were top notch.

It wasn't easy to get my hands on three hundred dollars so fast. I took some out of our savings account at the bank and borrowed the rest from my partner Manny. I asked him not to tell Markus.

Thursday came. I found a booth at the Famous Odessa in front by a window. Famous as it was, the deli only had nine booths along the wall and windows, and four tables in the middle. It was half full when I got there. The fragrance of hot pastrami, potato knishes, and cucumber-sized green pickles penetrated every pore.

One o'clock came and no Lipsky. I unfolded my newspaper and began reading the latest war news: Still no real action by the British and

French. I kept checking my watch. Fifteen minutes went by and no Lipsky. Then a half hour. Initial irritation at his tardiness turned to apprehension as the clock approached two o'clock.

A waitress in a brown-trimmed white outfit came over for the third time and asked for my order. For the third time I told her I was waiting for someone. She pattered off in her white nurses shoes. One of the men at a nearby table gave her a grab on her plump ass when she passed.

A cramped wooden phone booth stood in the back of the place. The deli was hot inside, so I left the door open while I lifted the receiver and dropped a nickel in the slot. The phone rang and rang, maybe ten times. I hung up, waited another fifteen minutes and tried again. Still no answer. I checked to be sure I was dialing the right number. After one more try, I left and nearly ran back to the tailor shop. I felt like I was wearing a sign telling every hoodlum in the neighborhood there were bundles of tens and twenties in my pockets.

"What's the matter?" Markus asked as soon as I closed the door. "You look like your dog just died."

"Maybe he did." I spilled out the whole story about my plan to rescue Lieb.

"You should have told me," he said. "I'll help with the money. If you can't reach Lipsky by phone tomorrow, we'll go to his office together."

I grabbed Markus and wrapped my arms around him. My little brother was a good man, and I was relieved I now had an ally. He pulled back and laughed. "Hey, he's my brother too," he said. But it often felt after all these years like any ties Markus, Ester, and Zelda had to Lieb dangled in a frayed fishnet.

Three more times I tried calling Lipsky's office that afternoon. I started calling again the next morning before leaving the house, then again as soon as I reached the tailor shop. By nine o'clock I had called four times. I slammed the receiver down just when Manny walked in the door with a newspaper tucked under his arm, folded to one of the inside pages.

"You'd better see this," he said. He held out the newspaper and pointed to a small article on page six. The headline pronounced the catastrophe.

TWO MEN ARRESTED IN JEWISH RESCUE FRAUD: A former Red Cross employee and a Jewish Rescue Committee employee were arrested by FBI detectives yesterday after bilking desperate U.S. relatives of European Jews out of tens of thousands of dollars. They duped benefactors by manufacturing daring stories about perilous rescues of Jews from Germany, Poland, and Russia. Criminal charges against Samuel J. Lipsky and Menachem M. Veinberg were brought in federal court in Manhattan. The two are being held without bail.

Under the article was a picture of the two men being led into the courthouse, their hands cuffed behind them. Lipsky stared defiantly at the camera. I wanted to hit someone. Instead I ran into the bathroom and threw up in the toilet. Then I phoned Sidney Berman to scream at him for putting me in touch with Lipsky. He apologized.

"We'll find another way," Markus said when I got off the phone. That was easy for him to say. He wasn't the one who had to find the way. And he wasn't the one who was out two hundred dollars. Thank God I hadn't given Lipsky the other three hundred. But I had already told Lieb a means was available to get him out of Russia. Now what?

Desperate ideas swam through my mind and then evaporated in the test of practicality. I even thought about going to Palestine and working from there. Aside from being impossible, I had promised Sara a long time ago that I would not leave her a second time.

My head was bankrupt. My violent stomach exploded again.

Daniel had no bright ideas, nor did Sidney Berman. Chiam Chernoff and Moishe Stepaner were trying, unsuccessfully, to come up with their own plans for getting relatives out of Russia. New Year's Eve 1940 came and went and still no one had any idea about what to do next. Do you know what it feels like, to be the only one who can save your brother and be helpless to do anything about it? I pray you never have to find out.

That winter was as cold and drab as any in memory. Snow and ice never left the streets and sidewalks. Winds off the ocean reminded me of the glacial gusts across the Ukraine plains surrounding Uman. Dressing to brave the outdoors took as much time and preparation as preparing for an Admiral Byrd expedition to the South Pole.

Evening frost whipped my face and bit my fingers as I climbed the front steps to the house. My fifty-eight years punished my every step. I fished inside the mail box, unwilling to remove a glove even for a second, and pulled out a thin envelope from Lieb amidst a packet of others.

It was the first one since shortly after Thanksgiving. In that one he seemed to say he was moving closer to a decision to leave. His new grandson strengthened his resolve. *I look at Elias, this little baby, and I think Hatikvah – hope. You can't live without hope, and what hope can Elias have here?* That's what he wrote in November. I hoped this new letter would say he was ready to go for sure. Yet if he did say "go," then what do I do?

I went inside the house and unbundled, hanging up my heavy black coat, wool scarf, and hat on the clothes tree by the front door. My galoshes I tossed in a corner like Uncle Yakov used to do with his army riding boots. Sara awaited me as she always did with a full-flush kiss and a hug. No courtesy peck like most old married couples. Then I sat down in my chair in the living room, put on my reading glasses, and opened Lieb's letter.

> *They have released Sergey, praise unto the Lord. They say now it was all a big mistake. No charges were ever filed against him. Such a mistake! They held him for over six months in the local jail. No one was allowed to see him. Valerya tried to bring food and clothes, but the police wouldn't allow it.*
>
> *My dear brother, it troubles me to tell you what condition Sergey is in. The socket around his left eye was broken with fists*

268

or a club. He is nearly blind in that eye. His nose was broken and has healed in an odd misshapen manner. Teeth are missing. His hair is thin and scraggly. Such a change in so short a time.

I asked him if Viktor Askinov had taken part in the beatings. He lowered his head and covered his nose and mouth with the palm of his hand. He sat there that way for a few minutes. When he raised his head, tears glistened in his bloodshot eyes. He didn't answer my question, but I knew the answer.

Valerya is a saint, tending to our dear friend with adoring devotion. She asks for nothing but is so grateful when Golde and I come to visit them, which we do often. Sergey is suspect, so no one else will associate with them. We are all they have left. He eats little, Valerya says, but he will always eat the soups Golde brings for him. Their children have been gone for some time, one in Moscow and one in St. Petersburg.

For several weeks Sergey could not move while his wounds healed, and would say little of his ordeal, or talk about much of anything. At first I thought the beatings had taken away his ability to speak. All he did was sit in a chair and stare out the window. Now he will say a little here and there but won't discuss anything of consequence.

They have given him a job at the tractor factory, but not the exalted one of director he had before. He is little more than a clerk doing menial tasks. This for a man of his abilities who has served them so well. He seems unburdened not to have to think or make decisions.

Joshua is now in a more important engineering position at the factory. He is as irreplaceable as any man can be in our times. That is why he has not been called up to serve in the army like everyone else his age. Many are jealous of his status and that worries me, even though he tells me my concerns are most certainly exaggerated.

Joshua says I should worry more about the Soviets getting in-to a war with the Nazis. If that happens, they will need many

many tanks, and they will need the tractor factory to make them. Of course we have heard about what Germany has done to Poland, but that doesn't concern me any more than it should concern you. It is not our fight. We know what the Germans think of Jews, but our motherland has the strongest military in the world. Hitler would not dare attack us. And if he did, we will dispatch those Nazis in no time.

I put the letter down and took off my glasses. My brother was obviously appalled by the beatings Sergey had endured, but his urgency to leave Uman withered rather than hardened. He brought this home in the next letter I received in mid-February of 1940, only a month later.

He said things had changed a great deal for the better in just a few weeks. Joshua received still another promotion and now was invited to spend time with the district industrial commissar, Leonid Demochev, a Russian from Moscow. He had been assured he was much too valuable to be drafted into the army. As a result of his promotion, the family's circumstances improved. They had abundant food, a new radio, and their own telephone – though they had no one to phone except Sergey and Valerya.

Lieb bubbled about his new grandson, Elias, as though he were the baby Moses. He thanked God again for the blessing He had bestowed upon him. *My last days will be spent where I was born,* he wrote. *In this house. In this village. My grandson Elias will come to visit my grave and place a stone on my tombstone as I have done and will do with Grandpoppa, Poppa, and Uncle Yakov.* I had to be sure to write him that Ester, Markus, Zelda, and I did the same at Momma's grave each year. Momma and Poppa were as separated in their graves as Lieb and I were in our lives. How sad, I thought.

Lieb was an enigma to me. How could he not want to get out of Russia as fast as he could? He kept finding hope where there was none to be had.

"Maybe it's not hope. Maybe it's just giving in to what he can't change," Sara said after she read his letter. "He's made his decision.

Leave him in peace."

Perhaps I had to leave him in peace, but I couldn't be happy for him. Nonetheless, his decision relieved me of the responsibility for finding a way to get him out. "It's for the best," Ester said when I told her. Markus and Zelda both said the same thing. I didn't believe it.

Sara said Lieb was a strong man to endure what he endured and still have the faith in God he had. That made more sense to me than anything else. Lieb was strong, stronger than me. It had taken me a lifetime to realize it. It was just that we had wanted such different things, as unfathomable as that was to me. "He's like Poppa and I'm like Momma," I said to Sara. And as soon as I said it, a great weight was lifted from my shoulders.

A magnificent late spring followed the wicked winter. And with spring's arrival, Hitler launched his assault on the western countries. By May 10, the Netherlands and Belgium surrendered, and by the beginning of June the beaten British army evacuated Dunkirk. The German army entered Paris in mid-June. France surrendered. American isolationists, like their champion Charles Lindberg, raised the pressure on Roosevelt to stay out of Europe's war.

I, on the other hand, wanted to see us in it. First, to protect my brother. Secondly because Hitler was without doubt a monster with an insatiable appetite. But there seemed little hope of American involvement. For the first time in many years, people had jobs and a little money. The European war was not their problem, any more than what the Japs were doing in Asia.

In July, the Germans began their terror bombing of Britain. In August, an assassin put an ice pick through Leon Trotsky's brain. At home, as the golden leaves of autumn covered the ground, America prepared for all possibilities by instituting a draft. And in November, we celebrated the reelection of President Roosevelt.

"Lieb and Havol are safe," Sara reminded me when my anxieties about Hitler's intentions ulcerated.

"For now," I said.

"We're safe," she responded more emphatically. I couldn't argue with that. Yakira and Isaac were safe; my grandchildren were safe; Ester, Markus, Zelda, their children, and my friends were safe.

My scheme to rescue Lieb was preposterous right from the start. It's easy to see that now. He had never given me much encouragement, and there were always achy doubts about Lipsky. But I always felt pinpricks of guilt. I promised Momma on her deathbed I would get Lieb to America, and so far I had failed. No matter what I told myself, that much couldn't be argued.

Sara always said I was like a bulldog who wouldn't let go of a bone. But this time I decided I needed to stop wrestling with windmills and accept Lieb's decision. At least for now.

CHAPTER THIRTY-TWO

March 1941

It is difficult to explain how I could love my nephew Joshua so dearly when I had never met him. For so many years, Lieb described him in such intimate detail and with such feeling I knew him almost as well as I knew Isaac. I could imagine how he thought and what he felt. He was a good boy growing up and an even better man, a good husband, a good father, and a good son.

Occasionally Joshua wrote to me himself. A recent letter included a picture of his family. Leya held their baby boy, Elias. Joshua's hands rested on the shoulders of their two daughters, Rebekah and Anya. Elias was now a year and a half old, the only one in the picture laughing. He looked just like Joshua. And Joshua looked just like Lieb as I remembered him – ears too big and hair parted on the right, a mop hanging over his left eye.

Joshua was the one who wrote to tell me they released Gersh Leibowitz early from his prison term in Siberia, rehabilitated along with many others. That should have been good news, but the Soviets didn't do such favors for free. It was preparation for something else: maybe new purges or maybe war.

Nonetheless, Lieb was thrilled to see Gersh. He returned to Uman in the midst of a classic snowstorm, fierce winds off the plains driving drifts as high as the eves of the house. *Siberia was not kind to him,* Lieb wrote. *He left a powerful, sleek horse and returned a pale, tired mule. The Party gave him a job, but as a lowly clerk, not like the important position he held before. He stays in Uman all of the time now, alone and silent. We share a drink at the old tavern once a week on the Sabbath, though he doesn't acknowledge the day as such. He warns me all of the time to be careful of the Cripple. That devil's influence grows stronger and his prejudice toward the Schneiders has not diminished. I do not understand such men.*

My brother could not understand Viktor Askinov, but I could. I was the one who shot him, and he spent his whole life scheming to even the score. Since he couldn't touch me, he tortured my family in Uman, knowing it would wound me.

The police came for Joshua at night to rip him away from his frightened wife. She and Lieb followed them to the police station but couldn't even get in the door. Joshua was held in a freezing cell overnight without a bed to lie on or a blanket to wrap around himself. They wouldn't tell him what he was charged with, only that a special person was being brought in from Kiev who would make him confess his crimes against the people. Lieb was certain beyond a doubt that it was all Viktor Askinov's doing. Joshua never saw the Cripple while he was in the Uman jail, but he saw his brother Olek and his lackey Igor Czajkowsko smirking when the police first dragged him into the station.

Joshua's vital role in tank production at the tractor factory saved him. By evening of the following day, he still had not been interrogated. That's when his mentor, the district industrial commissar Leonid Demochev, stepped in and overruled the local police. Demochev's concern was armament production, not politics and vengeance. Joshua's skills were important in that. So he was released in Demochev's custody after apologizing for any errors he had made in his service to the Party and the workers.

When Joshua got home, he was a tangle of anger and fear. He said things sure to get him in trouble if he continued. Leya cried, setting off all of their children to crying. Shaina and her children huddled in a corner in awe as Joshua stormed around the house throwing pots and pans to the floor, and an occasional plate. Lieb and Golde tried to quiet him down, and eventually he settled into Poppa's old chair by the fire with a large glass of *schnapps*. What my brother wrote astonished me:

> *As a result of this incident, my dear son has found religion. He repeats over and over again the story of Moses leading his tribe out of Egypt into the land of Avraham. Moses did not get to that land himself but Hoshea finally led his tribe into the valley.*

Lieb took dangerous liberties in his coded message. The land of Avraham was my land, America. And Moses called Hoshea by the name Joshua. Was this at last my brother's plea for help rescuing his family? I did not know how I would do it, but I could not live if something happened and I had held back.

Lieb ended his letter with a question. *Do you, dear brother, understand the story of Moses? It is important that Joshua knows his uncle has heard him.*

This time I had to talk to the rest of the family before I answered. That night we gathered in our living room: Ester, Simon, Markus, Sadie, Josef, Miryem, and Sara. I had talked earlier in the day to Zelda and read her Lieb's letter. Lieb's urgency screamed at all of us. There was no question what he was saying: Joshua and his family must leave, and do it quickly. I was cautious. Lieb had said such things before in one letter, and then changed his mind in the next.

Everyone offered to contribute their part of whatever money it took to get them out. But no one had any idea how to go about such a thing. The experience with Sam Lipsky was fresh in all our minds. Looking around the living room, I saw nothing but long faces and blank minds. Then Josef said one name: "Mendel Silber."

"He's a Communist, for goodness sake," Sara answered her brother before I could.

"He's a real son-of-a-bitch, but who better to get a Russian out of Russia," Josef responded.

All eyes fell on me. I was the one who had a history with this bad character. And we had to do something right now!

Before we went to bed that night, Sara said, "you know Lieb will not be coming with Joshua."

"Why not?" Her remark surprised me. I hadn't considered that possibility.

"Because Moses never got to the Promised Land." Lieb would never leave his daughter Brindyl to lie abandoned in her grave in the cemetery behind the old synagogue. And Golde would never leave her brothers and sisters still rooted in Uman.

The first thing I did the next morning was try to send a telegram to Lieb to tell him I understood his message. But I learned at the telegraph office private citizens were still not permitted to send cables to private citizens in the Soviet Union. The only option was mail. So I penned a quick letter to Lieb telling him I got the message. The Almighty prepared the path to Canaan for Moses and Hoshea, and so it shall be. I said a prayer for them.

I sent the letter by airmail, expensive as it was. I had never done that before and hoped it wouldn't draw too much attention from the censors on the Soviet side of the ocean. I stuffed in a few more dollars of bribery money before sealing the envelope and handing it to the postmaster. I bundled up as I left the post office. It was cold outside, and smelled like rain.

By the time I arrived at the tailor shop, I concluded Mendel Silber was the only choice I had, reprehensible as he was. So I picked up the phone and called the number Josef gave me the night before.

Mendel sounded curious about my urgent phone call and agreed to see me that very afternoon. We arranged to meet at a bookstore in Flatbush, a short walk from the Avenue J subway stop.

As I walked down the station steps, the shiver up my spine came from someplace other than the chill of the bleak early March after-

276 . Alan Fleishman

noon. The street was crowded, workers on their way home. I looked back several times to see if I was being followed. The government might frown on its citizens meeting with known Communists, even if Mendel was small potatoes.

The small book store was dark inside except for the light coming in through the two little show windows in front. I thought it was closed, but when I tried the door handle it turned. A bell tinkled when I entered.

A sales counter with a metal cash register guarded the entry, but no one manned it. "Anybody here?" I called. No answer. The worn plank floor creaked under my footsteps as I walked slowly down the aisle. The scent of old manuscripts touched the air. I stopped at a bruised display table and picked up a copy of Steinbeck's new novel, *The Grapes of Wrath*. A stack of something by Sartre sat right next to it, and another about the failure of the New Deal.

The little bell tinkled again when Mendel Silber walked in. He closed and locked the door, scanned the street, pulled down the window shade, and then flipped over the sign so it said "closed" to the outside world.

"You're early," he said. He was still as tough and wiry as the first day I met him on the train from Uman thirty-five years earlier, but his balding gray-streaked hair and deeply etched face showed a hard-lived life. "Follow me," he said, leading me to the small windowless room in back of the store. We sat down at a reading table. He opened his coat, took off his hat and scarf, and draped them over the back of an empty chair. His eyes never left me.

"So what's this about?" he demanded. There was none of his usual sarcasm.

I approached the subject as cautiously as one approaches a porcupine. Mendel was a Communist but I never doubted his loyalties were first to himself, no matter how vocally he expressed his passion for the working man, Stalin, and the Soviet Union.

I posed the issue as a hypothetical. "What if someone of little importance wanted to leave the Soviet Union? Could they do it?"

He chuckled without humor. It didn't take him long to figure out what I was saying. He came prepared.

"Yeah, I know a guy who can help," he said. "Works in the Soviet consulate in the city. Want me to give him a call?"

"Yes," I answered.

"There's going to be a price."

"We're willing to pay."

"The debt won't be payable in money."

"What's that supposed to mean?" I asked myself what I was getting into. But I charged on. I wished I had brought Simon or Markus with me.

"Better you talk to him. I'll set it up. Wait till tomorrow, then call this number." He pulled a small slip of paper from his pocket and handed it to me. His eyes followed my shaking fingers as I took it from his grasp.

On the walk home from the El station, I thought about what I had just done. Either my brother's family was on its way to being rescued, or I had committed a stupid mistake. The clack of heels on the sidewalk behind me set off fresh paranoia. I stopped to look at the display of Hadacol and Lydia Pinkham in the window of the drug store to see if anyone was following, just like James Cagney would have done. I glanced out of the corner of my eye. The clacking heels on the sidewalk turned out to be those of a pretty dark-haired woman as unmindful of the cold chill off the bay as I was a victim to it. I turned up the collar of my overcoat and pulled the brim of my Stetson down over my eyes. Imagination stalked me the rest of the way home.

"Dah," the deep voice on the other end of the telephone answered. I gave my name and explained Mendel Silber had told me to call. The voice replied in Russian with the accent of a Muscovite. He said little other than issuing a brusque order to meet him in front of the Herald Square subway station at exactly two o'clock.

"No one comes with you," he warned.

"How will I recognize you," I asked.

"I will recognize you," he answered. "Wait next to the newsstand."

A few hours later I sat on the BMT, the clatter and swaying of the subway car stirring anxieties I hadn't felt since leaving Russia. Markus offered to come along, but I took the Russian's warning as a threat. My brother was the only one I told where I was going.

The gray March lunch hour had passed but the square was still filled with shoppers. Macy's and Gimbel's, across the street from each other, drew a flock any time of day. I took up a position by the side of the newsstand and scanned around for someone who might look like a Russian spy.

I glanced at the headlines across the newspapers. Yugoslavia and Bulgaria had been forced to join the Fascist Axis. German air raids on London damaged Buckingham Palace. The Senate was about to pass the Lend-Lease Act, enabling the U.S. to supply the Allies with armaments, an act some said would drag us into this war.

A big man brushed up against me a little too forcefully. "Avi Schneider?" he whispered. I nodded. "Come with me." He pushed through the crowded sidewalk toward a gray Chevrolet parked by a fire hydrant half a block away. A policeman loitered nearby, unconcerned.

The big man opened the rear door of the Chevy and stood back. A stocky man with a bushy black head of hair and even bushier black eyebrows sat in the back seat on the far side. He motioned for me to come in. "*Pozhaluista* – please," he said. It was the voice I spoke to on the telephone earlier. The engine was running and the heater warmed my numbed fingers and toes. The odor of the gasoline exhaust united with that of a body which hadn't known a bathtub or a bar of soap in weeks.

He understood what I wanted before I even began to explain. He leaned toward me. "It is most unusual for someone to want to leave our country," he said. He sounded as if he considered such a request sinister.

"This person only wants to join his family in America," I said, as though not mentioning that the person was my nephew somehow provided protection if this didn't work out. How naï veit sounds when I say it now.

"Yes, yes. So your brother's family wants to join you in America." He leaned back in the seat and sighed as though this conversation was taking great effort. "We can arrange that, but it will be difficult. It will take some time, and it will be costly."

"How do I know you can do what you say? I don't even know who you are."

He reached into the inside pocket of his suit coat and yanked out a thin leather wallet. He opened it to reveal a credential of some kind, and then handed it to me. It contained a picture of him, his name – Aleixandre Korsenkovich – and the seal of the Soviet Consulate in New York. It didn't matter what it said his official position was, he almost certainly was NKVD. I handed the leather wallet back to him.

He gave me a dead smile lacking any goodwill. "You are from Uman. We are comrades. We do you a favor. You do us a favor. We do not want your money. "

"I am not a person of any importance."

"You underestimate yourself, Mr. Avi Schneider. People believe you are an honest man of great courage."

I didn't like where this conversation was leading. We were ready to pay bribes to anyone we had to pay. But this Communist had something else in mind. He looked at my fists clenching and unclenching, every muscle strung so tight it hurt.

"Be at ease, comrade. It is so little we ask. As a show of good faith, maybe you convey a friendly message to your friend Mr. Berman, Congressman Breuer's associate. And it would be a big favor if your brother-in-law Josef Kravetz could stop his union's opposition to Communist participation. For each favor you do for me, we bring one more of your family to America. Yah, a good deal, as you say."

My first thought was if I said no I would put Lieb and his family in more danger than if I had never started all of this. The next thought was of Uncle Yakov and what he taught me about courage.

"The price you ask is very high, Mr. Korsenkovich. I will have to think about it and discuss it with the family."

"Discuss it with no one." He slapped his hand on the seat. The smile disappeared, his cold eyes locked on mine. "No one!"

I opened the door of the car and put one foot out. "I've thought about it," I said. "Thank you for your offer, but the answer is no."

"You are making a serious mistake, comrade. Time is running out."

I closed the door of the car and nearly ran to the steps down into the subway station. When I got on the train, I looked around to see if anyone suspicious was following me. Then I leaned back in my seat, closed my eyes, and breathed. The car was nearly empty except for a couple of kids with Brooklyn Dodgers caps, a small Negro woman bundled up against the raw day, and four or five Hassidic men congregated at the far end.

The racket of the train jammed my jumbled reasoning and frank terror. If meeting with Korsenkovich caused harm to Lieb or his family, I couldn't live with it. But I wasn't going to be a Communist stooge for anything. There was no certainty it would even help Lieb. How stupid to get involved with Communists. What was I thinking?

Now what do I do? The first thing was to tell the rest of the family what happened, and maybe we'd come up with something else. I felt more desperate than ever, but anything would be better than this.

The next evening on my way home I stopped at the Rexall store to pick up some Aspirub and Pine Brothers glycerine tablets for Sara's cold and sore throat. When I came out, Mendel Silber waited with one foot propped up on the fender of a gray Plymouth parked in front. I walked over to him.

"Don't be a fool, Schneider," he said without introduction. "These are serious people you're dealing with."

The puffs of smoke from our frosted breaths collided. "Nothing doing. I've already been a fool, getting mixed up with you people."

"Help us. This isn't your country. Not as it is. We'll change it. Make it better."

"You're wrong." I turned and walked away. I never wanted to see Mendel Silber again.

Another, more desperate, letter arrived from Lieb the next week. He repeated the story about Moses, Hoshea, and reaching the land of Avraham to be certain I understood his first message. That night I answered, assuring him help was on the way, though I still had no idea how to save my brother or my brother's son.

While I wrote my letter, Edward R. Murrow broadcast on the radio the latest German firebombing raid on London. When he closed with "good night, and good luck" I thought he was talking to me. I needed some luck. Lieb and his family needed even more.

CHAPTER THIRTY-THREE

April 1941

Duv leaned against the railing of the boardwalk and looked out over the morning sea. The smoke from his cigarette drifted into the salty air. Word had it Duv was one of the mobster Meyer Lansky's lieutenants, involved mostly with gambling. Even now I couldn't imagine Duv killing anyone. But who knows? Life changes people.

Deep furrows showed around his eyes, but even in age he lost little of the handsome looks girls never could resist. He looked at me with a sincere smile sprinkled with sadness. "I'm glad to see you Avi, even under the circumstances."

It had been Simon's idea to approach Duv about rescuing Lieb. "He's a gangster," I had said, unwilling to get involved with any more unsavory characters after Sam Lipsky and Mendel Silber.

"There's been talk it was Meyer Lansky and Bugsy Siegel people who broke up those Nazi American Bund rallies," Simon answered. He told me he heard rumors they had rescued a few people in Europe and Russia. They got some to Palestine and a few to America.

As reluctant as I was to get involved with any more bad guys, time was growing late. Joshua couldn't hold out forever from the Communists, and Hitler threatened everyone. Britain was almost finished, and then nothing would stand in his way. I had no better idea so, repelled at the thought, I agreed to call Duv. I got his phone number from Thomas Kelly. Duv was still a regular at T. T. Kelly's.

Duv answered my phone call himself. His voice was hard as a hammer. At first he sounded surprised and suspicious, then curious. When I started to tell him about Lieb, he stopped me in mid-sentence.

"I'll meet you on the Brighton Beach boardwalk in front of the Ferris wheel," he said. "One o'clock."

Duv was overdressed for the boardwalk. A wide blue and black diagonal tie held in place by a diamond stick pin accented his stylish gray pinstripe suit. I thought I saw the bulge of a small gun in the left breast of his jacket. He took off his fedora. I did the same. The unusually warm April sun soothed my aging, achy bones.

"We can pay whatever it costs," I said after I filled him in about Lieb's plight. There didn't seem to be any point in trying to appeal to the sentimentalities of someone who had spent the better part of a lifetime making money illegally.

"What makes you think I can help?" he asked.

"There are rumors you've gotten people out."

Duv turned toward me, his expression soft and somber. The mischievous smile of the youngster I once knew was missing. "Lieb was my friend too," he said.

"How much is it going to cost?"

He took a long drag on his cigarette, exhaled, and then flicked the stub into the sand. "At least ten thousand smackers. It depends on the situation."

My heart dropped to my heels. "We'll have to mortgage the house," I said. "It might take a few weeks, but we can do it."

He shook his head slowly and decisively. "I owe you," he said. "This one's on the house."

I thought of Mendel Silber. "No strings?"

"No strings."

A flock of seagulls squabbled on the beach over the carcass of a fish.

Another pair circled in the blue sky above. Small waves lapped the shore. Duv kept his eyes on three younger men in bare feet crossing in front of us at the water's edge. The boardwalk was nearly empty except for two old men playing chess on a bench a few lampposts down.

"What about Havol?" I asked.

He turned his attention back to me. "That bitch? Why would ya' wanna' save her?"

"She's Sara's sister. She's been through a lot."

He nodded. "Let me see what we can do. But first let's get Lieb's son and family out of there."

His confidence made me think this just might be possible. "When it's all over we have to have dinner," I said. "Just you and me. Maybe Simon and Markus. Catch up on old times." He flinched when a gigantic wave exploded onto the beach, then looked around to make sure we were still alone.

"This isn't going to be easy. We fail more often than we succeed. Sometimes people get killed. You willing to take that chance?"

"I don't think we have any choice, do you?"

"No."

"How will you get them out?"

"Don't ask too many questions. I'll let you know when our people have made contact. In the meantime, you don't tell anyone else what's going on. Got it? Not your family. Not your rabbi." His eyes drilled me.

"What do I tell them? I have to tell them something."

"You want to get good people killed? This isn't child's play," he snarled. The dark demeanor of a gangster clouded over him for a moment.

I looked away and nodded my assent. "How long will it take?"

He relaxed. "Maybe weeks. Maybe longer. It depends. Find something to keep yourself busy. Don't try to contact me again. I'll get aholda' you when there's news."

"Thank you," I said. "Thank you." I must have looked like I was ready to cry. He looked embarrassed.

We walked along the boardwalk toward Manhattan Beach, side by side like when we were boys. "We were quite a foursome weren't we – you, me, Simon, Lieb," he said.

"Life was a bitch," I said.

"That Askinov kid was the devil's bastard. But there were good days in there. The best ones of my life." We had reached the end of the boardwalk. He paused, as if he had something more to say and didn't know if he should say it. Then he continued. "I told you once I wished I could be as good a man as you were. I still do." When we parted, he drove off in a black Packard with big white-walls, driven by a broad shouldered goon. I walked.

Duv would save Lieb. I had no doubt. He was a hard man, but just enough of my old friend must have remained for him to risk saving Jews from the most dangerous place in the world. Why, I wondered?

I'm in over my head, I thought as I turned onto Oriental Avenue. Lieb and Joshua were putting all of their faith in me. And I was putting my faith in the hands of a gangster. What if Joshua is killed? Or his wife and children? I could still ask Duv to call it off, I thought. But I couldn't live with myself if I did nothing and Joshua was killed anyway. Everyone treated me like the big brother who was supposed to solve everybody's problems. This time Ester, Markus, and Zelda had to carry some of it. But Duv wasn't kidding when he warned me not to talk to anyone. Not even Sara. What if they let something slip? Ester talked too much as it was, and Sara was always trying to please her, too much for my liking.

There was no reason to trust Duv, yet I felt some hope for the first time since Lieb's panicked letter first arrived. Uncle Yakov used to say courage was when you did something you were afraid to do, but did it anyway. So be it. Let's see where this is going, I mumbled to myself. The two well dressed matrons I passed on the sidewalk looked at me as if I were a crazy old man talking to himself.

I stopped talking about rescuing Joshua and Lieb. The family all guessed from my silence that something was going on. "Any news?"

Markus asked each morning when I walked into the tailor shop. I always shook my head or barked a sharp "no!" Finally he stopped asking.

Six weeks went by. The only contact I had with Duv was one brief, meaningless phone conversation meant to lift my spirits. I began to doubt anything more would come of this than with Lipsky or Mendel Silber. Maybe Duv was all talk, I warned myself.

I tried to put on a good face for the others but Sara knew me too well. She tolerated my moods and kept a distance when that's what I wanted. She plied me with food and numbed me with liquor. She cuddled with me at night, but worry was not arousing.

In the middle of May a letter from Lieb finally acknowledged my earlier air mail letter promising rescue: *Moses drank from the waters of the Nile. He thanked the Almighty for promising to deliver Hoshea and his people from the pharaoh. Avraham be praised. And Moses was at peace even if he did not reach the Promised Land.*

The Germans captured Athens and pushed the British forces in North Africa back to the Egyptian border. German paratroopers assaulted the British stronghold on Crete with success. London continued to burn under the assault of the German Luftwaffe, but the British air force got in a few licks against German cities. Heavy Allied loses to German U-boats bloodied the North Atlantic. President Roosevelt declared a national emergency when they sank the U.S. merchant ship SS Robin Moor – and moved us closer to entering this war, I hoped.

The late May day Duv contacted me was the day the huge German battleship Bismarck sank the British battle cruiser HMS Hood, pride of the royal navy. She also badly damaged the battleship Prince of Wales.

"This is Avi Schneider," I answered when I picked up the receiver. My mind had been lost in the design of a new silky-blue evening dress when the phone rang in the tailor shop.

"Your friend wants 'a talk to ya'. Go out the front door and take a left," a tough monotone voice ordered from the other end. "Go two blocks and turn left. We'll be waitin'."

"I'll be back shortly," I called to Manny as I grabbed my hat off the rack by the door and headed into a bright afternoon. Duv wouldn't have come all the way out from Manhattan if he didn't have news, good or bad. My heart pounded so hard I could hear it.

I nearly ran the two blocks. Duv's square shouldered goon leaned against the big silver grill of the shiny black Packard, arms crossed in front of him. As I approached, he nodded his head toward the open rear door. I climbed in.

Duv wore his broadest mischievous grin, along with a double-breasted blue serge suit. He looked twenty years younger than last time I saw him.

"You squeezed Sara's tit in the clearing at Sukhi Yar."

His vulgarity about Sara startled me. It took me a second to realize what he was talking about. "My god," I yelled. "Lieb is the only person I ever told that to."

"We made contact," he laughed. "Our man saw him. Talked to him and Joshua."

We yelled so loud his goon turned around and peeked into the car to make sure everything was okay. He would have seen me giving my old friend a huge hug and kissing him passionately on the cheek.

"Are they out, are they out?" I begged.

"Slow down. They haven't left Uman yet. But soon."

"Tell me something. Anything."

"I can tell you this. We've made first contact. Next we're sending in a small team. They'll lead them out."

"When? Where will they take them? Can you depend on these people?" My questions came faster than Duv could answer.

He held up his hand to stop, his look sober now. "We've got a long way to go, but we made first contact. Be happy with that for now."

Duv did tell me it should be no more than two or three weeks until they were safely out of Russia. The same rules applied. I was not to contact him. He would call me when there was any news.

"And one more thing," he smiled as I was ready to exit the car.

"Lieb and Golde are coming out too. Not just Joshua and his family."

I started to cry right there, with one foot inside the car and one outside. I couldn't help myself. At last, after all these years, I had succeeded. I didn't know if I could hide my excitement from the rest of the family. I had to say something. Duv agreed I could tell them we had received some favorable information. "You can tell them the odds of rescue have improved," a nice turn of phrase from a professional gambler. "Bet on it."

On the way home I stopped at the synagogue to see Daniel. "Come and pray with me," I said without explanation. He joined me in front of the ark, his hand on my shoulder. I bowed my head and covered my eyes with my hands. "I am going to see Lieb again," I said softly. Daniel pretended he didn't hear me.

I didn't want to get my hopes up, but on my walk home I began to think of having Lieb with me in time for Rosh Hashanah in September, worshipping next to me in our synagogue. I broke into something resembling a trot, eager to get home. Next we had to start thinking about where they were going to live.

CHAPTER THIRTY-FOUR

June 1941

The jangling telephone phone rang at six o'clock that Sunday morning, June 22. I sat up in bed trying to will myself awake. Sara moaned in protest and turned over. The phone kept up its assault. I got up and tromped downstairs to answer it. No one called us at this time of day

"Have you heard?" Markus yelled as soon as I answered. "The Germans have invaded Russia."

"What are you talking about?" I tried to shake the cobwebs from my brain.

"What are we going to do? We have to get Lieb out of there."

All he knew was what he heard from the announcer on the radio. Before we hung up I promised to call if I heard anything from Duv.

I turned on the radio and started a pot of coffee, wide awake now. Ester phoned right after that. "Have you heard they've overrun Uman?" She sounded hysterical.

"Ester, they're hundreds of miles from Uman. The Russians will stop them." I tried to sound calm and confident.

By the time I hung up with Ester, Sara had come down the steps in her bathrobe. "What's all the commotion?" She was grouchy at being awakened so early on a Sunday morning.

I told her what had happened while I leafed through an old atlas trying to find a map of western Russia. "The Russians are no match for the Germans," I said.

She poured two glasses of water and handed one to me. I took a sip. She took a sip. "Let's be hopeful," she said, as though one could choose such a thing. "We don't know what's going to happen." She put her glass down and then ran her fingers over my cheek. "You've done all you can," she said. "There's nothing you can do." I didn't believe that.

We gathered in the afternoon at the synagogue to pray. There must have been a hundred fifty of us, all wringing our hands. I hardly heard a word Daniel said. My mind was in Russia. I felt the same foreboding I did after the first Kishinev *pogrom* a lifetime ago.

On the way out, Moishe Stepaner asked me to come to the Blue Sail, a bar on a side street in town not far from the water. A group from Uman was gathering to exchange whatever news we had about the situation.

I'd only been in the Blue Sail a few times. I didn't even know the bartender. Everyone called him "Litvak" because he was a Jew from Lithuania. He owned the place. He was a big man with gray hair growing from his nose, ears and knuckles. Litvak didn't say much, unlike Thomas Kelly. The bar itself was about as plain and simple as he was, with ugly chrome tables and chairs on a floor of cracked green linoleum. There was no big mirror behind the scarred bar. The food offering consisted of a big jar of pickles and a basket of stale pretzels sitting on the bar. Sometimes he cooked up kosher hot dogs if he knew he was going to have a crowd.

The dozen or so men filtering in from the synagogue looked serious, but none so dour as Chiam Chernoff and Moishe Stepaner. They clung together, clucking like chickens about to lose their heads. In all these years in America, they still looked and acted like Russian peasants from Uman.

Not much was accomplished that first day. The meeting was chaotic, everyone talking at the same time. No one knew much beyond what we learned from the radio, so all we did was ask questions, speculate, and worry together.

Duv had warned me not to call, but I couldn't stand it any longer. When he answered, he didn't even admonish me for breaking the rules. "We don't know anything yet," he said, his voice as grim as an undertaker. "Try not to worry. We're trying to make contact with our people. Hell, maybe Lieb is out of there by now. It's possible. I'll call you when I know something." His encouragement didn't help much, but there wasn't anything to do but wait.

The meeting in the Blue Sail bar the following Sunday was more organized. Someone brought a big map of the Eastern Front so we could follow the progress of the war. Moishe Stepaner tried to appoint me to lead the meeting, but when I deferred he took it on himself. Despite my protests, they all looked to me as the military authority only because they thought the night on the barricades thirty-six years earlier gave me credentials. How ridiculous.

Everyone had a brother or sister, aunt, uncle, father or mother still in Uman. We got radio broadcasts, newspaper reports, articles in magazines and rumors passed on from one person to the next. Nearly all of the solid information came directly from reports issued by the German and Russian governments. Both sides forbade foreign journalists from traveling with their armies. The news we did get was not good. The Germans moved fast. They took Lvov and Brody in a week.

"There's no stopping them," Chiam Chernoff grumbled before swallowing a shot of bourbon.

"Lvov and Brody are hundreds of miles from Uman." I pointed to a place on the map. "Lots of time to evacuate the civilians."

"The Russians aren't going to do the Jews any favors," Judah said. He was short and round as a pumpkin, with a mole on his cheek. There was no nonsense in the man. I liked him.

"They have to keep the Germans from reaching the Black Sea." I indicated the obvious on the map. "They're not fighting to protect Jews. They're fighting for themselves." Many of the men mumbled agreement. I wasn't nearly as confident as I tried to sound.

I didn't think that much about evacuation until I got a call from Duv at home a few days later. The minute I heard his voice, I knew it wasn't good news. Sara hovered close by ready to celebrate or commiserate, whichever the situation called for.

"It's over." He sounded exhausted and saddened, not at all like Duv. "One of our team reached Istanbul. The rest were killed by fuckin' Germans and Romanians. Lieb, Joshua and the rest of the family are still in Uman."

"Are they alive?"

"They were alive when our man left Uman." He paused, struggling to regain control. I thought I heard a sob. "Don't lose hope. We hear Jews and Party chiefs are being evacuated to the east."

"Anything else we can do?"

"It's over for us. Almost all of our people are dead. Wiped out. We're done."

"You've got to try," I begged. "Please. I've got no one else to turn to."

"Russia's lost," he said, his voice choked with frustration. "And we can't fight the whole fuckin' German army all by ourselves. We got better things to do."

"Thank you for all you've done," I said, trying to hold back my tears. Sara came over and put her arm around my shoulder.

Duv's voice dropped almost to a whisper. "I'm sorry, Avi. There nothing else I can do. If I could I would. I promise you." He was close to the edge again. "Lieb was my friend. And so are you."

"If you ever need anything...." My voice trailed off, the empty promise unfinished.

"For your own good, don't try to contact me again. You don't want to be seen around people like me." The phone clicked. He had hung up. I turned to Sara and shook my head. We collapsed in each others' arms there in the hallway, clinging to each other, sobbing and swaying.

Simon and I had lunch the next day at the coffee shop. I needed the comfort of my old friend. No one knew me better or longer than Simon. He wore his fifty-nine years well. I don't know how he stayed so thin with Ester's cooking. The skinny kid I knew growing up in Uman was still there beneath the nice suit, horn-rimmed eye glasses, and a brush of a moustache.

Both of us only nibbled at our chicken salad sandwiches. "He's a gangster," Simon said. "So why'd he work so hard to rescue Jews?"

"I like to think it was because some good parts of our old friend survive."

"Too bad there isn't more of it."

"He said something. That growing up with us were the best years of his life. We did have some good times." I smiled just thinking about the time as young teenagers we peeked at the naked women in the communal bath behind the synagogue.

"Whatever he was then, he's a killer now, and don't forget it."

"I won't be seeing him again."

The Russian army was no match for the Germans. On that we all agreed. The Blitzkrieg rolled on so fast we had a hard time keeping up. Ester, Markus and I talked on the phone every day. Zelda and I talked a few times in the first weeks after the invasion.

On the Friday night after Duv's call, we met at Ester's for Sabbath dinner. We prayed for Lieb and his family, and shared memories: playing in Sukhi Yar, school, Lieb's marriage to Golde, and our fear of Viktor Askinov. I tried to give them hope. When Josef said, "There's no stopping them fuckin' Krauts," I said, "The rain and mud will stop them." When Ester said "There's no place to hide," I said "So they'll move east." When Simon said "Lieb's not a fighter," I said "But he's a good thinker and that's what he needs right now, a good head on his shoulders."

Sara held my hand all the way to Ester's and back. But on the walk home she asked, "Why do you give them false hope?"

I pulled my hand away. "Because I'm their big brother. If I say there is hope then there is hope."

"What will happen will happen," she said. I wanted more compassion than I was getting. Sara accepted her sister Havol's fate stoically.

"God's will," she said. I could not do the same.

Sara reached over and grabbed my hand again. She put her mouth to my ear and said, "I'm sorry." We held each others' hands the rest of the walk home.

It must have been the third week of July when the men got together in the Blue Sail bar again. "Give me some good news," I pleaded when I walked in.

"There's nothing good to tell," Chiam answered. "First it was Lvov, then Brody, then Ternopol."

"They're in Vinnitsa now," Judah said. He jabbed his index finger at a point on the map. "Right here. A hundred miles from Uman." He emptied his glass of beer and slammed it on the table.

"The Germans are after Kiev, not Uman," I said.

"The Germans are after St. Petersburg and Moscow," Litvak called out from behind the bar. "And they're going through Lithuania." Everyone ignored him, as though Uman was all that mattered.

"My sister and her family are in Kiev," a slim, bald man said from the corner of the room by the map. He mumbled something under his breath that sounded like a prayer, maybe Kaddish. Someone else said "Amen."

Moishe Stepaner had been sitting quietly beside Chiam Chernoff just like he always did, a newspaper in his hand. "The Germans passed through Vinnitsa. It says here some elements are confirmed at Zhitomir. That's only seventy-five miles from Kiev. Casualties on both sides are unbelievable."

Just as we were getting ready to leave, the map taken down from the wall, Pinchus Sklar walked in. He usually talked too fast for a man whose English was hard to understand. This time he was deliberate: "The Germans passed through Belya Tserkov, Southwest of Kiev. They're almost to Uman."

The German army had moved nearly six hundred miles in twenty-three days. We didn't know for another week, but the Battle of Uman had already begun on July 15. It didn't end until August 8. The newspapers and radio reported over a million men on both sides killed, wounded or captured. It's impossible to grasp such a large number.

A couple of weeks later we learned for certain that Uman was now firmly under German control. I tried not to picture Nazis strutting across the market square or camped in Sukhi Yar. And where was Lieb? What happened to him?

We went to synagogue, prayed and then traipsed to the Blue Sail. The despair of the hot August day smelled like a sewer.

Litvak took out a couple of bottles of whiskey and put them on our tables. The map we had been using to follow the battles lay in a corner, no one caring to put it up. What was the point? That week we drank hard liquor until we were too numb to speak. It didn't help.

"I heard Churchill's broadcast," Judah said. "He accused the Germans of executing thousands of civilians in the areas of Russia they overran."

"Not civilians. Jews! That's who they're killing," the thin, bald man in the corner yelled.

Chiam pulled out a Yiddish newspaper. "It says here that thousands of Jews were massacred by the Nazis in Minsk, Brest-Litovsk, Lvov and some other places."

"How do they know?" the Litvak yelled from behind the bar. "They don't know. They said the same shit in the last war, and it turned out to be nothing but propaganda."

"I've seen it in a couple of the other Yiddish dailies." Judah picked at the mole on his cheek until it bled.

"God's been watching over our people for five thousand years," Moishe Stepaner said.

"Well, he hasn't been doing a very good job of it lately," Chiam answered.

The German army moved on East like a horde of Cossack vermin. They took Kiev to the north of Uman and Odessa to the south on the Black Sea. Moscow and St. Petersburg would surely fall before winter came. My hope was somehow Lieb had escaped to the east. Let everyone else give up. I wouldn't.

When I walked home that hot August day, I felt Lieb as surely as if he were walking beside me. I had never wanted to go back to Russia. Now I had to, no matter what Sara said. When this damn war was over, I was going to find him.

We met again at Ester's for Sabbath dinner. It was more like we were sitting *Shiva*. Ester was solemn when she lit the candles, an old shawl from Uman on her head. I think it was one of Momma's. Josef and Miryem started joining us for Sabbath dinner most of the time, at least in part because we connected Josef to Havol.

"Let's say *Kaddish*," Markus said solemnly after we finished dinner and all of the plates were cleared.

I smacked my hand on the table startling myself and everyone else. "He's not dead." It certainly changed the mood around the table, and not for the better. None dared to challenge me.

After the fall of Uman, our Blue Sail minion only met at the bar every now and then. Someone said the friend of someone's brother-in-law heard that a number of Jews from Uman had been evacuated to Tashkent in the east. But no one could produce the name of the person who said it. Still, it made sense some would have been evacuated. I prayed Lieb was among them.

My letter writing to Lieb didn't stop. Maybe I thought as long as I kept writing he was still alive. I didn't get an answer. But of course if they were evacuated, the postal service wouldn't know where to direct my letters.

I was mad at everyone who had anything to do with making this war. I'm ashamed to say I got very angry at Lieb too for his irresponsible obstinacy, refusing to leave Russia for all those years when he had the chance.

Soon after Uman fell, I went to Saturday morning services at the synagogue. I needed some comfort. Daniel delivered a sermon on hope in the face of uncertainty, or something like that. It didn't help. But I still wouldn't give up. Not yet.

CHAPTER THIRTY-FIVE

December 1941

I was glad when America got in the war at last. I never doubted we would win. If there was a god, He was surely on our side.

We expanded our little tailoring operation and took to making women's uniforms: WAC, WAVE, Red Cross, and military nurses. Isaac converted his factory to making parachutes and knapsacks. Business boomed.

Every Jewish boy I knew volunteered to go fight. Young men in military uniform were everywhere, looking strong and handsome. Isaac, Ester's son Willy and some of the others tried to join but were told they were too old. I was glad of it. But Miryem's son Henry went. So did Sadie and Markus' sons, and Tillie's younger brother and a few cousins. By the time it was over, nearly six hundred thousand Jewish boys served. Tens of thousands were killed and wounded, bleeding just like the gentiles. And every drop of blood they gave earned all Jews their place as real Americans.

Our nephew Henry made me proud when I saw him in his Marine uniform the first time. He was as special to Sara and me as if he were our own flesh and blood. Though Miryem never would let Josef formally adopt her son, Henry and Josef adopted each other with an earned love no legal proceeding need sanctify.

As a kid, Henry loved coming to our house, and sometimes he spent the night even into his teenage years. I think now of the time I looked out the kitchen window to see Sara trying to play catch with him in our back yard. He must have been about eleven years old then. Here was this once-Hassidic woman in her pink and gray housedress, hair hidden under a scarf, chasing a baseball. Henry wore his Dodgers cap on his head and a mitt on his left hand.

"Keep your eye on the ball Auntie," Henry called. He tried to throw it as softly as he could. Sara's eyes and mouth opened as wide as they could get, hands apart, body taught as a banjo string. The ball bounced off the front of her chest and fell to the ground. "Good try, Auntie. Good try." Her failures didn't stop either of them from trying again and again whenever he came to visit. Five years later she could actually catch about one out of every two throws.

At twenty-five, Henry had finally pointed himself in the right direction and was midway through City College. But he joined up the day after the Japanese bombed Pearl Harbor. The Marines shaved off his bushy brown hair. He looked so handsome in his uniform the girls flocked to him like spawning salmon.

From early in the war, Henry flew fighter planes, Marine Corsairs, in the Pacific. Miryem started going to synagogue on the Sabbath and prayed for him as though his life depended on her prayers. Maybe it did. Such piety was something new for Miryem.

When Henry went off, I worried about what it would do to him. He was so gentle, and he was going to have to kill people. I prayed he would come back with a soul he could live with. I knew something about the savage inside of even good people. I swore I would still shoot Viktor Askinov if I ever got another chance. Only this time I would make sure I killed him.

Our little tailor shop wasn't so little any more. We had twenty people working for us now in two shifts. Most of them were women, and a few older men. Every moment I wasn't at the tailor shop I spent on bond drives, scrap drives, refugee relief, and service as a Civil Defense air raid warden in case we ever got bombed. They issued me a warden's white metal pith helmet shaped like a British soldier's, an armband, and a fire extinguisher you had to pump by hand. Sara fretted. "You have to slow down," she said, repeating my doctor. I couldn't. All of this frantic effort left me too tired to worry about Lieb every minute. Sara made me promise to at least hire a boy to shovel out the coal ashes from the furnace in the basement.

Sara volunteered to roll bandages for the Red Cross, but soon found herself driving an ambulance. It's a mystery how she ever learned to drive. "No one asked me if I had a license," she said. "So I just got behind the wheel and did what they do in the movies."

The world knew what the Nazis were doing to the Jews even though today most say they didn't. Maybe we didn't know the details, but we knew enough. As early as March of 1942, Jewish organizations reported the Nazis had already murdered over two hundred thousand. The BBC broadcast in June 1942 the massacre of over seven hundred thousand. The World Jewish Congress held a press conference in London, also in June of 1942, and told the world a million Jews had been exterminated. Some people didn't want to believe it. Some didn't care. After all, they were only Jews.

Ester and Markus pressed hard for me to accept Lieb's death, sit *Shiva*, and say *Kaddish*. Even Sara hinted she had a premonition months before about both Lieb and Havol. I refused to believe it. They had all given up on him before, during the 1921 *pogroms*. I hadn't given up on him then, and I wasn't going to give up now. "He's alive as long as I say he's alive," I yelled. "Wait, you'll see." There was hope until there was evidence. I got angry with all of them. I couldn't see at the time this was their way of dealing with their own heartache for him.

My faith seemed vindicated one hot, sticky August day in 1942 when I stuck my hand in our mailbox and grasped the thin tissue paper envelope. I took one look at Lieb's left-handed chicken scrawl and let out a scream that brought Sara running and caused Mrs. Epstein next door to look out her window.

"He's alive." I grabbed Sara and kissed her right there on the front steps for the whole world to see. Sara screamed, threw her arms around me, and kissed me back. My hands fumbled in my eagerness to tear open the envelope.

> *My Dear brother,*
>
> *The messenger from God has arrived unto Moses. And Moses told the messenger he will join Hoshea in the land of Avraham. Blessed is the Lord, and blessed is my brother. Soon we will drink together from the waters of the Jordan. If I were to die tomorrow, I would die with thanks on my lips that I have been given such a brother as you. I give you all the love I can give.*

That's all there was. Just this single piece of tissue paper with these few words. I turned it over. Surely there must be more. He's still alive but where is he? He sounds like he is still expecting me to rescue him, I thought.

Sara saw the joy on my face evacuate. "June 18, 1941," I said when I eyed the date on the top of the letter for the first time. "He wrote it over a year ago, before the Nazi invasion."

Sara covered her mouth with her hand. Then she put her arms around my neck and pressed herself to me. I wrapped my arms around her; we clung to each other like that for minutes. "This doesn't mean he's dead," I said, when I pulled back.

We listened when Edward R. Murrow confirmed some of our worst nightmares in a December broadcast. Reading it was one thing, but hearing Murrow say it out loud made it so. "Millions of human beings, most of them Jews," he reported from London, "are being gathered up with ruthless efficiency and murdered. It is a picture of mass murder and moral depravity unequaled in the history of the world. It is a horror beyond what imagination can grasp. There are no longer concentration camps – We must speak of them as extermination camps."

Soon after Morrow's report the New York Times carried a story of the atrocities on the front page. The Times usually buried such stories in the back, and so did many other newspapers. The Times' publisher, Arthur Hays Sulzberger, didn't believe his power should be misused to specifically help other Jews.

President Roosevelt warned Hitler and the Germans they would be held accountable for what they were doing to the Jews. A published warning, that's all he did. We loved FDR, but we still couldn't understand why, now that he knew, he wasn't doing something to rescue Jews destined for extinction.

In early 1943 the Manhattan Beach Jewish Rescue Group chose me as their president, deputized to voice our protests to the Democratic Party. I sought out my old friend Sidney Berman, regional chairman of the party with offices in Manhattan. Sidney agreed to see me right away, aware of the growing political influence of Jewish organizations like our rescue group. Rumors already circulated that FDR was going to run for an unprecedented fourth term. If he did, he was going to need us.

Slivers of snow struck me from all directions on the walk from the trolley. It felt good to get in out of the January cold. Sidney greeted me at the door of his modest office with the enthusiastic handshake and big smile of a veteran politician. He knew why I was there even before I started talking. And I knew the party needed money.

Sidney began his defense of Roosevelt with a patient lecture about the situation within the State Department. The congressman he used to work for was now on the House Committee on Foreign Affairs, so he had inside information.

"The Department's full of Jew-haters from top to bottom," he said, "starting with Secretary of State Hull. The old boys all knew each other at Groton or St. Paul's, then Harvard, Yale and Princeton. Wealth and fashion. It's a pretty nice club to belong to. The only Jews they ran into growing up were the ones in their college classes. You know, smart and pushy ones. If there wasn't a war on, they'd just as soon send us all back to the old country." He stopped his tirade long enough to light a cigarette, then resumed.

"We had the story of the exterminations as early as August of '42. But the State Department twisted arms to keep it quiet for awhile."

Sidney got up from his desk and walked over to the poster on his wall of Rosie the Riveter imploring us to buy U.S. War Bonds. When he started talking again I thought he was talking to her. "This guy Breckinridge Long. Ever heard of him?"

"No," I answered.

Sidney sat back down behind his desk. "If Jews knew what he's really done to them they'd fricassee him. Long's the Assistant Secretary of State. He's the one who directed our embassies and consulates to slow down visas so no more Jews were admitted to the U.S. Then he showed them how to do it with administrative tricks. So you know what happened?"

He didn't wait for my answer. "Ninety percent of the quota spots that might have gone to Jews from countries under German control haven't been filled. Only a handful of Jews have been admitted to the U.S." Sidney slumped back down in his chair; he took off his glasses and threw them on his desk.

"FDR's goal is to win the war, first and foremost. He says that's the fastest and surest way to save Jews and everyone else. I think he may be right in the long run. But he also wants to win reelection if he chooses to run again, and this issue's too hot to handle. You know, polls show a quarter of Americans still look at Jews as a menace."

"I don't know if he can hold on to Jewish support if he doesn't do something," I said.

"Who are you going to vote for? Dewey? He's such a yuck."

"So what do we do?"

Sidney picked his glasses up from the desktop and put them back on. "Pressure, pressure and more pressure. Keep it up. Work on the New York Times and other newspapers. We only get coverage of these exterminations in bits and pieces. Turn up the heat."

So we went on the attack. We organized. We wrote letters, held headline-grabbing rallies, protested, and raised money. And still we denied to ourselves the full horror of what we knew – what everyone now calls the Holocaust. How else could I hold on to hope for Lieb?

CHAPTER THIRTY-SIX

August 1943

War or no war, I wanted our fortieth anniversary to be the best day of Sara's life. She knew we were going to stay overnight in Manhattan, a rare treat, but that's all she knew. The rest was a surprise. She was a giddy little girl for days before, clapping her hands together and begging me to tell. Then she'd beg for just a hint. When I almost gave in to her, she giggled "No, no. Don't tell me." Then she wanted to know what she should wear. "Your blue suit with the little blue hat," I said.

Actually, she didn't have many choices. Since the war started there wasn't enough material around to make much new. So I cut down my old blue striped suit to make a suit for her. I varied a McCall's pattern to give it the stylish square shoulders and a skirt up to the knees. Sara looked spectacular in it, accentuating her still-narrow waist and shapely legs. She was self-conscious about her eye glasses and mostly-gray hair. I told her she looked glamorous, and it was the truth. The beautiful young Hassidic girl in rags I first met forty years ago had become this elegant woman.

While she was getting dressed, I slipped a hard-to-get pair of nylon stockings from my bureau drawer, courtesy of Isaac and his government contacts. She squealed and threw her arms around me when I gave them to her.

I transformed a couple of my own suits for myself so I wasn't out of style: no vest, no pocket flaps, no pleats, and no cuffs on the pants. I had some silver cuff links and a swell blue, red and gray patterned tie to go with my gray gabardine suit.

As we were about to leave the house, Sara took hold of me by the arm and pointed at our reflection in the entry hall mirror. I put on my fedora and tipped my hat to the swells in the mirror before we headed out the front door.

The August morning air was sweet as bees' honey after a summer rain. "You make me so happy," she said as we walked down the street toward the subway. She put her arm through mine and squeezed hard with the other one.

Sara was everything any sane man could want: loyal, accepting of my frailties, and quick to forgive and forget. She was the most honest person I knew, incapable of telling a harmful lie. She was a fantastic mother and an even better grandmother. We laughed. We shared good books and movies. She told me she loved me and was proud of our good marriage. She let her family and friends know it. And she still ironed my undershorts.

We had been at war for over a year and a half. We worried about all of our nephews in uniform, but none more than Miryem's son Henry. He had been in the Pacific for seven months, flying Corsairs against Jap fighters. He said little in his letters home to us or to his parents. He wrote more to Isaac, but much of it was censored.

Because Henry was in the service, Miryem got to hang a little flag in her window, a "Blue Star Mother." Every time I took a walk in Manhattan Beach I saw all these white flags with a red border and a big blue star in the middle. More and more of those blue stars were replaced with gold ones, meaning someone's son had died in action.

Henry was there when we won a big naval victory in the Battle of the Bismarck Sea and when we took Guadalcanal. The Allies drove the Axis out of North Africa. Jews in the Warsaw Ghetto rose up and fought back in vain against the Nazis. The Russians defeated the Germans at Stalingrad and went on the offensive for the first time. Maybe soon Uman would be freed too. Sara and I read the newspaper and talked over the latest war news every morning at breakfast. "We have a long way to go," I reminded her when she got ahead of herself. She accepted my analysis as authoritative, even if I changed my opinion the very next day.

We had a Victory Garden in back where Sara replaced her flower beds with even more beans, tomatoes and cucumbers. You couldn't get much fresh produce in markets any more, so Sara hoarded her pre-war cans of Stokely's corn, carrots, and peas. Everything was rationed – our coupon books our most precious possession. I longed for a good piece of candy, an extra pair of shoes, or a shot of Scotch. We held scrap drives for anything made of steel, tin cans, paper, rubber bands, or string.

Air raid drills always came in the evening, usually spoiling one of our favorite radio shows: Inner Sanctum, Duffy's Tavern, or Sam Spade just when he was about to solve the murder. When the siren sounded we turned off all the lights and pulled down the blackout blinds. I put on my Air Raid Warden pith helmet and armband, grabbed my baton and ran out the door to assume my duties. Sara took her post at the fire station as an emergency ambulance driver. We were sure Nazi submarines lay right off Manhattan Beach ready to attack us.

But the war couldn't spoil our special day. We drove up to the front door of the Barclay Hotel, across the street from the new Waldorf-Astoria. Sara lit up when she saw where the taxi was stopping. The doorman opened the door and helped her out while I paid the driver. "Can we afford this?" she asked, not for the last time that weekend.

After we checked in, we walked over to Broadway for a matinee performance of Rodgers' and Hammerstein's *Oklahoma*. It had been sold out for every performance since it opened in March, but Thomas Kelly could fix anything. After the final curtain calls the stars, Alfred Drake and Joan Roberts, came on stage and asked everyone to make a donation to the USO to support our boys fighting overseas. Wicker baskets passed down the rows and everyone threw in a few coins or a couple of dollars. Sara put in her own dollar bill with purpose. "This is for Henry," she said.

The sun was shining when we got out of the show and walked back to the hotel. Servicemen jammed the streets – Army, Navy, Marines, Coast Guard, and some from Allied countries. The officers tipped their fingers to their hats and nodded at Sara, begging with their eyes. They ignored me. Several enlisted men stopped to whistle. Sara was embarrassed and pleased. Except up close, no one would guess she was nearing sixty. I looked like her father in comparison.

She was never more gorgeous than that day. She squeezed my hand with each suggestive smile, leer or whistle, as though to reassure me. I was proud to have her on my arm. "They're wondering what this beautiful woman is doing with such an old man," I said when we stopped at the traffic light on Park Avenue.

"I love my Prince Charming," she answered, reaching up and kissing me on the cheek. "And you're not an old man."

Sara cooed when we walked into our room, met by the perfume of the big bouquet of flowers I had sent up. A bottle of precious white wine iced in a silver bucket on the small table, with some plump strawberries nestled in a painted china dish along side. She threw her arms around me. "This has already been the best day of my life."

I took off my jacket and threw it on the bed. She took off her jacket and shoes while I opened the wine and poured two glasses. I turned on the radio and found Tommy Dorsey playing Moonlight Serenade. I took her in my arms and we started dancing.

She laughed, "But you hate to dance."

"But I love holding you." She snuggled her head in my shoulder. We rocked back and forth.

"I was never loved until you came along," she said. I kissed her hair and ran the back of my hand along her cheek.

We washed up for dinner. I changed my tie. Sara replaced her little hat with a stylish white scarf tied in a bow on top, but she kept on the same suit. No one wanted to appear frivolous during the war, even when stepping out for the evening.

Thomas Kelly was waiting for us when we walked in the door of his crowded restaurant. Everyone in New York who was anyone jammed into T. T. Kelly's: businessmen, newspaper columnists, politicians, and every army officer above the rank of captain. Thomas no longer worked behind the bar. Now he wore an elegant tuxedo and greeted customers. Still handsome, his hair was as gray as mine, but he had a lot more of it. He also wore more of a paunch.

"Where did you find this lovely lassie?" He held his arms out to Sara. She gave him a warm hug and a kiss on the cheek. "My goodness, Avi, you look like a lad who has been smitten. Come. I have something special for you."

He motioned us to follow him to a small private room elegantly decorated with blue velour chairs, white tablecloths, and gold silk drapes. A waiter brought us three crystal glasses of champagne and a plate of chocolates on a gold tray. I hadn't seen a real bottle of champagne since the Nazis invaded France.

"Thomas, how did you get your hands on this contraband?" I asked.

He laughed. "An honest man shouldn't raise too many questions."

Thomas lifted his glass to toast us, serious for a moment: "May your love be in abundance as long as you live. Treasures in life are many, dreams realized by few, but I know the test of God's goodness is when he gave me friends like you." We clinked glasses and took a sip.

The lobby of the Barclay still swarmed with people when we got back. Our side was starting to win this godforsaken war and no one wanted to go to sleep until it was over. Sara swore she saw Bette Davis and Ernest Hemingway go through the lobby in spite of my insistence it wasn't them. That didn't stop her. Over the next few weeks she told everyone she knew that we had seen Bette Davis and Ernest Hemingway.

"What a fabulous day," she said, kicking her shoes off as soon as we got to our room. She kissed me. "I'll be back." She smiled seductively, her voice throaty. She closed the bathroom door behind her. "Get ready," she said from the other side. It was getting hard for this old man to get hard, but Sara still found her ways. She liked it with a small light on.

Afterward, we cuddled. Her breathing became shallow; I thought she had fallen asleep. "There was never anyone but you," she said softly. She had told me that more than once, but I always liked hearing it. I stroked her hair, kissed her forehead, and squeezed her a little closer.

There was a war raging outside. My people were being slaughtered. My brother Lieb might already be dead. But inside of me, I was at peace. Daniel once told me that if you can't give love, you aren't really capable of receiving it. "To be loved is a gift," he said. "To love someone else is a greater gift." He was right. After forty years, I was still madly in love with my wife.

I held Sara until she fell asleep.

CHAPTER THIRTY-SEVEN

January 1945

Soon after D-Day I began writing this journal. I still go to our small Manhattan Beach public library where I can hide in a corner, remember, and write. I hope I have time to finish it because there are a few more important things I need to tell you.

By the middle of 1944, our side was winning everywhere. On June 6, when the Allies invaded Normandy, it began to feel like the end was in sight. A cousin of Tillie's was killed but other than that, so far everyone in our family was still okay. The Russians pushed the Germans back beyond Uman. They'd liberated just about all of the Ukraine.

The first documented reports published said the Nazis had methodically murdered nearly two million Jews. Such outlandish numbers made no sense. Skepticism licensed me to believe Lieb was still alive when everyone else gave up hope. We all worked hard to find out what happened to him and his family. Information about specific individuals was still scarce, fragmented, and unreliable. I kept writing to him but got no answer.

When Sara and I went to the movies, they always showed newsreels of the war before the main feature. Sometimes there were shots of dogfights in the Pacific. We'd both learned to identify the outline of a Marine Corsair, the kind Henry was flying. She had to cover her eyes.

Sara called me at the tailor shop one January afternoon screaming for me to get right home. "Henry?" I asked, fearing he was dead.

"Just come home," she begged.

She waited inside the front door crying, her face the color of snow. I swear she had aged ten years since I left for work that morning.

"Josef called," she said, wiping her nose with a laced hanky she pulled from her apron pocket. "They got a telegram from the War Department. Henry's been shot down. He managed to crash land at an army airfield. He was wounded. They didn't explain how badly. He's on his way by ship to a hospital in Hawaii."

"That's good news." I wrapped my arms around her. She sobbed into my chest, unable to speak. "His war is over," I said. "He'll be home soon."

We didn't get much more information for a few long weeks. First Josef and Miryem received a letter. The next day we got one too. They were written by an attending nurse named Kay Nolan writing on Henry's behalf. She told us his right shoulder had been damaged, in addition to his leg wounds, so he couldn't write for himself yet. He was recovering nicely and would begin rehabilitation in a few more weeks. He would be in the army hospital in Honolulu for quite some time. Sara wrote right back, addressing her letter to Henry. She wrote him every week after that. I usually added a few words of my own.

Kay Nolan continued to write what Henry dictated. Once, a few months later, Henry telephoned us. We could only talk for three minutes because it was so horribly expensive to call New York from Hawaii, even with Bell Telephone's special rate for soldiers. Henry sounded cheerful. He described how beautiful Hawaii was, so enthusi-astic it sounded like he was on vacation rather than recovering from a battle wound. All Sara wanted to know was how he was and if he was eating enough.

"Yes, Auntie," he said. "The food is wonderful."

When we hung up, I mentioned how much older he sounded, like a grownup man. "He's still a little boy," Sara said, her eyes filling up. All I could think of was Sara and little Henry playing ball in the backyard.

Henry wrote his next letter himself, boasting about how quickly he'd recovered from his shoulder wound. He said everything was healing well and he was going through unmerciful rehabilitation on his leg. They had fitted him with a heavy brace that was a burden to drag around. Kay Nolan, his attending nurse, was a fantastic person and made sure he got everything he needed. He thanked Sara for sending his favorite peanut butter cookies; they reminded him of home and his auntie's cooking. She had to cash in a king's treasure of rationing coupons for the peanut butter. Sara examined the writing carefully and declared his shoulder still not back to normal.

The next letter told us they let him leave the hospital every now and then for a few hours. Kay Nolan took him to the beach three times. Every week he wrote more about Kay Nolan and less about his wounds. "I can tell where this is leading," Sara said. I wasn't sure how she felt about it.

When Sara mentioned it to Miryem, Miryem dismissed it. "She's a *shiksa* for heaven's sake. What would Henry do with a gentile girl?

In the next letter to his mother, he wrote: "We're in love and I've asked her to marry me. She accepted."

I could hear Miryem roaring on the phone to Sara when I got home from work. "He can't marry her." Miryem yelled so loudly Sara had to hold the phone away from her ear. "She's not even Jewish. How can he marry that whore?"

"Miryem, you don't even believe in God," Sara said in a reasoned voice. Sara surprised me. This pious Hassidic-raised wife of mine didn't seem to think it was such a tragedy.

"How can you defend them? Look at the way they're murdering the Jews," Miryem snapped back.

"You can't condemn her like that," Sara said. "You'll drive Henry away."

"Well you can bloody well have him."

Josef overheard the conversation on Miryem's end. He told me later that when she hung up on Sara she stormed out of the room and stomped up the steps. Josef sat down and read the newspaper, waiting for her to cool down. A short while later she came stomping down the steps wearing a light jacket. Before he could stop her, she was off to the post office to mail the heated letter she had just written to Henry.

Sara and I both agreed Miryem's reaction was more about her having to share Henry with a wife than it was about Kay Nolan being a *shiksa*. Miryem was jealous.

Sure enough, a letter came back from Henry two weeks later that was only a little less charged than Miryem's. He was hurt and disappointed. He sounded like he'd been abandoned. He begged Miryem to "be happy for me. Get to know her. You'll love her as much as I do."

Sara didn't wait. She immediately sent Henry a letter giving him our congratulations, love and support. She made excuses for Miryem, explaining how upset she was given her unbearable worries after he was shot down. Sara told him Josef welcomed Kay, as we did. She told Miryem what she had written before she mailed it. Miryem seemed disinterested but didn't object.

Sara's letter must have helped. The next one back from Henry to Miryem was apologetic but just as firm in his determination. In it, he said it may be better for them to be wed there in Hawaii, and that by the time she received his letter they would already be married. Miryem told Josef to answer it. He did, congratulating them and telling Henry how eager he was to meet Kay. Sara and I sent off a note of congratulations too and enclosed a fifteen dollar check as a wedding present.

The day Henry brought Kay home, Josef asked us to come over to their house. He didn't want Miryem and him facing them alone. We waited in the living room for them to arrive, none of us saying much. Miryem pulled the curtains back every five minutes to peer out. At last a yellow taxi pulled up in front. We went out on the porch. Nothing happened for a minute. Then the cab driver got out and ran around to our side to open the car door.

The first thing I saw was a cane poke out from the back seat, then the leg of an olive green Marine uniform, and finally the rest of Henry. He turned back to say something before Kay got out behind him. She tried to help him, but he wanted to walk on his own. It was difficult to watch him hobble toward us, leaning on his cane and dragging his leg behind him. He held himself ramrod straight like a Marine.

Miryem ran to him and threw her arms around him. Tears streamed down her cheeks in rivulets. "My baby, my baby," she sobbed. It was all she could get out. He held her for the longest time, stroking the back of her head.

"I'm home, Mom."

Kay and I connected with our eyes and shared smiles. I wanted her to know she was welcomed. The cab driver made two trips to the front porch with their luggage and Henry's stuffed duffel bag. The cabbie watched a scene he was going to witness a lot more in the coming months.

They moved in with Miryem and Josef for a time while Henry figured out what to do with himself. Miryem was gracious to Kay in a formal way, but she treated the next door neighbor's new daughter-in-law with more affection than she treated her own. Henry pretended not to notice.

Miryem's loss was our gain. Sara and I took to Henry and Kay as though they were ours. Sara treated Kay as warmly as she did Tillie, her own daughter-in-law, and Kay responded in kind. She called us Auntie Sara and Uncle Avi the second time she saw us.

"You must show me how to make your koo-gell," she said. "Henry's been telling me about it for months." And Sara did. Every time they came over Sara taught her something new. First kugel, then matzo ball soup, tzimmes, kreplach, and finally gefilte fish. You could tell Kay wanted to don a gas mask and garden gloves when dealing with the gilled ingredients.

Henry and I talked about his future and what he might do with himself. I tried to make it comfortable to talk about the war but he didn't want to. "It's over, Uncle Avi."

Kay was a nice small town Christian girl from Kansas, alone in a strange Jewish village. The poor thing looked as much like a blonde *shiksa* as anyone could look. She was plain but not unattractive, and she obviously adored Henry. She took care of his wounds, usually in private, with nursing skills neither Miryem nor Sara could equal.

I admired how hard she worked to fit in. She never went to church while she stayed with Miryem and Josef. Most people tried to make it easy for her, but not her mother-in-law. Miryem went out of her way to show how Jewish she was. She served the most ethnic Jewish foods she could find, like tongue and kishka, which she herself wouldn't even eat. I thought she was trying to starve Kay to death, but Kay gamely tried everything.

Miryem insisted we all go to Edelstein's Delicatessen, a very kosher place run by some Orthodox Jews from near Odessa. Miryem ordered first, a corned beef sandwich on rye with a Doctor Brown's Cream Soda. Kay went next. She was confused by the menu, never having seen a kosher Jewish delicatessen before. She followed Miryem's lead, with a few modifications. She asked for her corned beef sandwich on white bread with mayonnaise and a glass of milk. The waiter went berserk. "This is a kosher place, lady. No milk and meat. You vant milk and meat, you go to a *goyish* place." He vomited his words so loudly others in the crowded restaurant turned their heads to see what the commotion was about.

Kay was so embarrassed she wanted to hide herself under the table. Henry was amused. Miryem was triumphant. She explained to Kay what *kosher* was, and her horrible transgression, in the condescending tone one uses when explaining something to a four year old child. I was sitting next to Kay. I squeezed her hand under the table and grinned at her. She shrugged her shoulders and smiled back at me. She learned quickly. The next time we went to Edelstein's she ordered a corned beef sandwich on rye with mustard and a Doctor Brown's Cream Soda.

On Friday nights Miryem lit Sabbath candles, which she had never done in all of the years I knew her. She insisted Henry say the prayers since she didn't know them. When he started in English the first time, she stopped him, insisting he say them in Hebrew. Henry gave Kay an apologetic look, but did what Miryem asked.

After a couple of months, Henry was fully healed, though he was going to have to wear the metal brace on his leg for the rest of his life. I only saw the scars on his leg once. They looked like someone had made big scratches with a wide piece of white chalk. No hair grew there. His leg had withered to about the size of my arm. The leg embarrassed him; he only allowed Kay to see it.

I was proud of Isaac. He asked Henry to work for him in Berkinbury while Henry figured out what he wanted to do. Isaac and Willy had already begun converting their plant back to civilian use, making children's clothing again. Henry and Kay were eager to get their own place and start a life. They were also glad to get away from Miryem, though they didn't say as much. Eventually Miryem made her peace with Kay after their little girl was born. But that was still a couple of years off.

We saw Henry and Kay about as often as we saw Isaac and Tillie. We were in Berkinbury visiting them when they interrupted the radio broadcast to announce an American airplane had dropped this cosmic bomb on the Jap city of Hiroshima, vaporizing it right off the face of the earth. All living things, human and animal, were seared to death. I couldn't feel sorry for them.

I began searching for Lieb long before the ashes cooled.

CHAPTER THIRTY-EIGHT

August 1945

The war ended and the boys started coming home. Everyone in our family made it back alive, but the Ackermans down the street lost a son. So did other mothers and fathers in our synagogue. Gold stars hung in windows all over Manhattan Beach.

We read about Jewish refugees – concentration camp survivors and slave laborers – who wandered aimlessly across Europe. Orphaned children roamed like starving wolves. Jewish agencies in our country worked to feed them, clothe them, and connect them with any family they had in America. But only a few were allowed to enter. The Schneiders and the Kravetzs mobilized, checking every list of survivors, pursuing every lead to find Lieb, Havol and any survivors from their families. They could be anywhere.

We cheered when we heard any morsel of information about hidden Jews who survived. We took to bed early with each newfound massacre. The number murdered was too huge to imagine. The Russians took their time revealing who had been evacuated east when the Germans first overran the Ukraine. Chiam Chernoff, Moishe Stepaner, and everyone else from Uman ran into the same dead ends we did.

When we exhausted all of our sources and leads, Ester came up with the idea to write my old friend Sergey Shumenko. He was a Christian. There was a good chance he survived. So I wrote and sent it airmail with a few dollars tucked in. No answer. I wrote again. Still no answer. Then I wrote to the Soviet Embassy in Washington, D.C. to see if they could locate him. Next I tried the Soviet consulate in New York. No help came from either of them.

When we had all burnt ourselves out, Sara pleaded with me again to honor my dead brother and her sister Havol by sitting *Shiva* and saying *Kaddish*. "He's alive," I snapped. "Don't dishonor him by declaring him dead when he's not." She turned away, as though I had slapped her. The odds were long. I knew that, and sometimes I yielded to panic too. But if anyone deserved to live, it was Lieb. Until we knew for sure, I couldn't give up. Sara called me stubborn. I called myself determined.

I went back again and again to all of the refugee agencies until they knew me by name. No one lent even a thimbleful of encouragement. When there was nowhere else to turn, I tried Duv and Mendel Silber – against the advice of Sara, Markus, Simon, and Josef. Neither one would even take my telephone calls. It was a blessing.

Many days that winter after the war ended, I grabbed my heaviest coat and headed for the beach. The stormy seas quieted my turbulent mind. This is where God was, if there was a God, in the pounding surf, the salty air, the cold sand, and the infinite gray sky. I walked along the edge of the water, all alone except for the scavenging seagulls. Something told me if Lieb were dead I would know about it. He couldn't have come to his end without registering a sound.

One Sunday morning Daniel joined me; both of us bundled in warm pea coats, our knit caps pulled down over our ears. The sun peaked in and out from behind puffy clouds. We labored through the sand, our toes numbing. A family of sandpipers, early arrivals from the south, foraged along the water's edge.

"What am I supposed to do? I can't just give up. Maybe he's alive somewhere. Or one of his kids or grandkids. If they are alive, they're going to need me."

"Keep looking. Help all the refugees you can. Do good works. God will find you." I hated when the rabbi in my good friend fed me full of platitudes.

I stopped walking. "Don't tell me about God," I foamed above the crashing waves. "Not after all that's happened. Lieb never hurt anyone. He honored the Almighty even when he risked his life doing it. So what did it get him? First a *pogrom,* then a civil war, a famine that took his daughter, and still another famine. Purges that cost him a son-in-law and almost cost him a son. Then the Nazis came. Can you find God anywhere in that?"

"I'm told many went to the gas chambers saying the *Sh'ma*," Daniel said quietly.

They should have died fighting, I thought. Not in a gas chamber. I wanted to scream it into the wind but the words choked in my throat.

We trudged toward the boardwalk in silence, leaving footprints in the sand behind us.

Movie newsreels and photographs in magazines showed Americans the concentration camps and the fields of massacres, so I was prepared when I went to see Sidney Berman. He had gone to work for the United Nations Relief and Rehabilitation Administration, the agency set up to deal with the ocean of displaced refugees. When President Truman appointed Herbert Lehman to run the UNRRA, the former New York Governor asked Sidney to join him.

His sparse Manhattan office was in the annex of a large post office building on the East Side near the river. The place was a barnyard of people scurrying back and forth, ringing telephones, clacking typewriters, and mountains of file folders stacked on overloaded desks crammed close together.

Sidney knew I was coming. When he saw me, he hung up his telephone and hurried over. My usually-manicured friend was in rolled up shirt sleeves, loosened tie, and suspenders. His wrinkled trousers looked liked he had slept in them; his dark beard needed a shave. "Come," he said grabbing me by the arm. "Let's find a quiet place to talk." He led me down the hall to a small windowless office that looked like it had until recently been a big storage closet.

"There's no glamour in saving refugees," he said, motioning me toward one of the two wooden chairs.

I had told Sidney on the phone why I wanted to see him. He got right to the point. "I checked all of our lists. I couldn't find anyone with the names you gave me, or anyone from Uman," he said. "But that doesn't mean anything. The Soviets evacuated some Jews further east when the Germans first invaded. It's possible your family was among them. But the Soviets aren't being very forthcoming with lists. Stalin thinks everything's a capitalist plot.

"We keep getting more people coming into the camps every day from the east, many from the Ukraine. They're unbelievable people. They've walked halfway across Europe just to get to the Western Zone." My solemn friend shook his head and let out a long sigh. He had crevices in his forehead and etches around his eyes not there the last time I saw him.

He ignored my attempt to ask a question and kept talking. "Agencies helped over five million refugees return to their homes in the months right after the war ended. But that leaves another two million still in the camps. Many have nowhere to go. Their communities have been destroyed. When the Jews were taken away, gentiles moved in and grabbed their homes and their shops. Now they won't return them if a Jew does manage to get back to his hometown. Do you know when some of them tried returning to their homes in Slovakia and Poland, mobs attacked them? There was a big *pogrom* in Kielce. Many Jews refuse to return home, particularly to the Soviet zone. Can't blame them."

For the next fifteen minutes, Sidney gave me a dispassionate presentation of the mission to handle millions of displaced persons. The Allies set up camps to house them, mostly in Germany, with some in Austria and Italy. The majority of the Displaced Persons were former inmates of Nazi concentration camps, labor camps, and POW camps. But some were civilians fleeing in front of the Soviet armies, eager to get to the West. Russian and Ukrainian collaborators mixed in with the legitimate refugees. Things were too chaotic for the relief agencies to do much checking. These bastards served the German army willingly, and helped with the executions. They knew they would be hung if they went back to their homes. They hoped to slip into the United States masquerading as Jews to gain sympathy. Too many succeeded, as you'll find out.

One urgent task now was creating services to help survivors find their relatives. Sidney's agency, the UNRRA, set up a Central Tracing Bureau. Names were gathered and sent to rescue agencies and the other refugee camps. They published endless lists in newspapers and broadcast them on the radio. They took pictures of the children and circulated them too.

I had already tapped into these sources with no success, but the more Sidney talked the more encouraged I was about finding Lieb. I told him so.

"If he's alive, we'll find him," Sidney said. "But prepare yourself. He won't be the same man you remember. I've been there. I've seen them. Most of them are damaged. They're scared to death of authority of any kind. Many are depressed, and who can blame them. They've been through a hell we can't imagine. They move from camp to camp like ghosts, trying to find any family still alive."

"What about the children?" I asked, thinking maybe at least one of his seven grandchildren would have survived.

"Unfortunately, the young ones often don't even know their own names. Officials examine their luggage and their clothes for any speck of identification or hint of where they came from."

Sidney glanced at his wrist watch. My need for help superseded my reluctance to take up his time; I craved a crumb of hope. "So what do I do?" I asked.

He put the palms of both hands on the desktop and leaned toward me. "Don't give up. Keep doing what you're doing. There are many agencies at work on this. I'll give you a list before you go. Contact them. Use my name. Maybe it will get you a little extra attention. I'll keep checking the lists too. And be sure to check all the children's organizations."

Sidney dismissed my repeated offers of thanks when we shook hands at the door. "If they made it to the West, they'll show up on one of the lists," he said. It was all the hope I had.

Not long after my visit with Sidney, a few more Jewish refugees landed in New York, some in Manhattan Beach. Numbers tattooed on their forearms branded them like cattle. When I met one, my first question was always "Where are you from?" None were from Uman.

Sara volunteered with a Jewish relief agency helping to get them settled into new homes and jobs. She worked hard, but at times came home despairing of their ingratitude. "You'd think we were the ones who locked them in those prison camps. I'll bet some of them aren't even Jewish."

She was right about that. As Sidney had warned, impostors snuck in among the displaced persons, Nazi collaborators who only wanted to come to America. They found it easier to get in if they claimed to be Jewish, inviting the sympathy and assistance of a world shocked by the Holocaust.

One of those impostors had word of Lieb.

CHAPTER THIRTY-NINE

September 9, 1946

The jangle of the phone interrupted my quiet Monday morning. Sara answered it. "It's a Mr. Litvak," she yelled from the living room. "He says someone's looking for you."

I took the phone. It was Litvak from the Blue Sail bar. "There's this guy here. Says he's from Uman. Doesn't speak much English. All he says is 'Schneider, Uman, family.' He looks and smells like a dirty old goat."

I grabbed the side of the table to steady myself. Litvak couldn't tell me anything more. I told Sara about the phone call, and then walked as fast as my legs would go toward the Blue Sail. The September morning was as fine as any day can be, sunny and fresh from the previous night's rain. But I was so lost in thought I hardly noticed, and nearly ran into Mrs. Lefkowitz as I rounded the corner in front of Sloan's Army Surplus Store. I didn't even pause to beg her pardon.

I had spent the last thirteen months chasing every rumor, crawling down one varmint hole after another. They all ended in frustration. The hardest part was not knowing. What if Lieb was still alive somewhere, desperate for my help? The only thread I had left to hold on to was the old saying about no news being good news. Now this stranger pops up, waiting for me at the Blue Sail.

It wasn't time for the bar to open but the door was unlocked. Two working men I recognized sat at a table under the eaves toward the back having a drink and talking quietly. Helen Merrill crooned Bye Bye Blackbird from the radio atop the counter behind the bar. Litvak fiddled with a knob trying to tune in the station better. He turned around when he heard me come in and motioned toward an old man hunched over a table in the corner, his back to me. The closer I got to him, the more the smell of sewage rose around him.

The day was warm yet the visitor wore a heavy threadbare black coat, so frayed I could see his dirty white shirt through a hole in back. The oversized coat hung on him like a sack. The whiskers of his bushy gray beard twitched, his wiry gray hair sticking out like a wig of Brillo Pads. A worn brown cap with a short leather bill perched on top of his head. I hadn't seen one like it since I left Uman. He hunched over a glass of vodka.

"I'm Avi Schneider," I said in English, standing by his table.

He didn't look up. "Sit," he commanded in Russian, motioning me with his hand toward the chair opposite him. The vodka bottle and an empty glass rested on the small beer-stained table. He motioned for me to have a drink. I shook my head.

I sat on the forward edge of the chair opposite him. "You have word of my brother?" I struggled with my rusty Russian.

He nodded slowly. Nothing else moved but his head.

"Are they alive?" I demanded.

"I will tell you. Be patient." He lifted the glass of vodka to his lips, tilted his head and threw it down. He lowered the glass onto the table deliberately and began to speak in a monotone as though he were too weary to exert any more energy than required.

"The Germans surrounded Uman in late August 1941. The big fight was on the outskirts, but shells hit all over town. Your synagogue was damaged a little, and some of the buildings around the market place. Do you remember the market place?"

"Yes, of course. And my brother...?"

"Patience. I must tell you everything," he said. "A couple of weeks after the Germans took over, they herded all the Jews into the market place. There were thousands of them. The Ukrainian militia helped with the round up. We thought the Germans were liberating us from the Russians at first. We learned better, but back then the young militiamen were eager to show their cooperation."

I hadn't spoken Russian in decades so I labored to understand some of his words. When I asked him to repeat himself, he just kept going, unconcerned with whether I understood or not.

"The Germans put out a proclamation for all Jews to assemble so they could get an exact count of their population in Uman – men, women, children." He said the word 'Jews' as though cursing the dead. "They threatened severe punishment for anyone who didn't obey the orders. We already learned you didn't argue with the Germans."

"It was a fine September morning, cool, so many had on coats. A day like today." He looked out the small window and gestured with his hand. "I saw your brother in the first row with his family. He was wearing a long brown raincoat. You would recognize him at once - the dark eyes, the bald head, the big Jew nose. He was so thin. Standing in the middle of the children and women made him look taller than he was. Those wire glasses crafty old Jews wear. He seemed to understand what was happening better than the others."

I tried to picture so many Jews in the market place. Maybe it was crowded like it used to be on market day. I leaned forward resting my elbows on the table, holding my breath, anxious for him to get on with the story. His stink wafted over me. "Tell me what happened to Lieb."

He ignored me. He stared at the empty glass in his hand. "The Ukraine militiamen helped but it was the Germans who were in charge. You have to understand this. There were many German SS everywhere. They began marching the Jews out of town to a place where they said they would be registered. Thousands of them, but the Jews gave no one any trouble. All very orderly.

"One of the militiamen put a big red flag on a long pole and stuck it in the hands of Mordecai Klebner, the butcher's retarded son. Then he

326 . Alan Fleishman

put a Russian soldier's hat with a red star in front on his head, cock-eyed. The poor fellow looked quite ridiculous given the circumstance. He didn't know what was happening. He thought he was leading a parade. He strutted around, high stepping like a crazy Gestapo, waving the flag over his head, a stupid grin across his face. He was very proud of himself. Those Germans thought all the Jews were Communists and all the Communists were Jews. They hated them both.

"Your brother was in front I remember, holding one little girl's hand in each of his. Maybe his granddaughters? I don't know. The others around him might have been his family. Three or four more young girls. They all stayed together on the march to Sukhi Yar. Do you remember Sukhi Yar? It wasn't so far."

He kept his eyes down. I saw mostly the top of his head and protruding nose. I wanted to grab him by his grimy hair and make him look me in the eye. My heart pounded, jumping all over the place.

"Did they kill him? Did they kill Lieb?" The inside of my mouth tasted like lubricated metal. He poured himself another drink and pushed the bottle toward me. I ignored it. He kept his attention fixed on the glass of vodka, one hand wrapped lightly around it.

"They built a small airfield at the end of the ravine. They had to take down some of the old trees. The trees had grown very tall, very pretty." I could picture where the airfield was, a scar on the tranquil Sukhi Yar meadow.

"Have you ever heard of the Einsatzgruppen?" he asked, glancing up briefly.

"No," I answered. He nodded. The only sound in the bar was one of Litvak's cats meowing. It was insistent. Then it stopped. Litvak must have put it outside.

"The Einsatzgruppen. They were the ones responsible. Special SS action groups. They came in right behind the Wehrmacht – the regular army. Highly trained professionals. Their duty was to cleanse the area." He glanced up as though to be sure I understood what he meant by 'cleanse.'

I was there with Lieb. I could feel Lieb's terror, his despair, his desperation for his children and grandchildren. What was he thinking in those moments?

"Your brother was very proud. He held his head up high, walking with confidence as though he expected it to be a registration and nothing more. He walked like he was in a hurry, occasionally saying something to one of the granddaughters or turning to say something over his shoulder to someone else, maybe his old wife."

Tears welled in my eyes. I fought them back, cupped my hand over my mouth, maybe to hide my agony from this strange man who might be enjoying the telling. The look on his thick lips and cratered face didn't change. He sipped his drink and returned the half empty glass to the table. I didn't realize I was holding my breath, waiting for him to continue.

"At Sukhi Yar, there were German soldiers everywhere. More Ukrainian militiamen arrived in trucks, with SS officers commanding them. The militiamen had work tools with them and large bags of lime.

"The Jews came across the field by the thousands, all in an orderly way, guarded by many Germans. So many. They hit a few of the Jew stragglers with the butts of their rifles. As they got closer to Sukhi Yar, they saw deep ditches had been dug all along the edge of the meadows. The ditches were a nuisance in such a place, but it wasn't the worst thing the Germans did to Uman. When they left in 1943 they burned down some of our fine buildings and blew up one of the bridges crossing the river.

"The registration tables were set up near the edge of the ditches. Your brother was one of the first in line. The German clerk at each table had them sign a registration book. They ordered them to place all of their jewelry and other valuables in a bin to the side, writing out a receipt for each item. Many of the women, not knowing where they were going, had brought their jewelry with them.

"Then they had them remove all their clothes – men, women, children – all together. The young and the old. It didn't matter. There was one very good looking woman with a baby sucking at her ripe breast.

Your brother helped his granddaughters take off their dresses. He patted them on their cheeks and smiled at them."

The man finished his drink and poured himself another. I was so lost in his story I no longer smelled his filth. Instead I focused on the black dirt beneath every one of his fingernails.

"They were pushed and shoved to the edge of the ditch. Your brother – Lieb is his name?" I nodded. "Lieb still held onto their hands. He looked like he was standing at attention, head up, shoulders back, even though his old-man private parts were dangling there for everyone to see." He snickered. I wanted to smack him.

"The Einsatzgruppen did the difficult part. They moved in behind the line of Jews and started shooting them with automatic pistols and Lugers. Your brother and the two little girls fell into the ditch. Then the others in his family fell in too. A couple of the young girls looked like they had pubic hair and small breasts. Nice ones. Too bad. Such a waste.

"The next line of people was ordered to the edge of the ditch. The men were handed shovels and made to heave lime in the ditch on top of the bodies. Then they were dispatched.

"The Jews didn't fight back. How could they? There were so many soldiers and militia. The Einsatzgruppen were good at their job. They were quick about it. So organized you had to admire them. They seemed to be in competition with each other to see who could kill the most the fastest. Maybe there was a contest." I wanted this to be over, but I was as duty-bound to listen to the rest of the story as he was to tell it.

"Your brother was one of the lucky ones. He went first. It was worst for the mothers. The soldiers yanked some of the crying babies from their arms, held them upside down by their legs and struck them on the head with a club or a pistol, but so hard their skulls split open. Then they threw them into the pit and shot the mother. Some of the bodies in the pit were still moving, not quite dead when the next load fell on top of them.

"The smell of blood was worse than a slaughter house. And the smell of lime on top of it." He held his fingers to his nose, oblivious to his own foulness. "And the noise, the noise. It was awful. So much crying and shouting. The gunshots went on and on like they would never end. Even into the next day."

At last he stopped talking. He sat there panting. He didn't move a single muscle, and still didn't look up at me. Then he began rocking slowly back and forth.

"All of them gone?" I whispered.

He nodded.

"All of Lieb's family?"

He nodded.

"Havol Kravetz?"

He nodded.

"Bayleh Zuckman, Gersh Leibowitz, Meier Braun, Shlomo Zilberman?" I mentioned a few other names I remembered.

He nodded after each one of them.

"You didn't mention his grandson, the little boy."

"I don't remember a little boy."

"There must have been a little boy," I insisted.

"No little boy." He shook his head, equally insistent. "Maybe he got separated from the rest. It happened. But no one escaped. No one."

The thought of little Elias dying all alone, without the comfort of his Grandpa Lieb – it was too much to bear. I wanted to scream, to throw something, to hit someone.

Bile rose against my tongue. I forced it back and willed myself to think, to speak. "And what of Sergey Shumenko? Did he survive the war?"

"Ah, Comrade Shumenko. What a shame." He shook his head back and forth slowly, twirling his empty shot glass in his hand. He looked into it as though examining tea leaves in the bottom. "He tried to hide some Jews in his attic. The Gestapo found them of course. You couldn't fool those Germans. They could smell a Jew ten kilometers away. Jews have their own smell, you know."

He poured himself another drink but let it sit there. His right hand still gripped the nearly empty bottle. "They hung him from the big tree in front of your old synagogue. He didn't die easily. They say he squirmed for a long time. The Germans let his body hang there until it began to rot and the crows ate their fill. They made an example out of him. After that, no one in Uman was going to hide any more Jews. Shumenko always loved Jews a little too much. He should have known better." He paused. "Then they burned down the synagogue."

His entire story could be some cruel hoax, I thought, maybe for money. Blood-red anger transfused me. "How do you know so much? How do I know any of this is true?"

He slammed his hand on the table. "Because I was there!" The vodka bottle and glass shook violently.

"I don't believe you," I screamed back at him.

He yanked something from his coat pocket and slapped it down on the table in front of me. "There!" It was a small daily prayer book in Hebrew, with a scarred brown leather cover. "I took this from your brother's coat."

I recognized it immediately. I opened it to the Yiddish inscription inside in a familiar handwriting: *To Lieb from Momma and Poppa on your bar mitzvah. May you live a long and happy life.* I remember the day they gave it to him.

"Who are you?" I yelled, pounding both fists on the table.

He slowly raised his head and stared at me. Red rivers streaked the whites of his steely eyes. Even from beneath the mop of greasy gray hair and shaggy beard; even beneath all of the scars and lines of age; even from a distance of six thousand miles and forty years. Even then, I knew I was looking again into the evil eyes of the Devil.

"Viktor Askinov!"

His lips snarled, baring his rotting teeth. The Litvak told me later the sound that came from me was not human. "Smite him, Lord!" I raised my fists to the sky. "Smite him!"

The fires of Hell burned before my eyes, the sickening smell of cooked flesh assaulting my nose. Rifle and machine gun salvos thundered in my ears. I heard the distant scream of my own voice and a crash as I toppled the table between us. Bottle and glass smashed. I landed on top of the beast, carrying us both to the floor, pinning him beneath me.

My hands grip his throat and they begin to squeeze like a closing vice. All that exists is my mind and my hands, unconnected from the rest of my body, choking him. They belong to someone else. I squeeze harder. And harder. His face turns white, then red, then purple. His tongue sticks out of his mouth and foam drips from the edges. His legs kick, but gently. He begins to gurgle. Why doesn't he struggle? Instead, his plump, hairy hands rest lightly on mine. How long does it take a man to die, I wondered?

The haze in front of my eyes cleared enough for me to recognize his satisfied smirk. I looked down into his eyes. They showed satisfaction, not fear. He wants me to kill him, I thought. I squeezed harder. Just as his eyes rolled back in his head I released my grip.

"Avi! Let go!" Litvak screamed in my ear, grabbing me by my shoulders and pushing me off of Viktor Askinov. "Let go of him."

The two men who had been sitting in the corner helped this pile of shit to his feet. Litvak hauled me to a chair at one of the tables like a prizefighter between rounds. I gulped air, my chest heaving and my heart pounding without rhythm. Litvak kept one hand on my shoulder to make sure I didn't resume the attack. I buried my face in my hands and cried. The radio whispered Glenn Miller's orchestra playing Sunrise Serenade.

I looked up when I heard the slow thump of his steps. I saw only his back as he moved toward the door, leaning on his cane, shoulders sagging, dragging his right leg behind him. His cane and the scraping of his leg sounded on the worn linoleum floor until he disappeared out the door. The jagged neck of the shattered vodka bottle lay on the floor next to the overturned chair.

I sit there too numb to move, too dead to think, staring, feeling and not feeling. Lieb is gone, horribly gone, I realize. His whole family is gone. Why am I here, I beg to understand? Why am I spared? I hear Litvak speak to me but I can't tell what he's saying. He speaks louder and stares into my eyes but I don't see him.

"Do you want me to call someone?" I finally heard Litvak ask.

I nodded. "Rabbi Daniel." He went to make the call.

I stared at the closed door through which Viktor Askinov had disappeared. Then Litvak returned and sat in the chair next to me. He didn't say a word. He didn't move. He just sat there. My mind was locked, and I knew it was locked. I tried to get it to work. It wouldn't. I stared at the door some more. Litvak handed me a glass of water. I raised it to my dry lips, but my hand was shaking so badly I spilled much of it on myself.

How long did I sit like that? Who knows? Long enough for Daniel to arrive. "Come," he said, lifting me by the arm. "Let's go for a walk on the beach."

"I couldn't tell whether the look on his face showed victory or defeat," I said to Daniel. We sat on the rocks by the water's edge. The early afternoon sun lit the ocean in deep blues and frothy whites. "Why do you think he came all this way to tell me?"

"I don't know," Daniel said. "Maybe to be kind – to let you know what happened to your family. To give you some finality."

"More likely to boast about it, his final victory over me." I thought of all those times in Uman, those horrible times, when Viktor Askinov took such pleasure in torturing me. I saw him the night of the *pogrom* marching down Nevsky Street toward our barricade, leading the mob. "He was the Devil, Daniel. I swear it. I should have killed him then, when I had the chance. Why couldn't I kill him now?"

"What good would it have done? It wouldn't bring Lieb back to life."

"One more monster would be gone."

"Too many have died in God's name already," he said.

"God can't do all the dirty work by himself or He would have done it by now."

"They tell me you saved a lot of people's lives the night you shot him," he said. "Maybe that should be enough."

We looked out upon the gentle sea for the longest time, no talking between us. The crack of gunshots sounded in the unexpected crash of a wave. A bunch of kids playing in the sand chased each other and laughed, mocking my defeat. Viktor Askinov won. There was nothing more I could do. "How can you still believe in God after all of this?" I asked Daniel again.

"How can you not?" he answered. "Who do you think kept you from killing him? And if you killed him you wouldn't be any better than he is. That is what he wanted, to smear you with his filth. You're too good a man for that."

My mind shot off in a new direction. "Anti-Semitism is too ingrained in too many Christians," I said. "Even if all of the Jews die tomorrow, they will still hate us."

"And how about Christians like your friend Sergey Shumenko. He died for you, and for Lieb."

I cannot possibly understand his sacrifice, and I should have said that. Instead I asked, "What do you think Lieb's last thoughts were?"

"Avi. Stop! You'll never get an answer to that, so let go of it."

"I think he thanked God for giving him life, and for giving him Golde, his children, and his grandchildren."

"And for giving him a brother who never stopped loving him."

"Yes, that too."

Lieb was dead, his family snuffed out. We would be dead too if we had stayed in Uman – Sara, me, Isaac, Yakira, my grandchildren Max and Rose, and all the rest of the family. Instead we were safe here in America with a nice house, a new Hudson, and lots of money. Why? Lieb was a better man than me, better than any of us.

We learned at the Nuremberg Trials that over 20,000 Jews were murdered in Uman during those two days, the horror of it too much to imagine. We try to explain, to understand. But there is no explanation; there is no understanding. There is only good and evil. Sometimes good wins and sometimes evil wins. I know that now.

Daniel walked me home from the beach that fine September day. It wasn't until I climbed the steps to the front porch that I realized I might not be entirely finished with Viktor Askinov.

CHAPTER FORTY

September 10, 1946

Sara and I clung to each other all night long. They say the worst demons of the darkness yield to the dawn. They're wrong. When I opened my eyes, the horrors were still there.

I plodded down the stairs in my bathrobe; Sara was in the kitchen, the coffee perking. I went into the dining room, opened a door in the credenza behind the dining table, and took out a bottle of whiskey. I poured myself a drink, then another, and waited for the numbing. It was only nine o'clock in the morning.

Viktor Askinov opened a fear I hadn't known since I left Uman. The Devil was in our midst, right here in Manhattan Beach. I should have killed him this time, but I failed again, for the third time. One thing I knew for sure: I couldn't let him inflict his terror on Sara or my sisters and brother. So I told them Lieb and Havol were dead, that the Germans killed them. I didn't tell them the details of how they died, and I didn't tell them it was Viktor Askinov who delivered the news. When Markus asked about the messenger, I told him it was a refugee who passed through Uman.

As I sipped my liquor, I thought I would have to do something about Viktor Askinov. He couldn't be allowed to exist in our midst. But today was not the day to think about it.

By noon the house filled with family and friends. The whole scene took place in black and white as though I was watching a Hitchcock movie. Yakira and Tillie prepared the food. Jake and Isaac covered the mirrors, supervised by Daniel's wife Hannah.

Josef and Sara held hands much of the afternoon, trying to make some sense of the loss of a sister they never liked much growing up, but mourned now. When Sara wasn't holding Josef's hand, she was clinging to me as though her hold alone kept me from bleeding away. We said little to each other. We didn't need to.

Sadie and Miryem found a place in a corner. Henry and Kay tried to keep Rose and Max occupied. Kay was bewildered by her first exposure to a Jewish wake; Henry tried to explain the symbolism and identify each relative.

My old partner Manny, shuffling like an old man, came with Solly Birnstein. So did Sidney Berman, and my old roommate Gideon Katz, all the way from the Bronx. Bettino Rossi sent a nice fruit basket, and Thomas Kelly an enormous bouquet of blue and white carnations.

Chiam Chernoff and Moishe Stepaner brought their wives. They too had lost cousins, aunts, uncles, and old friends in the massacre at Sukhi Yar. They sat with Ester and Simon.

Nieces and nephews were there for their parents' sake. But they couldn't mourn a family they never knew.

The only one missing was Duv.

Daniel led the prayers. We said *Kaddish*. My mind wondered to Lieb's little grandson Elias, only two years old then. I pictured him wandering in the crowd alone on that awful day, crying, searching frantically for his grandpa, gunshots and screams surrounding him. I prayed some other grandpa held him by the hand when his end came. I thumped my heart with my fist and wailed: *"Sh'ma Yisraeil Adonai Eloheinu Adonai Echad.* Hear, O Israel, the Lord is our God, the Lord is one."* But it was the devil who sat on my shoulder. I saw Viktor Askinov's red-streaked eyes bulging as my hands squeezed tighter around his throat.

By late afternoon the crowd thinned. I stood at the front door to say goodbye and thank each person for coming to honor my brother. Ester brought me a small plate of hardboiled eggs, lentils, and a bagel. "Eat," she said. "You haven't had anything all day."

"Thank you." I took a bite of bagel.

She rested her hand on my arm. "You carried this all alone for all these years." She sniffled. "I'm sorry."

"I was never alone." I meant it. I touched her hand. She wrapped both arms around me and held on. She kissed me on the cheek.

At last all that was left was the family. Markus began telling stories of Sukhi Yar when we were young. Simon added some of his own stories. I hadn't told them the slaughter had taken place at our splendid sanctuary. Zelda joined in with some funny stories about mealtimes and chores when we were kids growing up in Uman. Ester tried too. I listened and smiled.

Nothing that day struck me as odd. Not even when one of those green and black wartime police cars stopped in front of the house. I heard the breaks squeak and peaked out through the lace curtains. A plain clothes detective got out on the passenger side and ambled up our short walkway. He knocked on the glass panel of the front door. I stepped outside to meet him.

"You Avi Schneider?" I didn't appreciate the threat in the way he said my name.

"Yes."

"Detective Frank Pierce." He pulled a badge from the side pocket of his rumpled tan suit jacket and flashed it too quickly to read. His loosened brownish tie hung at a sloppy angle, top button of his shirt undone. He reminded me of every cop in every murder mystery movie I'd seen in the past fifteen years. He walked like one, dressed like one, and spoke like one, with a faint smell of liquor on his breath when he stuck his head too close to mine.

A big uniformed officer got out of the police car on the driver's side and rested his elbows on the roof, keeping an eye on me.

"There's a dead guy in the morgue," Pierce said. "Thought you might be able to identify him."

"I don't understand. I don't know of any dead person."

"Didn't have no identifications. Only things in his pockets were fifteen cents and a piece of paper with your name on it."

"I can't imagine..." I started to get an uncomfortable feeling this detective wanted me for more than just identifying a body. "We're sitting *Shiva*. It's the Jewish mourning, for my dead brother."

"I know what Shiver is," he snapped. "Sorry 'bout that Schneider, but you gotta come with me. Won't take long." The uniformed policeman came around the other side of the police car and moved up the sidewalk toward us as if to warn me I didn't have a choice. I had always been fearful of any policeman, but this was beginning to feel like the Tsar's secret police, the Okhrana.

Just then Josef came out to see what was going on. Josef wasn't scared of them. The police were frequent adversaries of any union organizer.

"You're gunna' have to come with me, Schneider. Right now."

"Where are you taking him?" Josef asked, stepping between me and the detective.

Before Detective Pierce could answer, I said, "Just to the morgue to identify someone. It's okay. Tell Sara I'll be right back."

Josef looked puzzled but nodded and stepped aside. He didn't lift his sharp stare from the detective. "I'll be down to get you if you're not back in an hour," he said.

Detective Pierce opened the back door of the police car and gave me a gentle shove from behind. Then he jumped into the front passenger seat, not even taking off his fedora. The tires screeched when the driver hit the gas pedal too hard pulling away. Pierce lit a cigarette with the scratch of a match on the front dash.

The two of them ignored me. They cracked jokes back and forth about wops, niggers, and Hebes, which gave them both a good laugh.

"So where'd they find this dead guy?" the driver asked Pierce.

"A patrol car found him hangin' from a girder at the top of the steps of the Brighton Beach El station. Looks like he did himself in, but he might have had some help, if you know what I mean."

"So is he a Hebe?"

"Nah."

"How can you tell?"

"They didn't put his pecker through the pencil sharpener." They both laughed so hard Pierce's skinny face lit up like a bright red light bulb. I'd never heard a circumcision referred to as a pencil sharpener. I fought back a smile, refusing to give them that satisfaction.

My mind was so short of connections I didn't recognize how absurd this all was. Everyone I knew in Brooklyn had been in my house today, even my barber. So how could I possibly recognize this poor soul who had passed to the beyond? It must be some sort of black mistake.

The morgue wasn't far from the house, but it was in an industrial section of Brooklyn I wasn't familiar with. "Can you give me a ride home when we're done?" I asked as we got out of the car. "I need to be with my wife."

Pierce didn't look as benign as he did on the front steps of my house or the front seat of the police car. "When we're done with ya'." His manner would have put me on edge if my wires were still connected.

The sound of our footsteps echoed down the long gray tiled hallway. Pierce stayed close beside me, the uniformed officer immediately to my rear, as though they expected this overweight sixty-four year old man to make a run for it. We were the only ones there.

We paused in front of a pair of swinging metal doors. A putrid odor of chemicals and blood seeped out, like the sawdust and blood of Jake's butcher shop. "Ever seen a dead body before?" Pierce asked.

"No." My voice bounced off the sterile gray walls into the silence.

"It ain't pretty." He took my elbow in one hand and pushed the door open with the other.

The room was bigger than Ebbets Field. Bodies rested on six wheeled gurneys, each with a gigantic unlit spotlight over it.

"Hey Doc," Pierce called to the only person in the room, a thin bespectacled man in a white coat who seemed to be in charge of the morgue. "Let's take a look at that old guy. The one with the twisted leg."

Pierce's words froze me for a barely-perceptible second, but he didn't miss my flinch. My guts felt like they were being scrambled with an eggbeater. I mashed my teeth so hard they could have shattered.

The white coated morgue keeper would have looked good as a granite statue on a mausoleum. "This guy know him?" he asked, flicking a finger in my direction.

"His name was on the note in the bum's pocket. Avi Schneider."

Doc walked over to the middle gurney and turned on the big overhead light. Brown streaks and yellow splotches pocked the gray-white sheet covering the body. He lowered the sheet with two hands so the corpse's head showed from the chin up.

"Come here and take a good look," Pierce commanded, guiding me with a firm hand toward the dead man's head.

At first all I could see was the bristled wire of a matted gray beard and wild hair. "Can you identify this man?" Doc asked with judicial formality.

I stared at the face of Viktor Askinov. Even death couldn't wash the evil from his fat lips.

Pierce grabbed my upper arm. "Answer the man. Do you recognize him?"

I shook my head.

"Say it out loud," Doc ordered in a flat tone.

"No." But I couldn't look away from him. Vinegar rose on my tongue.

The detective lowered the sheet a little further, revealing the corpse's neck. "Any idea how he got these rope burns?" He pointed at a thick purple bruise mark around Askinov's entire neck.

"No."

"He hung himself." The way he said *hung* sounded like an indictment. His stare narrowed in on me. "Or someone hung him. Know anything about that?"

"No."

"You don't know much, do ya'?" He took a cigarette from a pack of Lucky Strikes and stuck it in his mouth, but didn't light it.

"Am I in some kind of trouble?" I tried to control my voice but I wasn't succeeding. I needed to go to the toilet.

"Just answer the question and don't be a wise guy."

"I don't know anything about that."

Pierce pointed at what appeared to be the bluish-purple imprint of thumbs where I nearly strangled him the day before. "And how about these other bruise marks?"

"Detective, I am a sixty-four year old man." I held up my two arthritic hands. "Do I look like I have the strength?" He took my answer as a "no," like I intended. Those fingerprints could send me to jail. I hope they haven't already talked to Litvak, I said to myself. If they had, though, I'd probably know about it.

Pierce walked around the corpse and toward the foot of the gurney. He beckoned me to join him, and motioned for Doc to lift the sheet. A tag was attached to the big toe of the corpse's left foot. The tattered right pant leg was rolled up above the knee.

Pierce pointed. "That fuckin' leg looks like the branch of a twisted tree. Ever seen anything like it, Doc? Look at those knots and scars." White streaks spider-webbed down the corpse's hairless leg starting above his knee and ending just above his ankle. The leg was no bigger than a child's. His foot was at an odd angle to the rest of his leg, his toes shriveled and curled into themselves.

"Looks like someone shot him in that leg a long time ago. Look here." The doc pointed with the tip of a scalpel. "It's withered. Poor bastard must have been in lots of pain his whole life, dragging that stump around with him."

I felt no pity. I felt no satisfaction. I felt no guilt. All I felt was a determination that no one in the family should know this monster had reached us.

Pierce turned to me. "You don't seem too sorry for him. Is there anything you wanna' tell me?" I felt no emotions, so I didn't show any.

"He already told you he doesn't know the man," Doc said, providing a welcomed interruption to Pierce's interrogation. "He's just one of those bums – one of them refugees trying to sneak into the country."

"Yeah. But why'd he kill himself?"

If someone had told me Viktor Askinov was dead, I wouldn't have believed him. You can't kill the Devil. But here he was in this morgue in Brooklyn. Still, I expected him to open his eyes and bare his teeth at any moment.

An impulse surged through me. I had to know for sure. So with the same compulsion with which I had attacked him in Litvak's bar, I reached out and grabbed his foot. I squeezed. It felt like slimy gray clay.

Detective Pierce grabbed my hand and yanked it away. "Still say ya' don't know him?" he demanded. His glare said I had just confirmed his suspicions. My stare remained locked on that contorted leg.

"I've never seen a dead man before," was all I said. He let it go at that.

As we walked back to the car, he continued to probe. "But I can't figure how he got your name," he mused.

"Maybe someone from the old country gave it to him," the uniformed officer said. "They do that, ya' know."

"Who gives a shit anyway," Pierce said to no one. "Just some bum who liquored up and hung himself. I got better ways to spend my time than on this kinda' shit." The two of them ignored me on the drive back, even when we pulled up in front of the house. I opened the car door and exited without a further word.

Josef waited for me on the front porch. "What was that about?" He asked.

"A mistake," I answered. Josef gave me a skeptical look but didn't press for any more answers.

Four days later a small article in the newspaper said a derelict hobo had hung himself. There were no signs of foul play. The unidentified man was buried in the Brooklyn Potter's Field in an unmarked grave. Pierce probably suspected me, but no one was going to spend any time investigating the murder of a nameless vagrant.

Viktor Askinov was dead. Why did I feel no relief, no joy, no triumph? Why didn't the fear go away?

A couple of weeks later, we forced ourselves to go to synagogue for *Rosh Hashonnah* – the Jewish new year – more from centuries of habit than devotion. Maybe some hoped to find an answer there. More were contaminated with doubt.

Daniel stood atop the altar in his finest black robe and yarmulke, his huge tallis wrapped around him. With body bent from age and a thick gray beard, he looked like the vision of a rabbi from the old country. He had the impossible task of trying to explain how God could let a tragedy like Sukhi Yar – like the *Shoah* – happen to his chosen people.

I didn't hear a word Daniel said in his sermon, and only heard the familiar prayers as a noise. My mind was vacant, my heart dead. For those two days and nights of Rosh Hashonnah, I clung to Sara on one side and Zelda on the other. Markus clung to Sadie, and Ester clung to Simon. Miryem sat next to Josef, but Josef did not cling to her.

For a moment on the first day of Rosh Hashonnah, I closed my eyes and was again back in Uman. I could feel Lieb sitting on my one side, as he did most of the time on the High Holy Days. Duv sat on my other side muttering jokes and mocking Rabbi Rosenberg under his breath so only I could hear him. I laughed out loud. Lieb poked me in the ribs and shushed me. "You're going to get in trouble with Poppa," he said.

When I opened my eyes, I realized it was Sara who had shushed me and poked me in the ribs, not Lieb. She had her prayer book open, absorbed in Rabbi Daniel's petitions to God.

But even with my eyes open, I felt a presence in the synagogue. Something caused me to look back over my shoulder. The real Duv Eisenberg stood in the back of the synagogue near the exit. He was solemn, the mocking grin he reserved for synagogue nowhere in evidence. When he caught my eye, a small sad smile brushed his lips.

I got up right in the middle of the service and walked back up the aisle toward him. A few heads turned, but not many. When I reached him, he held open his arms; we hugged and held each other as deeply

344 . Alan Fleishman

as two men can.

"Lieb was my friend too," he whispered. When we let go, we both reached for our handkerchiefs to wipe our eyes. "He's the best man I ever knew," he said after wiping his nose and sticking his hanky back in his pocket. "The only one better than you."

I motioned for Duv to follow me into the vestibule outside the sanctuary. Just as we exited, Duv looked back to the altar where Daniel was watching us even as he chanted a prayer. Duv raised two fingers to his forehead, a subtle salute. Though he now denies it, Daniel raised his hand inconspicuously to touch his own forehead.

"You know Viktor Askinov hanged himself," I said as soon as we were out of the sanctuary.

He nodded. He didn't look surprised.

"He was there when Lieb died. Probably had a hand in it," I said.

He nodded again. "I heard what you did. Almost killed him. I'm proud of you." Something in his manner hinted at a secret he wasn't going to share. I didn't realize until much later that Daniel was the only one who could have told him about my encounter with Viktor Askinov at the Blue Sail bar.

"For a minute I was afraid the police suspected I did it," I said.

"I wouldn't have let anything happen to you." He put a hand on each of my shoulders and looked me in the eye with a compassion I never expected from Duv.

A thought clicked in my mind and came out of my mouth before I could stop it. "Did Viktor Askinov kill himself, or did someone kill him?" Emotion drained from his face.

"Whichever you prefer," he answered, his vacant voice that of a killer.

I looked down at my shoes. "Three times I could have killed him," I said. "With that rock when we were kids; the night on the barricades during the *pogrom*; and a couple of weeks ago. I failed every time."

"You didn't fail. You are what you are, and I'm proud at one time you called me your friend. I'm just sorry I never lived up to that."

"And I'm sorry I couldn't be more forgiving."

"I got the life I deserved, and you got the life you deserved." Tears shimmered in his eyes again. "But Lieb didn't. He deserved better."

"Why did you come today?"

"To honor Lieb. And to be with you." A tear ran down his left cheek. He wiped it away. "I'm sorry I couldn't save him. Save his family." He sniffled.

I nodded. "You tried your hardest, and I'm grateful."

"I have to go," Duv said. "Give my regrets to everyone. Say hello to Simon and Markus for me. We were quite a gang back then, weren't we?"

I walked him out the front door of the synagogue. We grasped each other and hugged hard. Then he put on his hat and dashed down the steps, not looking back. His goon waited for him by his shiny black Packard.

Eight days later we were back in the synagogue for *Yom Kippur* – the Day of Atonement. It came on a Friday that year. I did not seek God's forgiveness for my sins. If I sought anything, it was an apology from God for what he allowed to happen to Lieb.

Twelve days later, they hung the first ten of the Nazi leaders found guilty at the Nuremberg Trials. Goring escaped his punishment by committing suicide the night before. Someone smuggled him a cyanide pill. Too bad. I wanted him hung with a short rope so he would strangle to death slowly and painfully.

Daniel said those executions were God's retribution. He said the Soviet rape of Berlin was God's retribution. He said Viktor Askinov's hanging was God's retribution. And to each, I said it wasn't enough. God owed us more than that. I didn't expect Him to deliver.

CHAPTER FORTY-ONE

Early September 1947

Six years had passed since the day Lieb was murdered, and one year since I learned of it from the mouth of Viktor Askinov. Most days I ate, I slept, and when spring came I sat in the back yard in a stupor. At first I tried to find a reason to believe Viktor Askinov was lying. Why should I believe a person like that? But independent verification from Western investigators soon put that notion to rest.

A few lucky refugees arrived in town, those with relatives in Manhattan Beach and Brighton Beach. In my time, New York had been the funnel for immigrant Jews coming to America – Jews full of hope. And here it was again, New York a funnel, only this time it was desperate Jewish refugees who had survived death camps.

Most had a number tattooed on their forearms like livestock. Some tried to hide it as if it was their shame. Others displayed theirs with the pride of a defiant survivor. Sara reached out to these poor people; I paid them no mind.

I should have given more attention to Sara's grief. Her sister Havol had been murdered the same as Lieb. And I should have given more attention to the grief of Markus, Ester, Zelda, and Josef. But I knew horrors they didn't know then and still don't know now: the details of how they died in Sukhi Yar that day, and that Viktor Askinov had been right here in Manhattan Beach within a hare's breath of us, just five blocks from my house. I'm telling you, that makes all the difference in the world. To think that Lieb made it through *pogroms*, purges, civil war, famine, and the death of a daughter, only to die in a ditch. I don't want to say any more about it. I don't want to think any more about it.

Others in town mourned their dead too, but I tortured myself with merciless anger and self-reproach. I took Lieb's death and the death of his family as my fault, my failure. Regardless of why, in the end all hope was bled out of me.

Daniel and I saw each other or talked on the telephone almost every day. I don't know why he put up with me, or what I would have done without him. Whenever I saw him I dared him to defend God. I wanted to get even with God, and insulting Him through Daniel was the best way I could think of to do it. I'm sure at this point, Daniel had his own doubts.

If I wasn't doing that, I was attacking all the gentiles who participated in the murder of six million Jews. Not just Germans and Austrians, but Ukraines, Poles, Hungarians, Rumanians, and half the people in the rest of Europe. One morning we had a cup of coffee and a piece of Boston cream pie at the Woolworth's counter. "They would have celebrated if Hitler had killed us all," I charged. "You watch. In a few years when they stop feeling guilty, the Christians will be back at it, hating and killing Jews."

"Hate can't kill hope," Daniel said. "God won't let it. You can't let it."

"What do you mean? Hate's already won."

Daniel threw his fork down on the counter, disgusted with me. "So you're giving up? That's what you're doing?"

"That's what I'm doing."

Daniel had nothing more to say so we left it there. But he recognized the anger born of grief. He only let me go for the moment. On the way home he said "Viktor Askinov's death brought nothing but joy to everyone who knew him. Glad he was dead. Think about that. And think about the grief everyone feels about Lieb's death, and their love for him. That is Lieb's triumph. That is the Lord's triumph." I wasn't ready to listen just then, but I heard his words and they stayed with me.

The next Monday we took an early morning walk along the beach. The children were back in school so it was empty except for a uniformed city workman picking up trash from the sands. We stopped and leaned against the boardwalk railing, looking out at the sun glistening on the blue sea. The only sounds were those of seagulls squawking and waves lapping. Neither of us wanted to break the tranquility.

"I woke up in the middle of the night seeing trains," I finally said.

"Trains?" He looked at me with a puzzled expression.

"I sprang straight up in bed, with this clear image in front of my eyes. Railroad tracks. The same tracks that carried me west toward America back in 1905; the very same tracks carried those poor Jews in boxcars east toward Poland and death camps."

Daniel turned toward me. He put his hand on my shoulder and stroked it. "My friend, my friend," he said. His dark eyes carried my pain.

"In my nightmare I see two trains passing, one headed for America and one headed in the opposite direction. In my train, everyone is laughing, full of hope. In the other one, children moan and mothers cry."

"You're not the only Jew having such nightmares," he answered.

"Maybe not, but it feels that way."

Daniel's sympathy didn't stop the trains. In my sleepless nights, the wheels clacked on the rails, a horn sounded every now and then, and the cars swayed whenever they rounded a curve. But more and more I saw the boxcars traveling east on those tracks, not my train of hope traveling west. My only relief came on the nights when I saw just empty train tracks with no trains traveling in either direction. It was going to take a miracle to end those nightmares.

Daniel usually didn't try to defend God. Instead he changed the subject and got me talking about Sergey, Valerya, Madam Shumenko, or other righteous gentiles. He mentioned friends like Bettino Rossi and Thomas Kelly often, knowing they would give me the shirts off their backs, or die for me like Sergey died for Lieb. He did it all with such a deft hand I didn't realize what he was doing, but he was getting through to me.

The first week in September Daniel came over to the house in the late afternoon. I think Sara called him and asked him to come. Her concern for me was reaching a breaking point. Daniel and I sat out in back on Adirondack chairs under the shade of the huge apple tree Sara had planted twenty years ago. Maybe the worst of the hurt was softening a little, but only a little. I leaned back in my chair and studied the ripe red fruit hanging from the tree.

"So, has Isaac joined the country club there in Berkinbury?" he asked, studying the same apples. That May Jack Shapiro, Isaac's friend, had forced the country club to admit him, the club's first Jew. Shapiro had seen fierce fighting during the war as a major in a tank battalion. He wasn't about to let a country club's board of old men deny him what he thought he had rightfully earned – a chance to play golf wherever he wanted.

"Yes, Isaac just joined," I answered. But Daniel already knew that before he asked the question. It was Daniel's way of reminding me of progress being made – this new generation of Jewish G.I.'s seizing their rightful place in America, just like Jack Shapiro did. "America's going to be different for our grandkids," Daniel said.

Indian summer was still a couple of weeks off. Overnight rain had cleansed the overcast September morning. The *Yahrtzeit* candle I lit the night before for Lieb hit me when I walked into the kitchen and saw it burning on the counter next to the toaster. It marked the anniversary of his death. It also marked the end of Viktor Askinov. I hate to admit it even now, but I get satisfaction when I picture Viktor Askinov dangling by his neck from the top girder of the Brighton Beach El station.

Sara made some eggs and toast for breakfast. When we sat down to eat, I didn't say much. She asked me if I was going into the tailor shop today. I grunted. She mentioned the adorable Japanese war bride Sam Spiegel's son brought home. Sara liked her. I grunted again.

For the past year, Sara had every reason to get upset with me on a daily basis. But the strongest feelings she ever showed me were compassion, with occasional frustration. This morning she finally had enough. She slammed the dirty frying pan into the sink; then when she cleared our dishes from the table she dropped one and broke it.

She let the pieces of the dish sit there on the floor and turned toward me, her hands jammed in her apron pockets. Sparks shot from her blue eyes. "The world is not all your responsibility. And God doesn't always do what *you* want. Maybe He can't. But we are here. We are safe. Our children are safe. Our grandchildren will have the life we wanted for them."

She pulled a hanky from her apron pocket to wipe her runny nose. "And all because you insisted. You made us come to America. All of us. We're grateful to you for it. But you are not God." She stuffed the hanky back in her pocket and took a deep breath. "Lieb decided for himself. Havol decided for herself. And you decided for yourself."

She picked up the pieces of the broken dish and threw them in the garbage pail under the sink. I didn't know what to say so I said nothing. Then she yanked off her apron and threw it on the back of the chair. She left the room without a word.

I couldn't remember the last time Sara had gotten so upset with me. Frustrated, yes, but not angry. Her words this time bit deeply, and this time I heard her.

I stared at the flame of Lieb's *Yahrtzeit* candle. Then I got up and went out to sit on the front porch, indifferent to the chill of the morning. A few neighbors passed by and waved. I ignored them. A couple of neighborhood boys, off school for the day, played in a mud puddle until their mother called them in. The whir of Harold Jacoby's lawnmower two doors down the street carried to our porch. It stopped periodically when he needed a rest from pushing. A muffled clap of thunder rumbled in the distance.

I don't know how long I sat there trying to sort out what Sara had said, and what Daniel had said a couple of weeks before. That look on Sara's face had been shared suffering, not anger; and I didn't like hurting her. She loved me. All she asked was that I love her back.

The front door opened and Sara came out carrying my jacket. "Put this on," she said. "You'll catch your death of a cold." I did what she said.

She sat down beside me on the bench and took my knobbed hand in hers. She lifted it to her lips and kissed it. We sat that way in silence for awhile, our hands locked in her lap. She took a deep breath before speaking. "We must mourn, but then God commands we resume our lives." She raised my hand again and kissed it. "We're getting old, Avi. Our days together are numbered. I don't want to waste even one of them."

I pulled her to me and ran my hand through her gray hair. "I will find my peace. I promise." Once I realized I had been punishing her worse than I punished myself, I knew I had to stop. I brought my lips to hers. She turned her head to meet me.

"Let's walk on the beach," she said.

"I'll drive," I answered. We had bought our first car last August, a 1940 navy blue Hudson Coupe. This luxury spared our weary old bones.

We groaned in unison as we got up from the bench. Our harmonic chord made us both laugh for the first time in a long time.

Only the determined few ventured onto the beach on a dark morning like this. When a stiff wind whooshed through, Sara stopped to pull her coat closer about her. We strolled hand in hand down the wooden pathway bordering the wet sand. I adored every inch of this woman, from her liver spots to her sagging breasts. And she loved me in spite of my widened waist and muffled hearing.

Saltwater and seaweed scented the air. Angry white waves from last night's thunder storm smashed on the beach. We stopped to watch a flock of gulls circle overhead and then sprint out to sea. A shaft of sunshine slipped through, cutting gray clouds and dark water with slender streaks of sparkling silver.

One seagull lagged behind the others. He circled and glided above us, not once but several times, before rushing off to catch up with the rest. At that moment, I swear I felt a firm touch on my shoulder. I turned to Sara. I was holding her one hand and her other one was in her pocket. Sara said later I looked like I had just seen the archangel.

We stood there, fixed on the seagull until he caught up to the flock and they disappeared into a low cloud. I don't believe in angels. You know that. But in the moment I was sure Lieb had touched me to say goodbye.

Sara used to say "you Schneider men are all so stubborn!" I thought she was only talking about Uncle Yakov, Poppa, Markus, and me – but surely not Lieb. Now I can see Lieb was more stubborn than any of us. He wouldn't let Viktor Askinov, Josef Stalin, or even Adolph Hitler expel him from his home. He would leave when he decided and not a moment sooner. He paid with his life. That day I realized in the end Lieb was also the bravest, the most heroic of the Schneider men.

When my seagull flew off, a certain peace came over me for the first time in a year, and maybe many years. Something told me life was not finished with me. But what more was there to do but wait for my end?

CHAPTER FORTY-TWO

LATE SEPTEMBER 1947

I was in the middle of a little afternoon snooze in my living room chair when the telephone jangled in the hallway. Sara answered it. I cleared my head enough to get up and turn down the radio.

Sara didn't say much to the caller other than "yes" and "I understand." Then she stammered, a surprised look on her face. "You'd better talk to my husband. His name is Avi Schneider. He might be the one you're looking for." She handed me the telephone and sat down in the chair next to the hallway table to listen.

"This is Avi Schneider," I said.

"Hello, Mr. Schneider. I'm Selma Hirsch from the Jewish Children's Refugee Agency." She sounded nice enough, but officious. "We've been searching now for six weeks for someone in New York named Avi Schneider. We've called everyone by the name of Abraham Schneider, Avriham, Avrahim. We even called Schenectady and Buffalo."

"Well, people call me Avi, but my citizenship papers read Abraham Schneider. How can I help you?"

"Mr. Schneider, we have this little boy here with us at our agency. Actually he's in our camp at Oswego, but he's due to be transferred to our orphanage here in the Bronx day after tomorrow. He was picked up in Austria and brought to America along with nineteen other orphans for resettlement."

"What does this have to do with me?"

"His name is Ilya Portnoya. Do you know anyone by that name?"

I thought for a moment. "No. I don't know anyone named Portnoya." I turned to Sara. "Do we know anyone named Portnoya?" She shook her head. "I'm sorry Mrs. Hirsch. We don't know anyone by that name."

"It's Miss Hirsch," she said, slightly defensive. "And like it or not, Mr. Schneider, there seems to be some connection. The woman who brought him to us was a Russian. She died the next day. She said your name over and over again until she couldn't speak any longer. 'Avi Schneider New York.' And the little boy says little else than 'Avi Schneider America.' You are the only Avi Schneider we can locate among the seventy-three Abrahams and Avrihams we traced."

"I'm sorry to disappoint you Miss Hirsch."

"He is an orphan, Mr. Schneider. He has no one to take him in. He's only a little boy. Probably seven or eight years old. Maybe nine." She sounded frustrated and desperate.

"I understand he's an orphan, but I don't know how I can help you." Though she could only hear my end of the conversation, Sara's expressions changed with each exchange, first concern and now sympathy. All of the Jewish war orphans we heard about and read about tore at Sara's heart. She spent half her days collecting donated clothes, food, and toys for them.

Selma Hirsch's voice grew more anxious. "Mr. Schneider. Do you know anyone from the village of Komarova?"

That got my attention. "Komarova? Is that near Uman?" My mind twitched but I couldn't place Komarova on a map.

"I don't know. All I know is it's in Kiev Gibernya."

When she heard me say Komarova, Sara's eyes opened wide. She nodded her head up and down repeatedly to say that "yes" we knew someone from Komarova.

"Hold on one minute," I said to Miss Hirsch. I covered the mouthpiece and turned to Sara. "She wants us to come to the Bronx to meet this little boy and see if we might know him from a picture or a resemblance. Do we go?"

Sara jumped up from her chair. "Yes, yes, we go." She tugged my sleeve. "Sergey Shumenko and Valerya lived in a little house in Komarova after he was released from prison."

So I promised Miss Hirsch we would be there on Wednesday at ten o'clock. I hung up, puzzled by Sara's reaction. She had a big smile on her face and was almost jumping out of her shoes. She clapped her hands together. "Don't you see?" she said. "There has to be some connection."

I myself didn't know what to make of it. Sara wondered if it could have anything to do with either of Sergey Shumenko's two sons. But their surnames were Shumenko, like Sergey's. I could think of no other possible tie, nor could Sara. Still, Miss Hirsch referred to me by the name of Avi. That nickname seemed unusual to her.

I plopped down in my living room chair, leaned back, and started thinking about this strange conversation I just had with Miss Hirsch. Sara went to say something - to tell me to call Ester. I held up my hand to stop her. A thought dangled just beyond my grasp, like it does in a dream. As I already told you, my Russian wasn't too good any more, but a Russian word kept turning over in my mind - *portnoya*. I couldn't quite remember what it meant, but something told me it was important.

Sara watched me, attentive. Miss Hirsch's accent rolled around in my mind, irritating as a pebble in your shoe. If I didn't speak Russian very well, Miss Hirsch was even worse. When she said the word "*pogrom*" she put the emphasis on the second syllable as though she were speaking Yiddish. Those of us from Uman put the emphasis on the first syllable, like the Russians. A thought began to form. What does it sound like when you put the emphasis on the first syllable of *portnoya*? I said it out loud: "Portnoi." Sara gave me an astonished look of recognition.

Then it came to me. Portnoi! *Tailor* in Russian; *Schneider* in

Yiddish. Could this little boy be related? A cousin from Odessa maybe? But a piece was missing. Then the name *Ilya* broke through. *Ilya* in Russian. *Elias* in Yiddish. Elias Schneider. It couldn't be! He had surely died with Lieb and everyone else at Sukhi Yar on that horrible day in 1941. But he was born in 1939: Two years old then, eight years old now. And Viktor Askinov hadn't remembered a little boy with Lieb that day.

"It's Elias," I shouted to Sara. The name just spilled out of my mouth before I thought it. I grabbed her and squeezed her to me.

She held me tight for a moment, and then pulled away. "It's possible," she said, though more hesitant than I would have liked, and with none of the exuberance she had shown just a few minutes before. "Maybe you should call Ester and Markus and see what they think." Sara's doubt was written all over her face. My fleeting certainty fizzled with the improbability of it.

I called Ester and recounted my phone call with Selma Hirsch. She didn't even let me finish speaking before she cut in She didn't remember anyone we knew named Portnoya. When I offered it might be Elias, she ignored me and went on talking. She said we had relatives in Kiev and Odessa - Poppa's sisters. "I'm telling you, if the boy's connected at all, it's through one of them. A cousin maybe," she said.

"But how? There were massacres in Kiev, worse than Uman. And Odessa too."

"Listen to me. In Odessa many got away to the east," she answered. "Simon has cousins from Odessa who were evacuated before the Germans got there."

I gave her my speculation that Valerya and Sergey could have taken Elias in, and then Valerya took him to Vienna. "Let me ask you something," Ester responded. "Why would this Christian woman, this Valerya person, take in a Jewish baby?" Ester's tongue dripped with bitter herbs when she said the word Christian. "If you ask me, someone's trying to put something over on you."

"We're going to meet him day after tomorrow," I said, deflated by her disbelief. "In the Bronx."

"Be careful you don't get dragged into something," she warned. "You're too good hearted, Avi. People take advantage." Just before she hung up, she told me a friend of hers fell for a similar hoax. The friend and her husband turned over five hundred dollars to some fraudulent agency for a child that wasn't even Jewish.

When I finished with Ester, I phoned Markus, expecting a more sympathetic reception. But he was skeptical too. "It's probably just a coincidence that *portnoya* and *schneider* both mean tailor," he said. "With a name like Portnoya, or Portnoi, he's without doubt Russian. And the name Ilya is certainly Russian."

"But what if his real name is Elias, not Ilya? Elias Schneider, not Ilya Portnoya."

Markus didn't answer right away. Then he said, "Avi, I want it to be Elias, too. But it's not Elias."

"Miracles happen." I slammed the receiver down so hard Sara jumped. She came over and touched my cheek. "It's possible," she said again, only this time with more conviction.

When I phoned Zelda, my little sister surprised me. "Of course it could be Elias," she said after I recounted my conversations with Miss Hirsch, Ester, and Markus. She seemed almost defiant in her assertion.

"You know, this is something Lieb would do, right up to the very end," she said. I could hear her sniffling on her end of the phone line. "If it's him, I'll come right away." In a second, I was sniffling too. She asked me to phone her as soon as I knew anything. Before hanging up, Zelda offered financial help if it turned out we had any relationship to the little boy.

I took a couple of shots of liquor before going to bed that night. It put me to sleep but didn't keep me there. A dark dream about a train roaring along its tracks woke me before dawn. The roar was actually thunder and a downpour beating against the windows. In my dream, I couldn't tell which way it was going, west toward hope, or east toward the death camps. But I saw a little boy on the train – a little boy who looked like Lieb. He brushed the hair out of his eyes with his left hand, and smiled at me.

I lay in bed, now wide awake, thinking. The truth was that the call from Miss Hirsch came completely out of nowhere. Even if the agency was legitimate, I could still be the wrong Avi Schneider. On the other hand, Sergey or Valerya might have told a neighbor about me, a neighbor named Portnoya.

I decided to call Daniel soon after the grandmother clock in our living room struck eight o'clock. He had worked with most of the refugee agencies, and at least he could tell me if Miss Hirsch and this Jewish Children's Refugee Agency were legitimate. His grumpy morning voice yielded when he heard it was me on the line. He woke up when I told the story of Miss Hirsch and my suspicion the little boy could be Elias. I asked him about the Jewish Children's Refugee Agency.

He had worked with them, he said. They were legitimate, and did lots of good work. Then there was a long pause on his end of the phone. "I don't know how to say this right," he continued. "I don't want to spread rumors. But sometimes this particular agency, and this Miss Hirsch, can be too aggressive about finding homes for their little charges. There's talk they make doubtful claims of relationships, trading on survivor's guilt, just to find a home for one of the little ones. You can't blame them entirely. The children need homes. But still, it's not right. I don't mean to be so skeptical. Just be careful." Daniel left me uneasy, but with a better picture of who I was dealing with.

I slowly put the phone back in its cradle. Sara witnessed my long face. "His name is still Portnoi – Schneider." she said. "We know that. And Ilya could be Elias, don't forget."

Right after breakfast, Sara left for the grocery store. She returned with two bags full of groceries. She unloaded both chocolate and vanilla Dixie Cups, sliced bologna, white bread, potato chips, canned peaches, and who knows what else. She took some hamburger meat from the Frigidaire. Later I found her peeling the shells off of boiled eggs to make egg salad.

"Are we expecting company?" I asked.

"He'll be hungry," she answered without looking up from the plate of eggs.

It wasn't dawn yet when I got out of bed the next morning, put on my bathrobe, and went downstairs. I boiled some water for tea and sat down at the kitchen table to drink it. A comment Zelda made on the phone stuck in my head: "Lieb would give up his life and everything he had, and die with dignity, comforting his children and grandchildren to the end. At the same time, he'd try to save Elias." It would have taken Lieb's courage and Lieb's faith to do such a thing, I thought. But let's say somehow he convinced Valerya at the last moment to take Elias in. How could an old woman Valerya's age have walked all the way from Uman to Vienna?

Sara came down the steps in her nightgown and slippers. She put her arms around my shoulders and kissed the top of my balding head before sitting down at the kitchen table next to me. "Tell me honestly," I said to her. "Do you think this woman mentioned in the agency's report could be Valerya Shumenko?"

She nodded. "Valerya was a friend, a good friend," she answered. "Look at how often Lieb wrote about her. There were times over the years when I thought his feelings for Valerya, and maybe hers for him, went dangerously beyond friendship."

"What if it is Elias?" I asked. "How are a couple of old people like us going to raise a little boy?"

"One step at a time," she said. "If we have to, we will." She took a sip of tea from my cup, and then looked off in the distance, her mouth moving before words came out. "Everything happens for a reason. Maybe it's why Yakira never had any children, so she and Jake could raise this one. Can you imagine how lucky that little boy would be to have those two for parents? And how much love he would get from *all* of us?" She took another sip of my lukewarm tea.

Sara put her hand on mine. "Does it matter so much whether he is Lieb's grandson or not?" she went on. "Whoever he is, there's an orphaned little boy out there who's been through hell. He needs someone to take care of him, to love him."

I nodded my head as if I agreed, but I was thinking it was about more than an orphaned child. It was about my brother. If the boy was Elias, a part of Lieb would live on. He would still be with us. He wouldn't have died for nothing.

The clouds from last night's rain passed momentarily and a beam of morning sunshine showed outside the kitchen window. Then clouds covered the sun again and the gray returned. "I'd better go shave," I said, getting up from the table.

"Avi, you've got to be prepared either way, if it is or if it's not Elias."

I nodded my head. But after the darkness of Viktor Askinov, and now after this little granule of hope, I wasn't ready for such disappointment. Like it or not, it did matter whether or not it was Elias.

Two days after Miss Hirsch first telephoned, we headed for the subway, bound for the Bronx. We decided to walk to the El station rather than take the car. Metal garbage cans lined the quiet street waiting for the garbage men. The snapdragons bordering the sidewalk in front of Mrs. Epstein's house released the flavor of honeyed vanilla. Sunshine and drizzle competed with each other, first one winning, then the other. When the sun shot through the passing dark clouds, the puddles along West End Avenue glistened like mirrors. I wasn't watching where I was going and stepped right in one of the puddles, ending up with a wet foot.

All during the subway ride, Sara held my hand with both of hers, resting them in her lap. We said little, the noise of the subway smothering any serious conversation. I stared at the placards along the ceiling of the subway car advertising Lifebuoy Soap and Duggan's Cupcakes, but my mind was on the little boy.

The Jewish Children's Refugee Agency was in a dilapidated walkup next to the elevated subway, surrounded by old apartment buildings that reminded me of our days in East Harlem. There was nothing but asphalt and concrete anywhere in sight, not a single tree or shrub. The last of the rain clouds passed.

Inside the front door, a hand lettered sign on a piece of cardboard pointed us up the worn wooden stairs to the office. This ancient five story building was a fire trap. Along the hallway at the top of the stairs, we passed several small rooms that served as classrooms and playrooms. The well-scrubbed quarters had the smell of antiseptic covering urine mixed with too many sweaty children's bodies packed into too tight a box. We heard some quiet words, but none of the commotion you would expect from a place filled with kids.

In the large open area, a few women worked at their desks, one on the telephone, and three others reading files and typing. I looked at my Benrus. It was ten o'clock; we were right on time.

As if on cue, a tight little middle aged woman in a gray smock came from the hallway at the far end of the open area. She smiled a weary smile and held out both of her hands, one to Sara and one to me. "You must be the Schneiders." Her voice was warmer than the officious voice on the telephone. "I'm Selma Hirsch."

"Come. Come," she said, motioning us toward two chairs next to an aged wooden desk that looked like it had been assaulted with chains and shovels. Just as we started to talk, we were interrupted by the roar of a subway train going by.

When it passed, Miss Hirsch began a drawn-out explanation of the colossal task facing the Jewish Children's Refugee Agency. These orphaned children they served had all been stuck in displaced persons camps until President Truman laid down the law: break through the red tape and get those in the American zone to America. Until then, if these children wanted to come to our country, regulations required they had to bring their birth certificates to an American consulate.

"How were they supposed to do that," Miss Hirsch asked sarcastically, "when some of them were too young to even talk? Most of them spent the war in concentration camps. They didn't know their own names or where they were born, no less have a birth certificate."

I drummed my fingers on the desk, impatient to hear about the little boy, Ilya Portnoya. Sara reached over and covered my nervous fingers with her hand. Miss Hirsch paid no attention. "The program's going to end in about six months. We've gotten about a thousand children into the country so far. Maybe we'll get another three or four

362 . *Alan Fleishman*

hundred in before it ends."

"What happens to these children?" Sara asked.

"If we're lucky, we find a relative who will take them in. If not, most of the time we find a Jewish family to adopt them, or be foster parents. A few times we had to settle with placing them with nuns in a convent." She shrugged her shoulders with a soft smile of grateful resignation.

My mind wandered while she talked. "Tell us about this little boy we're here for," I finally broke in. "Ilya Portnoya."

"Ah, yes. Little Ilya. We brought him in yesterday with nineteen other children, from Oswego. Nine girls and eleven boys. Ilya's a shy, well-mannered little boy. Alert and very bright, but he never smiles. He's been through more than we can imagine."

"What do you know about him?" I asked.

Miss Hirsch opened the thin file in front of her and pulled two pieces of paper from it. "I suggest you read this first." She handed the pages across the desk to me. "I'm afraid all we know about Ilya is in that report," she said. "How they got out of Russia and to Vienna we'll never know, but we have other stories just like it. Only in this case, unfortunately, the old woman died."

```
                      CLIENT REPORT
            JEWISH CHILDREN'S REFUGEE AGENCY


     CHILD'S NAME:        Ilya Portnoya
     NATIONALITY:         Russian
     TOWN OF ORIGIN:      Kiev Gibernya.
                          Village of Komarova?
     AGE:                 Between 7 and 9 years
     NEAREST LIVING RELATIVE: Unknown.
     CLASSIFICATION:      Orphan
     INITIAL PROCESS:     Seegasse, Austria
     DATE:                December 12, 1946
```

This child was brought to the Seegasse Camp by an elderly woman who said they had walked all the way from Kiev Gibernya in Russia, a distance of over 1,200 kilometers. The old woman spoke no language other than Russian and the camp had no Russian interpreters available at the moment she arrived. The woman died, probably of starvation, one day later. The boy speaks very little, but enough to determine Russian is his first language. He seems to understand some words of German, but speaks only a few distorted words.

The boy does not know how old he is, but he knows his name. He is small and thin, so it is difficult to estimate age. Our best approximation is that he is between 7 and 9 years old.

Sometimes he refers to the woman who brought him to us as Grandmamma and sometimes as Auntie Via, but he speaks so softly it is difficult to determine if this was her name. We determined from her before she died that her surname is not Portnoya, as is his. She did not have time to reveal what her name was before she fainted. We can tell from the way he calls for her that she was someone very close to him, whether aunt or grandmother.

The only family connection and lead we have is the final words of the old woman. She repeated what we presume to be a name over and over again. The name was Avi Schneider. The boy also repeats the name whenever anyone tries to speak to him. The woman mentioned New York once. The boy keeps saying Avi Schneider America.

END OF REPORT

I finish reading the report and hold it out to Sara to read. She shakes her head. I hand it back to Miss Hirsch. Neither the report nor Miss Hirsch can answer my question: who is this child and does he have any connection to me?

"Why don't I go get Ilya so you can meet him," she says. She returns the report to its folder, and then rises from her chair. "Wait here. I'll be right back." She turns to go.

Fear strikes my stomach with the force of a hammer. Any chance that a remnant of Lieb survives could end when the little boy appears. I am choked with panic. Delay is the only way to keep my brother alive for a few minutes more.

"Tell me first, is he circumcised?" I shout, trying to keep her from leaving. "I know he had a *bris* when he was eight days old." Miss Hirsch stops.

"Nearly all of the little boys are circumcised, Mr. Schneider. They're Jews." She turns again to leave.

"But is he left handed? My brother Lieb was left handed. So was his son, Joshua."

Miss Hirsch surprises me by coming around her desk and giving me a hug. She smiles as she separates herself. "Let me get the boy."

She exits at the far end of the room, down the hallway from which she had come. Sara gazes at me with the same radiance of the nineteen year old girl I met for the first time across the market square on that sunny day forty-five years ago. She seems excited, not scared like me.

While we wait, the compassionate ghosts of Momma, Poppa, Uncle Yakov, and Lieb crowd my mind. "It has to be him," I say out loud. My guts scream. It is almost more than I can bear.

A solo typewriter clicks. Another subway rumbles through, clattering on the tracks. I wonder which direction it's going, and what is taking Miss Hirsch so long to get the boy. Is there a problem? My heart shivers. I close my eyes and start shaking. My gripped hands turn white. "Hope, hope," I demand of myself. "Pray."

Sara clutches my arm. "Look Avi, look," she cries.

I open my eyes and there he is, walking cautiously toward us in his short pants and a blue striped T-shirt, one sock up and one sock down. He is a skinny little boy with dark chocolate hair and big dark eyes. He stops not far from us.

He gives me a soft smile and looks at me as though he recognizes me. Then the little boy raises his left hand and brushes his floppy hair from his eyes.

"My god, its Lieb," I say.

It was a fine September morning.

Acknowledgements

The encouragement and help I received from friends and family have been the great joy of writing *A Fine September Morning*. None have done more than my wife Ann, who was the first to read every line. I couldn't have done this without her constant enthusiasm, careful editing, sound advice, and passionate defense of my fragile ego against all comers.

Tom Brunner, Carol Whitely, Jim Meikrantz, Sandra Didner, and George Marcellino provided scrupulous editing and constructive feedback. Bob Berkowitz suggested many creative appellations for this saga. Steve and Marlene Kofman lent their tasteful convictions to the final selection of the title and cover design. Marlene suggested the back cover.

Lynda Steele forced me to alter and re-write the critical final chapter in its entirety, much to its betterment. She provided the final sentence, which now seems like the only appropriate ending.

Carla Skladany deserves special thanks for her unbridled cheerleading, and for specific suggestions, like noodles rather than pasta, and "*Holy Mary, Mother of God*," excited words shouted out by Josef's hot paramour, Maggie. Jan Skladany provided the gripping image of the same train tracks carrying Jews west toward the hope of America in 1905 and east toward Hitler's death camps in Poland thirty-plus years later.

Dr. Ted Merwin scrubbed late drafts for anachronisms and cultural accuracy. His own book, *In Their Own Image*, provided the inspiration for Sara's American assimilation via popular culture. All-in-all, Ted's input contributed immensely to the book's authenticity.

I might still be writing drafts and more drafts, endlessly, if not for my always-professional daughter, Beth von Emster, and my friend Andy Weir. They told me I was finished and ready to go to press. I trust their judgment.

Special thanks goes to Tom Kearns for being my dear friend and bringing so much pleasure into my life for so long.

ALAN FLEISHMAN

Afterward

A Fine September Morning is the sequel to *Goliath's Head*. It continues the saga of Avi Schneider and his family. While it is a work of fiction, it is real and true, founded on scrupulous attention to historical accuracy to the best of my ability.

While the plot and characters in the book are totally a product of my imagination, the broad outline of the immigrant story, timelines, and settings closely parallel those of my parents and grandparents. The specific addresses where Avi and Sara lived are those of my Fleishman grandparents, who in fact lived in East Harlem and Manhattan Beach.

The Spanish Flu, which nearly killed Sara in the book, took my grandmother's life while she was still a young woman. My father was only fourteen at the time; his mother's early death left a lasting imprint on him.

In the book, Isaac and Tillie's courtship and marriage shadowed that of my mother and father, including the date and place they were married. The story of the engagement ring Isaac gives Tillie is true. My wife Ann now wears that ring.

The town of Berkinbury, where Avi's son Isaac moves as an adult, is a stand-in for my hometown, Berwick, Pennsylvania. As with Isaac and his wife Tillie, my mother and father moved to Berwick in 1934. However, it was my maternal grandfather who, along with his brother, started a garment company in that town named *Lady Esther*. In the book, Isaac names his company *Lady Sara*.

Several critical passages in *A Fine September Morning* come directly from historical events and detailed records. The fire in the Becker Dress Factory is a facsimile of the 1911 Triangle Shirtwaist Factory fire in which one hundred forty-six immigrant workers died, mostly women. The account of the pillage, murder, and rape of the Ukraine Jewish community during the Russian Civil War is taken directly from the Red Cross report published in 1920 of its on-site investigation led by Ezra Heifetz.

Newspaper headlines are authentic throughout the book. They reflect what people knew at the time. Edward R. Murrow's 1942 first broadcast from London about the extermination camps for Jews is from a verbatim transcript.

The most difficult part of the book to imagine and write was Viktor Askinov's telling of the end of the Jews in Uman. I'm sure some of my distant Fleishman and Kravetz cousins were part of the carnage in the ravine at Sukhy Yar. The details of that event are a meticulous reflection of the eyewitness testimony of a young German army lieutenant named Erwin Bingel given at the Nuremberg war trials. I feel indebted to him for his honest and complete account.

And finally, my apology to those offended by the ethnic and racial slurs uttered by characters in the book, some even coming out from the mouth of a good person like Avi Schneider. It was a tough call about whether or not to include such language. But this is the way they talked then, and in my opinion including them was necessary to depict the prejudices that existed at the time. These commonly used racial and ethnic slurs reflected an intolerance that flowed in all directions. Such language was still very common in 1947 when Avi wrote this memoir.

Author's Profile

A Fine September Morning is the sequel to Alan Fleishman's successful debut novel, *Goliath's Head*. Prior to beginning his writing career, he was a marketing consultant, senior corporate executive, university adjunct faculty, corporate board member, community volunteer, and an officer in the U.S. Army. Fleishman hales from Pennsylvania where he graduated from Berwick High School and Dickinson College. The father of a daughter and twin sons, the grandfather of seven, he and his wife Ann live with their Siberian cat, Pasha, high on a hill overlooking San Francisco Bay.

www.alanfleishman.com

CPSIA information can be obtained at www.ICGtesting.com
Printed in the USA
LVOW11s0145280716

498072LV00001BA/96/P